Books by (Jasselin) Joseph G. Asselin

All published by Jasselin.com

Publishing since 1979

English books

A Pat on Your Back

Justice Now

When Justice is Death

French books

Perdu au-delà du Sidéral

Quand Justice est la Mort

Penser Succès

Une Tape dans le Dos

Réinventons notre Vie

Livres de recettes 1985

Les Recettes de la ferme (4 saisons) Tome 1

Les Recettes de la ferme (Pot-au-feu) Tome 2

WHEN JUSTICE IS DEATH

Special squad, fighting against
World economics destabilization

By: Jasselin (Joseph G. Asselin)

Jasselin.com
PUBLISHING

Adapted version for easier film script writhing
Main character names definition at the end

Library of Congress Cataloging-in-Publication Data

Published by; Jasselin.com (publishing since 1979)

Printed at the Point of Sale.

ISBN (Export Trade Paperback) 978-1-927652-09-1

ISBN (eBook) 978-1-927652-08-4

Readapted version, for easier film script writing

Extracted from the original French version:

Justice sur-le-champ & (Justice NOW translated copy)

Legal deposit to: Canadian National Library and

Quebec National Library. (Fourth trimester 2017)

Typesetting and designs by Jasselin.com

Rewrote, not translated, from the original French version:

Justice sur-le-champ

Jasselin.com - publisher

Format: (09_02_2018_350p_6x9)

SYNOPSIS

A lot of exciting action in true Joe Trakker fashion: this is an action-packed sweeping police intrigue of international economic fraud and financial extremism. In what, a virtual worldwide vast army of unscrupulous criminals, killers, mafias and cartels, that meet in a global Consortium; their chief weapon untold billions of laundered, but ever dirty money.

This is a HIGH-CALIBER POLICE STORY, on international economic fraud and extremism cells finance tracking

This criminal element had goals of forming their own most important 'World Bank' to drastically control the highly volatile but fragile world economy; they are buying at the lowest prices all the systems that they wanted to infiltrate and destroy, playing with the world economy, to enslave without compassion or mercy, the entire unsuspecting financial world; even killing to attain their dirty goals.

An elite squad known as (S.I.I.T.F), Special International Intelligence & Tactical Forces has been formed to fight more efficiently against economic crime, the subsidizing of international extremism cells and organizations. The intense action unfolds as S.I.I.T.F., with tactical and intelligence shrewdness unmasks and dismantles this complex woven web of worldwide major criminal organizations.

The beautiful intelligent Joa and the determined, but macho, Trojan highly skilled and extremely intuitive, both special agents, are helped by Joe Trakker who is inspired by supernatural images activated by SOMBRAJ. With a lot of foresight and determination, they lead the special Law Enforcement Forces through the complex and violent world of organized crime!

Can they save the world from global economic destabilization or, will the world become subservient to a worldwide mafias-like financial extremism dictatorship?

CHAPTER ONE

My name is Joe Trakker and I have the most unusual story for you. I am a seer of criminals, killers and morally corrupted distorted spirits:

"Shall we say that I am ... voyeur ... no, not in the usual sexual sense, but through the eye of my camera." These visions occur as I film, however, trying to convince authorities that these films and visions are real and depict injustices, which are in the process of being committed, can sometimes be difficult. It is obvious, that these stories merits to be told. The following is one such interesting case, so I will tell this story with conviction as well as enthusiasm.

As I become embroiled in telling the story, these facts, even if they are phantasmagorical, I will recount in detail. I believe it is my duty to tell you all the basics of this deplorable adventure as they are depicted and exposed on the viewing screen of my camera.

Here is first a view from afar which appears normal, as normal as could be applied to the 6:00 p.m. news: two gangs, who, without concern for their environment, are firing at each other in total disregard for the innocent all over the place.

Like me, you probably might say to yourself, who cares. Let them kill each other. It will eliminate some of the morally distorted criminals in this world we live in. We have become hardened as these occurrences are constantly being played out on the News and portrayed for us through the media and now even depicted in films whether on the movie screen or television. The reality is, we pay to see more.

But I tell you: "do not be worried, this story is not about gangs killing each other's. The macabre crime scene you will see is only the trigger that has revealed evidences about the most important international criminal organizations about infiltrating and destabilizing the whole world economy."

However, when you come and look through my video screen you will see a whole other dimension, so come closer!

COME SEE! COME SEE!

Joe Trakker, as if motioning to an interested crowd: "yes! Come with me! Become too, the voyeur"!

And the Action Begins

The quiet was suddenly shattered by the sound of gunfire and automatic weapons. Bullets filled the air with acrid smells of smoke and death. The asphalt parking lot was now strewn with a scene of bodies immobilized in macabre positions. Other more fortunate were running for their lives, zigzagging through the corpses hoping to avoid being shot, some firing on others, or simply fleeing death.

"It is a war which seems without mercy!"

"**Come closer**," as if Joe Trakker was addressing the entire world, "and see what I see on my video screen, do not be afraid to have the air of vulgar voyeurs, as this affects the whole world, without exception. What is taking shape there to your left is a precursor to the eve of a total change to the capitalist world as we know it! This may be the beginning of a world becoming subservient to a terrorist world criminal dictatorship without precedent!

And a little while ahead after the shooting: "see Joa and other members of the elite squad known as (S.I.I.T.F), Special International Intelligence & Tactical Forces, taking out seized documents of the highest importance, and computers, out from the presumed criminal Dennis Kildem's RV. They are transporting all those documents and computers down there to the left, appearing at the rear of that large Greyhounds kind BUS, which has been converted into a combination mobile fortress crime lab and intelligence center. Already at first sight, as she consults a list of the names and with a quick rise of her arched eyebrows, she indicates these names are known to her, and that she is aware she has hit the proverbial jackpot.

Joe Trakker, the seer of criminal spirit visions, cried out with much enthusiasm, "what luck! The 'Boa,' Joa's nickname, has just stumbled into such valuable and crucial information—even unimaginable to Joa!"

It is obvious but without those two gangs war, Joa would never have had the chance to get her hand on those crucial documents that she was looking for since so much time...

Let's Go Back Five Days Before

Prior to this crucial moment, you may not have heard this story. Let us go back five days to Fort Pierce before the Daytona Bike Week 2014; because you now want to know how it all began.

The story will unfold on the video screen of my camera. You will, as I will, live all the moments and I will provide a detailed narrative, perhaps sometimes disjointed, but take heart it will all make sense eventually. You will witness the possible dismantling of the international criminal financial dictatorship, the fight against economic crime and extremism cells finance tracking by the elite squad known as S.I.I.T.F.

It begins in Fort Pierce, Florida!

For the last twenty years, I have lived in the South of the United States during the winter months. And because I encounter people who speak different languages, I have been called by a variety of names to which I respond to, depending on the language and the country of origin of the person who is addressing me at the time. I might add that I speak, read and write many of these languages. I therefore adopted the name Joe, as it is very recognizable in many languages; my ear can easily discern the language and the country origin the individual is from.

I was in South Florida for that winter, late 2013 early 2014. I had not been there for a few years. The previous year, I had preferred to go to Texas for a period of six months, traveling far and wide on my motorcycle when the weather was nice or with my van on inclement days. I love the open air and the vast open spaces of the great state of Texas. Over the last few years, I have adopted a minimalistic way of life, as I own a Nissan high-top NV2500 HD van with a customized trailer and hitch that enables me to carry my Harley my trusty motorcycle.

The possessions I carry with me consist only of necessary things which allow me to live comfortably and to sleep in my van, or in a tent weather permitting.

When the weather turned cold, rainy, and especially if the winds became unbearable, I was having a ride to Roma, a town on the Mexican border. There, catching a bus to Monterrey where I was spending a week or two living in a hostel, simply because I love Mexico, the people and the culture. Unfortunately, I have not spent as much time in that wonderful country in the last twenty-five years as my soul desires.

So back to my Florida story and the way I did my traveling during 2014. The weather was cold to cool, and not ideal for the sun worshipers or people who love to go to the beach. I prefer the temperate weather because I do not like to lie in the sun and bake my skin to a crisp. When it gets too hot, I am not interested in writing, I prefer the open air and spaces, and so I get on my Harley and ride into the surrounding areas.

You must think that I am spoiled and lazy, indeed you may have reason to believe that; however, after an extensive period of research and writing, I sometimes have to wait a month before I pick up my pen and begin to write again. I know how I am and I must not force myself to the point of getting fed up with writing.

A Body Shop, a Strange Encounter

My van was beginning to show some wear-and-tear on its body. Some rust spots had appeared on the right and left fender as well as on the sliding door. It bothered me because every year I had the body waxed and oil sprayed, and the remainder of the van's body is original.

While wandering about in Fort Pierce Florida, waiting for the temperature to warm up so I could head a little further up North, I decided to stop in at a small body shop that I had noticed on my way to the beach where I often went to do some writing. I love sitting by the seashore, on a beach. Near the water's edge I find it is the ideal place to read or write. I tend to head to such a calm and beautiful environment as much as possible, even when the weather is still inclement. Maybe it is the reason why my permanent residence is located near the water's edge, even though it is up North where the winter is cold and sometimes seems endless.

This small body shop attracted my attention, as it appeared rather poor, but well maintained. For some unknown reason, it bade me to go and check it out. As I entered the shop, I was pleasantly surprised to encounter a gray-haired-dark-skinned gentleman. He seemed warm, with an inviting sort of old-school friendliness that drew me in.

As I entered the body shop, he took his paint respirator off as he had just come out of the paint booth, his kind unusual gray eyes like those of a wolf or a Malamute showed surprise to see me, as if white folks were not the usual customers in his body shop.

I told him about my concerns of rust now showing up on my van, and that it bothered me. I asked him if he would look at it and tell me if this problem could be resolved.

With a warm and kindly smile, and sweeping gesture from his massive arm, he beckoned me wordlessly to follow him into the interior of the body shop. Over his shoulder, he told me his name was Joshua, or Josh Bonitos. As we entered his office I could see two chairs, and as he motioned me to sit I thought to myself it was time for his coffee break. True to my instincts he poured two cups of full-bodied coffee, handing one to me in such obvious southern-style hospitality that I could not refuse, even though I was not in the habit of taking a second cup of coffee in the morning.

His coffee was so good, sweet, and creamy and to my taste, and this all without even asking me my preferences, as if he knew them. I am not a suspicious person, so this did not scare me. I was not afraid, even if this was strange, especially his eyes. We talked about a variety of things, but we did not discuss my van's rust spots, and that left me with ever such a slight feeling of uneasiness. He began telling me a story. He was very knowledgeable on the history of the South, and in a two-hour monologue revealed a hundred years of history. As far as I was concerned I had all the time in the world and was all ears, as I am always on the lookout for good ideas.

I mentioned to him that he was a good storyteller, and that he should write. His response was, "I am not well-educated," and added that his personal life was mostly spent in the body shop among the smell of paint.

When he mentioned paint, I should have quit and run out of there because I am extremely allergic to chemical products, especially automotive paint. There is some chemical compound contained in automotive paint which is very harmful to me, whether it is the vapors from solvents or accelerators, I do not know. Not being wise in chemistry, I simply must always avoid these.

Chemical Compounds

Which Can Cause Choking

It has happened to me a few times. I choked while eating after painting; however, I was fortunate to have someone there in those instances to do the Heimlich maneuver to help me.

On one such occasion after having used automotive paint, I decided to go and have a hamburger. After taking a few bites, I began to choke and could not breathe. I spotted a very heavy-set strong man at another table and gesticulated to him that I was choking. At first, he thought it was a joke, but finally his friend, noticing my distress, told him that I required immediate assistance or I would choke to death. With great skill, they began to help me dislodge the offending piece of hamburgers which was stuck in my throat.

I have concluded that I was definitely allergic to volatile chemicals, and that I will have to avoid contact with them at all costs. I do not want to mislead anyone that I have been affected (no I am not deranged or disturbed) because I choked a few times or that I have been in prolonged contact with chemical compounds, but that I must be vigilant when these products are present.

Automotive paint allergies

And the symptoms

Following several choking episodes after having painted, the symptoms I experienced were pronounced and immediate. The fact of the matter is, these chemicals affect me adversely, and can have life-threatening results. My airways constrict and my body no longer responds or functions normally.

Getting back to my automotive body work specialist, he said: “do not be concerned about the little bit of rust on the van. It can be mostly removed with abrasives and some strong chemicals I have.” Without a second thought, he cleaned the rust and applied the necessary paint, then a clear coat of fast dry. He refused payment as he said, the pleasure was his, as he had enjoyed telling me about the history of the South and he would not allow me to lessen his enjoyment. I shook his hand warmly and thanked him for his kindness and the wonderful day I had spent in his company.

My travel plans.

They say: “life is what happens while we are making other plans.”

My original travel plans included spending a few months in Miami and then making my way up North as the heat of the South became unbearable for my taste. I had enjoyed a moderate temperature during the three months I spent in Hallandale, which is situated between Hollywood and Miami. There I had worked very hard on the preparation of four books, including two French single pot recipe cookbooks that I was going to republish for a special 25th Anniversary

Edition. They were like old friends to me, four-season farm recipes, and comfort foods from the warmth of an old-fashioned kitchen. Their popularity was not surprising and they had been the backbone of my writing for some time. I wanted to repay this by bringing new life to my old friends. In addition, I felt my old friends would then in turn add new life to my electronic book Website.

The first has always been a big seller, its recipes are easy and quick to prepare depending on the availability of seasonal produce. The second was a little neglected, but could be made just as popular because it contains treasures for the palate, the kind of recipes grandma would prepare. Many of the recipes were sent to me while I was the editor of a farm magazine.

During these three months in Hallandale, I took the opportunity also to reroute two books which were waiting for me to make the last corrections and then release them on the internet. The first book, 'RÉINVENTONS NOTRE VIE' (formerly: Terre des Femmes) written in Hollywood, Florida, 89 to 92 was completed after hurricane Andrew in 94; the second, "Un Monde à Revers," began in Florida, 1999 to 2002, after an amazing and exhilarating hike in the Everglades on Route 75, when returning from Naples where I had visited friends. And finally, I wrote the first original version of this book, in French in 2014, and here is a rearranged English version that I rewrote, simplified with more details for more easy film script writing with more dialogues.

These few paragraphs of self-description are only to illustrate the diversity of my hobbies, and as a preamble to this quite strange exciting story.

Now, and most importantly for the task at hand, my other hobby is photography and filming. They have always held a special interest for me, almost a passion. My camera very seldom leaves my side; I am always searching for something interesting to capture. This capturing of interesting moments on any media is enjoyable and seems to make the days go by too fast. Several of these small stories form parts of a growing file of interesting cases which also need to be told at some future time. For now, this story began with me, or more specifically: what did happen to me for being invested with supernatural visions concerning criminals.

CHAPTER 2

Heading North

After spending the last ten days in Fort Pierce where the weather was more to my liking, I decided it was now time to head north to my wonderful little cottage located in the country on a river side. I have enjoyed many wonderful periods there, in the calm and peaceful surroundings, writing and just relaxing while thinking of my next adventure which might be captured on my camera's video screen.

So, the next morning I set out. I did not pay attention to the unease I was feeling, and without further thought I headed to my friend Josh's auto body shop in my now clean van, towing my Harley, my friend, my trusty old Harley. For some unknown reason, I felt drawn to go there. In hind sight, it was more than to just say goodbye and thanks before I left for the coast. I was not feeling very well. Perhaps stopping to see Josh might be a good idea as his delightful personality and listening to his unlimited ability to tell accounts of historical yarns might do to me a world of good.

Allergies Can Kill

As I entered my friend Josh's interesting body shop, the smell assaulted my senses. A dreadful feeling of unease set in; something was going to happen, yet I could not quite put my finger on it. I should have turned tail and ran like hell, but alas, I continued to enter to locate my friend.

This moment of indecision has thrown my whole life into total turmoil. There, deep in the shadows of the shop, I saw what I believed was a cat, sitting by a chair. That shadow suddenly faded into the others, and then like an apparition, there stood Josh as if he was waiting for me. Making his way into the sparse light, I noticed his quirky smile as he offered me a mouth-watering jelly donut covered in white icing sugar. Unable to refuse such a treat, I accepted the succulent donut and thanked him for having repaired the rust spots on my van. Despite the fact that my stomach was still churning, I could not resist temptation and took a huge bite out of the enticing donut, and immediately began to choke. The body shop chemicals had me in their death grip.

Panicked, I indicated to Josh that I was choking and that I wanted him to perform the Heimlich maneuver, but he seemed unable to understand what I wanted him to do. In sheer desperation, I flung myself stomach first onto the back of a chair. It was a desperate attempt to knock the breath out of myself to dislodge the offending piece of donuts stuck in my throat, blocking my airway. Slipping into unconsciousness, I could see Josh running around me like a dog chasing his tail, and I had a sudden thought, "Santa Cachucha! Is this how my life ends, death by donuts?"

Thinking This Is the End

Exhaustion was now setting in. I felt my life force ebbing away at a rapid rate. I could no longer focus on what was occurring around me. Finally, as death became imminent, I could only faintly hear, or thought I could hear in the distance, Josh...

There on the precipice of death, and in a state of euphoria, I began to see through my body, like a super imposed image, as it slowly rose into the air. Like it was a time-lapse photography, I could see myself lying there on the floor, lifeless.

The brain can play tricks when deprived of oxygen. I could see Josh's spirit in the form of a white mystical vapor slightly to the rear of his body. In my mind, this was a strong spirit; however, here I lay dying and his spirit could not intervene and save my life.

The strangest thing was, there seemed to be another more powerful spirit watching me with interest, a spirit in the form of an iridescent radiant vapor with nobody in sight. With no knowledge of such phenomena, my perception was of extreme power yet at the same time the image of this entity was a strange co-existence with an incredible beauty. I kept seeing a blue shimmering ... what? ..., A butterfly? ....With seemingly fragile transparent wings, yet no earthly butterfly ever possessed the forces that I could sense in this fluttering presence. Perhaps it was, maybe, a spiritual manifestation born from my love of butterflies. I am captivated by their kaleidoscopic color and wonderful dance in nature. This presence, this beauty, in slow motion like a prima ballerina, shimmered without concrete form about my body.

As a last resort, and with the remaining strength which I could muster, I tried to concentrate my brain to engage Josh's mind, to have him apply pressure to my stomach. Alas, this desperate attempt was not working either; even his spirit did not understand that my body was dying. Oh my, I thought as I was watching myself die: "death by donuts—that is difficult to digest"!

The Spirit Speaks

(And It Was to Me)

OH! My gosh!

Believing I was now dead, I could see out in the distance the iridescent radiant presence standing alone, not near a body. It was bizarre as that spirit began to speak to my spirit in an unintelligible manner. His words and sentences were a little strange, like that of a child just learning to communicate, but I understood what he was saying as he spoke in a stilted stumbling manner:

"Me, am SOMBRAJ. Me, goal is to eliminate the shadow of what exists and is to come that is bad in this world, in thee, words. Me, believe it means justice must prevail. Thee, friend Josh is known as BRAJ, helpers to SOMBRAJ. Me, fight against the intolerable injustices which are now underway and indulging the good ones."

I had come to believe that I somehow had died and been put in this situation because of my clumsiness. I was unworthy to continue to live. Immediately without hesitation, in a very loud and raspy voice SOMBRAJ exclaimed:

"NOT! Me, know thee. Thee, fight for justice all life. Me, need thee powers of human on earth. Thee, have knowledge to help SOMBRAJ to assert justice and rid world of distort."

Gasping for air, I felt ... my spirit ... whatever was left of me respond as if in a dream: "tell me the truth, did both of you kill me to get me to join you for your supposed fight for justice? Come on tell me, out with it?"

"NO! NEVER BAD! Thee, never bad. Live good life. Thee ate big piece of sweet donuts and breathed bad chemicals body could not tolerate. Thee, not pay attention to warnings."

I felt myself addressing SOMBRAJ: "if I speak to Josh's spirit, will it understand?"

The shimmering entity that called itself SOMBRAJ replied: “NO! His spirit does not have that power. What thee want say to Josh, me will say.”

So, the dream me whatever I was, spoke to Josh through the SOMBRAJ: “really Josh! Did you not know how to help me?” Josh, with great disbelief that I was speaking to him without moving my lips, was extremely upset. He exclaimed in panic mode: “NO! NO! It is true! I do not know how to help you! Please tell me what I need to do”! Josh was still running around me in complete distress. SOMBRAJ intervened. He had the power to calm Josh.

Everything I describe now was happening rapidly. Time, in the spirit world does not exist or has stopped, I do not know. Once SOMBRAJ had calmed Josh, he began to try to make me understand that I could be saved, if I acquiesced to his proposition. But he was still speaking with bizarre, saccades intonation, a little difficult to cease...

“Me, not have power to remove the offending piece of donuts which is blocking thee airway. Little time left before thee, body dies. Most important is that me, enter thee, body, so me use spirit powers to remove obstruction.”

I had no idea if this was a dream or reality, but whatever it was, the one me, or the reality that the dream was in, pleaded, I’ve yelled with the least energy I had, mentally: “oh please! Hurry up! Hurry up! My body no longer moves! Oh my! It is turning blue!”

“Me, must have thee permission, to enter thee, body. Need to meld our spirits. So, me, can have the power to intervene immediately. As if it was me body. Need thee, consent, for me to go into thee, living body.”

I heard, or felt myself suddenly rebelling:

"Damn you! This is blackmail! I prefer death rather than loss of self. I would never let my body be occupied by another spirit unless I had control. I definitely do not want to be an accomplice to murder to punish murderers. Yes, a murder is murder; however, I believe in justice running its course. Who am I to judge as there are greater powers than I, who will deal with these shameful characters?"

The spirit replied calmly: "No, not to murder but justice by Spirit."

I was less disturbed now and responded: "I do not understand, why take my body to administer justice by Spirit?"

SOMBRAJ informed me in his own thoughts:

"Justice as thou know deals with the living being, but the Spirit Justice is on a different plane. It deals with the spirit and makes the spirit suffer. This transcends the limit of any physical pain that a human can endure. The Spirit Justice will remove the Shameful human from life itself, if need be, by applying the appropriate Spirit Justice."

I countered that:

"To take a life is murder according to our laws. If we take justice into our own hands, then we too are criminals." SOMBRAJ as if speaking to a child replied:

"Yes, in life, not in the spirit plain. Life is landed gift only, on humans from the Spirit and this can be taken away at any time." I still was not sure, I needed more answers but my life was slowly ebbing away:

"If as you say, life relates to the landed gift of the Spirit, why do you have need of my body and mind to bring Spirit Justice to Shameful humans?"

SOMBRAJ, knowing time was short, was getting exasperated and with a last-ditched effort, he said:

"The suffering of so many victims now had reached such limits of intolerable proportions that there is need for unconventional action. Murderers, rapists, drug peddlers selling to children as well as the network of prostitution rings are causing extreme hardship and suffering before maiming or killing their victims. This has become so rampant that it now requires extraordinary measures. If this crime spree goes on unchecked, the violence will continue to multiply at an alarming rate taking advantage of the innocents, to satisfy their pleasure, as they will not fear punishment at the hands of human justice."

Frustrated I said: "well! What are you waiting for? Use your great powers to rid us of these shameful humans, if as you say their life is a temporary lent gift, why do you let all this suffering go on when you can prevent it? I do not understand." And after a few second:

"STOP THE SUFFERING, DAMN YOU!"

In a calm manner SOMBRAJ said:

"NO! It is not as easy as that. This suffering is global and not specific to one or a certain number of shameful individuals. If we eliminate them one by one, then others will take their place. These shameful individuals are part of a huge and well-oiled machine and the judicial systems currently in place are incapable at this time to combat such a force, any attempt will worsen the situation and those distorted injustices will go unchecked and continue to spread alarmingly."

This had gone on too long, so at last with what I thought would be my last breath:

"Santa cachucha! Do I understand you correctly, SOMBRAJ, you need me, Joe Trakker, to infiltrate these global organizations of shameful individuals to play policemen and get me killed by these unscrupulous killers? So... SOMBRAJ......Great spirit, you are asking me, a small-time ex-journalist and writer, to find these networks, that experienced highly skilled and advanced technical global police forces are unable to do?"

The Power of a SOMBRAJ

SOMBRAJ affirmed: "yes! They do not have the powers of SOMBRAJ to guide them in the right direction. My being paired with you, Joe, will enable us to accomplish many things they are unable to see or understand."

I suddenly was able to feel very deeply the value that is this spirit. Without further words, I understood what his intentions were and what I was getting into. He assured me if he had wanted to, he would not have waited for any consent, if it had been someone else; but that he needed my help to accomplish what in the past I would have liked to do, concerning the injustices that were now taking place. However, I could not have undertaken such a horrendous task on my own. He reaffirmed it again, that it was necessary that we combine our efforts and work together to fight the global crime networks and organizations, to eradicate this world of epidemic corruption.

"Me, agree to special arrangements, thee, not just a small writer, thee, good judgment and thou abhor injustices! Hurry! Hurry! Thee, body will no longer be recoverable without damage within the next nine seconds."

"OK! OK! Do it! Do it! You promise, yes? I will always have control of my spirit and body concerning my deep principles until my true death, OK?" He confirmed acceptance of my requests.

Now Alive Again

I write about them now, as witness to what happened. We know, of course, these conversations between spirits could not have been recordable. You must have lived it like I did to know that it really did happen.

The Return to Life

In a fraction of seconds, I felt a great burst of energy penetrate my immobile body. Suddenly my throat was no longer constricted. I coughed, the piece of donuts dislodged itself, and I began to breathe almost normally again. Even the unease in my stomach vanished. Again, I started to cough and I shouted with surprise:

"WOW! This can't be real"!

Josh was so happy that he began crying, as he helped me up and put his arms around me in an embrace with such strength, that he almost knocked the wind out of me again. I thanked him as I looked for a chair to sit on. Spotting the overturned chair which I had knocked over when I fell, I raised it back on its legs and promptly dropped my sorry carcass into it.

It was then that I realized SOMBRAJ had entered my body. I had an entity living inside me, with ME! The full impact of what would occur has hit me, confirming my thoughts on how my life would be changed. We had become supposedly one in spirit and body; therefore, we would be inclined to think and act according to what we see and hear.

With lightning speed SOMBRAJ had entered my body through what I believed was the center of my stomach, my belly button, and not by penetrating my brain through my head as we often see it depicted in movies or TV. The SOMBRAJ spirit was not taking over my thoughts or memories but becoming part of my living spirit. Suddenly this was becoming an exhilarating experience. I was in total awe of him but not fearing the familiarity.

I also came to realize and understand but would never have imagined SOMBRAJ materializing as a butterfly, like the one that kept flitting around my head when I was fighting for my life. This self-appearance of materialization, was only one of his many scary exteriorizations that he has the power to achieve, accordingly to the cause.

SOMBRAJ confessed to me that his manifestation as an iridescent blue or other color butterfly with gossamer wings was necessary to express important things. He let me wonder on the usefulness of the butterfly of any different color, again probably because of my fondness of butterflies. I am always impressed by their stunning colors, and the metamorphoses they undergo to become butterflies.

Confrontation with SOMBRAJ was not long in coming. His English was improving quite quickly. Not being of our morals and value system, he had no compunction in telling me that I was now OK to take my place as an assistant in order that he can accomplish his work:

"YEEKS! This was going to be more difficult than I first thought."

As we all know, it is problematic for two lovers to get along and come to an understanding on certain matters; however, two spirits should show more intelligence and wisdom. I guess it is like everything else. No one, not even spirits want to give up control when one shows signs of a certain weakness no matter if only temporary.

CHAPTER 3

Northwards Journey

We followed the highway northwards along the Atlantic coastline, the view alternating between blue ocean scenes, incredible mansions of the rich and famous, palm trees and dunes. The ever-changing hypnotic beauty rhythmically unfolding around us as we traveled enabled us to further adapt to one another. It was time well applied as we slowly metamorphosed from an internal awkwardness to two learning to function together, if being compared to a well-oiled machine could somehow describe this process. Our relationship, even if strange, was progressing well. However, it was not easy as we all tend to protect what's ours and often even desire to be the head honcho. I realized that the SOMBRAJ spirit also has the same tendencies as we humans.

Like me, SOMBRAJ became enthralled by the beauty of the wonderful landscapes and it was such a thrill for me to see his reaction and incredible pleasures as he experienced the beauty of Mother Nature. SOMBRAJ for the first time, through the eyes and indeed, the feelings of a human, was discovering, experiencing and enjoying what we humans take so much for granted, life itself. The pleasures of a SOMBRAJ spirit must be unfathomable as they travel the universe but we also have incredible pleasures in life itself on this planet, the earth.

These last enjoyable days, as we motored along, were awesome. We discovered myriads of incredible beaches from

Indian River up to Cape Canaveral, spending some time in Floridana Beach enjoying the beautiful weather as we meditated and made decisions on our assimilation. We continued our journey and SOMBRAJ became more entranced with the beaches and their captivating beauty, so we decided to extend our stay in Melbourne and Cocoa Beach. I did not mind the delay as it was so delightful to watch SOMBRAJ walks on the beach, enjoying the sensation of the sand between his toes, the smells, the beauty of sunrises and sunsets which he saw for the first time as a human. SOMBRAJ was like a child. Who in their right mind can resist watching and delighting in a child enveloped in the enchantments of discovery.

As we left Cape Canaveral, oh how I would have loved it if there had been a launch, just to see SOMBRAJ's reaction. We then traveled without stopping until we reached Edgewater and New Smyrna Beach. He admitted, tongue in cheek, new for him, that it was the first vacation he has had in the last few hundred years. Then he stated with such passion:

"Shameful characters are bad shadowed spirit. They have roamed earth since the dawn of man. There is no rest for the SOMBRAJ spirits because sick distorted mind permeates the earth; we have a lot to do and it requires urgent attention!" SOMBRAJ told me.

Confrontation between the Spirits

After this initial union with SOMBRAJ, I felt uneasy, and decided it necessary to set a few personal boundaries. Hence, if SOMBRAJ thinks he can dominate me in any way until he deems it necessary to use my lesser powers as a voyeur spirit, he surely has something else coming. Thinking he can control me with his greater powers, he does not know who he is dealing with. My powers, however, compared to his, can cause a considerable number of difficulties for him, more than he could ever imagine. I knew then, he would want to work with me as if we were partners, as opposed to a lord and master. SOMBRAJ knew that I had nothing to lose, considering that I was almost dead before he intervened. I may let him go for a while, but...

SOMBRAJ's first attempt at having a physical body was a challenge for him. As he tried to stand up from the chair and walk, he lost his balance and unceremoniously landed face down on the grimy workshop floor. After struggling to get up, and expounding in words which were foreign to him, he said that this was a new experience. He had never used the body of a human before. He had always controlled the BRAJ, from the exterior, like operating a TV remote control, but now this was totally different. Now he was inside, and the feeling was quite like, poles apart. When inside it might be difficult to control the TV.

With tongue in cheek, I suggested that I help him to get to my van. This compromise, even if it was small, would enable us to work in harmony and accomplish things as a team.

So, unceremoniously I informed him:

"Hey SOMBRAJ! I know this body and all the little hiding places where I have put my memories." Then, with greater emphasis I asked:

"SOMBRAJ, REMEMBER OUR AGREEMENT!"

A little less emphatically I added:

"We also must decide in advance to separate the physical and mental tasks; however, we must protect the body, then we can improve... OK? Remember, you must be aware SOMBRAJ. This fancy new travel package you are in is unlike yours, quite mortal, and I rather fancy doing things like breathing." I sensed he reluctantly acquiesced, even if he did not respond.

I would not let him control me as a puppet, and put my life at risk again. I could even learn to live in the same body with SOMBRAJ, and accept the fact that I did not hold a monopoly on the truth; especially when it came to the direction which should be taken. I had to give him the benefit of the doubt and allow him to take the lead, at least for a short period. Things usually work out in the long run at least that was my experience.

I told him about the travel plans I had decided upon prior to our meeting. He agreed that we should continue with those plans; they would enable us to get to know each other and allow us to come to a consensus, on how we were going to deal with issues during our association.

SOMBRAJ told me that functioning in a human body was exceedingly more difficult than he first imagined, if he thought it was difficult for him, I said:

"Here I am, in my body, in the company of another spirit who is trying to perform some basic physical functions like standing up, walking without tripping, or even trying to do simple things like urinate." And beginning to be contradicted, I thought:

"Santa cachucha! His difficult education was about to unfold." Well, for the next few days, even if he tried hard. SOMBRAJ was like a child in the body of an adult, encountering and dealing with many of its functional idiosyncrasies.

Two Spirits in the Same Body

Oh my! I guess it was bound to happen. For the next part of the story I will need to relinquish my body to SOMBRAJ. The discussions were now on another level and were occurring at an excessively high speed. There was no longer any need for us to spend so much energy in discussion; we were finally on the same wave length as our exchanges of ideas were instantaneous. I mentioned our disagreements, the difference of opinions in dealing with various situations; however, there will certainly be others, because we are two spirits with strong characters as well as opinions on how things should proceed or be handled. I left him to stand on his own two feet to deal with various human functions, and I would only intervene in serious emergencies, or as needed to maintain my personal boundaries. I would at all costs, retain primary ownership of SOMBRAJ's new transportation.

If you think it is easy to occupy a body, think again. For example, what SOMBRAJ had to experience, the feeling of hunger and the need to eat; when he needed to go to the washroom, do I stand or sit; walking without falling on his face and determining when he was required to run, jump—to speak, laugh, yes cry—the appropriate time to lead or follow, dealing with sexual feelings and sensations, and so forth. These being only but a few all of which were new to him.

He also had to deal with my reactions and emotions to things which were second nature to me. After all it was a previously owned body still occupied by its owner and this was now quite a challenge for him. SOMBRAJ had to learn to speak; understand the feelings I had when I encountered certain women who pleased me, how I dealt with conflicts, my natural gestures, my fears as I face danger, my worries to do well... Oh, so much to learn! The term co-exists had new meaning, for both of us. It was becoming much more than a standard adventure.

As time went by, he would learn and we would no longer have to concentrate or worry too much about the physical requirements of my body. It was now time to concentrate on the assimilation and acceptance of two entities which were becoming united. It was not a question of... WHO would control WHO ..., but rather, would we become a team? That was the real issue at hand.

I hoped that in a while everything would calm down and we could function in a state of normality. I felt that it was necessary that I let him learn by himself after giving him a few pointers. He would realize that he needed my help when it came to consult my memories and share the many tasks that lay ahead.

The other alternative was not viable with SOMBRAJ. That would involve remaining on the exterior telling me what and how to do things. After many attempts, he realized that it was a waste of time trying to reinvent the wheel. As I suspected earlier, he came to prefer that we pool equally our new knowledge of one another, especially our skills, education, my memories and the reflexes and habits of my physical being.

He thought he knew my spirit, but he was in for a big surprise when he finally realized that my physical being communicated in many different languages. He became very quiet and readjusted his way of thinking, showing more appreciation for my ability to speak with people in a variety of dialects. When he saw me speaking to various people in their native tongue, SOMBRAJ felt a little inadequate in this area, as he only spoke one language, and still poorly at that.

In time, I got him to understand that he should use his great powers in ways which would make things easier for both of us. However, here we were two beings in a still very new and very strange relationship trying to occupy the same space. It was bound to be difficult. Yes, he did save my life, sort of. However, I am the type of person who does not like to be manipulated, especially where my freedom and convictions are concerned. So, I did not make his life easy, this was my life not his.

The greatest difficulty for him was that everything occurred too slowly, just like molasses in January. The struggle for me was to deal with his rapid-fire thoughts and opinions. Of course, he wanted everything to happen immediately, or yesterday, I had to point out to him this was not possible. He had to learn that occupying a physical body meant being governed by physical and temporal laws.

In the previous paragraphs, I had to elaborate on some of the more difficult moments we encountered in the early stages of our developing relationship, or perhaps I should say, meeting of minds. Those physical bumps, bruises, ah yes, and those ever so present embarrassing moments. But I was giving a chance to our relation, for a while, thinking to our mission.

Mutual Respect and Confidence

Changed Our Outlook and Behavior

I was reluctant to changes of any kind, until I finally began to understand that his world was without falsehood or deception. As soon as I told him that I now had growing confidence in him, everything changed for the better. Therefore, I had rid myself of most concerns caused by doubts and fears, which I had had as they pertain to him and Josh his local BRAJ. I was no longer afraid that they were trying to put one over on me. I knew that I was not merely a pawn in fighting their war against injustices now being waged on earth.

Asserting one's point of view is important, however, discussing them in an intelligent manner and coming to a consensus on the correct solution to deal with such matters, can make things much easier in the long run. I was never one to hold a grudge for very long. It works or it does not, life goes on. SOMBRAJ told me that that is what he liked, but that he was still concerned about our assimilation to accomplish the tasks we were going to undertake. This was the last time he would discuss with me the governance of my body. Hence forth our combined knowledge and new mutual respect made our relationship much easier. At long last, after many difficult encounters, we had become a team working together to eradicate the criminal elements now plaguing earth.

Taking a Motorcycle Ride

(Saddle Angels-Saddle Bums)

Looking ahead and behind, we could see more and more motorcycle headlights as they made their way towards Daytona for Bike Week. An urge to take my motorcycle for a spin was becoming more prevalent and so informing SOMBRAJ I removed my bike from the trailer.

The thrill and pleasure of feeling the hot wind of the sea, with its unique scent, the caressing of the skin by the rays of the southern sun, were only some of the reasons why I towed my bike behind me wherever I went, regardless, of the hazards. What a contrast. The bikers that we passed, just in passing, one could sense some of them, thinking:

"I wonder what their reaction would be if they could equally perceive our mission, and who we are in their reality."

I suppose that anyone who rides anything of two wheels and propelled with an internal combustion engine can be considered as bikers, be it a spine rattling Harley or a Honda scooter, alike drugs that is somewhat the same for all, the freedom, the wind, all simply a cult alike pleasure that must be experienced. One cannot describe it with mere words. For this I endured the ritual of hauling the motorcycle behind, and the associated hazards. Once in the saddle, the costs evaporated to nothing.

During our short motorcycle ride in the opposite direction of the bikers, who were riding towards Daytona Beach, I was surprised by the extraordinary number of looks which were directed our way, however, the old habit of those who ride, of waving was a common occurrence. SOMBRAJ benefited from these encounters to make eye contact with some of the Disgraceful characters, even if only for a few seconds; that was all he needed.

I told him that for the next ten days, the largest gathering of motorcycles in the world known as Bike Week was taking place in Daytona Beach, Florida. Since he enjoyed my motorcycle and had made eye contact with some shameful characters, how could he refuse attending such an event so rife with opportunity for our mission?

Advertising was displayed everywhere and you would have to be blind not to see it.

WELCOME BIKERS

TO BIKE WEEK, DAYTONA BEACH

This is an opportunity for bikers to celebrate and parade their bikes; it is a cherished ritual, especially by American, Canadian and some European bikers. Going back to memories of when I was young, one such occasion comes to mind. I had prepared to travel to Daytona Beach with some friends to take in Bike Week; unfortunately, this dream was never realized as circumstances beyond my control dictated otherwise. By attending this gathering of bikers, I would fulfill that dream.

As I shared these memories with SOMBRAJ, he came back to reality because for a little while he seemed to be in his own little world as if he did not know where to begin the real task at hand.

Windows to the soul

SOMBRAJ had made eye contact with some of the bikers and more than a few showed signs of being dreadful individuals, but those he dismissed as being not what he was searching for, or so he thought. I had to make him understand that it was possible to encounter bikers who attend this big event but for all intents and purposes are part of the distorted doings and large organizations that hide, as well as operate, organized crime.

I could see SOMBRAJ beginning to realize that he must delve deeper into the individual through this new window called eye contact.

Ah yes! I began to have confidence in our functioning as a team as I sensed his new awareness through our becoming one. It was time to change primary focus from our assimilation and start our hazardous task of eradicating the world of morally criminal inclined (cold killers). Perhaps things would have been easier if I had let him take over my body because of the huge differences in our two spirits, however, it would have necessitated me leaving my memories, feelings, ideas, and impulses by letting him control my physical body. I am not that easy to manipulate so it did cause difficulties in us adapting to each other and forming a strong bond which would be required to deal with bad shadow spirits. I also believed in the end, we could better accomplish the impossible with both spirits united to fight our common cause: unfair criminal biased mind on earth.

The Spirit Comes Alive

SOMBRAJ could also sense the change occurring on my part as well. He suddenly became focused and very animated, no longer distracted. It was a fantastic moment for both of us. I felt invincible, that we would be able to do anything we set our minds to. Finally, we were ready and the timing was perfect. I felt his contentment and I needed him to realize that it was time for us to get started on our mission, and that we were both going in the same direction.

How can two spirits co-exist in one body?

I know it is strange that two spirits could live in the same body and yet be two different entities at the same time! I felt the same way until by faith I began to experience these phenomena. Here is a plausible explanation:

As a very young man I was once captivated by a group of Brazilian musicians; totally fascinated by the percussionist's adeptness of the instruments he was playing. His skill of using his hands in turn on his congas and bongos, you would think there were two people involved. (As I explain it to you, I review those images in my mind.)

During the intermission, I proceeded to ask him how he performed this tour-de-force: play two instruments at once, which had different timing and tempo. He explained to me in a few minutes, how he could separate the left side of his brain from the right, he also told me if you wish to accomplish this, it is possible: "do not get discouraged as this takes practice."

I do not get discouraged easily and practiced the technique over many years; finally, years later seeing the light, I had mastered the skill as if there were two musicians within me.

The wonderful skilled percussionist repeated the instructions three times to be sure that I understood and retained this technique:

"With your left hand in front of you, left palm down, move your hand around as if you were caressing a child's head. With your right-hand palm facing your belly, move your hand around as if you had eaten too much. Then move each hand circling around in the opposite direction, then inter change the position of each hand. Do these movements repeatedly for a long period; however, do not get discouraged and some day you will have the skill to change the circling of one hand while not affecting the direction of the other and vice-versa."

And the same brain expression applies for left hand and right-hand keyboards partitions. My mother having studied classical piano had tried to teach me this technique, so that I could realize my dream of playing the piano. After many years of repeating the technique over and over, I finally understood it. To my mother's delight I was finally able to play certain classical pieces as well as a variety of other musical genres.

At this point, it was time for SOMBRAJ and me to allow our spirits to work as one. I wondered, if SOMBRAJ was the left or the right in my brain, will you tell me for I do not know? We had become the perfect couple but we are two spirits, even this seems odd, however, things work better when we act as one.

Now you can comprehend why I must say we and you must wait for the adventure to begin. You will appreciate that we are two different strong characters but at this stage we are only in the preliminaries of working together or should we say of one mind. Remember our mission. We had become a fighting unit, and that I believe was of critical importance.

Our intervention begins

SPARKED BY THE SUFFERING VICTIMS!

SOMBRAJ is not a singularity, according to the need; they can deploy anywhere it is necessary to carry out a major operation. According to SOMBRAJ:

"If money had been the only element of concern in this vast network of shameful criminals, the SOMBRAJ spirits would not have had to intervene. It is the suffering, imposed on their victims and their families that had triggered this operation. Too much suffering was going on for such a small planet." This he repeated many times over.

The plea for intervention was requested by all the victims that were being tortured, kept captive or died as well as for the hopefulness of the living victims who ask that justice be done. Nothing can stop the cold killers, it's in their predator blood, and even if the penitentiary system would keep them lock in jail forever, Justice is done only: When Justice is Death, and it has to be death.

A World Tendency

SOMBRAJ had to be very sensible and determine from where the suffering originated. Poverty, family separation, accidents, sickness and all related problems associated to our systems and structural contradictions can cause other kinds of suffering.

Human kind on earth tends to oppose each other causing frustration. SOMBRAJ must channel all his resources to alter or adjust what needs immediate attention and correction. SOMBRAJ had a good concept of organized crime and this was his focused targets. Our internal union had enabled him to see clearly or at least in a better fashion, the human concepts of politics, human corruption, and our various organizations and how those human failings, manifested themselves in varying degrees. He saw with greater clarity the differences and meanings of terms such as Mafias, gangs, cartels, political greed and warfare, and a much better perspective on the full spectrum of human, good, fair and honest or slanted.

CHAPTER 4

Target: Bike Week

We arrived at Daytona Beach for the beginning of the 75th Annual Bike Week which began on Friday, February 2014. Hundreds of bikers where gathering in groups of varying sizes. They made their presence heard especially when it came to the well-known characteristic sound of the Harley Davidson.

This did not impress SOMBRAJ. Most of the time humans who are involved in the world of crime are rather inconspicuous and rather reserved with their gaze; however, they seemed to have a knack for recognizing each other. Making eye contact with the bikers was not conclusive, that the individual was part of organized crime; we needed to find a way to infiltrate their group.

I knew that he wanted me to somehow get their attention as he needed more direct and connected eye contact. But with poorly timed and a poorly contrived effort at humor, I joked that I was too much of a prude, and with a north wind it was too cold for me to get naked. Normally, even though, SOMBRAJ is within there is a presence of respectful separation. I know he is there but he observes my privacy and if necessary, I can now enforce that privacy.

However, at this precise moment I thought: "Oh no"! As he entered my thoughts, no problem SOMBRAJ said:

"With my energy and power, it is possible to maintain a normal body heat for at least two hours and again one hour after one hour of rest." Everything for him was so simple, but for me, it was difficult to believe his sometimes disconnect with human quips, and his differences between humor and reality.

SOMBRAJ communicated to me clearly that something had to be done to catch the bikers' attention. It was like he made a film clip in my mind and the images were very disconcerting. I doubted and feared but SOMBRAJ reassured as he could, and before I could raise any further objections I found myself in a biker chick clothing store, stepping into some leather clothes. First a pair of very tight black leather shorts and sandals laced up to the knees. We topped it with a pink camisole without sleeves and a tight black leather jacket or should I say straight jacket. To hide my face so that I would not be recognized I put a nice pink leather cap and completed my outfit with an exquisite big pair of black-rimmed glasses with yellow lenses.

To further disguise my new persona, I purchased makeup and applied it to my face. How SOMBRAJ knew how to do this I did not dare ask.

With my long well-shaped legs and small butt, I could now pass for a beautiful sexy biker babe, as long as they did not look too closely. Looks were sure now coming my way to the point where I was being asked or shouted at:

"Hey! What's so good did you sniff? Followed by typically crude made comments.

I was totally embarrassed, hoping I would not meet or be recognized by anyone I knew. I was now in another world and had lost the remaining ego I had left. At that one moment, the cause that we were fighting for was in the forefront and of most importance of my life.

Attracting Attention at Any Price

As I have said we needed to attract attention, so we could make eye contact, in order to build a viable data base of characters possibly planning to take part in, or already part of organized crime. He told me many times, that this was the only way that he knew as being in a human body. According to him:

"Eye contact tells you everything as they are the windows to one's soul," which was especially true with SOMBRAJ.

Even if eye contact is only made for a fraction of a second, the human becomes an integral part of the network SOMBRAJ is building. Once the first eye contact is made, the network will continue to grow in an exponential way, by including individuals the first contact knows and so on and so on. The eyes as one's said:

"Eyes are truly the window to the soul," especially if you are a SOMBRAJ. But a specification that the soul is the educated part sustained by believers, but the soul is not the spirit.

For me this was at first difficult to believe, but after a few firm contacts were made, he made me see the results. SOMBRAJ plunged me into the feelings of his contacts; believe me in the chills this bitterness gave me. Not all we encountered were involved in crime; you will find good people everywhere! Even among bikers.

It is for this reason that he was so excited, to participate in this extraordinary gathering during Bike Week, to build his database. As this database grew, he began to eliminate the paths that did not lead to organized crime.

Criminal organizations from all ethnic mafias, cartels, gangs whatever you call them, are often linked in some way or other through criminal networks. Birds of a feather it seems, they tend to stick together. SOMBRAJ only needed to touch an object which came from an appalling character; he was then able to follow the clues which would lead him to the head of that crime organization. Like animals that have a highly developed sense of smell the SOMBRAJ spirit is a highly developed entity in the spirit domain. For them nothing is impossible as their flexibility of freedom to deal with injustices being imparted on humans will be released in the right direction.

Tracking down these snakes in the grass who worship the almighty dollar, at any prices even killing innocents, are those who SOMBRAJ is in search of. These useless nefarious humans run amuck because they are attracted by the power of the almighty dollar and believe themselves invincible in the eyes of any law, even the invisible universal one!

The triage began in all earnest. Many of these bikers were without history of current organized crime, however, some were being kept aside for future reference as their personality indicated a high probability of future contact or association with a criminal human or organization. SOMBRAJ with his insight could already tell that the heads of some of these organizations were highly placed in respectable organizations, even within management and their distorted powers and egos, led them to believe themselves to be untouchable.

I detected a pleasure in the way SOMBRAJ communicated that I had never seen before, as he makes me feel with considerable emphasis:

“A shadow can infiltrate through the eye of a needle if need be, it also has a long reach.”

A feeling of surprise has set in me, as I had not felt that pleasure that seemed almost of the hunter on the trail of his prey. SOMBRAJ has discovered, experienced something akin to joy or pleasure in doing well by fighting morally distorted criminals and especially cold killers. Anyways, it's like drugs, they beguine with the light one and then it goes to high sensation; Money gives powers, but they never have enough, even if they have to kill to get more.

The Shadow Has the Long Reach

This process has requirements and the timing must be perfect. The database SOMBRAJ was mentally building was like a road map of the criminal networks operating on earth and running amuck. It was imperative that these disreputable distorted humans and organizations with little or no sense of humanity are destroyed, before they become more established and imposed more hardships on humanity.

These individuals are useless in a normal society, so one must eliminate them by hitting them where it hurts:

- Disrupting their communication networks;
- Eliminating their electronic means of financing;
- Infiltrating their networks using propaganda to have them turn against each other, causing them to fight among themselves in hope that they will eliminate each other;
- Informing and providing authorities with irrefutable evidences on their crimes and the location of the corpses;
- Informing authorities on their organizations such as contacts, bank accounts, transaction, places of crops, manufacturing, arrivals and distributions and all their sources of incomes.

- And for the consortium operation: Informing authorities such as fiscal paradise's transactions, money laundering and founds movements from suspicious banks all around the world.

It is imperative that the highly placed sources of financial support, whether they are legitimate or corrupt, one must ensure that the criminal and terrorist elements be eradicated by turning them against each other. Showing the ne'er-do-well that you cannot trust the criminal elements, no matter how resourceful or intelligent they are and the magnitude that they believe themselves to be. Diverting any electronic funds, when possible, to charities sanctioned by SOMBRAJ. Destroy their trust and disrupt their finances. That is sure recipe for chaos and downfall.

One must also be aware that these notorious characters and criminal organizations often have contacts in the hierarchy of the corporate world and in government.

The most effective way to disrupt the criminal element, wherever it exists, would be to make the civic simple guy to comprehend that drugs and prostitution are fueled by them and without their participation and support this rapid-fire growth of a currently lucrative supposed business would begin to extinguish itself.

One must also keep in mind that these distorted masterminds, help the smaller criminal elements, feed on the weak, who quite often are individuals who have dependencies on drugs, alcohol, sex, etc. Much of these dependencies are quite often brought about, by contemptible characters, by enslaving them and by nurturing their habits on light drugs, shiny trinkets, and better life.

The Limitations of a Body

After SOMBRAJ had mapped and laid out his network, we needed to go to the next step, which was that justice should follow its course and assert herself that this form of morally distort doings would no longer be tolerated. Justice must prevail come hell or high water, for them most assuredly hell was very much on the menu.

I was always told that I had a great deal of imagination, but what will occur as I continue to tell you about this operation exceeds by far what I would have dared to suspect or expect:

"How will SOMBRAJ administer Spirit Justice without creating an injustice in turn?"

As I had so many times told SOMBRAJ that I did not want to participate in anything illegal, or get involved in any type of criminal activity that would land me in jail with those dreadful characters, I hoped he had not forgotten his agreement of our arrangement. He had agreed and told me that I was not to worry about how he would administer Spirit Justice. However, I would live on the edge and encounter diverse actions he would take that would make anyone's hair turn gray. I have not yet lived long enough to have seen everything.

For us to carry out our enormous and dangerous mission of justice, I constantly had to remind him that my body was flesh and bones and not a vapor like him. SOMBRAJ was determined and focused on the task ahead and wanted to be at the forefront of all the action, I constantly had to rein him back and say:

"Hey SOMBRAJ, I can be killed you know? That would certainly put an end to our cause, therefore, I must protect this body as it is our vehicle and you had promised not to put it in danger, no? Remember our commitment to each other!" SOMBRAJ acquiesced to my request stating that he was still getting used to the limit of a physical body compared to the fluidity of the spirit entity. He would need to slow down his urges to sync to this new living and unfortunately, rather fragile vehicle.

DISCOVERY of Many Networks of Criminals

We had now created many networks but SOMBRAJ was looking for something that I was unaware of at that time. Yet to my eyes, these were criminals in the worst sense of the meaning of distorted ones, individuals who have no respect for life. I was asking myself, and in a way I was also querying SOMBRAJ:

"How can such individuals continue to exist with such impunity, and making victims and believing that the long arm of the law cannot touch them?" Here I was standing alone shaking my head and talking to myself, not knowing that I was doing it in a loud voice:

"Where in heaven's name is justice for the victims? Is there only one type of justice which allows criminals too much power?"

SOMBRAJ answered me, because I was now in a monologue which looked like it would never end. Using my voice, he made it reverberate in my inner ear causing the answer to echo in my skull which left me with chills running up and down my spine.

With great emphasis, he told me: "our ranks are growing and this assemblage of humans and their own beautiful kaleidoscopic butterfly 'BRAJ' will search out these morally distort shadows."

"Very well," I replied!

SOMBRAJ added: "we will have helped. Other SOMBRAJ and BRAJ spirits will be responsible to gather irrefutable proof to destroy them for good."

As far as I was concerned I had not yet seen anything that would impress or astound me, but according to SOMBRAJ, things were about to happen rapidly. And with a deep vibration through my whole body, SOMBRAJ express himself:

"The temperature is growing, something very important will soon be revealed, and just a little more effort on their part and then everything they have ripped apart will turn against these appalling characters."

SOMBRAJ explained to me mentally: a SOMBRAJ vision is like a thermometer which indicates the amount of suffering being imposed in this world. It points out, how close we are to the source and whether we are heading in the right direction. And it's something similar with the bad shadows spirits, the assassins, with the difference, that is pressure, closer we're getting in the worst criminals' network higher the pressure is.

Our Exchange of Ideas Was Becoming More Fruitful.

We have been living in truck stops since returning to the land of the living five days ago, prior to our arrival in Daytona Beach. A few small local leads were exposed but SOMBRAJ showed little interest. He seemed to have bigger fish to fry, at least that is what I sensed.

SOMBRAJ knew that I had questions, he apprised me of certain things which might help me understand. He seemed a little impatient but made me aware of the following using his totally improved English communication skills:

"We must not waste our time tracking every nefarious or distorted characters. We must strike at the heart of their organization and disrupt their operations. We must ensnare them, causing in-fighting among themselves and then between each organized gang." He elaborated even more by imparting that:

"There is worldwide corruption crime and slanted actions taking place and it is running rampant. We must concentrate our efforts on these criminals and organizations to which they belong."

I felt such a great pleasure, SOMBRAJ had used, we. We finally started to exchange ideas which we both seem to enjoy. SOMBRAJ notice that I too had many talents and skills such as contacting people. It was not necessary for me to make eye contact but simply attracting attention to myself was sufficient.

Martial arts:

Physical prowess or an art form

Those who intensely practice the skill of martial arts know what I am talking about. You often have watched the individual's prowess, in films, when the use of martial art skills is being depicted. A case in point when the enemy arrives from the rear and suddenly, the maybe eventual victim turns, just seconds before the head gets cut off. This is possible once you have honed the skills and senses to a high level of proficiency. I am not at this level of skill however, over the years I have developed an intuition which is exceedingly very sensitive to anyone who casts their thought or their gaze on my person thus reaching my inner self.

The secret for me is meditation; by being oblivious to oneself and having an inordinate amount of self-confidence through practicing the art of self-defense as a way of life. This may help some people to achieve a deep innermost level of sensitivity to one's surroundings. This innermost level of sensitivity within ourselves has enabled us to expand our network more quickly.

CHAPTER 5

My name is Joe Trakker:

THE RACONTEUR OF THIS ACCOUNT OF INTRIGUE!

In essence, we are all cameras. We see, we experience, we capture, as we go about our lives. We capture images, memories, and we all become stories and we go about life becoming the other that we choose. For me Joe Trakker, life itself has become like my heroine, my drug of choice. So, in all senses of it, as I have said, I use my camera but also, I had over time become my camera. Not only do I see the magic of life but I will relate on how a traveler, through the video screen of his camera, becomes a seer of morally disturbed spirits (very sick guys). We can, as I have said, even use the word voyeur in this case, because everything is about seeing other personal things, acted or not; even if it's through our TV screen. Still, we want to see more, even if it is about killings movies.

Up to here, you don't have to worry: "I still have a lot of crucial views to show you through my camera viewer. But, stay close to me!"

I am Joe Trakker and because of my own stupidity, or perhaps lack of better judgment, I was first a victim of circumstances but the powers that have been determined was, I had enough talent to deserve a second chance. I was born in a wonderful small community of Stansted P.Q. just on the border of Canada and the USA. The border separates our municipal library with a white line traced on the middle of the floor; each side separates our two nations. We had the advantage of two somewhat dissimilar cultures and of two diverse visions of different countries, by the diversity of our friends, and by the choice of two compilations of different books available in the same building. This was my beginning.

In reality, I am a gypsy. My permanent residence is what piece of ground my shoes, on bare feet currently occupies, and be it my van or my cherished Harley, an old burgundy, Harley. However, on a few rare occasions I feel the need for old familiar walls, my library something solid that smells and feels of home and peace. Some place where I can guard parts of my life, memories plus a sense of solitude and beauty. For those reasons, however poorly explained, I have a small waterfront property just off the Trans-Canada Highway. It had been in my family for generations and willed to me on the passing of a favorite uncle some years ago, and I cherish it, however, seldom I am there. It is like my emotional life saver. I feel better knowing it is there, and put it on when necessary.

Half of my life was spent traveling to several interesting corners in the United States and I visited many of the beautiful quaint regions in Canada. These two countries may be different as it pertains to their culture, and, of course, the way that they make the policies, but when it comes to their beliefs as to oppression and extremism they stand together as brothers in arms and will fight for justice and freedom for all. There is so much to learn by visiting these two wonderful countries.

When I am fortunate to have an audience I often say:

"The USA has the American dream, but for me, Canada is my birthplace and living there is reality of what life entails (not a dream)! For me, it is 'home,' and all that that word implies."

In my vision of the written word or my writings, I believe earth should belong to all mankind and we should be able to travel anywhere regardless of the disparity of the regions, as these differences supply the stimulation of different ideas even if our beliefs are not similar. In the end, we are all part of human kind, the world belongs to all of us and we are all mere children on our planet Earth. It's never them, and us, it's always us.

It is difficult, however, in this supposedly evolved world of today (globalization), to imagine that groups of people remain with ideologies of simple mindedness, that parts of countries should be separated due to old racial grudges, or believing, usually fed by their inability to respect or to communicate with people who are different than their perfect themselves; quite often caused by the inability to learn other languages or being unable to emancipate their one track believing and upgrade their mind that others could be good too and so, having a good believing too.

As said, my first name is Joe and I am the story teller and our common family name is Trakker. I say our family name, as SOMBRAJ and I are now as one.

Much more than a hobby, as an ex-journalist editor I write for pleasure and from this I take a great deal of fulfillment. When an opportunity arises, my brain takes hold of the ensuing incident and begins to run with it, quite often during the night. For me to get some sleep I must get up and write down what is going on in my head or I will find it a long sleepless night.

When describing myself to others, it is difficult for me to describe with full intimacy my vocation. Writing for me is a hobby, and my love, my passion, is my camera. When others ask about who I am, and what I do I laugh and jokingly say that for me my life, my camera is a sickness not a hobby. It is hard to describe a mistress that for me is so demanding, so captivating, so incredibly beautiful and fulfilling.

I began with an old manual 35 mm; however, now I take advantage of the new digital technology. I added to my arsenal an HD video cam with wide-angle lens and this wonderful technology allows me to observe through my video screen a whole other dimension.

My latest toy is a mini digital camera, whose advanced capabilities and versatility enables me to make videos or photographs. I love the flexibility of this camera, because of its great variety of adjustments which makes it possible to photograph exactly what the eye has difficulty seeing, capturing images and actions which are impossible for the human eye to realize.

Each scene or adventure begins with what I see through my video screen. Another photographic acquisition of mine is a miniature video camera I have installed in my cap, to not miss any action or sound. So now, armed with technology and all it offers, the challenge of capturing life in all its reality gets rather exciting. In my hands this technology will assist in netting nefarious characters who will no longer be able to remain unseen.

"Come with me and live this story!"

I have described to you my relationship with life via my cameras. What I have seen experienced and captured, I will now lay before you on the written pages, so that this word picture may carry you also into the same experiences as I, enabling you also to become a voyeur and live this adventure through your own personal internal camera.

We now leave the past five days which has changed the life of several of us forever. As the story progresses, it will change and cost the lives of several others. Come closer!

CHAPTER 6

Meeting the magnificent Joa: on her ride

During our first visit to Daytona Beach, we were passing by the beach and we noticed an innumerable number of bikes in the Daytona Inn parking lots. Suddenly out of the corner of my eye I spied a magnificent ride which was attempting to overtake me on the right. Seated on this fantastic machine was a beautiful and graceful woman who was in total control, as if she was born to ride.

Like a moth to a flame, it was instantaneous attraction, or perhaps animal magnetism is more apt a description. Whatever the label, I had to meet her, and despite the trailer behind, I managed to swing across four lanes of heavy traffic—a mini—Daytona 500, and, U-turn completed, I backtracked to the same entrance and wheeled in. Her deep purple and black custom Harley, was there before me in the front lot, alike motorized artwork breathtaking in its intricate beauty. As luck would have it, I could pass between other parked cars so my van was there beside her custom machine. It carried the Harley logo, but whomever the customization; they knew what they were doing. This ride was no longer just a Harley, but indeed a piece of artwork with wheels, and attitude. The vision that I saw passing me on this machine was not there, so I got out to admire this exquisite machine.

After a few minutes of admiring this amazing ride, I saw its female rider approaching from the south side of the Inn which led to the beach. Even from this distance she was beyond striking in appearance. She seemed to be looking at something on the beach next to her feet. Suddenly, I saw movement almost as if it was my imagination, but it appeared to be a Siamese cat encircling her feet like a shadow, then as quickly as he appeared it was gone. I love animals but it for some reason left a small fishhook in my attention as I sensed for some reason this cat somehow meant something out of the ordinary.

Raising her head and looking in my direction, she noticed that I was examining her motorcycle. As she moved into earshot, I was inspired by her well-proportioned body and beautiful slightly bronzed skin which indicated her Latin heritage. Her long dark hair that reached below her waist was tied back in a tightly braided ponytail. In all truth, fitting with her carriage and appearance, the braid reminded me of an Indiana Jones's whip. The only thing missing was the hat! Smiling appreciatively, I said to her in Spanish:

"¡Que motocicleta y que manejadora!" (That is some bike and what a stunning looking biker.) And I added a little tentatively:

"¿Puedo Tomar Fotos de su misma, sobre su motocicleta?" (Would you allow me to take some pictures of you on that magnificent machine?)

With the raising of a beautifully shaped eyebrow, she looked at me and gave me a charming but cautious smile. I wanted specifically to present to SOMBRAJ a deep visual eye contact, an understanding on his level, even if it was evident that she was not part of the criminal element.

In a gentle melodic voice, she said in Spanish:

“Thank you but, no! I am not a model.”

She countered, still smiling, still cautious, and she added some personal boundary works by saying:

“I do not particularly like the camera as it does not like me, I am not photogenic.”

I said with such emphasis in my voice that I may have startled SOMBRAJ:

“Impossible! Not photogenic! That is not true because everything I see in front of me is beyond amazing, and that includes the bike!” My compliment and perhaps my manner put her at ease somewhat and she managed a smile and laughter.

It was easy to give her compliments as she was a natural beauty, friendly and humble to boot. Then she spoke to me in very good English asking me:

“What is your nationality? Are you on holiday? Are you a biker? By the way your Spanish is OK.” She laughed at her own good-natured jibe:

“But it certainly is not your mother tongue.”

To an amateur like me, her manners, deportment, and even her rapid-fire questions had not quite clued me in on who she was or might be. SOMBRAJ, however, because of his tremendous insight and abilities, could determine quickly and with great certainty that for all intent and purposes this awesome woman was in law enforcement. If I had not been so enthralled with her beauty, I would have noticed, on closer examination of her belt, which she was carrying, even if it was partially hidden by her casual clothing.

I instinctively felt drawn to answer her many questions in a way that she would not determine who we were until it was necessary. Her rapid-fire questions kept coming and finally with a grin on my face I promptly said to her:

"You would make an excellent police officer. You have the art of interrogation down pat."

Arching her beautifully sculptured right eyebrow for the second time, she replied with disarming sweetness:

"Really? You truly think so?"

Being careful not to divulge too much, I told her that I was an ex-journalist and writer to Daytona Beach for a few days, and that I would be heading north as the temperature began to warm up.

With maybe a little bit of envy on her part she said with a hint of envy in her voice:

"That is a perfect life!" Touched by her friendliness I agreed, smiling:

"Yes, the perfect life." Turning back to make her way to her Harley, she shouted to me:

"What is your name?" I shouted back to her:

"Joe Trakker, and yours?"

"I am known as Joa." Laughingly, she shouted back, "Joa Kara." And I said, laughingly too:

"Goodbye, keep safe. Hope we run into each other again, literally I mean."

This encounter would take place sooner than later as SOMBRAJ enable me to be privileged to some of his visions. We had now made a friendly contact and the energy which passed between the three of us seemed to be very positive, and without the slightest suspicion.

As she gracefully straddled her machine, and before leaving through the Inn parking lot she said farewell to a very well-dressed tall bald man who was, probably, also a law enforcement officer.

SOMBRAJ had felt a certain unusual chemistry and perhaps something else which he could not quite fathom present between them. What was it that passed between the two as their eyes met? They seemed surprised to see one another in the same place, perhaps each of them thinking this was their own territory.

SOMBRAJ, go for it, not waiting to encounter chances!

Later we strolled down the many picturesque pathways in the surrounding area, taking in the many sites and having lunch at a wonderful little eatery situated on the boardwalk. We had returned to the Daytona Inn, and by happenstance or by the subtle urging of SOMBRAJ I know not, we entered the lobby and sat off to one side casually not reading a non-paper.

There was a nondescript man there that SOMBRAJ took note of. He was carefully being non-noticed, as we were. Shortly the tall bald law enforcement officer entered and the two spoke briefly in the far corner of the lobby near the coffee machine.

SOMBRAJ is a spirit. At this point in time I am his home; however, he also can occupy any other living being, or beings, to learn what he needs to know. His only limitation, as in my case, is that he needs permission from a higher order sentient being to enter. In the case of a lower order form of life, he does not, and can freely enter one or more living creature to accomplish what he wishes. In that particular case we are close to the same, we take the ownership of anything that we consider lower than us and we even eat them.

It was a rather interesting experience for me, to say the least, to have SOMBRAJ present in me, and at the same time he was also able to enter smaller life forms to become closer to someone he needed to make eye contact with, or listen to their conversation. Indeed, if he was spiritually close to someone via a physical proximity using an animal as a vehicle, it was sometimes possible for SOMBRAJ to gently prod some unsuspecting person into saying more than they normally would. I did not understand well this aspect of him. It was not on my level and difficult for me. I knew that occasionally he could. However, I was not able to completely fathom how or why it was or sometimes was not possible.

So discreetly, we could determine that the tall bald handsome male law enforcement officer had an undercover contact at the Inn. SOMBRAJ, using a lower life form, he could approach close enough to hear their conversation. The gist of it was concerning the arrival at the Inn of an important gang from Miami during Bike Week. The contact revealed that he had discovered that the Inn management was not happy, as they had not been made aware who these guests were. The bookings had been made by an outside agency and the Inn had to honor their commitment.

The undercover contact further stated to the law enforcement officer: "this gang is recognized as extremely noisy, dangerous and always looking for a fight. It is important that we keep an eye on their activities or we may end up in a considerable amount of trouble."

The tall law enforcement officer then left his contact and entered the main lobby. SOMBRAJ could follow him, as the officer approached the Manager who was standing behind the desk in deep conversation with his desk registration assistant.

The Inn manager was obviously frustrated, as he turned and made eye contact with the tall officer who was in the process of addressing him. In an agitated voice, the manager proceeded to advise him that his bosses do not like having this group of characters on their premises. To lessen the Inn manager's concerns, the officer stated that he would keep a close eye on them, as he is familiar with this gang.

He thought but not saying it: 'seven years ago, as a detective on the Miami drug squad they had tried to put some of this gang behind bars; however, the attempt failed.' And the conversation ended. However, I felt SOMBRAJ's interest peak. This told me that a significantly serious part of his network was taking shape.

The day ended without anything further of importance happening, so we returned to where we had parked the vehicle. I am not a fan of impersonal hotel rooms; I tend to try and find a quiet place to bed down for the night. Sometimes I end up at the rear of large condo development, or a quiet visitors' rest area on one of the highways. When I travel and while writing, I rarely spend more than two to three days in the same location. I do not find it necessary to spend money on a hotel room, to occupy only for a few hours to get some sleep. I am usually backed on the road very early in the morning the next day, until I stop for breakfast.

Daytona Helps to Show Bikers' Color Association

Except for the bald man case in the lobby, the previous day had passed without any important or significant contact being made with regards to the type of criminal individuals we were interested in. However, more and more of the bikers were now showing their gang association and were growing in numbers.

Bike Week leaves Daytona packed. It seems half of North America is there on two wheels, occasionally three wheels. Interspersed in this milling crowd of wan-n-a be gypsies, we could see the groups' colors in their leathers, wearing their patches, but they blended in with the scenery. To the casual observer, it was fiesta time. We were focused on finding a faction and they were there. The ones we were interested in were not movie extras. They did not flaunt their badness. When they partied, it was in private if possible. One did not get one's colors in trouble.

As indicated by the variety of license plates, some were coming from as far away as the Canadian provinces of Quebec, Nova Scotia and Ontario as well as New York State, Ohio, even California and arrived with trailers loaded with several motorcycles. It was impressive to see these highly organized but diversified convoys, which consisted of not only of every day bikers but of the rich with their expensive trucks towing luxurious trailers or massive trailer homes driven by a chauffeur. We were focused on a very particular group or type, and feeding SOMBRAJ's mission was not always easy.

Having a Lunch Quietly, Waiting for Hell to Break Loose

Later, sitting at a table by the window, eating my home cooked meal of scrambled eggs and Canadian bacon in a wonderful but very busy little restaurant located on US1, all was well with the world as I went unnoticed since I dressed to blend in. I wanted to be invisible part of a large crowd. The feasting and party had begun, not only here in the restaurant, but throughout Daytona, people were passing around a lot more than full-wine skins, and it appeared no one was too anxious to stop these bikers from celebrating during these ten days of the annual Bike Week.

One never knows when a turn of faith will occur, one minute you are enjoying the peace and quiet to almost boredom and then suddenly, all hell breaks loose. With these characters enjoying their libation, fully, it was only a matter of time before things would reach the boiling point, I was hoping it was not going to be the case in this wonderful little restaurant.

After having eaten my huge delicious breakfast, SOMBRAJ and I began to summarize the various exchanges of glances between us and some of the characters we had encountered. Although we had made many contacts, SOMBRAJ felt they were not important enough to be of any value.

Then out of the blue, SOMBRAJ got an idea and requested that we return to the Inn where we had met the beautiful Joa the previous day. I was under the impression that SOMBRAJ was laughing at me. He was now learning to recognize the feelings that a human being could enjoy yet, still could not quite understand them. In this case, he sensed my interest and physical attraction to the vivacious Joa and believe me, it was not just her magnificent motorcycle that caught my eye.

After paying the waitress and chatting with her for a few minutes, I wished her a wonderful day and thanked her for the enjoyable coffee and delicious breakfast. I am one of these people who are never in a rush in the morning. I left the restaurant and made my way towards my vehicle which was parked a few streets back. I could not help but admire the wonderful bikes, which were lined up like peacocks on the side of the road. It had been impossible to park amid the huge conglomeration of motorcycles and makeshift shops set up for the occasion. The shops carried many different items and quite often were very colorful, one would say like a kind of bazaar, atmosphere.

Even the fields which were usually void of activity were being used and becoming filled with trailers and big motorized RVs. Many of the usual parking lots were being utilized by vendors to exhibit motorcycles and by a variety of shops. As for me, I like my motorcycle, but it is limited to wander the country side and not to spending a week to celebrate watching bikers drink and become immature in admiring other motorcycles.

A luxurious RV stood out

ALIKE A NEON SIGN, IT WAS A WORK OF ART

On approaching the Inn, where we were at the previous day, I saw a golden-brown and beige RV decorated with black and white lines going in all directions as they crisscrossed one another. This was an expensive yet sensational graphical beauty and the art work executed by the artist was astonishing. I mentioned this art work, because I have already spent over three months carrying out an intricate work of art on my own RV, that I had 10 years ago, and it was only half that size.

I did not want to draw any attention to myself while admiring the exquisite art work, so I decided to park a little further from the maddening crowd. As a precaution, I felt that I needed to hide my cameras but kept the miniature camera well concealed in my cap.

In the distance, I could see a tall extremely dapper man with a shock of straight black hair. On closer approach, I noticed his very deep inset black eyes; one would say the eyes of a falcon or a hawk. He was directing approximately thirty well-dressed men, pointing and explaining something to the men about the bikes which seemed to be his babies. The men nodded and apparently were guarding the three strikingly super modified bikes, the type of motorcycle you would see on display at an exhibition or at a very expensive dealership. The three motorcycles were painted in the same graphics as the luxurious RV. The colors, however, were more vibrant, they were, I assumed with great certainty, the property of the owner of the resplendent RV, and obviously worth a King's ransom.

My instincts told me to stay at a safe distance to admire the art work on the vehicles in question. I had the opportunity, however, to make eye contact, even if quickly; with the tall man who I believed was owner of all these magnificent jewels of great value. The look in his deep-set black eyes gave me the feeling that he was cold and pretentious yet powerful and influential. Also, after another quick glimpse, he left me with a feeling that he was obsessed with possessing whatever he wanted or desired and if he did not get his way he could be very malicious and destructive.

SOMBRAJ had had the time to view this individual's criminal history through my eye contact with him, but he went around for an extra butterfly ride. What SOMBRAJ was also able to ascertain regarding the entire group of his men, gave him a detailed history of all criminal operations of this organization. I was happy not to have brought a regular camera, I feared this group, I felt a great deal of hostility; but my miniature camera which was well hidden, was doing its work. And it is what you are seeing too, through my viewer...

Back to Day One

Joe Trakker addressing directly to viewers:

"You remember those first viewings at the beginning? Watch out and stay safe, on my site, for not to be shouted down to death." Joe Trakker addressing to the voyeurs as to him too: "Be alert, the worst is close to unroll before your eyes!"

"But stay close, as a witness! And still have a sight through my camera viewer!"

Trakker's Bad and Deep Sensation

My excitement began to build, as SOMBRAJ told me about the big luxurious RV group which had just arrived on the scene. He could determine through our eye contact with the leader and his men, that this gang of criminals was one of the wealthiest, most influential and dangerous in the world. The complicity and involvement of his men, had painted a graphic picture of their crimes, and at this point SOMBRAJ admitted that he had never felt such a bad and deep sensation. I also felt this malevolence. It became untenable that we needed to leave this place and find a location on the other side of the street. Keeping a low profile, we stayed close by to ensure that we could view what was going to develop.

We concluded that the luxurious RV group had just arrived and that his men were responsible for removing the motorcycles from the trailers. The big boss would surely not be doing this type of menial work even if the machines were beauties. Being the master, he would have his underlings take care of ensuring that his needs were met, whatever the case may be:

Whatever the boss wants—the boss gets it—yes, sir!

I could feel SOMBRAJ's excitement; it seemed stronger than ever before. If somehow, I had not known of SOMBRAJ's existence in me, I undoubtedly would have felt it during these intense moments of excitement, without any doubt. He was still linked to all of them and it made me feel that he had not yet finished viewing the list of all their crimes. These types tend to be without scruples and usually have a very ugly aura hanging over them.

This last encounter was what he had been looking for, and why he had come to this world. This had been a profitable morning for SOMBRAJ, as all expectations of gathering information had been surpassed, especially as he was the only one who knew that another gang had arrived at the Inn less than an hour previously. These two gangs were each unaware that they were now guests at the same Inn, let alone, attending the same Bike Week as the other.

Once SOMBRAJ had completed augmenting his network with information gathered from the large numbers of questionable characters coming from all over the world, he would transmit and dispatch orders and precise information to all other SOMBRAJs and BRAJs who were positioned around the world. Only then would he be able to eventually coordinate and sanctions the required action to be taken; this because he was the only one, to know what will happen from the NOW moment.

Things happen sometimes by what we think is chance, fortunate or otherwise, but not for the SOMBRAJs. Evidently this is what SOMBRAJ was waiting for, and finally got what he expected or needed, and maybe prepared. Upon delving deeper into these criminal's mental history of their distorted activities, it was worse and more widespread than he had expected.

He then said to me in his usual matter-of-fact manner, to make sure that we were both on the same wave length:

"Something very, very important is happening on the global stage!" He was in that crucial moment, so in tune with me, that I heard him in a high voice, as he wanted everything to be clear in my mind.

These statements left me a little confused but I knew that sometime soon SOMBRAJ would explain to me what he meant or I would come to understand it by myself.

When all the craps are meeting, it smells deeply!

I rather sensed that SOMBRAJ did not openly share some of his wanderings as a butterfly or at least that I was being kept in the dark about him being another entity. He did not reveal all his excursions but I had this awareness that they existed. I had the feeling that something was important inside the nice RV and also, about what the 30 men were dealing along their private discussions. SOMBRAJ was turning around and according to others SOMBRAJ, the same meeting was happening all over the world. When all the craps are meeting it smells deeply...

We knew the inevitable was going to occur and it appeared that it would be sooner rather than later. These two gangs would finally confront each other and like a bomb, some incident would set it off. I believe, or should I say suspected, that SOMBRAJ was setting up some kind of plan or trigger to do just that.

In all his excitement, had SOMBRAJ forgotten our agreement? He seemed to be secretive and I felt he was keeping me in the dark. He had made many short visits, also, to the rear of the Inn where a cement bunker held huge garbage containers. At the rear of these containers lived a homeless man known as, 'The Pouilleux.'

SOMBRAJ, after a few shorter butterfly reconnaissance flights, and also hearing some of their investment discussions while flying in the Dennis's RV, it became urgent to deploy the whole SOMBRAJ high-level spirit summit. SOMBRAJ unified to all other SOMBRAJ worldwide, now in ebullition, did their job: opening the eyes of the complete unified world investigation agencies, about important and crucial information waiting into the Dennis Kildem RV.

Crucial Moments to Unclench the Worldwide Operation

This is a crucial moment, the S.I.I.T.F. headquarters, and all worldwide Law Enforcement agencies and armed forces are connected and aiming at the same goal. Never ever was an international united force of that amplitude.

Since a while, Joa had already warned her local and international S.I.I.T.F. Headquarters that something imminent will explode and reveal its dynamite contains. Be ready she told them.

While Joa was connected with her S.I.I.T.F. Headquarters, only for more confidential and secured operation, her Headquarters were dispatching and managing the whole operation worldwide. They were all connected together for instance efficiencies. The US Armed Forces were General Bentall's authorities and was synchronized to protect the operation, according to Maxim Kgnu.

While in standby waiting for Joa's move, the worldwide S.I.I.T.F. Headquarters, diffuse Joa's verbal curriculum vitae kind, in open waves, for those who didn't know Joa's competencies:

"Hi everybody! I'm Maxim Kgnu the mentor of Joa, who is one of my best intelligence and strategic experts. It's easy, giving you a brief appreciation of the best disciple, I ever had to train.

"At first glance, even dressed as she was, as all of her team, Joa would not inspire one to believe that she was the person she was, doing the job that she did. Hers is not a simple description. If you asked her, she would state her career simply in three words—I'm a cop—or perhaps seven, with, 'married to my job,' added for effect. All of which, although true, falls far short of describing what she actually is, and is capable of, if and when required."

"Standing five feet eleven in her stocking feet, and tipping the scales at one hundred and forty pounds, plus or minus a few ounces, not one of which is fat, Joa would easily pass for the last word in understatement. Despite the tied back hair and efforts to dull down her appearance, Joa is physically beautiful, with her black hair and bright eyes and slightly bronzed skin hinting of the trace of Spanish blood she carried. Most have a family, with careers and hobbies attached. With Joa, her career, her hobby, her family, her passion, was law enforcement, and Joa lived, ate, and breathed her passion. It was not what she did, it was what she was."

"She was undoubtedly a bit of an enigma among some of her peers. To her, her life was almost her faith, although she had that as well. She ate and exercised in ways that would leave those who wrote textbooks nonplussed, as she seemed to measure how she lived with a mental micrometer. Simply put, she loved what she did, and made doing it better than what was considered possible, her lifestyle and lived that better than what was considered possible."

"She had graduated from the police academy, from her military training, and from several universities always at the head of her class. Easily classified as super intelligent, as well as physically capable includes several languages, but fluency in Spanish, German, Russian, French and several dialects in Arabic, including Yemeni. She is a master's master in martial arts, trained with the US Special Forces, has worked globally as a special agent, and holds various rather advanced degrees in international economic law enforcement and mass-oriented psychology."

"Within S.I.I.T.F, one such focus that she regularly applies her degrees and experience too, with uncanny efficiency, is that of profilers and her command of that end of psychology and criminal sociology had no match. All of that, yet the personality that carried these things seemingly so effortlessly were for the most part happy and captivating. It was a respectfully affectionate department joke that God needed a special agent to shake up hell, so he made Joa the Boa."

"She refused advancements adamantly to continue working in the field. Her supervisors had long since mastered the art of asking her what and where and how. The shoe was not on the wrong foot, simply on the foot required by Joa so she could do what she did best."

"If needed, her credentials could carry her with little effort into 1200 Pennsylvania Avenue or Number 10 Downing Street. She knew on a first name basis the US Secretary of State and others of high standing. Only a few years into her career she received the Police Medal of Honor for bravery on the job, stepping between the bullet of an armed robber and a father trying to protect his children. Despite being terribly wounded she calmly and coolly disarmed the assailant using only words, and had him in handcuffs before collapsing from loss of blood into the arms of her backup."

"In her short career, she had in total five white scars where bullets had found their mark. Joa was also, eventually picked up on the S.I.I.T.F radar system, recruited by Franck Chavez, who was also head of Special Ops in the United States Navy, Homeland Security, and Lieutenant Dominic Dulorme's, head of the DGSE in Paris France when he was not serving S.I.I.T.F or the UN."

"How does one person accomplish all of that? After having been made an orphan at an early age on the untimely death of her beloved parents, Joa was raised by her older sister, who was a highly sought-after archeologist. Hence Joa's love for Egyptian archeology and her total fascination with the Egyptian Mau purported to be a mystical cat. Her academic background includes Egyptian studies which she would have continued had it not been for her love of law enforcement and her need to rid the world of morally distorted criminal powers and their infectious belongings."

"It is said that: (it is the fire that makes the sword). Her beginnings had been difficult, and from her beginnings she determined that the difficulty would not win, and so she diligently applied the natural gifts she had, and a remarkable life was forged from the fires of life."

"Thanks to all, and have a good game against world crooks!"

Joa was listening but getting a little shied, wishing the end of Maxim's praises shower.

Precision had to be revealed

Till this moment, nobody was aware of the SOMBRAJ's existence. Everything was on the Joa's shoulders, even Joa; she ignored completely the existence of SOMBRAJ. Everything was intuition and about feeling or seeing something.

Precautions Have to Be Taken

Joa did advise all of her teams, to be ready and all her helicopters and the Commander Brigit Herckel and her team, to come closer to the Inn site, she said:

"Because we have to do something to get those evidences, waiting for us in Dennis Kildem's RV, and also, accordingly with what, NOW, S.I.I.T.F. Headquarters required: 'find the way to get the evidences out of there!'"

So she had to precise to her teams, to the whole world, all the S.I.I.T.F.'s offices and the S.I.I.T.F. Headquarters, that were now all connected together for the next coming operations:

"So, be receptive, we have an enormous task, the world is attached to our moves."

"Money is something about we all know that is governing the world economic stabilization. But when the most important part of that money, as never before, is transferring dangerously in the wrong pockets, a world action has to be taken."

"In particular, when a crook's World Bank (WTB), owned by a known criminal Consortium controlling many fiscal paradises inlets and dealing and laundering cartels and multinational companies and organizations dirty money, the whole world cannot let that happen."

Joa received an important call from her Headquarters

Operation CONSO-DOWN: in standby.

SOMBRAJ did convince Joa easily; she had now the intuition about the most important meeting taking place at Daytona Beach Inn. Joa received a call about the most important world craps, known crooks coming from all around the world, building up at the same meeting.

Orders were from S.I.I.T.F. Headquarters: "Operation CONSO-DOWN now on STANDBY." That signal was instantly sent to the all cooperating unified Law enforcement agencies all around the world:

"Standby for: operation CONSO-DOWN!" Joa and 54-TI were now, permanently connected with the S.I.I.T.F.

Headquarters, who were also connected to all other World and US armed forces, including the Pentagon monitoring.

Joa had the order to arrest 4 members that had an international warrant against them: Julien Patois from France, Heinz Darker from Germany, Roberto Benito from Mexico, and Petro Capitez from Columbia. It was a pretext alike, go in and get evidences that they extant to Joa, but she thought loudly:

"No need for opportunism be patient, I could not go in there and arrest those guys by myself, they might be 30 guys, armed, and known as dangerous," but she had to wait for the proper moment:

"At least, being patient to have enough of my team on the spot or, I ..., hope something else..."

Will two gangs, long-time enemies, finally come to blows?

Meanwhile, unbeknownst to each other, two of the most powerful gangs were now in the same Inn. The bad lifeblood between these two gangs after twenty years of competing for the same territories was legendary. Occasionally they had fought, even drawn blood, but somehow had managed relatively peaceful coexistence avoiding all-out war simply because it was not cost effective or perhaps, a clear-cut opportunity for all-out victory had never manifested itself to either leader. Now, these were as it seemed two very large rats in a very small cage. It appeared, according to the SOMBRAJ's ebullition, that things were about to happen.

And none of them knew the presence of their worst enemy at the same hotel.

Joe Trakker, ready and well camouflaged

To capture the action, whatever it may be

"Being proactive and always ready to record interesting activities on my video cam, I made my way to the parking garage on the other side of the street. During my stint in the Army I was known as the Ty-Kid Kodak, carrying with me, cameras equipment which was available at the time, and I was always at the ready to capture anything and everything that may or may not be significant or crucial. As I entered the second level of the parking garage, I made my way to a wall where I had a panoramic view of the front of the Inn, the parking lots and the south side of the Inn where the beach was located. I positioned myself behind the wall which allowed me to remain unseen to prying eyes. There, remained waiting to capture any type of activity which might be unleashed. With my thumb on the red recording button, I waited patiently for the action that SOMBRAJ may have had a hand in the making, figuratively speaking, of course."

What will trigger off?

SOMBRAJ, perhaps had an idea as to what the trigger would be, which would cause events to take place; if he did, he was not making this knowledge public property between him and me, or perhaps he had not worked out the precise details. Sometime SOMBRAJ relied on improvisation or happenstance. SOMBRAJ was the only one who knew what was going on in his one spirit.

I began to wonder if the homeless man known as, the Pouilleux would be playing an important part in the unleashing of mayhem during that boiling moment! He had been in the area for the last few weeks and drew attention to himself, when he came out of his shelter of cardboard boxes, behind the dumpster. One could hear him talk in a high voice to an imaginary person, often with such animation, that no one would approach him for fear of being accosted. The employees of the Inn seemed to tolerate his presence, as they had not even advised the management that The Pouilleux existed, let alone lived on the premises. The Pouilleux, as this man's brain was not operating on all cylinders, he was, as they say, a sandwich or two, short of a picnic.

Only SOMBRAJ had the powers to understand and possibly use any hatred which this man had accumulated within himself. This hatred centered around the powers that be, his family, and for all intents and purposes the world in general. In his mind, everybody was guilty for the misery that was inflicted on him. Even his hobo acquaintances were cautious in their dealings with him. It appeared that no way or hope for this man to return too normal was there, but only suffering.

When necessary to do so, to carry out universal justice, SOMBRAJ could help to free this type of most unfortunate man while serving a good cause. This kind of justice does not burden authorities with paperwork or long procedures, for which we never know if the issues were reasonable or unreasonable.

Unaware to me at the moment that the action was about to begin, I remained in my hideaway ready for the first shoe to drop and telling you:

"And I feel that you might all do feel the same as me?"

"But, keep an eye open!"

The Miami Southern Fire Gang

Now in Daytona Beach

An informant had already told a tall well-dressed law enforcement officer bald head, known as Lieutenant Detective Gordon Trojan that Southern Fire gang was in Daytona Beach. Given that they had booked the rooms after the Tampa Dennis Kildem group, the Southern fire gang's vehicles had been parked at the northwest side of the Inn parking leading to the beach.

Southern Fire gang arrived barely an hour before the Orlando—Tampa group and had already parked all their vehicles, motorbike trailers, and bikes. The Miami gang had pulled out their beautiful bikes, to be viewed and admired. Bikers love to hear the engine on these outrageous machines. They were all loud beyond loud, as if Southern had decided to focus his hatred on just the human ear drum. Not just Harleys, but every form and makes of two-wheeled thunder imaginable: BMWs, Kawasaki's Suzuki's, Goldwing's, Indians, and other restored relics and antiques. Some of them were valuable beyond belief, polished, chromed, gold plated, and each one seemed with its own unique sound, however, never tolerable and always over the edge of auditory pain.

Finally, after all the necessary time in posturing and ego boosting was spent in the presence of these mechanical wonders, the Southern fire gang was moved off to a small bar on the beach. Their voices became very loud and boisterous as they shared, of course, in the bikers' angel's nectar .... BEER.... A few of their number remained around as guards, going back and forward from the beach bar to the Inn parking.

After a while, drinking, forgetting the bikes, Tonito Thunder Vasquez, a muscularly built, medium height, rugged Puerto Rican and the uncontested leader of the Southern fire gang with affiliation to the drug cartels, seemed a little preoccupied with his surroundings. Turning towards a group of his men, he shouted to his right arm man, his younger brother:

"Hey Ramon! It is your turn, CUIDASE (you, be careful in Spanish). Go check around to ensure all our toys are OK. Have a look on our beauties! OK?"

Then laughingly Tonito shouted in broken English to his men on the other side of the bar:

"We do not leave our beautiful toys without supervision, too long, especially in Daytona Beach during Bike Week! Not? Ah! Ah! Ah!"

Yes, something is close to happen, but how it will start the killing? Only Joa knows and this will be confirmed later in Joa's crime-scene report. Joa needs to reassemble the whole puzzle in her own professional way...

At the same time like in a spider's web being spun, other activities were taking place near the Daytona Beach Inn and surrounding area. This activity would now become the components which would make up a film captured on my video cam:

"And as me, you do not want to be missing a single action frame.

Trojan's Law Enforcement Officers

Lieutenant Detective Trojan was fully aware that the Miami Southern fire gang was now arrived at the Daytona Beach Inn. He had done a thorough check of the area, just barely fifteen minutes before their arrivals. A voice of one of

Trojan's undercover team came over a portable radio telling him:

"Everything is under surveillance, they are now gone to the small bar on the beach and the partying and drinking had begun in earnest." Trojan instructed his undercover man to apprise him of any changes or the slightest movement from any of the gang members. He then said:

"Until later or call me if the situation changes!"

Lieutenant Detective Gordon Trojan was a very impatient, yet thorough law enforcement officer, who tended to be also very quiet and secretive. He did things his way regardless of guidelines set out by the upper echelon. He had kept mom about some valuable information and had not observed orders given, according to new conventions stating that all law enforcement agencies were to share all valuable information if falling under the national security guidelines. But for him it was only a bad Miami gang, he didn't see other things other than a drug servant gang to watch closely.

However, during this time, the resourceful and intelligent Joa had been updated by her own informant that he had overheard the conversation between Trojan and his undercover man. According to him everything was under surveillance on the beach and the surveillance information was fed back to Trojan.

Joa on Her Way to the Inn

Joa was now upset with Trojan. It appeared that he was taking things into his own hands and might destroy her secret investigation. Without a moment hesitation, her Harley baked to life and she made her way to the beach. Joa had a fear feeling going her way, to the Inn.

"For now, let stop me cam and let me explain to you why, and how come, Joa was

there. There was a very worldwide spider web building up, all in the same time, so after a few more explanations we will get back to action, but stay close."

Joa and Her Undercover Team

She as well was playing a very secretive game but had a good secret reason. Her undercover team was set up in 54-TI, a high-tech mobile com center, and com laboratory. She worked in secret with this team, on the capture of an international money launderer, which entailed billions of dollars.

Her immediate concern was Dennis Kildem, one of these so-called money launderers that is the great-grandson of Benjamin Den Kildem, one of the co-founders of an important financial consortium owning a World Bank known as WTB (World Traders Bank). Dennis Kildem is more commonly known as part of The Kildem Family Trust. Dennis, supposedly a business man, respectful in name only, had been under surveillance for a long time by a large Special International Finance Task Force & Tactical Forces known as S.I.I.T.F. This so-called businessman had just walked into the Inn with his following, and with an air of great authority, sent the Inn staff rushing in all directions to accommodate his needs.

Joa, a very savvy special agent and profiler had been in Daytona Beach for the past two weeks, supposedly working with Trojan's team which had been temporarily organized to deal specifically with Bike Week. However, she had been working undercover with her team for the last three months on an extremely sensitive assignment with S.I.I.T.F. Headquarters. It was imperative that the secrecy surrounding this assignment to be protected and not be accidentally revealed. This is the way Joa would do at any cost.

At this time, Joa did not know that Southern fire gang was at the same Inn as Dennis Kildem's group. Nor was she aware that Kildem's cut-throat criminals coming from all around the world and well known by law enforcement were also there too; the bookings did not indicate who had been registered and which rooms had been assigned to these individuals.

The Mobil-lab, 54-TI, also a surveillance team

The Mobil-lab, 54-TI, with its equipment and surveillance team was located strategically just off site. They had been collecting videos and pictures for barely an hour, and were now in a monitoring mode. Next to the Inn, in the adjacent parking lots, was a recreational vehicle service center that also held a diversified collection of yachts, small mobile homes for sale by owner separated by their small office. Between all those disparate and unconventional bizarre things for that luxurious area, 54-TI was hiding there. Maurice had deliberately left it dirty so as not to attract attention. Their traffic to and from their Mobil-lab was masked by several stacks of used tires. But it was an excellent command center with a perfect spying view on almost the whole site.

Since the arrival of the Dennis Kildem group, they had not yet done any research on any of the individual as no one had attracted attention. However, they were watching this group, closely. The information which had been gathered was that Dennis Kildem, head of a well-known organization, would be at the Daytona Beach Inn for a business meeting. Reservations had been made for 30 rooms, a suite, a large meeting room, and 35 parking spaces in the northeast parking lot at the front of the Inn.

54-TI, arranged with the Inn management, had installed gadgets all around in the meeting room and private rooms for hidden surveillance equipment. The devices they had rooted hidden, however, were all new technology, microscopic, and undetectable by any current technology. Anyways, Kildem was getting careless with his large ego getting larger time to time.

As requested by Dennis's Executive Secretary in Tampa, no specific name was to be assigned to a specific room.

Joa's intuition was ON for the big fish

Joa, in her usual efficient preventive way and after being hit by a strong intuitive feeling, she jumped into action and as precaution, demanded that Code Red and code 23 hold to be initiated by her team; once she had been made aware that Southern fire gang was on the beach. At that very instant, computers were put in action to search and gather information on all persons present on the Daytona Beach Inn site.

At the same time US armed forces, air and land, as ask by the S.I.I.T.F. Headquarters, were in the code red and 23 hold ready too for action, and synchronizing with the world operation: CONSO-DOWN standby. For other than Joa, it would have been premature or overstate precautions but everybody at the S.I.I.T.F. high command was following Joa's professional decisions very seriously.

The International law enforcement community, managed by S.I.I.T.F. has requested that special attention be paid to Dennis Kildem and his well-oiled organization, while another faction of S.I.I.T.F. was taking care of the (KFT) Kildem Family Trust and their consortium associates. And the same request was made all over the world, even on the higher level of the members, personally, of the Kildem family and to the all-known members of the Consortium's WTB (World Traders Bank).

Trojan Was Suspicious About the Big Concentration of the Miami Gang

Trojan was suspicious, maybe influenced by SOMBRAJ too. He had requested information from the FBI and the CSI Miami drug department about Tonito Thunder Vasquez and his gang known as Southern fire, connection to drugs and Mexican and Colombia cartels.

The research and analysis would subsequently show the extensive expanse of the array of crimes related to the Southern fire gang. And this request was now captioned by the 54-TI's teams, as for the S.I.I.T.F. Headquarters now permanently connected to Joa's operation since the call on operation CONSO-DOWN standby. The suspense was worldwide, waiting for Joa moves.

CHAPTER 7

Preventive CODE RED alert and code 23 hold

Joa, animated by her so now intense intuition, was in a hurry. She straddled her Harley and headed for Daytona Beach Inn, doing the slalom through opposing vehicles. Arriving quickly at the Daytona Beach Inn, Joa had missed Trojan by at least twenty minutes. Her haste in reaching the site after she had heard from her undercover agent regarding the conversation Trojan had with his own undercover contact had left her quite perturbed as to how Trojan was handling the Bike Week assignment.

Of course, her main concern was on how it would impact S.I.I.T.F. investigation. Since she had put 54-TI on red alert and code 23 hold, the information on at least a dozen names linked to or part of the worst of the Consortium organization and the other side, drug cartels were starting to emerge on reports from the highly sophisticated international computerized communication systems, which fell under the mandate of S.I.I.T.F. The names, photos, and information which appeared on their screens and paper reports, were well-known and recognized by law enforcement everywhere in the world. It was a rapid and an incredibly efficient two-way data exchange system. When it was fully manned and in high gear, as it was now, it was like a living science fiction movie, but this was real business.

Joa was now seriously concerned and needed urgently to talk with Trojan too. His undercover contact had no idea of the larger law enforcement operation in progress there and he needed to be stopped, now, before he inadvertently blew everything out of the water.

"Damn"! Thought Joa,

"I don't need this to gum up the works." She was now dealing with standby events at Tampa, Orlando, the Daytona Beach Inn and all its complications, and now an undercover contact she did not know was like a loose cannon rolling around in the middle of her now unorganized organization.

Passing by, as she approached Trojan's mobile office trailer, one of his men was just leaving. There was mutual recognition, and without waiting for her question, Captain Carl Rayner a State Trooper simply spoke: "he's not here. Left twenty minutes ago," and waited for Joa's reply. She did not give one. With a muttered, damn! Not quite under her breath she wheeled about and headed towards the main Inn entrance.

SOMBRAJ Sensed Something More Crucial

SOMBRAJ felt more than a tingle from Joa, as if he had become part of her as well. It was not only that she was concerned about the two operations being carried out but, SOMBRAJ sensed something more crucial, like keeping her out of harm's way. SOMBRAJ would nudge Joa's intuition to trust her well-honed observation skills and to take all necessary precautions to avoid accidentally rushing into a gang war that I was feeling, close to be triggered.

"This is the instant just before the images seen in my camera viewer: you remember, at the beginning where we were feeling as voyeurs?"

Joa in danger: Gangs Conflict or Warfare.

As she reached the entrance to the Inn, in a surreal image, Joa saw the shadow of a Siamese cat stealthily cross the entrance; then like a flash it was gone. She was beginning to think she was seeing things, however, her intuition told her otherwise. For some reason the image left an uneasy feeling within her. She continued with greater care to the parking entrance of the Inn. As she reached for the massive oak entrance sign, a shot rang out missing her head by mere inches, hitting the sign pole beside her with a sharp, Thwack! Again, she heard more gun fire, but this time the shots originated from somewhat further away.

Suddenly, bullets seemed to be flying everywhere and those firing did not appear to care who they hit, their targets seemed to be everything and anything that moved. Her initial caution and her quick response had probably saved her life.

“Damn”! Joa thought: “Gangs warfare 101, it looks like we have World War II point fives!” It seemed as if the bullets were coming from all directions. Some had already found victims as several bodies were strewn about the parking lot; some immobile in grotesque positions, others bleeding but still moving ever so slightly:

“What a macabre scene,” Joa thought to herself:

“Damn! How did this begin?”

She suddenly had another bullet whistling close to her head, from a guy with a machine-gun, she turns over in an agile move and fired to stop him. That guy felt down, but already had received many other shots before falling down; hopefully the Joa’s shot was the definite one.

54-TI on Code RED Transmitting ORDERS

Previously, Maurice had had 54-TI-tech squad cover not only Dennis's nest, but literally the entire public portion of the Inn and its parking lots with video surveillance and the various feeds were available to them in ultra-high-definition colors and sounds. Her earpiece began spitting out information coming from 54-TI, her Mobil-lab team who was now briefing her on aspects of the action taking place in front of her that she could not see in its entirety.

As she adjusted her earpiece, the voice of her Belgian tactical S.I.I.T.F law enforcement officer, Maurice Deschenes, was saying:

"Be prudent Joa, there is a major gun fight between two gangs taking place in lots close to the beach. People are running in every direction and bullets are coming from everywhere, as Inn patrons and gang members are trying to escape the terror being lashed out whether they are innocent or not."

In the same time, Joa shouted to her team via her earpiece mike: "**URGENT!**" "Send reinforcement to the Daytona Beach Inn, armed confrontation taking place between two gangs, gunshots in progress. First responders isolate the area, do not allow rescue on-site until we are secured." A lost bullet came close to hitting her for a third time, burying itself in the post beside her head.

Recovering quickly from the near miss, her training kicked in, and with a steady voice shouted orders to 54-TI team:

"Get reinforcements using the code words: BRAVO, DELTA, and URGENT ASSISTANCE are REQUIRED? This was the trigger which would put into motion the assistance of land and air teams who were in the vicinity, including Bridget Herckel and her cleaning team and the General Bentall's armed forces.

Code RED "BRAVO, DELTA, URGENT ASSISTANCE REQUIRED."

Joa's 54-TI had taken over operations once she had spoken the trigger words, "BRAVO, DELTA, and URGENT ASSISTANCE REQUIRED." Only then did Maurice, the 54-TI tactical officer and her team gives her more specifications of the ever-evolving scene, as well as details, on other shots emanating from the beach area. The team was now in full—Code Red—operation modes as well as in control of all communications going out over the air. Like a well-oiled machine, it had already requested the ambulances, helicopters and land forces. Joa's team had full priority on all local and regional services once she had pronounced the required coded message. 54-TI was equipped to take total control of events as they pertained to acts of war, extremism or terrorism, financial intervention or crimes on a grand scale, domestic or international.

With the code RED, it was initiating the scrambling of all communications pertaining to the current operation, but the team was to allow the local force to only communicate among themselves on things which fell under their jurisdiction. This was to avoid their interference in the main operation and possibly eliminate more casualties being incurred.

That is why; reinforcements and medical aid were deployed as quickly as they were once Joa had unleashed the trigger words, BRAVO, DELTA, and URGENT ASSISTANCE REQUIRED.

Anxious to get in the Kildem RV

She was waiting for the massacre to stop, for entering the Dennis sumptuous RV, to cease something like compromising documents; she was feeling like a magnet to get in there. And her Headquarters were anxious too. Maurice, in full contact with Joa and her Headquarters monitoring the whole operation, was ready to move faster than fast. She said:

"Maurice, it looks like the RV occupants had fled, hoping they're not gone with any pertinent evidences that we need. Many bodies are around such as the three corpses now lying near the RV. These three had tried to defend the RV and perhaps, Dennis and some of his close allies, until they were obliged to flee the scene under fire."

"Still wait my signal Maurice!"

At the same moment, Trojan arrived at the scene, but looking a little fuzzy. Some shots were still heard around and in the Inn.

Trojan Arrivals at the Crime Scene, Trojan Concerned

While all those happenings, Trojan, who had been listening to the high volume of chatter on his hand-held radio, wondered if war had been declared to require such a large deployment of force, especially coming from another area outside his temporary Bike Week assignment. The situation at the restaurant was becoming very uncomfortable, and Trojan was beginning to get anxious as to why he had not been informed of the situation. Blake grimes, sensing the anxiety of his team leader, was also becoming frustrated but in an attempt to lower the tension quipped with his sometimes-droll humor, saying:

"Criminals these days just have no respect for higher orders of law enforcement; we can't even get a damned donut break in."

Yes, he was late but, not being in proximity of the Daytona Beach Inn and seeing the adjacent streets to the Inn being inundated by so many blacks and whites with sirens blaring, he could not make his way into the melee quickly enough for his satisfaction.

Trojan with a show of impatience, finally arrived at the shootings, said to Joa:

"You're OK Joa you are OK, not hurt? OUF!"

Joa said to Trojan:

"Thank you for your concern and my gratitude is genuine. You know as well as I do that technically we are both cops, and that is all part of this bargain. It comes with the territory. I took a few near misses. Not the first and not the last." Trojan answered her with an air of relief in his voice, now knowing that she had not been hit:

"Bravo Joa! ¡Bravo 'PIQUANTE' Fuego!" With a sincere look of concern in his eyes, those were Trojan's first words to her after placing his hand on her shoulder to show he genuinely, not just professionally cared about her.

It was certain that Trojan had scored points in her heart in so acting, because she had expected a much different reaction on his part. She would not have blamed him of it, if he had reached with a greater distance or coolness because she acted on her own authority and had implemented a plan which was a coup-de-grace and had not involved him. He never let on and seemed truly concerned about her personally.

Trojan was not just another law enforcement officer, even if he just got caught with his pants down, this time. He is very competent and cool-headed when it came to these types of serious and volatile situations. He might not know how come he had been assigned to his temporary bike-week job, but the future will reserve some understandings.

"Job well done Joa!" Trojan was sincere.

Joa kept under wraps information pertaining to Dennis's association to international money laundering, which came under the mandate of S.I.I.T.F. She also did not mention her involvement with S.I.I.T.F. as this information was on a need to know basis and Trojan at the moment did not need to know.

Joa was not obligated to disclose what she knew or had on Dennis Kildem. She did, however, tell Trojan:

"We had my team and I Dennis under surveillance, as he was the known head of a very wealthy and well-run organization located in the Orlando-Tampa area. This very influential man could remain incognito, for a long time and it had only been recently that he had come to light, as to his association with local and international organized crime. When information, which had been gathered, indicated Dennis and some of the members of his organization would be staying at the Inn, as well as making an appearance for Bike Week, new and sophisticated electronic gadgets of all types had been put in place everywhere in the Inn."

Trojan Is There to Cooperate

Trojan, surrounded by his men who were now arriving too on the scene, affirmed to Joa that he had Tonito Thunder Vasquez, undisputed Southern fire's gang leader known as under surveillance. This gang is the most dangerous in Miami and had been for a long time, related to cartels.

Trojan agreed that they should have exchanged certain information which could perhaps have avoided this confrontation by these two gangs. Trojan, shaking his head and feeling a little guilty said whether it was to Joa or anyone who was listening:

"Yeah! Two gangs as powerful and dangerous as these two should never have been in the same area at the same time.

Something was bound to happen, as they have been enemies for such a long time and anything could set off this powder keg."

"I do not agree," Joa said, but did not push the matter further as Trojan was unaware of the importance of Dennis's participation in the international world of organized crime and what it posed now to global national and international financial security.

Now almost ready to get in the Dennis RV, smiled and shouted to Trojan:

"I think the contrary, but I cannot say any more or I might have to kill you!" This left Trojan with a bewildered look on his face but continued to walk off to join his men.

54-TI, approaching slowly, waiting for the GO order

Her team anxious and 54-TI was in running slowly mode, coming closer, waiting for the OK. Her team was there for that exactly moment, they needed to quickly enter the RV to gather, remove and protect the valuable information, and perhaps some unexpected original evidences. While the firing slowed down a little, Joa and two of her team ran to the RV. They came in securely in case somebody was still inside. Outside there were still shootings, one shot here and there, but Joa cried with enthusiasm to Maurice:

"Maurice! NOW, GO! Come closer with 54-TI! Be prepared with your team, you need to get ASP in the RV and get those evidences things out of there!"

Now, the scene was quiet, subdued, unlike the gun battle that had taken place earlier. Everyone had been running to escape and save their skin and many had headed for the beach while others had found hiding places in behind buildings, bushes, washrooms, cabanas and even under cars. The opportunity did present itself to Joa and her team, to spontaneously sneak over to the Kildem RV which was now riddled with bullet holes, no longer a work of art, but a survival of terror.

On his side, Trojan and his team, cooperating, were running everywhere to arrest those that still had guns and machine-guns, while Joa was doing a fast acknowledges of the RV's stuff that she dreamed at and wanted so much: "yaw! These evidences will finally help the consortium investigation!"

Finally Gathering Evidences, from Dennis Kildem RV

The occupants who had not fled had died and she suspected she would find a valuable treasure trove of information including some surprises within. Thinking to herself:

"People like these mentally sick and distorted doers and reprehensible characters, after having killed and stolen for the past 20 or more years, and acquire the feeling being untouchable; finally, they make mistakes. That is why sooner or later they always end up being caught, because they become careless and complacent."

In front of Joa, in full view of everyone, lying down on a table was Dennis's briefcase, working documents, personal files on his men and some of his associates, extensive compromising documents with lists of millionaires and billionaires from all over the globe. Some of these were already known to S.I.I.T.F because of their somewhat dubious reputations.

When she first went inside securely, with two of her team and without hesitation called Maurice telling him to come closer and was so happy to yell:

"We have hit the jackpot of information!" But there was more. It was an almost unbelievable bonanza. In an adjacent area lay a laptop, a desktop computer and a top-notch CPU tower, the last word in new technology. The main computer was connected to a Wi-Fi antenna which was high-tech. She could tell by looking at it that it was as exotic as illegal means could attain. Sitting on a shelf behind the mainframe was three external hard drives. Joa said:

"How could they have been so stupid?" Taped to the screen was a list of passwords and more on one side of the tower. This was Christmas on steroids! They looked at one another speechless for a moment, with grins and head shaking and open mouths that said it all. Joa, a true professional in law enforcement that sometimes she seemed to have ice running through her veins, could not help but shout to her team:

"What a find! Holy cow! What extraordinary discoveries! For the last three months, this is what we have been looking for! Here we have even more than we had hoped for!"

She couldn't wait calling personally her Headquarters, telling them:

"On a fast look it's enough to hit them to the hearth, and there is a lot more to get them down for a while! There is so much stuff, big tower with 3 tetra hart drives, so much stuff. As soon we get in 54-TI I'll send transactions and names. But we will need a strong protection, because what we have worth more than a billion... And finally, almost crying, she shouts to everybody."

"I think we have struck the mother lode!"

Trakker's exclamation: "You may remember Joa's expression and mine too, at the beginning! Stay closes and sees through my viewer!"

And more, all those men coming from all over the world had an iPad, a tablet or a laptop lying around, and some of them still had their suitcases down under the floor in the baggage compartment. The timing was perfect, almost no one had checked in their room yet, and any of them were gone at the beach for a foot bath and all their personal things were still in their car, parked in the front parking lot. What a gift for more information.

Joa, as a professional, took inside photos of the RV, of all the stuff and everybody who were witnesses, any of her team and Trojan's team and send a fast copy to her Headquarters. Precautions have to be taken in front of their Consortium's lawyers that may contest the material reality of those computers, hard drives, laptops and all the information that they will try to get rejected. Videos from the gadgets installed in the Inn will be collected by Commander Herckel at her arrival, and send to 54-TI, for extra evidences on the shooters at the crime scene. Trojan men were taking photos too. Today's numeric technology is wonderful.

Finally, and in 54-TI, six specialists were already devouring all the stuff while sending only a fast, general sample to S.I.I.T.F. Headquarters. After a quick look through names and evidences, transactions of money laundering with numbers and bank's accounts and a quick look through the big computer tower and laptops, she had the evidences to get the OK from the S.I.I.T.F. Headquarters, The State Secretary and the Secretary of Defense too, to unclench the immediate code 23 with no more hold for the US operation. Till that code 23, everything was on its way to protect the evidences. She needed conclusive evidences, according to national security rules, to release the Hold on the code 23 regional.

Operation CONSO-DOWN Released and Now Unclenched Worldwide

Joa had already determined the importance of the operation and the key was Tampa. She expressly communicates again with S.I.I.T.F. Headquarters to verbally certify the importance of the discovery, mentioning that all the computers may release a lot more and that all the passwords were available as a gifted, beside the main screen.

She specified:

"Only 54-TI has the technical electronics for a fast and secure uploading and scanning quickly all that huge information, so 54-TI will need armed support all their way to Tampa."

As soon documents were in 54-TI, Joa had ASP a few other samples with names and transactions to S.I.I.T.F. Headquarters. There was a euphoric reaction all over the world unified forces... The whole Joa's teams received the Headquarters orders in the same time as in the whole world:

"Operation 'CONSO-DOWN' unclenched from now on, the most important ever operation worldwide highly related to the Kildem meeting at Daytona Beach Inn. Interpol, CIA, FBI, GRC Mounted Police, Scotland Yard, US state and county sheriff and US marshals, are all aiming, connected and cooperating, in unison, on that ever-vast operation against the consortium economic destabilization tentative, the Kildem

Family Trust implication and their World crooks bank (WTB)."

Even if the Kildem RV information was not appearing as the utmost to throw down definitively the Consortium, it has been sufficiently important to invade and arrest and handcuff many criminal heads of the consortium and put a hold on their Bank activities (WTB).

Taking out evidences ASAP

Leaving the confines of the once luxurious Dennis RV, Joa, made her way to Trojan who was now approaching her. In a professional coolness, she said to him:

"OH! Gordon! Commander Bridget Herckel and her cleaning team are coming to take charge, getting all those vehicles towed, and FBI and CIA, have something about those guys, they might be here too, very soon. So, you may be freed off soon for your Bike week job."

"I think you already noticed FBI and CSI Miami drug department, no? They will be here soon either."

"OK! Joa, thanks, I will get everything straight for you."

"HO! Trojan! I'm so nervous; I have to get out of here NOW!"

In the same moment, 54-TI was loudly coming in. Nobody could miss it but Joa needed to speed up to Tampa.

"Trojan, you hear that loud sound? My Mobil-lab is coming in right now, and I will be taking all the documents and computers that are contained in that bullet riddled RV."

"Gordon, I have to move so fast, would you have a few men to help to get the RV's stuff out?"

"I am sorry I cannot tell you more as it is a matter of National Security and on my sight since more than three months. Please understand I will apprise you of the situation once I get the OK." Trojan, in a matter-of-fact voice said:

"Need any warrants?"

Joa had already turned and was making her way back in the direction of Dennis's RV where her Harley stood, and said with a smile:

"It is not necessary. Thank you though! We have standing NSA warrants."

Trojan, watching her turns back towards her Harley but while she was still close, said with praise and admiration in his voice:

"OK Boa 'using her nickname,' this is your show, and a pretty good one I might add. After all, you developed and implemented this plan, it is all yours. I got-a say it.... I'm impressed, but, please be careful. Please be vigilant." Then, with a bit of a puzzled smile, said:

"Lab? What Lab? Huh?" Laughingly she turned around and leaning her head towards the noise of the oncoming 54-TI said:

"You will see. Here it comes"!

54-TI pushing its way in

Everything is happening within minutes. 54-TI was unceremoniously announcing its arrival with loud crashing noises. The short strip between parking lots was blocked by two nose-to-nose police cruisers with their blue lights still flashing and two on guard Daytona regulars watching with grins and wide eyes as the diesel of 54-TI barked. The Mobil Lab 54-TI extended its push bumper, and with one growl from the massive diesel simply ate its way through and pulled in behind Dennis's RV.

It appeared that no matter what the obstacle before it was, this behemoth of a motorized tank would be able to clear its path to get to whatever destination it decided it would get to.

Joa had made her way back to the Dennis RV and her Harley, and with a matter-of-fact air of confidence was preparing to bring the show on the road to Orlando and Tampa. Inside herself, she was pleased, and warmed somewhat by Trojan's words. Not all her feelings were purely professional and she caught herself as she donned her helmet, she looked back towards Trojan, and could not help flashing him a smile, then stopped herself again abruptly.

Her attention was diverted at this moment by several law enforcement officers assisting at Dennis's RV, who whistled and cheered, as the massive 54-TI pushed through the obstacles that had been in front of it, as if it was moving through paper and potato chips. The S.I.I.T.F agents within the Dennis RV now in custody were already moving boxes and bags of evidences out the door towards the open maw of 54-TI.

" Hurry up guys; we may have an advance on Dennis before he gets to Tampa!"

She saw Trojan shaking his head and she knew the look on his handsome face and in his eyes was not just admiration. He was pleased, not by her attention so much but pleased for her, because she had been so successful in this part of the operation: the Kildem RV treasure of evidences.

This is the 0 second at the beginning

Remember, when you came closer to me, looking in my camera viewer, as a voyeur as I was pleased too, showing to you?

All happening in the same lapse of time, when Joa join her team who had made their way to Dennis Kildem's luxurious RV, she was anxious to enter the RV to discover the treasures that might be awaiting there for the Joa's team, the SIFTS Headquarters, and for the whole world satisfaction; but that treasure was the beginning of hell for Dennis and certainly a big knock-down for the consortium. But Joa knew she had no time to waste, she had to leave and make her way towards Tampa with 54-TI, and her helicopter to be there faster, because of the unexpected situation: Dennis was completely disorganized, so Joa had a 30/45 minutes gain on him. No time was to lose!

Happening in the same time, stay close to me for not missing anything

- The 54-TI arrivals, to upload the RV's evidences.
- Trojan arriving after the killing
- Captain Bill Trapp, 2 minutes later.
- Commander Bridget Herckel. 5 minutes later.

- Medical aids helicopters and ambulances.
- Bunch of TV news helicopters and all kinds.
- And FBI and CSI Miami drug department. And a few CIA agents had something going on with Dennis Kildem about industrial and commercial espionage. And for this national and international security, FBI and CIA have been appointed to cooperate with S.I.I.T.F. Headquarters represented by Joa.

The sky was full and the surrounding too.

The not-any more untouchable Dennis Kildem and his organization thought they were untouchable and could avoid any trouble with law enforcement because of their association to many political influential people. Dennis was heard to say:

"Men as influential and rich as me and my associates cannot be touched by anyone, or any law enforcement agency! They would not dare!"

Dennis must have been foolhardy, or on the verge of being crazy, to take such risks by making this trip. A risky move could and will cost him dearly and throw his life and organization into complete turmoil. Dennis and his men must have been discussing some serious business interests as they left Tampa on their way to Daytona Beach and Bike-Week, because, lying on a conference table which had been adapted to the luxurious RV, for everyone and anyone to see was this enormous amount of paperwork, briefcase and a couple of state-of-the-art laptops. Joa needs to get in the computers but her team will do it expressly.

Keep silent for giving us a chance to hit the big lot

At this moment, The Consortium was not aware about the carnage happenings in Daytona area, Joa, had a chance to act fast, until Dennis Kildem organization reorganize with those who are still alive. He was calling his men one by one and had rung in the dead bodies only, with no more energy to get their hand on their phone. SOMBRAJ had made his job efficiently.

When justice is death, **means: it has to be death!**

SOMBRAJ was effective:

"Justice had to be served. Those killers did not have the right to live, for killing again and again!" Enough is enough makes me feel SOMBRAJ.

Joa had asked her Headquarters and Maxim Kgnu to not expand information about documents and things grabbed in Dennis RV. She said to Maxim:

"We need time to get to Tampa for the big lot, just imagine what we may find, this we have maybe a little compared with what we may discover!"

"Dennis will badly want to get back his compromising effects and he's going to run desperately for it. But we don't want the whole Consortium after our ass right now, at least not before we get the big Tampa treasure portion and not before we get the air force's support and all law enforcement agencies, to block roads and entrances on I-4."

"I do not think that the Consortium or anyone knows about the crazy stuff that was standing there in the Denis Kildem RV. So, please, try to delay information at TV channels." Maxim agreed and specified:

"Be secure Joa, we are all aware of what you are asking."

Joa has stood federal warrant to requisition and take hold of everything

It was an extraordinary situation. Joa, totally gob smacked by her powers as a special agent of S.I.I.T.F, was permitted to take everything. She had a standing federal warrant and did not require the local authorities getting involved. Her mandate, under the prevalence of national security, was if need be, to requisition everything either in or surrounding the scene. That is why they can act fast, not losing time waiting for papers.

Under this standing order of authority, the Code 23 Local and 23 Regional was initiated and certified by the US High Commandment and the S.I.I.T.F. Headquarters.

The entire investigation, which had been in place for about three months, had now come to fruition. The plans that were now implemented, allowed Joa complete authority on the activity that was taking place at the Daytona Beach Inn and its surrounding area. This meant that the local team was to enter immediate action and that her own helicopter, a Sikorsky Raider but her other Black Hawk was still in Tampa for local requisitions while on her way to Tampa. She needed to and make haste towards Tampa, but her Tampa teams will do and prepare her arrival.

Joa's Armed Helicopter Sikorsky

Anyone fishing off the coast of Florida that day would have been startled by the sights and sounds of the low-altitude military-style attack helicopter streaking westwards at top speed. The lone Sikorsky Raider, sans rocket launchers and standard battle fare, was, however, well-armed, and carried a dedicated fighting force, which there were few, if any, equals, past, present, and most likely future as well. Joa sat on the floor with her legs splayed around the mount of one of the fifty caliber SAR's and reclined against several cases of ammunition. She focused to start preparing her crime-scene report, intently on the tablet on her lap and the report slowly building on its screen.

No Casualty, All Dead

This horrific death scene was kind of bizarre as the corpses that were strewn everywhere had received multiple gunshot wounds as if fired by a sub-machine-gun. There had been no requirement for medical assistance by the EMS team but the ambulances removed the victims to the morgue to have death certificates done on them. Even the helicopters returned empty-handed, this was very unusual, to say the least:

"Was this a rendering of accounts of some sort?" She was suspicious but there was no need for extensive research, the killers were on the scene almost all dead and the dead bodies were killers too. There was no mystery but she had an idea who or what was the trigger.

No one was expecting an operation of such magnitude except for Joa and 54-TI's tactical team which fell under the mandate of S.I.I.T.F and of which nobody knew existed. But even for Joa, there was a mysterious happening around there. Death was flying. She was seeing things like butterflies but...

To the unseeing eye, a beautiful iridescent blue butterfly had a job to do and was fluttering around every elongated body, to ensure that they were truly dead. This was to ensure these distorted recognized killers would not encumber hospitals leaving these facilities available for eventual victims. There would be no impact on the judicial system but the morgues would be filled up, possibly running out of refrigeration units. Once assured of their demise, the beautiful butterfly took flight with each of their borrowed spirits, as said by SOMBRAJ:

"Life is gifted, but in theory lent for a while only, and killers do not need a spirit, in a spoiled living body, to kill again, more and more innocents."

This was part of this being's plan, to ensure that the media in reporting these killings, stated that they were deemed to be a rendering of accounts and that justice had been served, for all the innocent victims who had been touched by these morally distorted sick doers. **When justice is death** means that those killers as Dennis Kildem and many of the Consortium's members, do not deserve to live...

When it's the only way to protect innocents, justice has to be done, and SOMBRAJ was there to assure that those guys were not being able to buy justice agreements with their big money...

The NOW moment Joa was waiting for

Till this NOW moment, Joa had the OK for anything she needed to do and she had the complete approbations of the US secretary of state, the General Frank Bentall of the US defense department and the SIFTS Headquarters authorities for any armed support she needed.

Joa requested that the Sikorsky Raider the Tiger pick her up at a point to be disclosed to the pilot. For security she had to look like going in her Mobile Lab with the Kildem RV's treasure. Joa had dispatched the Black Hawk to Tampa as advance requisitions of the DK palace, Dennis Kildem's headquarters.

Joe Trakker Has It All

"Meanwhile, back at the parking lot garage faced to the Daytona Beach Inn, the other side of the street, where I, Joe Trakker had been well hidden from the action, but excited and scared. Not having enough hands to hold my cameras and thinking it would be nice to have had someone—one of you—helping me and sharing the excitement of taking pictures of the chaotic scene that had taken place in front of me." But Trakker was not really alone.

At the same time SOMBRAJ lived intensely while the carnage was taking place, and as for me perhaps I was living it just as intensely as that of a voyeur. In the reality of the real world what is the purpose of an ex-journalist and writer, if not, but to report what was happening, on the spot, at the Daytona Beach Inn? After all we humans are all intensely interested and watching TV's and social media to get as much information that is available concerning all and any violence like was happening anywhere in the world. So, in a way everyone has become as I am, a voyeur of type.

While the action was taking place, SOMBRAJ, mostly in the form of a butterfly made many sorties, and I was for some reason physically exhausted, but too energized by the events to be preoccupied with him. I knew that he was not going out for a walk or a stroll, because he was gathering information and avoiding the gun shots which were coming from everywhere.

These acts of violence and associated activities were not random. This incident would change forever the life of several of us and would also cost dearly by several others losing their lives. This killing scene is not what counts in this story, it was only the trigger to finally put upfront the madness of a man in what way did not deserve to live. All the documents and computers seized from Dennis's RV will put that criminal organization apart and may, with more evidences, throw them down forever. Joa's aiming still the international consortium and their Bank (WTB).

US General Bentall Deployed Armed Forces as for a War

When the CONSO-DOWN operation became activated, the S.I.I.T.F. Headquarters asked cooperation on the name of National and International Security, from the State Secretary of Defense. General Bentall was ordered to deploy all forces necessary for Joa's operation; as every armed force around the world were engaging armed forces on that important world economic happening.

Instantly, Joa was advised that she had to certify the coordinates for an important forces deployment to be ready to protect 54-TI and its treasure of vital information.

US Air force bases were ordered to deploy their war jets, armed helicopters and armed ground forces were also already merging to Daytona, they had the OK for an eventual conflict with criminal mercenaries and diverse criminal armed elements. They have been informed that a world crooks' meeting was concocting to enslave the whole world by controlling and destabilizing the world economy that would cost millions of jobs.

So, the message from the General Bentall was:

"We have first to protect and show-off in the same time. The whole world is frozen to their TV screen, and we have to parade our war forces, all done in the same time, for showing to the world and especially to those refractive countries that may have a dream to play armed nuclear balls with us."

The whole unified world Law enforcement forces were on the ready too, having a sight at any known and anyone, hordes of criminal organizations. Everyone had the same momentum:

"We would never accept or let a world crooks' organization to control the world economy and enslaving us all!"

In that consortium's bank (WTB) case, close to attaining to their ultimate phase, of capturing billions more founds, to become the most important bank in the world; many other world banks were close to be obliged to convert to their financial power.

The whole financial world has been advised instantly and now unified against those crook's consortium bank (WTB). Enough is enough, the world economy has suffered inadequately, now their dirty money will be seized and after that operation the whole criminal crooks' junk will be on their way to hell, where they belong to... The same will happen with the crooks followed inlets transactions with fiscal paradises specializing in cartels money laundering and for those big fortunes for not paying taxes.

Ready to Protect and Show Off

In addition to already active forces, others were on standby, waiting to intervene when the Code 23 regional was activated; that meant that all regions specified under this plan were to stand at the ready and wait for further orders, including the Cape Canaveral air force bases to be ready for more active armed support. And those were including the county sheriff office, and state marshals, to protect their moves along their way to Orlando and Tampa and any local police to block local streets.

In the case of Dennis Kildem, many scenarios had already been considered prior to—Code 23—being set in motion to encompass the whole perimeter of Tampa, Orlando, and St. Petersburg. Monitoring of banking activities regarding the Kildem organization were in place at several Miami bank institutions, however, nothing had been set up for Tonito Vasquez and his Southern Fire gang as it was believed to be a local matter and did not yet come under the mandate of S.I.I.T.F high finance investigation.

Armed jets, helicopters, armored Oshkosh JLTV, and all Florida's county and City's sheriff were ready to block roads to protect 54-TI on its way to Tampa with the Kildem RV vital information. National and international security was a must at high levels. The full worldwide operation was on the GO, since Joa had a certification of compromising evidences being confirmed with the S.I.I.T.F. Headquarters, against the consortium or the Kildem Family Trust.

As already said, everything is happening almost in the same times, on the crime scene, when Joa was preparing to quit urgently to Tampa, and while Trojan was still taking care of the crime scene. Local police and many other police corpses are still fighting in competition against each other for territory or case supremacy, instead of competing against criminals. Here is one of those known scenes.

Daytona Beach Local Police, Bill Trapp:

Want to take matters into their own hands

At the busy moment with all the commotion going on, the arrival of Captain Bill Trapp and four of his men were almost anticlimactic but during such volatile incidents, tempers tend to run high and quite often important people seem to get pushed aside and left in the dust.

Moments after the shooting had broken out at the Inn, the immediate roads were filled with 911 first responders. Civilian vehicles had stopped to permit their passing and the ensuing traffic jam had essentially blocked Trapp, and his men, of being earlier at the crime scene.

By the time Trapp arrived, he was angry at everything and at everyone and no one. This was his timepiece, and eventually all this egg cell would be pretty much destined for his appearance. He had not been overjoyed from the beginning, when the city informed him that his zone would have state troopers and other outside assistance, for bike week, and worst, none of them would be answerable to him. So, arriving on the spot, he addressed Trojan with his guttural growl, and with all his frustrations present vented his anger directly into the towering Trojan's nostrils. In any other situation, it would have been comical but hot here.

Bill Trapp was a good cop, well known as one of Florida's untouchables. No number of bribes, threats or duress in his work could sway him. He believed deeply and passionately in his job, and those who trained him to do it. With him, everything was by the book. It was joked that he would not give his own mother a break on a parking ticket. Thus, his nickname: Bible Bill.

When they trained him, they trained him in police procedures. However, Mr. Congeniality, he would never qualify for. He had all the tact and diplomacy of a lead pipe in a back alley.

No matter whom you were, Bill Trapp was a most unforgiving mirror, and you found out quickly what he saw, and Trojan found out at that moment how sacred Trapp saw his job and his territory, and God help anyone who deliberately or inadvertently trod on Trapp's sacred cow or ground as Trapp let it all out, standing facing Trojan:

"OK, Mr. Miami Vice! Your job is peacekeeping re-enforcement. This is a murder investigation. My show! Not yours! So, take your talent scouts back to your fancy parking lot digs. Not your jurisdiction! I'd let you watch a real cop work but I haven't got time to nursemaid anyone."

Turning very slowly, Trojan the utmost professional, despite his quick temper, walked off without uttering a single word. Bible Bill had not finished debasing the mighty Trojan and threw after him, just loud enough for everyone to hear:

"If I need any help, I'll call you!"

"Don't call me! I'll send over donuts"!

Trojan stopped, and from the sidelines almost out of nowhere, the 5 foot 5-inch burly Sergeant Blake Grimes, quickly and stealthily for his size, stepped in front of the six-foot-tall muscular police captain Bible who did not get a chance to say another word, and facing each other nose to nose, one could interpret this as a comedy scene from the Mutt and Jeff series. Blake knew Trojan's volatile temper. One gang fight was enough for one day, and he stepped in to protect his team leader from further insult and an all-out war of fists, because in any duel between the two, verbal or otherwise, Blake knew that Trojan would win, hands down, and he knew they both needed each other at this moment. The situation needed to be cooled down fast. With a forceful voice, Blake said to the still fuming Captain Bill Trapp:

"A little respect please, OK Captain Bible!"

Then in slow motion the sergeant turns to his left and like the grim reaper of death pointed his finger to the corpses lying down everywhere in many different poses of death, and in a gruff and sad voice said to the Captain:

"You! Ah-h! ... You know all these dead, there, Colombo?"

Caught off guard by Blake's question, and suspecting Blake knew something that he did not, the Captain responds in a suddenly cautious voice:

"Uh! ... No! I do not but..."

Blake cut his words off in a most authoritative voice saying:

"Well, hell if you don't, Sir! I do! These are two of the most dangerous gangs in Miami and Tampa! They control most of the drug trade in this area. Hell, it all the southeast USA! So, maybe the ever so vigilant Colombo does need our pathetically inadequate help after all."

"Do I hear a yes or no? I need a straight answer from you. Any Bible Passage will do!"

Blake had effectively defused the situation and Captain Trapp responded with a somewhat sheepish laugh while his men look on:

"No! I have no idea who they are. OK! I admit, they must have been flying under our radar!" Blake, saw he had accomplished what he wanted, and stepped back a pace and replied with a grin:

"OK then! Colombo, this is yours or would you like to be included in Tampa and Miami? Sort-a, seems to me, your jurisdiction just shrank a whole lot. The reality is, we both need each other. We work as a team, remember! OK?"

Bill had been bested and he knew it, but Blake had done so with tact and skill that Trapp did not know existed. He looked down for a second, then looked at Blake once again purely professional and replied:

"Yes, of course, we are a team! Leave me to do my job. Tell Gordon I will be over to his office shortly to brief him on where things are. Right now, I have work to do, and every second count."

Trojan grinned the slightly, and without turning, walked on.

Blake knew enough to withdraw at that time. Both had their own personal share of kudos, or victory, and no further pushing was required. He nodded to Trapp and turned towards Trojan who was now at the opposite side of the lot near Joa who was attending her Harley.

Before making his final exit and still trying to get the last word in, Bill fired another barb at Trojan as he saw Joa getting on her Harley a little further away. He cried out at the top of his booming voice when he saw a news team had just started filming:

"Hey the Boa! Job well done! Go for it! You rock and it shows who is running the show here!"

Joa had been watching from the corner of her eyes, she was an excellent lip reader but made as if she did not hear the comment from the captain, because she was revving her bike. Instead she turned her full attention and admiration towards Trojan, smiled and winked at him as she manhandled her Harley up the lowered back ramp of the BIG articulated BUS-LAB and disappeared inside. At that moment, everyone was thinking:

"WOW! What an exit by the Boa"!

Joa, the Boa, Leaves Trojan in Awe

And Almost Speechless

Joa had nothing to prove to anyone. She had everything under control including herself, after her brush with death.

Just prior to the arrival of Captain Bill Trapp and her departure to join 54-TI, she had asked Trojan, if he could provide her with a different view of the scene at the rear of the Inn where the garbage bin enclosure was located. As she approached Trojan, she said to him in a very low melodic voice while displaying a beautiful smile:

"Just pretend that we are chatting in a very friendly way because up there on the Inn side someone has been filming and taking pictures of the scene." Trojan with a discreet look of surprise acknowledged Joa's request:

"Ah yes! What tipped you off"?

Being very precise with her words and speaking in a modulated manner, she said:

"I will walk slowly to the other side of you, and then you can look towards the center of the building, to the rear, a floor above the balcony with the red canvas chairs but be careful. Do this very discreetly, someone is still using a camera behind the two French windows located at front." She then began to move slowly turning her back towards the center of the building to allow Trojan to have a good look, without attracting attention to him.

Trojan responded by giving Joa a very rare broad smile which softened his facial expression. She thought to herself:

"He should smile more often because he is a very handsome man and those blue-green eyes are wowing killer." Trojan spoke, bringing her back to the situation at hand, and still smiling that wonderful smile, he said:

"OK Joa! Good observation, I will reserve a copy for you, OK?"

She nodded and smiled as she had now moved again to give Trojan an even better look at the area in question. However, for a moment, he seemed to be focusing more on Joa's lovely smile then what she had said about the camera being trained on the macabre scene. Noticing his moment of hesitation, she said:

"Thank you, Gordon it's nice when we cooperate. Never too late for that, is it?" Trojan was pleasantly heartened that she remembered, let alone called him by his first name. Just for one passing moment he had allowed himself to be Gordon, instead of Lieutenant, and he liked it more than he cared to admit.

Still smiling and showing her wonderful pearly whites, she said as if reprimanding an errant child, and with a little concern in her voice:

"Gordon, are you listening? I will send you an email or a fax whichever method you want, providing you with information on the dead which were found on the site. Is that OK with you?"

Finally, realizing his moment of hesitation had been noticed and he had been caught concentrating on her smile and not what she had said, he replied a little sheepishly:

"OK! Email will do when you can send the information to me. Thanks!" The thanks were warm and a bit more than a professional thank you, and she noticed that, and despite his tan, a slight blush, and it did not displease her, this subtly knowing he was attracted to her.

Then Trojan tried unsuccessfully to put on an air of nonchalance said:

"See you soon?" Then he turned and made his way back to his men. Then, not knowing what else to say grinned sheepishly and turned awkwardly to make his way back to his men.

Trojan's clumsy exit delighted her to her core, the sudden revelation that she could have that much effect on him, and hand over mouth to hide her giggle she made her way back to her team. That story goes fast, you understand why I have many cameras, to not miss a single frame.

CHAPTER 8

Let's take a break, my camera off

"I, Joe Trakker, must tell you directly out of my cam viewer, what you want to know about: why Joa was there at Daytona? And how come that huge operation was taking place at Daytona Beach? And why she was rushing to Tampa?"

"OK, let's get my cam on! Action"

Joa Gone Fishing for Key Information

The Joa's special squad on economic crime and international extremism had been coming up short and finding nothing of significant value pertaining to the operation of organized crime associated to Kildem and Kildem Family Trust. Joa had been assigned for more than three months, and when she had seen that her teams had come to a standstill regarding the findings on Dennis Kildem, she decided that she would take a chance and go fishing for whatever she could find using a different approach. Her intuition and her determination to get to the bottom of things, come hell or high water, always paid off in diggings. Hence, no one would blame her if she hurried to Tampa, with some of the best tactical officers on Trojan's team, in search of the still elusive key information.

She had been following Dennis's movements for the last three months and she was confident that she would find what she was looking for. Dennis's movements, associates, bank deposits and his general lifestyle, did illuminate a bright neon light in her mind that flashed: a huge organized criminal activity. She was not nicknamed Boa for anything. Surely, inevitably, her coils of justice would tighten unavoidably around this piece of walking criminal garbage. She worked on the simple and logical premise that Dennis Kildem was not God, therefore he will make mistakes, and she knew that with enough scrutiny his mistakes would come to light and from them, she would build a big trap for a big rat. But, nevertheless, Joa had to be equipped with the best tool for her and her professional teams, then was born 54-TI, that was first named—FIGHT for TECH and INTELLIGENCE.

"I, Joe tracker, I have to take a break again, because we have to go back to the Daytona Beach Inn, when she was in the ready to hurry to Tampa, for more evidences at DK Palace. The so wonderful machine 54-TI was the only one who could, securely scans and upload extremely fast, all the evidences she got out from the Dennis Kildem RV.

"OK! Let's get back to my cam viewer!"

Gathering the treasure trove of information in 54-TI

Joa, however, prior to riding off in 54-TI with her little army of special agents and police officers, had mounted her bike and shouts out orders to some of Trojan's team: to bring her all the Dennis RV's documents, computers, as well as different weapons and private objects belonging to Dennis's guests.

Joa, asks Sargent Grimes to help them, carrying all the materials they had gathered from the crime scene and put them into 54-TI. She also told him to make sure that copies of all videos and photographs were there or will be available for her as well. She then advised him to take over and ensure the scene of the crime was secured and he was to continue the investigation into the individuals who had been murdered until Commander Bridget Herckel (SIRS) arrival. She made it very clear that she wanted complete and up-to-date dossiers on every individual involved, up to what their dog ate for breakfast and what color their underwear was. Joa was beyond thorough, saw everything as important until proven otherwise.

Blake had acquiesced to her request but had given her a bit of a quizzical look:

"Umm! What will Trojan say about this? Hope he does not explode when he finds out!" He then proceeded to turn and leave to take care of matters at hand. Joa didn't know yet but her intuition was telling her to act this way.

She knew that ultimately; the professional Trojan would override any chauvinist ego he may occasionally trip over. Bottom line, despite a few issues he was a good man, and one hell-good cop. Also, she reminded herself that the Dennis investigation had nothing to do with his temporary office, which had been set up to deal with problems specific to Bike Week.

Back to the Arrival of 54-TI near Dennis RV

As the huge 54-TI had threaded its way through the obstacle course around the crime scene, it gave only a slight impression that it once had been a regular articulated big one-of-a-kind bus, which had been rebuilt and retrofitted to do a specific job. In a little time, this behemoth of a vehicle despite its size, had managed to find a path to the heart of the crime site. Trojan and everyone else had stood in awe of this beast that had just arrived with such quiet fanfare. Trojan kept shaking his head as if he could not believe his eyes, however, if Joa had anything to do with this monstrosity it did not surprise him in the least.

The arrival of 54-TI had prompted Detective Sargent Blake Grimes to exclaim:

"Hey! Great balls of fire, do you see what I see? What in the hell is it?" Everyone stood in near total amazement. The other shoe fell when Joa had made her entrance into the BIG-BUS-LAB using the back-side ramp of the behemoth and was heard yelling to Trojan:

"Lieutenant Trojan, duty calls! Hey! I will let you know what I find out and any new developments that occur. Talk to you soon. See you when I return, "Ciao!"

The activity there had once again been temporarily stopped because as impressively as 54-TI had arrived; it was now preparing to make a quick departure. The small discrete markings on the side door read S.I.I.T.F. This had not gone unnoticed by Trojan's eagle blue-green eyes, at which point a small smile came to his sensual lips:

"Definitely more than just a pretty face he thought." The imposing machine left as quickly and as quietly as it had arrived, taking all the valuable materials which had been harvested from Dennis's RV. Trojan sensed that the team within the beast was already devouring and processing the evidences.

Joa Has Swallowed a Few of Trojan's Finest Tactical Men

After the departure of 54-TI, Trojan returned to his work, but it left him concerned that the behemoth had also swallowed a few of his finest tactical men. Tom, Dick and Harry were nowhere to be found, scooped up by the veritable Joa. You could not miss these three Musketeers as they stood out among the rest of the men. Tom was six feet seven, and looked like an emaciated scare crow; Dick may have been six feet but looked like a tackle in the National Football League. His nickname was the refrigerator for his immense bulk and strength. As far as Harry was concerned he was just five feet, if lucky, and fairly rotund, you could almost call him a beach ball. He was, however, one of the most brilliant computer experts on the planet. It was joked that he could hack his way into heaven, or hell, depending on his choice of the moment.

Trojan was still a little pensive, thinking that Joa had maybe had chosen his men well before, maybe, her setups the whole crew...? As he returned to his men, they suddenly exclaimed in unison as if they had been orchestrated:

"Hey Trojan! What the hell was that monstrosity?" A little taken aback by the questions, he showed a certain amount of annoyance and began to frown:

"Oh hell! They are gone but they are a fine bunch of agents and police officers." He then replied in a devil-may-care manner:

"You boys saw it as well as I did? What it is and what the Boa is doing, we will find out soon enough and only when she is ready and able to provide that type of information. Now, however, my biggest concern is if she only knows where she is off too, with so little protection, and she doesn't seem to give a rat's ass who is left worrying about her."

Trojan shook his head and said laughingly to his men, who were currently the only ones in earshot:

"My educated guess would be Tampa for a lot more than just simple ride, and she has left us holding the proverbial bag, and whatever has caught her attention in Tampa. All I can say to them is, my condolences!" While Joa is gone, there are still things to take care at. She was flying to Tampa hoping or had an intuition of finding more evidences. While that lapse of time other things were happening at the crime scene.

The Press Stupid Questions

A few minutes went by, while they were getting the scene secured, when noises began emanating from the furthest parking lot from the Inn. Blake shouted to Trojan:

"Oh hell, speaking of bags! Here comes some of the content now. The press with all their paraphernalia, vehicles, and idiots complete with their standard collection of stupid questions." The team began to chuckle and continued working, when suddenly someone shouted:

"Hey! Is there someone here who can tell me what is going on? Was there a gun fight at the Daytona Beach Coral?"

One of the TV journalists had broken away from the herd and made his way pass the police tape and barricades to the front of the Dennis RV. Trojan briskly walked over to intercept the wayward journalist and give him the standard line used in these cases:

"Everything is only at the preliminary stage of an ongoing investigation. We have no concrete information to add or release to the press at the moment." Trojan unceremoniously escorted the reporter to the proper side of the barricade system and told him loudly for all of them to understand:

"You move again this side and I have you arrested for contaminating the crime scene, OK?" And he left the rest of the army of journalists standing behind the barricades which had been set up to protect the crime scene. Police officers had been posted to ensure security, and they did their job well, and quite enthusiastically. Not many of them were overly fond of journalists.

After dealing with the press, Trojan returned to discuss with Blake, how the crime site should be secured until Commander Herckel arrives. Both were a little concerned about how this would be done as the site was very large and very open. Trojan said to Blake:

"Joa knows, do not be worried, we bay be released from here very soon." Another concern was the influx of tourists due to Bike Week. Trojan shaking his head said to Blake with a smirk:

"Oh hell! Boa knows when to take her leave and go chasing after trouble. However, she has warned me often enough to let her do her job. Wish the hell she wasn't so good at finding trouble!" AND MORE noise came from the sky.

Joa's Message

Prior to her departure, Joa had left a clear message to all the law enforcement forces, currently at the crime site; this also included the very persistent press she knew that would make them always and ever annoying appearance. It didn't take much of a blood hound to sniff out the story played out here, and details as well as horrific videos and images would be fed to the various media outlets with various reporters feeling like they had done something absolutely amazing.

Joa wanted the others to know that she was part of a bigger picture and they should let her do her job. She had often said the same thing to Trojan in the past, but her work for the most part was secret and Trojan knew little, except that it was dangerous. Secretly, she liked that he was concerned about her, and hid that concern poorly. This battle of wills had become a constant conflict within them, and often Joa, with lightning speed and not mincing her words could establish exactly what her position was, nothing more and nothing less.

For her, it was only about her job, and never a question about ability or superiority or anger. This was one of her characters stretches, and one of the reasons why Trojan had nicknamed her Boa, but also one of the reasons he founds her so captivating, not just attractive. He knew that she really was that so good. Sometimes, what she did seem like a natural skill that she did the best without really trying.

Trojan, on a Need to Know Basis Only

While Joa was on her way to Tampa the crime scene was on Trojan's responsibility until Commander Herckel arrives. Once they had put their plan in place to secure the crime site, Blake interrupted his thoughts with:

"Hey Trojan! I guess you will let the Boa do her job? Am I correct"? Trojan replied a little impatiently at his Sergeant and close friend:

"Oh, the nymph with you! Did you not see that rolling monstrosity of a traveling wagon she left in, eh? I bet you, she already knows what the hell occurred here and I suspect it's a hell lot more than what meets the eye at this crime scene. However, she told me she would contact me with whatever information she could as soon as she was given the OK. I guess I am on a need to know basis only."

Blake addressed Trojan:

"My friend! You were smart not to give a detailed version of the incident to the press. Bet your bottom dollar, Boa would once again have had her own version, which will be completely different. Once it all comes down, you rest assured it'll be a lot more exciting than the gong show."

Trojan looked at Blake and said in a very complimentary manner:

“Yeah! But I tell you, that lady has a lot of what it takes to be an excellent law enforcement officer. Between you and me she seems to see everything we do not see. Call it intuition, law enforcement skills or just that she never gives up whatever the outcome may be, whatever it is, we must be honest and give her the just dues that are hers. She is so damn good at what she does and I have to admit, has a gorgeous looking.”

At that Trojan nodded to Blake and turned to leave. There was greater than urgent work to be done at the crime scene with his name written on it. He had only begun making a few preliminary mental notes when he heard Blake coming up behind him and mumbling something, he turned and waited for him shouting loud enough for Blake to hear over the noise in the parking lot:

“Hey Blake! Did you get a good look at that monstrosity of a Mobil Lab and the equipment? I could not believe my eyes, when the side back of it opened up and away went Joa up the ramp with her Harley and off she goes just like in a bloody Batman film.” Laughing Blake asked:

“Do you know where she has flown off to”? With a grin on his face and a wink he said to Blake:

“Really, now do you need to ask? She has gone to Tampa for some FISHING purposes. Pity the bastards she is after.” Blake in his usual joking way, looking at Trojan while rolling his eyes and said:

“Well, do we head out after her or do we sit here and keep holding the bag?” Trojan’s perhaps a little too quick response was:

“Hey, Blake! We have a job right here to do. She will cope very well without us; she’s a big girl now and does not need a nursemaid, especially the likes of us." After a few minutes of silence as he worked, Trojan added:

"Anyways she cannot be everywhere! I will look after calling the Miami Dade office to tell them of the death of some of Tonito's boys! At least the ones we could identify. I will solicit their help in getting information on the others by providing dental and finger prints wherever possible, maybe you can talk to Carl 'Skeleton's Bakker the coroner, and get that if they are ready." Blake agreed without hesitation and replied:

"I will get on that and keep you posted ongoing as the team finds out more from the crime scene data that we are now accumulating." Blake headed out towards the far end of the crime scene on the side where the beach was located to check out some data the team had provided him with.

Stepping out from the grassy area near the bullet riddle RV and making his way down the road on the West side of the Inn, Trojan headed for his car which was parked a considerable distance from the death scene. Once he had gotten into his blue Beemer, he made his call to the central office in Miami and asked to speak with Captain Sammy Longbow, his long-time friend and his former captain:

"Eh, Sammy! Have you seen the broadcast on TV of the carnage at the Daytona Beach Inn?" In a gruff calm voice, Sammy says:

"Yeah! Quite a massacre I would say. 'Probably' bring a lot more rats out of the holes over this one." Trojan agreed and warned him that things will start happening very soon down his way as well. However, the Captain stopped him and says:

"Yeah Trojan! The Boa has just sent me a fax. She has listed a dozen names and addresses of known dubious and somewhat colorful characters that reside here in Miami, especially in Dade County. I thought all of them had retired and were now living on their mega yachts enjoying the good life and leaving us in peace." Trojan response was a resounding:

"I thought so too." After a pregnant pause, the captain laughingly says to Trojan:

"You know, this is a lot bigger than we think. We need to watch our step and keep our eyes and ears open on this one or we will wind up like today's news, cold and dead." Trojan responded on an equally serious note:

"Yes, you are right, they will continue killing each other and nothing will change because others will take over their place. That is what is so sad, because we cannot seem to stop the vicious cycle. Well, Sammy, watch your back, my friend. Keep in touch."

When Trojan had finished talking to Captain Sammy Longbow and knew that the Boa had filled him in on the situation, he remembered that his next steps would be waiting for Commander Bridget Herckel to take over the crime site.

Trojan Sets the Record Straight

Trojan tried to always be sure of his facts and usually he was on top of everything. Unfortunately, this time he came too quickly to a conclusion. He believed that this was a settlement of accounts between the two rival gangs which also encompassed drugs and prostitution. For him, The Pouilleux was there simply at the wrong time.

Perhaps he was distracted by some of Joa's very quick observations; thankfully he had responded to the insistent press the way he had in deflecting their repeated and persistent questions. His public relations training had helped him in responding in such a vague way as not to anger the press, who after all were doing their jobs. Another reporter at the back asked again about something that had to be kept under wrap so for the thousandth time he said:

"Everything is only at the preliminary stage of an ongoing investigation; we have no concrete information to add or provide to the press at the moment. Thank you, ladies, and gentlemen. I must return to continue investigation. We may have information for you later, but for the present I must say that it is an ongoing investigation."

Seeing they were unable to get information from Trojan, various journalists left, followed by their camera men and entourage, and rushed towards another source of information, someone they did not actually like, but the grass might be greener there. Their bosses' criteria were: **boost the ratings**, so they were told to try and obtain whatever information they could get from local police, in this case, it was Captain Bill Trapp. The press wanted, images and video of the actions, so they could keep the public entertained and boost their ratings, which, of course, was a source of revenue for them and it's even why they are there.

Conflicting Revelations by Local Police

The venerable Captain Bill Trapp, with a mountain of work on his plate and the current world very heavy on his shoulders had almost made good his escape from the crime scene, but it was not to be. He was identified, overtaken, and surrounded by media, which normally he avoided like the plague, and for him at this moment, they were worse than Armageddon and a visit from his outspoken teenage daughter combined. It was a feeding frenzy and he was, for all intents and purposes, their intended lunch. Bill Trapp was better than a group of journalists. Much better. The questions rolled over him rapid fire and so he took control of the problem by simply standing quietly in the center of the microphones and cameras, looking downwards in a zoned-out fashion. His power over them was near tangible, almost as if an invisible switch had been thrown to the OFF position, and they became silent.

He pointed, received a question from one reporter, and spoke quickly without a second's hesitation:

"I will tell you what facts I am able to tell you. When I stop, anything further will be speculation, which I do not do, and at that moment this press interview is over and I leave. I have work to do. Is that clear?"

Bill Trapp's presence was unassuming, almost clumsy, but when Bill Trapp needed to be Captain Bill Trapp, one simply knew that one did not argue the point. There were a few nods, and the silence continued, so Captain Bill Trapp did too:

"What we do know is that there was an armed altercation in the parking lot. There were present and involved in this altercation, members of two different criminal organizations. The body count is incomplete, but what I can tell you is that there is at least twenty-three or more, dead or injured. At this time, we do not know what or who triggered this criminal activity and I know that what you do not want to hear is that the investigation is ongoing. You now know as much as I do. As soon as there is more concrete information to release, the police media representative will advise you. Good day ladies and gentlemen."

He smiled. His professional smile was multi-use, like a psychological Swiss Army knife, and the crowd parted as before the staff of Moses as the good captain strode off through the sea of journalists to do what he was paid to do.

Captain Trapp's comfort zone with the media came in the form of organized press conferences where he was a contributor as opposed to being ground zero. Prepared, he was more than skillful in his communications prowess and took great pride in reporting, not just his own, but police accomplishments in doing their job. He was after all a team leader, and it was a normal and a given for him to laud his officers, simply because they were good and he believed in them. When the situation was impromptu or uncontrolled, he generally elected to say little rather than to risk making his beloved police department a target.

The press corps was surprised but not shocked by Bill's short presentation of the facts pertaining to the incident in question. It was usual for Bill, to illustrate on any police activities as well as the legalities involved, and his department's involvement in highly volatile incidents. The media hounds had no bones to pick with the Captain; he had provided them with minimal information and knew they would not get anything else for the moment so they turned tail and left.

"Ho! You may have that... FBI might take the case right now, look up there" he had with a little mouth-corner-smile.

As said, everything is happening in the same time, Joa has hurried to Tampa, and the Commander Bridget Herckel arrival was just after Joa hurried to quit for Tampa.

Bridget Herckel (SIRS) arrival

Trojan, had received the orders putting S.I.I.T.F. in charge of the investigation, at the crime scene in Daytona Beach. She felt bad that she had not had the chance to tell him what was happening with a little bit of, why? To smooth any feathers that may have been ruffled by the move. He apparently had been told by a one of the team leaders of the (SIRS), Swift International Retrievers Squad which was one of the many international mandated Forces of S.I.I.T.F. that he would be advised that they were assuming all further responsibility for the crime scene; and he and his men were

going to be relieved in an orderly fashion to avoid compromising the crime scene and for giving him the opportunity to take care of his important charge, the Bike Week security.

The Daytona Inn was now officially closed, OFF LIMITS to all press and local law enforcement. Now that it was clear that this was a global issue (SIRS) were there to protect evidences and crime scene integrity. They had requested and received additional re-enforcements from Cape Canaveral. A special division of S.I.I.T.F., some of their Swift International Retrievers Squad; or (SIRS) had been brought in, complete with weapons armed vehicles, and helicopters.

No one could come into contact with any material, or witnesses, until such time as the (SIRS) investigators had interviewed each and every one of them.

Trojan had also been told to keep his team on-site, until the Special Forces were in place and briefed. All other people no matter who they were, must be removed from the site as quickly as possible. So, Trojan knew that he was going to be released to his appointed Bike Week duties. But the first step as Joa had asked Bridget was to define the S.I.I.T.F. interest concerning the Daytona crime scene and then dispatch to FBI, the drug concern not pertaining to Dennis Kildem S.I.I.T.F. investigation.

There Were Two Different Cases Here

A global understanding had to be precise to everybody. Joa, on her way to Tampa, asks Commander Bridget Herckel about a fast briefing to Trojan's team on the next steps appending at the crime site. To not lose time, she has tuned her radio on a special channel covering all forces around and specified:

"Hi! This is Commander Bridget Herckel from the (SIRS), division of S.I.I.T.F., in charge of the whole crime scene. I have to precise which is concerning our investigation: The Dennis Kildem and Joa's S.I.I.T.F. investigation is ours and the other part of the drug gangs that Joa was not interested in will be yours. But there were many other investigations going on with different law enforcement agencies, FBI was drugged concerned, CSI Miami was following Southern Fire gang, CIA was investigating since many years on industrial's espionage and money laundering on Dennis but didn't know anything on Tennis personally; or, didn't want to know because too complicated. So, to anyone concerned about a part of the present state of this investigation, you have to be knowledge that this is only the beginning part of an important, ever, worldwide criminal and money-laundering investigation. So, as soon it's possible, maybe tomorrow or a coming day, you will be informed. Thanks, I'll be very busy, so please let me do my work!"

Bridget is always clear and clean, and she has the character and the corpulence to impose.

Security Established: Bridget Herckel on-site

The Powerful Net of (SIRS) is spread

Indeed, Trojan knew about (SIRS). He had been hurriedly almost informed by Joa as she departed that re-enforcements from S.I.I.T.F. would be on-site very quickly. The quality of very quickly caught him a bit off guard, and the manner of 'very quickly irked him somewhat, to say the least. Very quickly came in the form of two Mi35M transport helicopters. Not as fast as their stock Euro copter X3, but the latter was unavailable from Cape Canaveral. The Mi-35M disgorged the (SIRS) teams, any one of whom had no idea of what the words slow or easy meant. The men and women exited like their transport was about to explode, they knew

exactly where they were supposed to be, who they were supposed to talk to, or with, and what they looked like.

Their commanding officer was an ex-field commander from NATO by the name of Bridget Herckel and she had earned both of her positions with minimal difficulty. Commander Herckel was German and stood six feet two in her bare feet, weighed in at one hundred and forty-three pounds; none of it was fat. She was tall, she was beautiful, and with one glance, you knew you did not mess with her.

Bridget was a professional Soldier and in all reality was quite typical of an S.I.I.T.F officer. Everyone had very special but differing skills, and Commander Herckel's skills were, on first impression, very obvious. She was very clearly not short of a briefing before her arrival and already knew most of the, who, what, where, when and why? Of the extensive crime scene. The rotors had not stopped turning, when her troops deployed to push back the perimeter, gain stricter crowd control, and search out who she needed, all orchestrated before she arrived. Herckel dispatched one of her troops on a dedicated mission to fetch Trojan, whom she knew by the detailed dossier given to her, and that she had all words, image by image in her memory. Before her arrival, he was the liaison between law enforcement and S.I.I.T.F., and, to her understanding, was strengthening the initially undermanned S.I.T.F. team.

When the S.I.I.T.F. agent caught up with Trojan, the latter was already aware that something was going on. The activities of the perimeter control were loud and impossible to go unnoticed. Trojan had already spotted Commander Herckel and reasoned that she was either in charge, or at least important and he was making his way towards her through the press of parked vehicles, when the (SIRS) agent accosted him indicating with a hand gesture and simply said:

“Lieutenant Detective Trojan, Commander Herckel would like to speak with you, now, sir.” Trojan paused briefly, and nodded at the agent wordlessly. Then continued towards the commander, he knew exactly what he would say to begin with, and was as they say, not in his happy place.

Trojan was the same height as the commander, and with a terse, excuse me stepped around in front of her, and between the commander and the agent she was speaking with, interrupting that conversation somewhat abruptly. Trojan immediately became aware of her, her badge, her uniform, her rank insignia, her physical presence of power, and her piercing ice blue-green eyes; and the importance of whatever words he had had ready simply ceased to exist; instead, he stated with straightforward Trojan simplicity and strength:

“I am Lieutenant Detective Gordon Trojan, temporary in charge at this active crime scene.”

Commander Herckel met his gaze and spoke simply but effectively:

“Yes, Lieutenant Trojan. Thank you. I am aware of whom you are and I will speak with you in just one moment, as soon as I have dispatched my agents.” Trojan turned enough so that she could continue her instructions. She spoke but a few seconds and the agent left for his mission.

Commander Herckel turned to Trojan to address this next issue. She was Commander in all respects, and had an excellent command, not only of her staff, but of all the skills necessary to lead them, only some of which were diplomacy and establishing dominance, which she did now in such a way as to assume complete control of the crime scene from Trojan, without the necessity nor the opportunity of a single verbal shot being fired. Not happy, but completely outgunned, Trojan had no choice but to hand his authority over to her, and guarantee that within the next 10 minutes his men would be ready to debrief her in the Dolphin Room at the Daytona Inn, and present any evidences they had to support her investigation.

Under her very capable tutelage she had within a very short period of time all the vehicles belonging to the two gangs identified, marked and ready to put on tractor trailers. Bridget had ensured there would be enough of these huge trailers and escort teams to haul and protect the vehicles. Everything was synchronized as planned since ever.

The trucks had now arrived and were in a queue waiting for their escort team, to take the evidences away to a secured area. They had been ordered to wait for their escort team leader, and then on his order, to pick up all the vehicles which were identified and displaying a yellow tag in their side windows. The truck driver and the team leader were to make sure that the doors were properly sealed to safeguard against anyone entering the vehicles. Any deviation from these orders would incur Bridget fury, and no one wanted to have that happen. All trucks and trailers were escorted, with heavy security, to a hangar located at a nearby FBI yard. It had been commandeered cleaned, and the owner's protests rapidly silenced with monetary compensation. It was, in a sense, a large holding area in which the crime lab teams could, at their leisure, comb through all vehicles for the smallest grain of evidence and also for identification to dead criminals on the crime scene. The FBI cooperation was helpful and they knew what kind of evidences Bridget needed.

The sky was still littered with several media helicopters, who had been warned to leave the crime zone or risking being ordered to land. If so, they may be charged with obstruction of justice by the special forces of S.I.I.T.F., who had the F.A.A. on their side. With the magnitude of the crime, and the sudden influx of forces from outside, the media were now electrified and on high alert. On-site security forces were now very hard pressed to control both the masses and the media. All were demanding to know what was going on. They had a right to know, it was after all, their backyard.

The Whole World Rocked by Macabre Scenes in the Media

The authorities poured over the crime scene like ants at a macabre picnic. Meanwhile, very shortly after the massacre, Channel 18, DBN News shocked the international community with video footage of the carnage shot by an amateur who, at this time, had refused to come forward, insisting on remaining anonymous. This, all in a statement made by Sylvia Hall, station manager, well respected and highly-sought-after journalists in her right and daughter of well-known retired owner of Channel 18 DBN, just prior to the footage being aired on the news.

Ms. Hall made the statement in conjunction with the announcement that the footage was extremely graphic and although, some of the images had been blurred to conform to FHC laws and regulations, that viewer discretion must be used due to the extremely violent nature of the footage.

The News Channel, then followed with live-on-the-scene footage of all the various law enforcement officials and first responders on the scene, but the officials had pushed the police crime scene barriers so far back from the carnage, that even the best of their telephoto lenses were not equal to the footage first aired.

The News Channel Banners Kept Rolling

"BREAKING NEWS – GANG WAR ARMAGEDDON at Daytona Beach Inn–STAY TUNED TO CHANNEL 18...... GUNFIGHT AT THE DAYTONA CORRAL,"

And the news announcer continually interrupted the live broadcasts, with short clips of the incredible gun battle that had taken place. Even the news helicopter was hard pressed to show anything of interest, as the police helicopter had taken over that section of the skies and the news station pilot had been issued an immediate and terse warning:

"Keep well clear. Do not interfere in police work in any way, or face possible arrest and seizure of your aircraft by United States Air Marshall."

The events were rapidly growing in stature in such a way that even the seasoned news personnel from Channel 18 were struggling to keep up. This was brought home to channel 18 with sobering clarity when the story was but an hour old. The station phone lines, hot to the touch with other stations requesting INS. Then, three men dressed in ominously dark suits, strode unceremoniously and unannounced into Ms. Halls office. They brandished federal badges and rather convincing documents that on initial examination gave the impression that the ink was scarcely dry, and the authority therein was ultimate:

"Surrender the original video and all copies, and the identity of the videographer, employee or..." Ms. Hall smiled grimly at the stone-faced agent and wordlessly turned to the copy machine and photocopied a paper from her desk, handing it without fanfare to Mr. Suit.

What it essentially contained was an obviously hastily written agreement, signed by Ms. Hall that simply stated the bearer of the original document was the sole proprietor of the video, was in possession of the original, and that Channel 18 would pay standard news copyright fees to the rightful owner. First Mr. Suit turned to his friend Mr. Suit and said a quiet:

"Son-of-a-witch"!

Ms. Hall spoke matter-of-factly, but coldly to first Mr. Suit, handing him a small video card and at the same time regaining control and dominance of her personal queendom:

"Here! Take this! You can see from the contract that there is no 'original,' at least not in our possession. We do not know the identity of the person in question nor his or her whereabouts. We have reciprocal agreements with six other networks and we have eleven outgoing feeds. That video is in cyber-land and, if you want all available copies..." And she paused just enough for effect before muttering the word:

"Gentlemen!"

"I would suggest, you get a warrant for the arrest of Planet Earth. Now if you would excuse me, I have a job to do. In case you forgot, the door is right over there." As if connected by an invisible string, all three noses turned in unison and filed unceremoniously out of the indicated portal. They had sufficient enough intelligence to realize that not only, were they beaten, they had shown up far too late for the fight and had lost by default. The reality is that there is so much agencies competing against each other, tailing for the same information that it's hard to issue to a salvation.

Once they had left, Ms. Hall sat quietly just for a moment, surveying one of the monitors mounted on a wall in her glass-enclosed office. Despite the fact that she was a war-seasoned news correspondent and had risen through the ranks to her present job, the scenes of carnage had taken charge for a moment. This was different. This was her home. That was where she entertained guests and held news conferences. She felt personally violated, with an even more determined sense of journalistic duty, to make sure that everyone got the story, all the story. Only in this way, only pure raw truth could serve whatever justice must take place in that particular case.

Then the professional in her, reclaimed composure and she began planning the next broadcast format. If a picture was worth a thousand words, this video was most certainly an entire library in its impact and meaning. Because of the legal implications and the graphic nature of some of the content, she had to be very careful in what she released. Also, she thought grimly, she recognized some of the faces that had appeared in the video, and knew that those therein were of the highest echelons of organized crime.

She did not want her station, her employees nor did she personally put at risk. There was a small part of her, in recognizing some of the crime heads of state lying in the grotesque positions they assumed in death, thought for a brief moment, innocence lost.

Well, live by the gun, die by the gun. You may have saved us the cost of a trial, but it was still far too expensive. We still lose.

Dennis caught in cold killing action!

Exposed by video cam footage

Prior to the killings and Dennis being caught on video cam, Joa had been unable to make the connection between Dennis and the other supposedly well-established gangster known as Tennis. These rather dirty characters had quite similar profiles but there was something, some piece of the puzzle that for the moment she could not fathom. She knew something was there, her instincts and intuition told her that there was more but just what that more was still a mystery. Perhaps too, it was SOMBRAJ, giving her a little nudge as he had felt her struggle with this conundrum. Then slowly, a suspicion grew, a light began to slowly illuminate in her sharp mind and thought:

"Was it possible that these two characters, in reality, were one and the same person?" Joa never jumped to conclusions, but she trusted herself. She knew there was something to her instincts, and she would not let go until it was clear and solid. The question marks only fired her determination more. The Boa's coils were slowly beginning to close around her prey. One question in her mind was just:

"How had these two, triggered all the actions?" Prior to this Dennis had flown fairly low under S.I.I.T.F radar and he seemed untouchable, because of his high political associates and friends, which gave him an air of respectability. Dennis was no longer persona-non-grata, since the video which was taken had been aired on the regional TV news channel DBN 18, showing the scene of the cold-blooded murder which had taken place at the Daytona Beach Inn; clearly showing an angry red-faced Dennis as he shouted:

"Kill that damn Puerto Rican dog! Kill that son-of-a-witch! What the hell are you waiting for! Kill the good-for-nothing bastards PORCO-RICO!"

Running over to his man who was standing motionless, frozen in place by the unfolding events and words emanating from his boss, Dennis had torn the revolver from the man's hand and shot the victim point blank, simply because he had the look of a Spaniard. The poor unarmed innocent victim had fallen to his knees, but Dennis had fired without hesitation. Even, in the slightly blurred video, the look on the face of the cold-blooded killer sketched chills and a sense of repulsion to anyone unfortunate to view that hatred racist cold-killer scene.

It was obvious that Dennis, who on one hand was an unquestionably intelligent and savvy business man, also had a twisted distorted mind with delusions of grandeur and power, causing him to lose control of his otherwise brilliant financial mind. In these instances of rage, tantrums and power struggles he had been heard to saying, those damn Puerto Rican dogs. No matter how successful or brilliant the individual was, if the person was Spanish, Dennis detested them. Whatever the cause of this hatred, no one had ever dared ask him. According to him, they did not have the right to live, and in his sick twisted mind he had the right to kill them. The man was not just a criminal, but a psychotic sociopath. It seems to have a similar distortion as kamikazes...

Tennis, Dennis's Dual Personality

At this time, Joa was still unaware of Dennis's dual personality; it had been and was still a well-kept secret within the echelons of crime. The name Tennis had been linked to an individual who was allegedly leader of one of the most significant networks of drug trafficking, killing contracts and illicit money laundering, and as well as one of the most important financiers of organized crime operating in the world. Even FBI and CIA and Interpol were interested about Tennis activities, as a part of his international industrial and commercial espionage activities.

She had been following Tennis's activities even before her assignment to S.I.I.T.F., this individual's name had come up again and again whenever trafficking was involved, whether it was drugs, weapons, diamonds, white slavery or simple racketeering. Whoever this elusive character was, she was impressed with his reputation of cold blooded, indeed ice-cold-blooded brutality and ruthlessness in his dealings.

To gather more information on these dubious characters and hopefully find out more about the almost legendary Tennis, she was anxious about heading to Tampa and on his big Yacht too, with her team, even if she was only fishing for more evidences. But, according to what she got from Dennis RV, Joa was driven by a magnet to get the Consortium's biggest fish.

But who and what is that Dennis—Tennis?

Nobody seems to know him—oh no—not any more since his face is encrusted on the TV screen and seen at repetition. He is now the most, wanted dead man, on the planet Earth... Anybody will now help the investigation because no one would be scared of him, anymore. His name is known as a rapacious that any Latin would like to see dead, for paying for his crimes.

The investigation revealed that the man, Dennis Kildem, presumable Tennis, killed with a bullet to the forehead as he fell to his knees, was an American businessman of Colombian descent who had no affiliation with the Miami gang. Unfortunately, the victim was at the Inn for business purposes with the Inn management regarding hotel linens, a twist of fate had made him a victim.

Joa was still pondering the various aspects of the investigation and the identity of the individuals who had been killed, when again her mind returned to the elusive Tennis. Tennis was still flying low under Joa's radar. She kept wondering and had doubted:

"Who is this guy? He seems to be well hidden in this web of intrigue? I will find you, if you exist, mi amigo! ¡Cuidase mucho! Careful, I am coming for you!"

One Victim Identified

Paolo's family, after being called for congratulation, the TV was quickly inundated all around the world, with news regarding the man who had been murdered at the Daytona Beach Inn. Apparently, this man was a patron of the Inn, and all of the employees knew Paolo Caballero, a gentle, kind, and friendly man, small stature, but with a big heart. This family man was leaving behind, a wife and three young children. The staff at the Inn loved and admired Paolo. They saw him at least once a month when coming to talk to the management of the Inn, about his wonderful linen products.

The report aired that Paolo had been shot in the middle of the forehead after he had fallen to his knees. The reported shooter, a well-known worldwide businessman, Dennis Kildem, apparently had murdered the victim in cold blood as he begged for mercy. The story evolved on a grand scale on social media and TV, its repercussions growing quickly to an international scale.

The Voyeurs of the Whole World, Enraged, Irritated

The public understandably was enraged and irritated with the almost unbelievable savagery of Kildem's sickening crime. This outrage, it seemed, now fueled a new and intense wave of public feeling; one that demanded more justice. They wanted to see the story unfold, the criminals brought to justice. The public energy on this one crime had apparently become focused like never before, and it seemed every law enforcement officer on the globe was now attuned to that one word, Kildem. It was also now absolutely certain that Kildem's associates, everyone up and down the criminal food chain from him, would be closely watching this situation unfold. This one event had sent shock waves through the entire worldwide criminal adepts.

Racism touches everybody and awakens even those who have an unknown to themselves tendencies. The Dennis Kildem racial crime vision was spread out to our voyeur eyes by this wonderful media, television. It was unrolling before our eyes as true as images can manage our imagination and deeply inflame our comportments with others and disrupt someone's sensitivity. This is why Medias especially TV could be hazardous or beneficial to viewers. In this case, everybody wants Dennis Kildem dead, especially those who speak Spanish.

TV Channels Concentrating on Dennis Kildem the Assassin

As Joa ask her Headquarters, to postpone the information about the Kildem RV's treasure trove seizure, for an hour or two, just to give an advance to the Tampa DK Palace requisition, the S.I.I.T.F. Headquarters have arranged with Ms. Hall from DBA channel 18. The answer was:

"Yes, we already have enough readings for now with the assassin Kildem, thanks, see you later Maxim."

"Oh! Maxim, you know that leak can come from anywhere, with a case of that prominence, billions of dollars are talking, so we have to be very restrained.

Nobody knew anything about what 54-TI had from the Kildem RV. Nobody would ever imagine somebody, stupid enough, to carry in his RV, so much incriminating evidence.

So, after the now, on and on, Dennis's cold killing event repetition on, about the Dennis Kildem appearance on TV all over the world, Joa's hopes, is for little more time to fulfill the Tampa operation.

Dual death conviction, by the media, and the whole world!

The media did their job well in airing the videos. They efficiently acted as his judge, jury and convicted him without a judicial trial and they acted as the trigger for any executioner or rites of wrongs. He has been found guilty for the atrocious racial killing of an innocent, both on the media and globally, and the verdict is death. Dennis is on the run and has no place to hide, or does he? Anyone Porto Ricans want him dead for what he did to one of them. Anyone Spanish speaking want him to be dead for his hatred racist words against Spanish-born blood human being. Anyone in the whole world now knows his face. He is, till this moment seen on TV, the most wanted dead man, that no one would like to see him alive in any country. Every 2 minutes, the same video repeats, and everybody wants to see it again and again. It is possible that, in everyone self, that there is a message for most of us: are we really different from others? Are we not all humans, so Brothers?

CHAPTER 9

Trakker gives more explanation on sequences

Even if images worth a thousand words, as through the video cam where the action is being depicted as if in a movie, sometimes it is important to give a little more explanation on things which appeared commonplace, but, quite often have a bearing on the story, as a whole. So now, Trakker addressing directly to the voyeurs as we all are:

"I know that you need more explanations because everything was happening in the same time, within half an hour to other things an hour. I was then closer, on the crime site with my cameras until the killing was over and right after Joa hastened away to Tampa with 54-TI. Till that moment after Bill Trapp did his show-off, almost all, of any law enforcement agencies were trying to get a part of the cake. But there was no cake, it was only doing things the right way to finally stop criminal doers."

"So now, let's go back through my cam viewer!"

See what was unrolling before everybody's personal stakes. And everything became crazy and give rise to competition. And every single law enforcement and local agencies wanted to get a part of the cake. They were there to justify their job, or hoping to get a promotion out of it, but they were not there to cooperate in anything, it was becoming a battle of power. Who was the highest in the echelon of supremacy?

- First, for Trojan, it was a Bike weak case, OK, there was BIKES around.
- Bill Trapp, it was my territory.
- FBI had that drug case in hands since years.
- CIA had two different cases: Tennis and a different Dennis since years, it was an international case in cooperation with Interpol, Scotland Yard, and GRC, since years. Tennis case was for several criminal offenses as killing and Dennis Kildem case was for buying and selling information from industrial and commercial espionage, money laundering and counterfeit transactions all over the world.
- CSI Miami Drug Department were the only one asking for later on information.

So, Commander Bridget Herckel had to make the point HERE:

"Hi, every one of you! As I said on radio, but I understand that no one had listened: any agencies of yours are on any of those cases since too long slipping time, that's why S.I.I.T.F. has been formed, to act fast and internationally. So, tomorrow or the next day you will be, for those interested, briefed accordingly to the Daytona's crime scene, but, concerning The Kildem's and the Consortium, you will be informed about what has unfolded at the crime scene only. National and international security secrecy will be divulged accordingly to your so dear state of interest echelon supremacy. I'm telling you, only what I'm authorized to tell, by my Headquarters; nothing is a source of my one personality. And we are also here to help any law enforcement agencies without competing or preferences. Thanks to all of you, and please let me do my work! Will see you in the next coming days, for the meeting."

Bridget had the tone to be understood without compromise, and everybody was now there to cooperate. She asks Bill Trapp to take care for security while FBI really had their hands at work.

Anticipation Was a Key

Earlier, long before Joa was leaving the crime scene, she had been anticipating a move by Dennis. When it came to law enforcement skills and instincts, she was second to none by the assessment of her peers, and she was all too well aware how severe the consequences would be if precautions were not taken to protect 54-TI, her people, and the evidences gathered within their criminal investigation.

Triggered by her intuition or perhaps nudged a little by SOMBRAJ, she had requested backup and additional forces. Her first concern after Daytona was going to Tampa. While going chasing she had first to protect the pit of the fruit Kildem's office and then, the big 65' yacht in Tampa Bay, and for more precautions his house in Orlando, even if he goes there once a month.

As soon Joa had the hold release on code 23 regional, she gives the order to requisition the 65s mega yacht Big Bang and haul the yacht in the middle of the Tampa Bay, far from any civilian area, in case Dennis had it exploded to destroy documents. And then ordered to occupy the DK Palace and get everybody out and protect the environment, and also the Orlando house. The Orlando house was only to get his wife out to a next closer Hotel, in case Dennis had hidden something compromising. His wife Jermain, has cooperated and said: "he has nothing in my house, I see him once in a while for bringing some money for expenses and we don't even talk about anything since many years."

And after a little minute, she wanted to precise, in a cold manner:

"He never stays more than 5 minutes and never goes anywhere in the house and never in the garage either."

Once the CONSO-DOWN has been unclenched

Since Joa initiated the code 23, she asks Maxim at Guardia Fortress:

"Maxime, be prepared to send teams close to the DK Palace," and when she discovered the treasure of evidences and after the S.I.I.T.F. Headquarters had unclenched the worldwide CONSO-DOWN operation, because they had enough evidences to do so, she called back Maxime:

"Go Maxime, what we have may not kill them but will hurt, I already upload to you a lot of incriminating evidences." Both of them were enthusiasm.

"OK Joa, Commander Francis DuFour is almost ready to go!" And 5 minutes later he called back Joa to reassure her, telling her that everything important is going to be treated immediately as soon they enter in Guardia Fortress.

"Joa, Francis is gone with five strong men and a trait body truck, to load everything needed and two Oshkosh JLTV, with nine men for help and protection. Local police and county Sheriffs will secure the area while we get all the Kildem's DK Palace office papers and evidences out of there."

National and International Security Forces Deployments

All known related institutions to the Consortium and (WTB) banks, businesses, multinationals, fiscal paradises inlets, syndicates, Trusts, were invaded by S.I.I.T.F. and allied police corpses everywhere in the world, but were put on hold, waiting for more documents evidences to close them down and arrest the concerned criminals. Even if they had evidences to arrest them, S.I.I.T.F. Headquarters wanted more evidences to kick them off for good.

The S.I.I.T.F. Headquarters according to National and International security now on a COMMITMENT, everybody was concerned and had to move fast.

For a little while, in 54-TI and when her helicopter joins her to fly to Tampa, she was with her little army but close to Orlando, and finally arrive the U.S. Air Force's armed war jets, helicopters hauling suspended Oshkosh, Humvees as a deployment as a war.

When 54-TI went mobile for more than a few moments or a few miles, there were also at her disposal 2-armed helicopter gunships sporting M134 Gatling guns, rocket pods with laser-guided air-to-air or ground missiles, and a complement of six fighters in each that could put the fear of hell into El Diablo himself.

Air force bases from Cape Canaveral and Tampa were coming soon on the party too. Tampa air forces were on their way all along I-4, patrolling from Tampa to halfway from Daytona. Cape Canaveral air force as fast they arrive close to 54-TI and other war jets were appointed to protect Joa on her way to Tampa. On land, armored Oshkosh JLTV, armed to the teeth were to be deployed all along I-4 to protect from mercenaries to surprisingly get out from the bush and trying to destroy 54-TI carrying the Dennis RV's documents.

Even though the 54-TI's body was constructed with bulletproof carbon fiber equivalent to an armored tank and was armed to the teeth with the most sophisticated weaponry; there was no doubt in Joa's mind, that Dennis and what was left of his organization would do anything to retrieve this treasure trove of evidences that she now had in her possession. By now, Joa was well aware that they all knew she was in possession of a hangman's noose, with their name on it, and she recognized the fact that they would not be happy. But Dennis assassin's face was on TV in repetition, the surprise for him will come later on, and he may lose some partners after they see what he has done; adding the hater's intolerance on him, he has created against him, might give a delay to Joa's teams.

Trakker explanations are sometimes necessary: While Joa was on her way to Tampa with General Bentall's armed protection, a lot of security was taking place all around Joa's operations. Roads, streets, fields around highways were in the process to be blocked and scout around for eventual mercenaries. All law enforcement agencies were unified for the first time ever and this all around the world. Bravo! That's the success ways...

Joa, flying high and fast to Tampa!

The Mobil Lab 54-TI on the move to Tampa

Joa had barely managed her escape with her 54-TI and her small but effective army, small in numbers, perhaps, but quite deadly when necessary. The Tiger had been notified earlier by the team in 54-TI, and sitting at the ready near Cape Canaveral. Once Joa had pronounced the code words—BRAVO, DELTA, URGENT ASSISTANCE REQUIRED, it was airborne to rendezvous as required. That rendezvous completed, it had left the small airstrip with its complement of passengers. They were now headed to Tampa to join the Black Hawk which had left much earlier on Joa's orders. Other local police and state marshals were assisting S.I.I.T.F. agents, keeping away any Dennis intruders. Coast Guards have hauled the Big Bang 65' yacht far in the middle of the Tampa Bay, and they got a specialist with a sniff dog and help to disconnect the batteries and any electrical system disarmed on the yacht to prevent Dennis to trigger destruction.

The tactical officers and the remainder of her agents were to join her ASAP at the designated secluded area in Tampa, then the force would head to an office complex known to be Dennis's DK Palace. Joa had obtained any additional local warrants necessary to local assisting police and all were now on their way to Tampa with a small army of specialized men and women, trained to deal with economic crime and national security. This was an impressive group of brains, sophisticated arms, and tactical assault training second to none which would be working in close proximity with the 54-TI tactical team and the Guardia Fortress.

Guardia Fortress, a Central Stronghold for Richness

Guardia Fortress is as a fortified citadel alike, to keep money and expensive values as diamond, gold and important papers against destruction or war bombing. The Tampa site is one of the strongest, indestructible, impenetrable, and fortified underground safe in the world; because Florida is one of the busiest money transits in the USA. And there is the US, S.I.I.T.F. Headquarters either and different allied united intelligence factions of the world.

Back in 54-TI, then Joa's brain team was deeply immersed in the job of dissecting the documents for information and evidences and purging the computers detained from Dennis's RV. They were to protect these evidences at all cost and if something unforeseen occurred, the information would be able to continue its journey through the legal system. Joa, before living 54-TI for her helicopter, the tiger, said to Maurice and his team.

"Here is why 54-TI has to go fast to Tampa, 54-TI is the only up-to-date intelligent machine to rapidly secure, scan, script, and upload all that so important information, and we may need to do the same with some information we might get from Dennis's office, and help our guys already on the spot. For the first half-an-hour we may be OK with our 4, armed helicopters but the air force and land forces are coming, so do not be disturbed to do your job. OK guys! I'm going up there with the tiger, rendezvous to the Tampa air force base."

Joa was already feeling something, as electromagnet, pulling her heart too secretive strange visions under big buildings pertaining or attach to Denis Kildem. She thought loudly:

"I feel enthusiasm for what we have done.....But I think, there is more, a lot more, that's why I feel as I ever felt before. OK! I'm coming to you alien!" We have to conclude that it is not being mentally hill, talking loudly to you, sometime..."

Bonanza of information to protect at all price

LISTING NAMES OF INTERNATIONAL CRIMINALS AND THEIR ACTIVITIES

Joa had been able to obtain an all-encompassing list of names identifying many international criminals from the documents seized from Dennis's RV. Some of these criminals were already known and being hunted by the international law enforcement forces of many countries. However, Money Talks, in this case it seemed to be able to say "S-h-h-h" very well, and so they were seeing other names hereabout believed to be respectable business magnates. Others were in positions of well-respected power, who for the first time could be shown directly connected to dirty crime and really dirty money. In an instant, their respectability and protection had evaporated. No longer were they hidden with their billions. Even known as good guys were transferring big money to (WTB) it was supposed to be the future, especially for crocks.

The data on the seized laptops was essentially a collection of hangman's nooses. The money laundering process in place was detailed in exacting and damning clarity. Some of it was extremely sensitive, incriminating some very lofty individuals and high-top politicians.

To avoid launching or triggering political pressures, Joa did not dare name well-known individuals who now appeared to be directly involved, at least for the present time. She knew that pressures of all kinds could come from all side and quite often from someone or something one never even suspected. Therefore, Joa played her hand close to her chest until she had a clear picture of everything she had at hand. Forewarned is forearmed and she did not want to lose a single one from her snares. In that special case, she was uploading everything to her hidden data bank and specially coded and scrambled that nobody could break.

Joa's Powers under Her International Mandate

Joa's powers under her international mandate were far and wide and allowed her to keep under wraps what she thought necessary to protect the furthering of her investigation. This mandate incorporated incidents where an economic crime affected more than two countries. The power of direction and priorities fell under the international mandate. This meant that, for the entire operation, Joa, and the upper echelon of S.I.I.T.F were depended on Federal Level Agreements signed by all countries involved.

This mandate guaranteed that a concerted effort first, and foremost, could be taken at the international level and simultaneously at a national level. This power had been agreed to by all signatories, in order to be able to fight effectively and internationally against economic crimes and extremism. Joa reported directly to the upper echelon of S.I.I.T.F when the incident had an international impact and secondly to the United State agency responsible for these types of crimes when they were committed and pertained to that country only. In addition, S.I.I.T.F had a liaison officer connected to the United Nations Legal Counsel Office.

To Catch the Big Fishes: Joa Needed More Evidences

She needed more than names to launch her all-out attack. She needed to have strong tangible proof and compelling evidences of fraud and specifics of crimes that had been committed. She needed hard evidence, paper trails, Bank Statements, emails, correspondence, proof of funds transfers, and signatures. She had the smoking gun but she was playing a game where the opposing forces were rank with power. So, the additional evidence she sought was essentially, the irrefutable eye witnesses. Money does talk, but she knew so does any kind of paper with a signature. Otherwise, she would find herself in a very precarious position and her investigation could die before she was able to make it count.

But, more than hopes she had about the Tampa Dennis office...

A Critical Situation: "I, JOE, Must Act!"

I am not a SOMBRAJ, but I am a journalist in the spirit, and that is something I have always known. I am a journalist in the truest of sense. It is something not encompassed with the word skill. One must have a feel for this and even the word feel, or any words for that matter, cannot describe what it is. For me, I just know where the story is; where things are that demand the light of day. Some stories are good, some bad, but all whisper in a voice that only a true journalist can hear. I was not just a voyeur, in the truest sense of that word. Nor even with the presence of SOMBRAJ, a mere puppet, or witness to the SOMBRAJ. Perhaps that is why I was chosen by him—it—she. I don't know. SOMBRAJ tells me of knowledge of other journalists, and I was chosen. Nothing more. SOMBRAJ has reasons, and I feel justifiably partnered with this entity.

As a journalist, I knew that I always should, could, and would take the initiative in going after information pertaining to stories which I discovered. It was never a question of courage or even morals, but simply who and what I was. A leopard cannot deny their spots. Sometimes the analysis and research would take me into the web of situations that had the potential of danger but I never hesitated, always persisted doggedly with confidence in my instincts, and always ensured the facts I held were indeed facts and not fiction before surrendering the story to any media.

SOMBRAJ and I needed to be in the midst of the action, but also stay secure and keep our anonymity intact, especially when it came to the criminal element which was at present our prime focus. It was rather high on both our priority lists, to avoid being on the lower end of the criminal food chain. That sort of thing had the capacity to spoil an otherwise good day, and I rather held to the idea of avoiding it.

An exception to those basic instincts had now become a reality for us. Joa up there and 54-TI, the both in their ways were heading into great danger, not just at Tampa. Dennis was desperate and would never let the evidences, in the hands of Joa's team, to explode into the hands of law enforcement. He and his personal organization would make a concentrated desperate attempt to retrieve or destroy it, no matter what's the cost. Dennis was well aware of what those costs would be to him, should he fail. Dennis faced the specter of the hangman's noose on two fronts. Not only was he in trouble with the law, but now there were many connected to him and this evidence, like dominoes standing in line on the gallows, and they would not be pleased with his stupidity. If they went down, it was a given that no matter what, Dennis would go too, and it would not be a mere prison cell that would be his forever home. It would be a most unpleasant trip indeed.

I had to put my skills as a negotiator into action to convince Trojan that Joa critically needed his assistance, NOW!

As far as, the consortium ignores what is in the Dennis RV's files and computers, Joa still has the big side of the baseball bat.

Convincing Trojan

It was imperative that I, with SOMBRAJ's support, convince Trojan that somehow, he must forget the investigation at Daytona and make his way to Tampa to help Joa because she would be coming under attack at any time. I had no idea that Trojan had just been dismissed from the primary responsibility of this massive investigation and was once again overseeing law enforcement around Bike Week.

I was afraid that getting to Trojan in his mobile office would be a bit of a feat. He was not regular police and I needed to get past Lieutenant Carl Rayner. I simply stated to the officer I had urgent evidence that Joa was in critical danger and I would speak only to Trojan personally. Perhaps SOMBRAJ assisted on that one, or perhaps the officer knew how important Joa was to Trojan.

At any rate, I found myself standing in front of Trojan's desk. He looked up and made immediate eye contact and spoke with abruptness:

"I didn't hear you knock! How, did you get in here?" and he looked past me for an explanation from his lieutenant. There had been any number of wan-a-be-s and knows-it-all, during the parking lot fiasco who had inundated him and his force with their drivel. I had to show him with rapid crystal clarity I was different. I spoke quickly and urgently:

"Lieutenant Detective Gordon Trojan, I have extremely important information for you concerning the safety of Joa." Trojan was on his feet and his manner was now not just police. This was personal. This was Trojan, on steroids. He knew, I knew something but who was I, and most important, how did I know it?

His eyes shifted to me immediately, and without waiting a second for his question, and with help from SOMBRAJ that I could sense, I spoke tensely:

"Joa needs your help. Hell is about to break loose in Tampa and you needed to get yourself over there with as large a force as possible. You have no way of knowing that Dennis's men and a force of highly armed mercenaries, both ground and air, are headed straight for Joa and the treasure trove of important information and evidences she has in hold." Trojan's cold and authoritative reply was immediate:

"How in Hell's name do you know this? How are you connected to this and how do you know about Dennis and things no one should know? No one knows of Joa's whereabouts. How do you? Make it good!"

The cavalry of one SOMBRAJ came over the hill to my rescue and gave me the key I needed. The images and voices flashed into my mind and I said to Trojan:

You remember when you arrive at the Inn, from your coffee break and finally arrived at the shootings, said to Joa:

"You're OK Joa you are OK, not hurt! And she said: "Thank you for your concern and my gratitude is genuine. You know as well as I do that technically we are both cops, and that is all part of this bargain. It comes with the territory. I took a few near misses. Not the first and not the last." Then you answered her with an air of relief in your voice, now knowing that she had not been hit:

And again, SOMBRAJ let me use Trojan voice.

"Bravo Joa! ¡Bravo 'PIQUANTE' Fuego!"

For the briefest of instants, one could have parked a truck in Trojan's open mouth, before he used it, and a steel-cold voice quite forcefully to cut me off:

"No one could possibly know those things. You had better tell me how you do! I had better like your explanation! And you need to start talking some really believable details. NOW!" Trojan walked around his desk and we were too close. The situation was out of control for him and it was his job to have it just the opposite.

He stared rudely at me like I had an eye in the middle of my forehead, then asked in a way that I knew he meant business, and he wanted answers, and I knew I did not have what he wanted. I also knew he would know if what I told him was on the level or not. For a brief moment, I was at a loss for words so I turned inwards to SOMBRAJ, hoping that this entity could help me to answer Trojan in a way that I could get him to believe me and acts.

Help Needed From SOMBRAJ

SOMBRAJ had already begun the process of being more SOMBRAJ. I knew from experience that SOMBRAJ could give me an idea, a feeling, intuition, instinct, or call it what you wish, and make me feel like it came from me. After all, SOMBRAJ was SOMBRAJ. But so far, his subtle prompting had been insufficient because Trojan was intensely focused and certainly not listening to any—inner voice—personal or otherwise.

Trojan was on high alert. Not just from current events, but I had triggered several additional alarm bells by knowing things impossible for me to know, and saying things the way I was not supposed to be able to say. He felt the existence of an undefined threat. So, I spoke as quickly as I could:

"NO! I know little of this myself, but you must listen to your instincts, just like Joa did. You look like you are ready to punch me out or throw me out, but you must believe me. I am on your side and I can help you, but only if you listen and believe me. Why else would I be here?"

SOMBRAJ picked up on the fact that what he was doing was not enough and it continued to help me:

"It is you who is so disturbing; in the manner you treat Boa, by constantly undermining her in your macho ways."

Trojan was listening and I ran with the opportunity. The more we made eye contact and I spoke, the more he realized that this raving idiot in front of him was perhaps not so crazy after all. I leveled my voice a little and continued:

"Listen Trojan, the activity here has died down, but unfortunately, the bikers linked to Kildem's organization are heading to Tampa and are not far behind Joa. They are ready and willing to do anything to retrieve the documents which were obtained from the Kildem RV. You need to help Joa now! There is no time to lose; otherwise you may well lose someone very important to you. It is not important at this instant; you know how I know these things. It is important you act on your instincts now, before it is too late. The explanations can come later."

I could see it in his face that I had hit a nerve, and that he was beginning to sway, so I said to him in hope of finally getting him to take some kind of action:

"Trojan, I know you will think I am off my rocker, but I know and so does the spirit in me, knows your every thought. The same spirit, intuition, whatever you call it, that is in you and Joa. Listen to it! Do it! This is urgent and Joa is in danger. Look, I am going with you so if I'm wrong—just how many years would I get for interfering with police business in this manner?" SOMBRAJ was feeding me and I knew for that precise moment, that, Trojan's attention was mine and I had to make it count:

"Hey! Another thing, why she's gone with any of your best men? Why she didn't tell you? Why she didn't ask you to come with her if it's not because of your macho behavior? Why she liberated you from the crime scene? So, it's a clear message, no...?"

Ticket to Tampa or Ticket to ride:

Heading to Tampa to assist Joa

I took a deep breath and got my second wind, "look! You have a good friend less than ten miles from here, Coast Guard Commander Jeff Clark, and he has two very fast: HH-65's at his disposal. Talk to Commander Herckel, tell her to give you four of her forces to accompany us, and you can bring a couple of your own men. You have arms, and Herckel can give you extra 50 calibers she has."

I stopped cold. This was information impossible to divulge that had gotten Trojan literally between the eyes. This had been both barrels and I had Trojan beyond arguing the point, the ball was in his court. I sensed rather than felt, SOMBRAJ give Trojan one last sharp poke, as only SOMBRAJ could. He looked at me in total disconnect for the briefest of seconds. For him, it was as if I really did have a third eye, which, when one considers it, really was the truth. Trojan was, in all reality, one hell of a law enforcement officer. He did not know all of the, how, but he was convinced that it was real, and he swung into action.

Trojan the law enforcement officer was instantly in high gear. Phone in one hand, radio in the other, he summoned one of his lieutenants from his off watch as the phone made the call to his old Coast Guard friend. I could see the light of friendship in Trojan's eyes as they made their connection, and I got Trojan's side of the conversation as he apologized for long-time-no-see, and a call for police business. The friendship was solid, the emergency explained, and Trojan disconnected with a sincere thank-you my friend, knowing that two: HH-65's would be airborne in ten minutes for his location.

Trojan turned to Lieutenant Carl Rayner, his second in command and told he was heading to Tampa. He expressed to Carl his need for four men, who they were, and the arms he wanted them to be carrying, and Sargent Blake and what was needed of him. Wordlessly the Lieutenant Rayner raised his eyebrows slightly at the orders, spun on his heels and was gone. Trojan glanced briefly at the floor, then looked at me as only he could, saying with words that matched his look:

"Unanswered questions, I will have from you all of those answers. If you fail me in any way, it will not be the law you are answering to." He poked tersely with his chin, and Sargent Blake was in for a surprise.

With the sight of the two HH-65's, and men sporting fifty caliber automatic rifles clambering aboard to assist him as show and tell, it took Trojan less than two minutes to convince the commander Herckel the emergency was real, and for her to part with four of her best men, two of whom were cracking snipers. She spoke to her aid to get the arms and men Trojan had requested on board immediately. It was amazing. Less than eight minutes after their arrival, both helicopters were airborne and streaking eastwards at full speed. With the twin fifty calibers in the cabin it was a little close, but they arranged their gear and with the AR-50's deployed out the open doors, they suddenly had transformed into a formidable killing machine.

Armed Support, Trojan on His Way to Tampa

The only task now was to inform 54-TI that they were on routes as armed support that they had information that Joa's operation was being threatened. With Joe's urging and some help from SOMBRAJ, Trojan spoke to Commander Herckel, and before they had lifted off she was in communication with Maurice to inform the group of incoming, were friendly support, and what their in-flight signatures were.

As the two HH-65s helicopters toured eastwards, Thomas, one of Trojan's oldest and most trusted friends, broke the verbal vacuum over the noise of the twin turbo.

Grinning, he poked Trojan with his foot, as much to break the tension as anything:

“Lieutenant, you are muttering. What are you muttering, SIR?”

He had spoken over the noise of the engines and everyone took notice. Blake mistook the friendly poke as a jibe and was immediately poised as if to have the other for lunch. Trojan grinned and gestured to Thomas with the irreverence reserved for macho guys who just did not know how to express that level of friendship in public. He thought for a moment, then even though the others could hear, Trojan zoned them out and spoke to his friend:

“Just wondering about something... I don’t know. Every time I see Joa, it’s sort-a weird. I see this butterfly. Or this damned cat. Except it isn’t a cat, or a butterfly. They are like shadows or something. Ah-h-h! Sometimes I think I must be nuts.” Blake was there because of his skill as a marksman. There was no pause-to-consider, no measurement of words. Tact borne of wisdom was not one of Blake’s strong points. So, when he spoke, it was as his norm to commit verbal social suicide:

“Damn Trojan! You really got it bad for that damn, eh? You see Boa and you see butterflies. Whoa-h-h-h! Trojan’s having visions!” Blake then unknowingly saved himself somewhat:

“The only time I see butterflies is when somebody punches me and I get my bell rung!” Thomas seized the moment with: “of course, Blake! You’re so ugly your right hand wants a divorce!” The tables had been well-turned and everyone laughed, including Blake. He was not the most polished of gems, but he did have the ability to laugh at himself.

One of Trojan's best marksmen, asked his comrade-in-arms point-blank:

"So, what gives with you two anyways? You look like your puppy just died," Trojan reply with a wave of his hand:

"Ah-h-h! Damn! You all know she means a lot to me. I feel like a shit not seeing this in advance and offering her more help. I should've seen this coming. Any good cop would have. It's not like she can't or... Hell, everyone here knows she is the best of the best. Brilliant, though, I'd take all of you on at once in a heartbeat before I'd go one-on-one with her. Level-headed, best law enforcement officer I've ever met. Yeah, she means a lot to me." Everyone was silent for just a moment. Even Blake could recognize the reverence in Trojan's voice. Then Thomas, his pilot, spoke up, his voice kind, but it cut to the truth bringing a stupid grin to Trojan's face:

"Hey boss! You ever think 'o telling' HER that?"

Their banter and conversation and the speed of the 65s had carried them not far, when suddenly their reverie was cut abruptly short. The intercom blared out just as the waist gunner shouted:

"Heads up! Incoming!"

Still far away from Joa, they are trying to catch up to 54-TI and their force, and it appeared that their journey may be harder than they think.

Trojan and Trakker on the Move

Once having embarked in the Coast Guard helicopter HH-65 and underway towards Tampa, Joe needed to make Trojan understand what was now transpiring, but he struggled with the—where, when, and how—with the others present, and not willing nor able to begin to divulge his source, which, of course, was principally SOMBRAJ. With a nudge from his inner partner, Joe begins to extract his video-cam from his bag, when Captain Thomas Montgomery after the friendly teasing of Trojan shouts: "incoming."

Capt. Thomas points to the radar screen, which shows two unidentified helicopters southwest just ahead of them and they seem running in the 54-TI's direction. As the two well-camouflaged Airbus Armed Scout and a Bell UH-1 Iroquois come into view, Capt. "Thomas," also notices as he gently banks his HH-65 a little towards the east that appeared as if a ground force is also in pursuit of 54-TI. Thinking to him:

"No fair, let's get an equal playing field here." He says to Trojan:

"Did you see that on your left? Looks like there is an incoming mercenary ground force headed for 54-TI, no? So only passing by, maybe we can give them a little help, no?"

"Yaw, let's take a minute to shout them few dozens of prunes." Trojan makes his decision in a heartbeat:

"OK Thomas! Let's even things. See what your 50 can do to the tail rotor of the Scout. It's only because we are passing by, we have no time to lose, and being to Tampa is our priority."

"OK! Trojan." The sound of the barrage of fire leaving the confines of HH-65 was loud, however, the contact with the Scout's tail rotor was even louder. As the Scout begins its spiraling descent towards the ground spreading large chunks of tails and rotor in its wake, the Iroquois breaks off and follows the disabled helicopter to a glen in the proximity of Orlando. Perhaps the Iroquois had been ordered to pick up the crew and what was left of the armaments of the downed Scout.

After a few moments, Thomas's Coast Guard HH-65, with Trojan and Joe on board proceeded towards Tampa at a fast clip. Moments later close to Orlando and seemingly from out of nowhere a Bell ARH 70 swept up from tree top level on the starboard side of Thomas's HH-65. The side cargo door was open with a mercenary in camo braced, and there on a harness, an assault rifle cradled in his arms. Before Thomas could react, ordinance from the M16 raked through the open door of the Coast Guard HH-65, for a brief second catching their gunner off guard, and showering the interior with shrapnel.

A split second before the burst of fire, Joe experienced an almost violent "image push" from SOMBRAJ, and without knowing why, launched himself against Trojan, throwing both of them into a tangled heap behind the pilot's position. As quickly as it happened, the ARH 70 was gone, down again to tree top level streaking off to the southeast. The waist gunner spun the caliber's 50, towards the escaping foe, but could not open fire. Below them and beyond the fleeing enemy were civilians on I-4 and on the ground. Pursuit was out of the question; an aerial dogfight over populated areas beyond any justifiable risk.

Trojan after extricating himself from the entanglement with Joe turned to his left where Joe was now sitting and said:

"Thanks."

Joe, never one to mix words, replied as a matter-of-fact, yet with concern in his voice:

"Your pride was not the only thing hurt. Look! You've been hit, and are now bleeding from a wound on your right arm." Trojan grabbed at his arm, grimacing, and lied:

"I am OK Joe; it is just a superficial wound."

The copilot grabbed the first aid kit from the bulkhead, scissored open the Armani shirt sleeve to expose the wound and applied a temporary bandage as quickly as if he were pouring a cup of coffee.

"Look Trojan," said Joe: "you will need to have it looked after when you get back on the ground." Trojan with a smile on his lips says to Joe:

"I have had worse; this only adds to my collection. You want see?" All laughing, it was as if he were more concerned with the loss of a two-hundred-dollar shirt than a half cup of blood.

Finally, from all sides, armed jets were passing by joining 54-TI and Oshkosh JLTVs coming from everywhere at full speed and chasing any enemy's forces away. Helicopters were now passing too just when we were over Orlando.

Joe Receiving Crucial Information From SOMBRAJ

Joe was receiving SOMBRAJ information, as people tendencies to believe in super power, it is not the odds in reality. SOMBRAJ was not predicting gypsy things or reading tarot, he needed to be connected to somebody's mind, and that person had to be in a scared position to release some information about what that person was scared to lose.

In that special momentum, SOMBRAJ was directly connected to Dennis's mind and his chakras, where everything is happening. The head is there for memories and deploying energies to do things, but the chakras are the real brain that governs our whole life.

Joa needed time to upload and secure the Dennis RV evidences, while Dennis's life was close to explode, thinking about what more he had to keep away from Joa.

That was what SOMBRAJ needed, Dennis, the very intelligent man was living the opposite of his mental disequilibrium and opening his real scary bipolar nature; so, the perfect state to get it all.

After all of what he was scared to lose revelations, SOMBRAJ went for a fast cruising true the DK Palace and has discovered the top-of-the-pot. The whole underground hidden basement of DK Palace was a bunker all interconnecting around the whole buildings agglomeration, with possible connection to an old church basement for fast escaping.

Joa was shaking alike, letting Trojan think he was scared.

"No! Trojan, I'm receiving huge and crucial information! We will have to warn on Joa, she is going in the rough place; she needs to know where the jackpot is, ever so huge. She will get it; we have about 30–40 minutes in advance from Dennis. No time to lose!" Joa was on her way to Tampa while 54-TI was securing the Dennis RV's treasure trove of evidences.

Handling and Securing the Dennis RV's Treasure Trove of Evidences

All the time during her helicopter ride in The Tiger, Joa was receiving encrypted messages and information from her team, who were now heading at top speed in 54-TI to Tampa Kildem offices DK Palace, so she thought. With the assistance of three of Trojan's men and especially the wiz kid Harry, they had been able to obtain sensitive information by deciphering it from the abundance of documents and extracting it from various hard drives, especially the desk top and two personal laptops which had been sitting on the conference table unprotected in Dennis's RV. Joa was impressed and pleased, but not surprised by the team's skills at getting some of this information to her in such a short period of time.

Coming closer to Tampa, Joa was happy with a sigh of relief when Maurice advised her that the most crucial part of the information and data were in the completion stages of being totally secured by the team, in accordance with the guidelines and procedures, as set out by the Charter of the International Constitution of S.I.I.T.F. under the auspices of their UN legal team. This Charter was established as a precaution, to enable the independent handling of such information outside of all politics, in order to ensure an international sponsorship equal to all countries, without regard to the importance or the involvement of one or several countries.

More precautions had to be done about the scanning and securing data and documents. Joa has the right to hold or publish, anything she discerns to be destructive, to the whole world economy; at least, not before deep professional analyses from the entire S.I.I.T.F. organization. So, to prevent temptation from individual or faction pressure, Joa has her one data bank preservation and everybody knows about that particular attention, it is written in their one constitution. And no one person alone can have access and manage or decode that particular information. Everything is first coded in 432k and then scrambled before to be uploading...

Some of the principal guidelines to protect the collected documents and information from Dennis's RV were to copy, encrypt, and transfer the three Dennis's computers data on the 54-TI hard drives and simultaneously upload to various data banks via the 54-TI satellite, in order to prevent any compromise or loss of evidences. They also had orders to secure all documents, by sending encrypted copies to her temporary office in Tampa, at Guardia Fortress and to the S.I.I.T.F. headquarters. In addition to ensure total security of these important documents and sensitive information which could compromise certain highly placed individuals worldwide; encrypted copies were to be sent to other data banks known only to the upper echelon and senior management of S.I.I.T.F. and one other known only exclusively to their most trust worthy partners.

Joa knew that the attack on her little army would not be long in coming; she also knew 54-TI and her team were at the ready. But with all those air patrolling armed jets, helicopters, and on the ground, armored Oshkosh JLTV now in the convoy and with the cooperation of all the county's sheriff officers well-armed and blocking any vehicle, all along the 54-TI route way; it would be almost impossible to interfere with the 54-TI security at least for the time needed to secure the documents and all the data.

54-TI, Armored and More Armed Than a Tank

Joa decided to take a few minutes to recharge her battery, looking around the interior of the helicopter she knew she was not sitting in the lap of luxury, but a very well-equipped Sikorsky Raider. Spotting a thermos, she poured herself a cup of java and leaned back as much as she could in this well-armed flying juggernaut.

Thinking about the rapidly unfolding events, Joa felt no guilt in denying Trojan the nickel tour of her Mobile-lab as he referred to it. Top secret in nature, it couldn't be further from an accurate description. Laboratory it was not. More accurate, it was as Joa laughingly described it, a well-armed 200-million-dollar telephone. To S.I.I.T.F, its designation was its celestial address, GSS54TI or, Geo-Stationary Satellite 54-Tactical Intelligence, or 54-TI as they called it (name given by the team: FIGHT FOR TACTICAL INTELLIGENCE) or fight for justice (54) justice. Within its confines, some rather exotic devices most dedicated as Joa said, to communications, but communications the likes of which few had ever imagined. It literally was science-fiction stuff usually seen on movies.

There were but three work centers or consoles, and a device that Joa lovingly referred to as her magic wand. Via the five-channel satellite, which was always directly overhead, she could upload or download any encrypted information or data, or images, or voice communications to any place in the world, at Terra bytes per minute. A digital photograph set in one of the scanners would be in Moscow, or Sri Lanka virtually instantaneously. She was linked to the criminal data bases of some 83 cooperating nations. Her magic wand as she called it, was a cubicle containing a device cloned from NASA, part miniaturized scanning electron microscope, X-ray interferometer, molecular gas chromatograph, capable of analyzing materials then transmitting the information to any of a number of scientific institutions for study and analysis. It was the closest mankind had ever come to making real the humor of fax me a beer.

From tissue samples, chemical compounds, or fingerprints; all were analyzed, digitized, and transmitted to all and any point on the globe in less than one minute. Usually it could be done in less than one. From the communications consoles, any type of data could be passed to any point on the globe instantaneously. Joa's cellphone was set to her own voice, fingerprints, or Iris. If she could touch, see, or talk to it, it functioned. To anyone else, it was dead. With voice recognition, she had instantaneous access to any one of five geosynchronous satellites, and thus to any person she wished to speak to. It too was linked to the lab. All frequencies and transmissions both in and out were beyond secure.

Tom and Harry worked two of the consoles; Dick was responsible for the magic wand. Any information Joa wanted, on any subject or person, regardless of who they were, was hers for the asking. Recessed into the roof were various communications dishes and antennae; to power it all, a silent but powerful small diesel generator, with back up solar power from the roof.

54-TI was a Tactical Command Center; information on steroids as she put it, that was its principal armament. It did, however, contain some small weaponry that Joa was particularly fond of. She was beyond Olympic marksman capabilities with all of them; her favorite that she carried with her at all times was either a Glock 18 or a Sig Sauer 2022 9 mm. An assortment of other additional weaponry consisted of a few exotic toys they kept for special parties, including but not limited to 12 Gage Taser shotgun shells, a 25 mm chain gun, colt anaconda 44 magnum, Sig Sauer 2022 9 mm—Joa's favorite, and a Glock 18. They also carried a Tarus Judge 25 Gage, revolver shotgun; Dragons Breath exotic shot gun ammo, short recoil Jerico or Desert Eagle 50 caliber; Semi-hand-gun. There were also a few almost conventional heavy weapons mostly of the automatic variety. The ammunition carried on board, where it discharged at once in the proper way, and was almost sufficient in its power to launch 54-TI into orbit.

There was an arms locker stocked with 2 McMillan TAC338 sniper rifles, 2 Barrett M107s, several M16's, a 50 caliber SAR and two weapons that officially did not exist; both were Laser based. The first one was a modified version of Lockheed Martin's ATHENA Laser and packed a 50 KW punch, powered by an array of rooftop capacitors, fed by the small diesel generator. The other one was a La-WS based laser that they could use its beam to fire an electromagnetic pulse, rendering any vehicle inoperable. The inherent problem with both devices is the amount of electricity to charge and fire these weapons. The La-WS gun was the low-powered version to apply the EMP against vehicles, both air born and land-based.

Although it was not intended as an attack vehicle, it could carry a compliment of 4 SWAT-type personnel, and the walls were constructed of carbon-fiber material capable of stopping the majority of small and medium arms fire from standard weaponry to just shy of anti-tank missiles. It had been heavily armored, but for its equipment and capabilities, was amazingly lightweight and capable of impressive road performance powered by a specially engineered Caterpillar Diesel and power train. If any military had ever wanted a Lamborghini disguised as a rolling fortress, 54-TI was it. All this rode on 10 puncture-proof military tires.

Joa, her Mobil-lab lovingly known as 54-TI, and her very specialized team had to make their way to Tampa before Dennis, hopefully, and his band of cut throats. Would her escort arrive in time?

The Cavalry Has Arrived and Not Too Soon Either

Joa knew in her gut that the attack on her little army was imminent. She breathed a sigh of relief when two highly sophisticated Apache Longbow and a Magusta, Attack helicopters finally caught up to escort and ensure their safe way to Tampa. Maurice, with the 54-TI high-tech radar noticed on his screen, two blips approaching quickly, but they were luckily taken in charge by the huge General Bentall Air Force power and were taking care on the ground by many Oshkosh JLTV just joining the party.

On the ground, the 54-TI-sophisticated satellite fed intelligence system was feeding Harry's main screens and digital warnings now had everyone on high alert. The screens were showing the approach of unidentified helicopters and ground vehicles. Aboard "The Tiger," Joa's pilot Commander Jamari Tarpin was now pointing to her the radar screen activity while at the same time he radioed ahead to Captain Wayne Franklin, waiting for them in Tampa, in the Black Hawk; that hell was going to throw a party and like it or not, they were invited. The attack Joa had feared was imminent.

But they were encircled again by the General's much organized force. Even if there is a strong force up there, somebody or mercenaries can be hiding somewhere and wait until 54-TI or any helicopter pass by and shout badly with a rocket launcher.

However, the would-be attackers would have been in for one hell of a big surprise because they would be running into the 54-TI, who could hold its ground quite well. This strike force of mercenaries and criminals was also unaware that they would be attacking an extremely well-equipped small force of experts who had unimaginable fire power right out of science fiction bordering on the Star War variety. Her order was simple and explicit: "Take them out! No collateral or civilian damage."

"Do not wait; shoot first to protect your comrades! They are armed to kill, so shoot first!"

"Do not wait until somebody hiding somewhere down there in the bush, waiting to destroy us with a Rocket launcher. That kind of weapon is deadly for us, up here, in helicopters."

Joa used a very simple reasoning, when whoever it may be is armed to kill, the law must be very specific. Their Charter was quite clear on these matters:

"Criminal elements on the levels we expect to encounter could be assumed to be well armed and prepared to use deadly force. If the attacking party ignored the warnings, they were fair game under the law to shoot them down."

Yes, there was a lot of dead, but they died, for the good, for the whole world economic stability. With all those crooks' names, bank accounts, password, and money laundering transactions gifted by Dennis Kildem, it will surely make a big hole in the consortium World Bank (WTB) that was in a deep end formation; the Bank was in the process to control the global world economy.

And finally,

The whole General's air and ground forces were there as a real war deployment?

CHAPTER 10

General Bentall's air and ground forces arrivals

As requested by S.I.I.T.F. Headquarters, General Bentall was there to protect 54-TI on his way to Tampa.

Commander Jamari Tarpin, turned and looked at Joa who had just put down her tablet and was taking a sip of her now cold coffee. From the look on her face, you could not tell what she had read but oh those eyes spoke volumes. She would provide him with the information he needed, in her own good time. He turned back to the task ahead, and that was flying The Tiger.

Joa had been apprised that the battle was underway, but initially appeared well in hand by her team in 54-TI, which also included the air support players ensuring that 54-TI would be adequately protected. She knew that 54-TI was capable defending itself and Maurice had the order for using the Maximum power to freeze them down. She said to Maurice:

"Do not take a chance, they are there to kill, so, as soon they come close enough, freeze them down! Our mission is so important; do not take chances because Kildem is going to do everything. Be sure of it!"

Joa, detailing the Daytona Crime Scene while on her way to Tampa

While heading to Tampa, she had to do something to kill the traveling time. Joa with a cup of hot coffee in her hand was mentally going over the action which had taken place in Daytona. They were making good time towards Tampa. Finally, not one to procrastinate, she grabbed her encrypted tablet and hooked her leg around the mount of the machine-gun to brace herself, and began formulating the crime scene investigation narrative and observations. Always well aware of an inordinate amount of power at her finger tips, which would allow her to substantiate whatever she put in her report for eventual dispersion to the necessary authorities, she saw it as simply responsibility, and so she began to form her initial report.

The observations were preliminary, but would be impartially complete and accurate because of her expertise in police forensics and crime scene evidence and the information obtained from her team in 54-TI. These observations would be given credence, once the results from the various analyses were received from the different labs and law enforcement agencies. Joa was quite capable of contributing information and analysis as to what had occurred at the crime scene, by using the information, witnesses' accounts, and videos provided to her by the extremely thorough and well qualified 54-TI team. She was also able to provide an eyewitness account, in the area visible to her, because she had walked in as the incident in question was taking place.

Conclusions would be based on videos, eye witness testimonies, and forensic indices which will include the location of the bodies, type and position of wounds which were inflicted, the direction of blood spatters after impact as well as powder marks or residue, the analysis of blood samples for identification and matching to the various profiles and bodies; determining the type of the weapons used, number of shot fired according to witnesses' accounts, the position and number of spent cartridges as well as their trajectory. Trojan has arrested 9 witnesses that were unable to fly away as others and they were a good source to identify dead friend bodies; and he gives his report to Commander Bridget Herckel.

Many questions had to be answered by other authorities, so for now she thought:

"Let's go back to my NOW mission. Later on, I'll have time to complete this report."

CHAPTER 11

Dennis Scared to Death

Yes, Maurice was taking care of others much farther, preventing them to engage with his very busy protectors around 54-TI. 54-TI was able of protecting itself but Maurice knew that the Dennis's mercenaries had the order to get the documents that Joa got out from his RV.

Dennis was obliged to fly away while still shouting and when he saw the dead guards lying down, close to his RV. And because a Spanish alike unknown man has pointed his harm on him, he thought:

"That's it! It is finished, I'm dead, and I won't need my documents anymore." And to save his life he had to obey to that man and his gun. But still alive without knowing why yet, he was at least able to reorganize and give orders to mercenaries:

"Get my documents at any price, get that 'Big BUS' on its way north on I-4." He was terrified and was offering money as I would be a Bank by himself. He ordered and has precisely and repeated as if he was getting crazy:

"Stop them first and get my documents and all my own things and destroy them, I want them brought to dust as they deserve to be."

For sure he was losing his head but more, he was entreating himself as a god...

Dennis on the Run

Always in the same physical time, thing where happening from all sides and back to the still shooting Daytona crime scene:

As Dennis and Dino exited the Daytona Beach Inn fire escape door, to their surprise and shock, a man leaped out of the bush near the rear of Dennis's RV and came face to face with them brandishing a very large caliber handgun. Pointing the rather fearsome weapon point blank at Dennis now pale face, the young man said in a clear cold voice:

"Gentlemen put your hands on the wall, feet apart and well back. Move it quickly. I will shoot either one of you in a heartbeat. I have absolutely nothing to lose."

He then proceeded to remove the weapon from Dennis's outstretched arms and frisked both men to ensure no other weapons were to be found on their person. Dino, on turning to face the man, went to make a move towards him, but smirking, the young man said in a voice that stopped the other cold:

"Do not even think about it or your boss will get his just dues, right now."

Motioning with his gunned hand for the two to head for the tree line at the end of the north parking lot, the young man told Dino to get into the driver's seat of the dune buggy parked there, and drive towards the south and to the beach. All this time Dennis's anger was building. He could detect a faint

Latino accent in the young man's dialect as he spoke English. His English was impeccable but there was something not quite right in his manners and damn that slight accent.

Dennis, a hunted man but next to limitless cash to buy anybody

Dennis was now a hunted man, and Joa believed that so far, that he would not have had the time to reorganize, but because his organization was so efficient and well-structured she had to be wary of the capabilities of any of his remaining lieutenant's contacting mercenaries. There were many guns for hire. Joa had met a few of these creatures, "on business," and she did not want to underestimate them. They were anything conceivable as far as criminal capabilities. Cast-offs from various armies and militias, well trained in hand-to-hand combat, martial arts, explosives, weaponry, and well equipped with whatever weaponry was available. These were the most unscrupulous and immoral characters imaginable. She had no fear of any of them; however, she had the most professional respect for them. Not good to ever relax in a viper's den.

The Dennis she knew about, had next to limitless cash and she knew that if the world mercenary's craps were not already out, it would be shortly. She and 54-TI were essentially the Bait and the rats who wanted it had really big teeth. To them, life had no meaning or value. There was no loss unless, of course, you died trying but they were ice-cold men of no conscience and so, of course, the latter part was of no concern to them. There were many of these networks providing this kind of service and Dennis's men would know who they were and how to locate them. The Dennis organization's money was still intact and available for the time being, but not for long.

Joa knew that the key to her investigation was the core of the Kildem organization. She had alluded about this to Trojan and was a little embarrassed to have left him holding the bag at the scene of the crime while the investigation was still in progress, but there was no place in her mind, for that precious moment, for personal sensation.

Several SOMBRAJ and BRAJ at Work

During the decisive moments of this operation, there were many SOMBRAJ's and BRAJ's at work gathering information which would be passed to Joe's SOMBRAJ. This information was obtained from the inner most thoughts of Dennis. All of it: his elicit criminal activities, the hiding place of information, how to get into this secure bunker which was the hiding place for his organization's files, data, precious objects, information of many of his high-profile contacts, bank information and most importantly the activities performed by his deepest dark secret =Tennis. Let it be known, Joa would kill to have the information on Tennis. The only information she had was that Tennis was one of these best tennis fighters, but he had to win or you were becoming a potential enemy.

Trojan and Joa were now becoming sensitized to the fact that their intuition was being helped by something or someone who was beyond their understanding, but for some reason believed that this or these entities were here to help. It is not easy to entrust one's own judgment or life to an intuition, but there are exceedingly intelligent people like Joa and Trojan who with some persuasion, even if sometimes not plausible, will see the bigger picture and acquiesce to the action required to handle the situation in question.

This particular one deals with the impending impact by a consortium of unscrupulous criminals who were in the process of creating their own "World Bank" which would control the global economy. No less are the other malicious crimes now plaguing this world. The dedication of individuals like Joa and Trojan, to name a few, is one of the reasons that the criminals have never been able to control the world and yet they do not cease to try.

Thoughts Are Energies That Talk

A SOMBRAJ is pure spirit, not a soul goody as many would like to think and there is no god's miracle things too in what they could do. A Thought is deployed energy that gives some information about anything, especially when a person is weakened about being scared of losing something extensive. One says that you are what we see in your eyes, so we are to what we think. Since a while, Dennis Kildem had a SOMBRAJ attached expressly to himself. Anything he was thinking or scared about was important information that was feeding all and everyone SOMBRAJ in the same instant. After he fled away to save his life, he had to abandon a part of his life right there. And when he coldly killed Paolo Caballero at the Inn corridor, it was stronger them himself, he lost his maniac-depressive temper against the all-time enemy Southern Fire Spanish gang. In his head, he was as a supernatural being with, dead-on, on anybody's life.

Dennis, scared as ever been, fled off the Daytona site without being able to think about what he was living behind, in his RV. For the first time of his life he was scared to death, he didn't know that he was going to react that way. For himself he was ashamed of himself, it was as fleeing as a chicken.

Only later, when he came down to think, he was able to evaluate the lost, and the move he did. He didn't even think about the loss of friends and partners, dead forever in the Inn parking lot.

SOMBRAJ was permanently connected to his mind, sooner or later he was going to reveal something crucial for the mission. When he heard about Joa on the news and about the carnage, he finally starts to think about his full of information Bunker, saying to himself:

"That Boa witch... She thinks she's going to find my secret Bunker by going to Tampa. Ah no! Nobody knows! Nothing is in my office not as well at my wife's home. And has a sick guy, everything was turning in his head, not able to stop thinking.

And the worst had to come, killing his little hopes, when he heard on the news about the cold killing of an innocent business man that had the only default to be a good for nothing Spanish, as he said... He, then, was looking badly for a TV set, hoping not to see his face attempting that unscrupulous crime as the radio news saying it loudly.

SOMBRAJ Connected Permanently to Dennis's Mind

SOMBRAJ was registering, and more he was scared more Dennis was revealing crucial information, his mental was sending pictures as the same kind you see yourself in a colored dream. Dennis, affected and losing control, was delirious...

- Oh! No... No... No, they can't get in my bunker, they don't even know about my bunker!
- "No... they don't know how to get in; no, no, saying in his head, no, they don't know how to get in. I'm the only one, ho! Ah no! Dino knows how to get in and where it is. No! No! Dino is not a turncoat; he's with me since, 20/22 years, no! It can't be him... Or... Maybe... I'm going to cut his throat off his head!"

- "Explosion: "no, anyways if ever they find it, they're all going to crash dead under the explosion forever, has ... ha ... ha!"
- "The Mega Yacht: I hope they stay away, far from 'Big Bang' they might don't know, it's on my sister's name anyway. But there's not too much stuff in there... Ah! Hope not I always wash everything after every throat cut off and my videos are hidden so deep under a keel compartment."

And so, on and on, he was revealing his real nature of a sick man; revealing so much information for helping S.I.I.T.F. squad to bring down the dirty heads, managing the Kildem Family Trust, the consortium and their Bank (WTD) the World Traders Bank.

CHAPTER 12

Joa getting closer to Tampa

Joa put her tablet down and spoke to her pilot:

"Jamari, please let me know when we are 30 minutes close to Tampa. I want to check with 54-TI as to their progress. Inform Captain Wayne Franklin from the Black Hawks, waiting in Tampa of our present coordinates and ETA pertaining to his current location and to await further orders." The tone of her voice was different, and Jamari knew she was troubled.

The pilot replied straightforwardly:

"OK Joa, we will be closing on that shortly. Our current position is forty-five minutes east of Tampa."

Joa was remembering the whole actions to be taken and it was a big bothering thing in her head:

"Hey Joa," Telling her:

"The whole world depends on the next coming hour. That crooks' Consortium and their bank have to be put on HOLD and their crook administrators send behind bars. We have the first shot with the Kildem RV's things, so now let's get dynamite evidences to blow them off for good!" It was her way to prepare herself for the next operation that she was feeling important. SOMBRAJ was working on her, on Joe and anyone concerned by the next important action. SOMBRAJ knew who is now Dennis, it took some time but he has revealed all its unscrupulous crimes and Dennis was the key reason why SOMBRAJ had to come alive.

Joa's Authorities, Under S.I.I.T.F Decree

Joa's authority to proceed with necessary force fell under S.I.I.T.F mandate and her freedom to do so was clearly defined. How she obtained results were her responsibility and solely hers. With eyes closed she appraised every agent in every position, every piece of intelligence, every movement planned, every plan "B," in case something went wrong. Success meant more than victory over crime. No losses. She would tolerate no losses. That was her burden, and the biggest personal cost, ever with her; keeping under wraps, what she thought necessary to protect the furthering of the Kildem investigation or to avoid launching or triggering political fallout. Joa did not dare name well-known individuals who may or may not be directly involved, at least for the present time. She knew that the power of this morally distorts influence came from power. Those of big power that was guilty, those were the cockroaches that did not scatter when the light came on. They were more apt, and quite capable of killing and eating the electrician, and worse, wore the appearance of clean, respectability, society.

Things of that nature were powerful protection in themselves and Joa must tread with absolute care and precision. Therefore, Joa played her hand close to her chest until she had a clear picture of everything. She needed to topple the unscrupulous Kildem organization and its affiliates. Also, she did not want to scare the bunnies that appeared clean or pretty, into diving into their respective holes. The fact that they felt safe and were still playing openly at their game was to her advantage.

Ongoing Kildem Investigation

On her way to Tampa, Joa was now sure that she had met all requirements under S.I.I.T.F. mandate, pertaining to the gathering and dissemination of the treasure trove of information collected from the Dennis Kildem RV at the Daytona Beach Inn. She knew she must, however, turn her focus on the possible recovery of more evidences and perhaps highly sensitive information she was hoping to find at the offices of the Kildem Organization in Tampa. Joa needed to add more substantive evidences, identifying Kildem's contacts the world over, and shed more light on the material recovered from the Kildem RV, as well as identify what activities Dennis and his cronies were currently involved in or planning.

She knew that she must be on solid ground when ensuring that the evidences, being gathered, could not be refuted in any way or by anyone. Therefore, she would continue to follow the trail that led her to Bike Week in Daytona Beach and on to Orlando and Tampa. Months earlier, Joa had been given the responsibility of handling this particular case. It had become stagnant and seemed to be dead before it got underway. Joa began going back over the occurrences of the last few months, making mental notes of the important aspects of her investigation. With an operation of this magnitude and importance, Joa first processed everything in her mind, determining her next steps from the beginning, going over every detail and searching out any weak points or things overlooked.

Months earlier when she was assigned to S.I.I.T.F., she began to follow the movement of capitals (money) transactions of a questionable nature around the world, and was immediately captivated by the enormity of the crimes and how well hidden they were. Crimes of all kinds, for the killing is a right, because it is for getting more and more money, more powers; no matters whom they kill for getting more power.

The illicit global movement of billions of dollars into the wrong pockets could severely influence the world economy, sending it in a violent and maybe non-recoverable tailspin. This type of activity was well beyond even the control of governments. Three months earlier, S.I.I.T.F team now headed by Joa, had obtained a file from the World Traders Bank (WTB) which led her to look into the domain of an important group of financiers with clandestine operations in Orlando and Tampa. The main culprit was an organization called Kildem, headed by a savvy financier known as Dennis Kildem. It was not a coincidence that Joa, her more than impressive team and the utter magic of 54-TI found themselves in Daytona Beach during Bike Week. And she prepared finely for the possible unknot of something close to emerge out of the smoking guns.

Joa, had found out, through one of her contacts in Daytona Beach that a very important meeting of a questionable organization, was to take place at the Daytona Beach Inn during Bike Week. The head of this organization, Dennis Kildem was seen to be gathering many of his important friends from over the world, and what had been most interesting to Joa, and which she also found strange, was the meeting included some of Dennis's former classmates, lawyers and some known politicians. Interestingly, Dennis had been discreet and was not in the habit of frequenting large crowds over the last twenty years. This meeting was not a one-and-only. Intelligence had discovered that several meetings of this kind would be taking place simultaneously in many parts of the world. So, that has put Joa's team-high beam on...

Under the S.I.I.T.F directive for this operation, Joa was mandated to identify, flush out, and most importantly, obtain concrete evidence against the individuals responsible. As to the best estimates of S.I.I.T.F, as much as 30% of all global finances were being drawn off by these criminal elements by direct theft, money laundering, tax evasion, embezzlement, insider trading and any number of other criminal activities. This criminal organization literally had its financial hands around the economic throat of the world, killing its trade and prosperity. The amount of poverty generated was staggering.

Joa, Under the Guise of Helping Trojan

Therefore, under the guise of helping Trojan and his team during Bike Week, Joa and her team would be able to observe the ongoing Kildem organization which they felt able to enable S.I.I.T.F to dismantle this group of nefarious characters and their organization. Her team earlier on, prior to Bike Week, had installed new types of undetectable cameras and listening devices on the Inn premises. The data collected would be supplemented by the Inn's own security equipment. They knew Kildem was not the All. But what they were sure of, Kildem was a keystone. Destroy him and perhaps the rest would topple.

Profiles on many of the individuals attending this secret meeting had been provided by Interpol, Scotland Yard, CIA, and FBI, GRC and US Homeland Security and more international law enforcement agencies. It was known that the group included major business magnates and often powerful politicians involved in the same illicit movements of money, currencies and stock market manipulation. It was global, like a medusa snake with many heads.

She needed more than names to launch her all-out attack. She needed to have strong tangible proof and compelling evidences of fraud and specifics of crimes that had been committed. She needed—hard evidence—paper trails, Bank Statements, emails, correspondence, proof of funds transfers, and signatures. She had—the smoking guns—but she was playing a game where the opposing forces were rank with power. So, the additional evidence she sought was essentially, the irrefutable "eye" witnesses, hard material evidence. Money does talk, but she knew, so does any kind of paper with a signature. Otherwise, she would find herself in a very precarious position and her investigation could die before she was able to make it count. Or the damage to be done to the consortium would not be a dead shot.

Earlier on, she had requested S.I.I.T.F be prepared at a moment notice to send an extra team of well-qualified financial experts with a support contingent of armed individuals to protect them. They were to be brought into The Guardia Fortress in Tampa and would be provided with information, paper, electronic and maybe even eye witnesses.

A simultaneous search was made in several commercial areas belonging to Dennis as well as many other questionable companies in several regions and countries. All pertinent information on these companies would be forwarded to S.I.I.T.F. at the Guardian Fortress in Tampa, Florida.

The Guardia Fortress on Worldwide Contributions

The Guardia Fortress housed the offices of a Special Task Force having been established in the last decade by the Unified World Bank (UWB) at the request of NATO and the global financial community at large because of impending threats and extremism to the global financial security needed to control and eliminate the dirty money. At that point the (UWB) Unified World Bank, NATO and the financial community determined that this special force should fall under the S.I.I.T.F mandate. It was unanimously agreed to that this new Branch would be called International Finance Task Force (IFTF) was to be headed by no other than Maxim Kgnu a well-respected and highly intelligent international financier. Thus, S.I.I.T.F had several (IFTF) banking offices set up globally, but no one is open to public.

S.I.I.T.F needed a connection to the banking community. Not just the banking community but the Global Banking Community, and that meant everyone. Bad guys and very dirty money, but was badly connected with the Consortium bank (WTB). One of the major sources of finances for the Consortium outlet was illegal arms sales and thus literally billions of dollars of this dirty money from dirty wars and drug Cartels. Hence NATO's involvement by the rear door without knowing it but suspecting it, but suspecting is not enough to intervene in a bank business.

CHAPTER 13

Trakker Briefs Trojan

And Requests His Help to Convince Joa

After the strafing incident with the enemies' Bell ARH-70, Joe returned to the task of briefing Trojan. Joe cleared his throat and said:

"Trojan, I was in the process of telling you what appears on my video screen, when we were rudely interrupted by that barrage of bullets and shrapnel. Now that the helicopter bandits have stopped shooting at us, so to speak, I will show you what I believe will transpire in the next hours in the Tampa area. It will amaze you, as it has me. However, I am getting more familiar with what my intuition known as SOMBRAJ provides as indices, to enable us to assist in the elimination of wicked, currently causing havoc on this planet."

Joe, reaches over to pick up the camera bag, where he had left it moments earlier, hoping it had not been damaged.

"Oh, no!" Trojan looks perplex at Joe's comment.

"What is it Joe!" Joe, all in a tither looks at Trojan and tells him:

"My camera bag is gone! I hope it did not fall out of the open door during the shouting." Trojan with a bemused look on his face picks up the bag which was out of sight near the pilot's seat. Picking up the heavy leather bag, he turned to Joe:

"Here Joe, you must have shoved it there when you pushed me out of harm's way." Joe looking relieved, takes the heavy leather camera bag from Trojan:

"Thanks Trojan, but no, I did not have time to shove both, you and the bag. As I mentioned to you previously, SOMBRAJ can perform tasks without us humans being aware. Now do I have a convert? What you will see next is quite unbelievable." Joe with what seemed to be a note of concern in his usually deep relaxed voice:

"Joa needs our help and soon."

Joe extracted his cam from the bag and pressed the ON button to engage the video screen. He noticed the cam bag had been pierced by a fragment of shrapnel and turned to Trojan and said:

"Have a look Trojan!"

Joe was not referring to what should have been fatal damage the camera had sustained but what was being depicted on its mysteriously still functioning screen. Trojan was totally engrossed in the video unfolding on the tiny screen before him. Perhaps mesmerized a better description, it was a drama the likes of which had never been seen before. This was no TV police drama. This was real, and the reality of it raised the hair on Trojan's neck. It was an explosion while Joa was in the bunker, that's why she needed SOMBRAJ for the specific timing.

Thomas, wondering what was so engrossing to the mighty Trojan, informed him, Joe, and the team, that he will let them know when they are close to the rendezvous at Tampa. At which point it would be important that Joa be contacted on the secure frequency for further orders. Being military, he did not want to encroach on whatever Joa was in the process of undertaking, as it seemed of a top-secret nature.

Joa Meets SOMBRAJ

SOMBRAJ was having difficulty contacting Joa using her intuition, because she was under so much pressure, having to contend with Dennis's organization. He needed an open line so to speak, to get through to her much occupied mind in some way and quickly, but at the moment all her lines in her mental switchboard were "busy." SOMBRAJ at the moment could not get through to her mentally. Her mind was thoroughly occupied, trying to deal with multiple tasks and situations; all of her faculties were engaged in resolving various issues. However, it was urgent to attract her attention and soon. So, I was thinking:

"Plan B—SOMBRAJ." SOMBRAJ would use Joe Trakker (me) and help me to use conventional methods, such as the secured frequency of the helicopter via 54-TI to contact Joa.

SOMBRAJ was now aware that Trojan was watching the critical video on Joe cam screen, showing future events and how they would occur at Dennis Kildem's headquarters. SOMBRAJ in his usual fashion was adept at getting Joe to act. It was essential for him to convince Joa of the danger she would be facing and the importance of the how and when of: that which she needed to do.

With the help of SOMBRAJ Joe made his move. Plan B—SOMBRAJ was underway. Trojan and Joe's video would be well applied to get Joa to listen to what he had to say. If at first you don't succeed, get a bigger hammer.

Time was of the essence. Joa was still airborne just south of the Tampa rendezvous; it was time for the call.

SOMBRAJ had turned his attention to Thomas, Trojan's pilot, enveloping him in a warm sensation and poking his intuition to get him to contact Joa. Thomas was a little confused as to what he was hearing Joe tell Trojan. Without analyzing it, he begins the process of trying to contact Joa through 54-TI. The nature of SOMBRAJ's mental intrusion to others was very effective. However, it was very subtle, and when necessary, could easily leave the subject without the slightest inkling they were being used or manipulated. Thomas keyed in the frequency. His mike was voice activated and with professional precision, that in this instance was not quite one hundred percent, he spoke.

"54-TI this is Coast Guard 4137. Captain Thomas Montgomery. I have urgent traffic, over." There seems to be complete silence and then.

"Roger Thomas, 4137. This is Maurice, 54-TI. How were you able to access this secure frequency, over?"

"Roger, 54-TI this is Coast Guard 4137 (Thomas). We have critical traffic for Joa, will explain later, over." There was a pregnant pause before Maurice replied. He was completely mystified by this communication coming over an assigned frequency no one knew existed as theirs. It was simply allocated as: military-banned, when seemingly a warm sensation enveloped him and he responded.

"Roger, Thomas 4137, this is 54-TI, what is the traffic, over?"

"Maurice, patch me into Joa, it is extremely, life or death, important, over."

Maurice, still not sure of the voice on the radio was busy keying the information into 54-TI's intelligence system, and to gain a few seconds more, challenged the caller using military Z codes to identify themselves:

"4137 please identify, Zulu Golf, Golf, over." Thomas reciprocated and immediately identified them as: friendly strike force aircraft using the same code:

"54-TI, this is 4137 Zulu Golf, Golf, one... Please advise urgent incoming traffic for Joa from one Lieutenant Detective Gordon Trojan, over." Maurice connected with the name Trojan, his screen gave him the identity, location and pilot of 4137, and he replied immediately.

"4137, this is 54-TI, stand by for patches."

"4137, this is 54-TI, we have your patch. You are clear to transmit this frequency. Go ahead 4137. 54-TI out."

"November Alpha 3 Sixers, this is United States Coast Guard 4137, over."

"4137, this is Two One Sixers, Joa here. Go ahead with your traffic, over."

"Two One Sixers this Lieutenant Gordon Trojan Joa, I have extremely urgent traffic for you from someone whom you have met. I have seen his evidence and it is 100%. Repeat. 100%. Please listen to Joe Trakker. Go ahead Joe."

"Joe who? Gordon what the hell is going on, how did you get this secure frequency, over?"

"Roger, Joa this is Joe. Joe Trakker, remember the guy with the camera you talked to in the Daytona Beach Inn parking lot, over?" Joa a little stunned to hear Joe calling her on this secured frequency said:

"Roger, yes Joe. How did you get hold of this secure frequency, over?"

"Roger, Joa things will become clear to you momentarily, I know this must be quite confusing and a little unorthodox but I had to get in touch with you. Trojan with the help of our pilot Thomas was able to get in on your frequency by contacting your 54-TI. As I said, things will become clear as I proceed with this most important call. Please listen. Your Operation 'BULLSEYE' is dependent on the success of the recovery operation of irrefutable evidence concerning all of the criminal activities of Dennis Kildem's organization and documentation which perhaps includes information on an individual going by the name of Tennis, also data on the International Organization of the consortium of criminals on track to succeed in the greatest economic fraud in history, with the aim of controlling the currencies of the world! There is no way I could falsify this information, over."

Joe Definitely Had Joa's Attention

Joe definitely had Joa's attention. Now extremely concerned, she countered:

"Roger, this is Joa. The information you are divulging is top secret. Be clear! Be quick! Know this! There are many lives at stake and I can and I will if I deem necessary, have your aircraft brought down. I am all ears, over." Joa's intuition told her that she had made it very clear to Joe what the consequences were if she doubted the credibility of what he had to say. What he knew, about their operation and how he knew it was both beyond her. At this point, security for her operation demanded her full attention:

"Roger, I will be as quick as I can but it is important that you understand. Remember our meeting and you found it strange that I recognized that you were a law enforcement officer, over." Joa with a note of suspicion in her voice replied:

"Roger, I remember and you also asked in Spanish if you could take my picture. How do you know that I am a law-enforcement officer, that is confidential and this frequency is secure? State your business and be quick about it, over?"

Joe was concerned that the conversation would head in the off-beam direction so he pulled out all stops:

"Roger, Joa, there is not much time, you are heading for in the wrong building. I am pleading that you listen to me. Remember the shadow of a cat which you saw at the entrance to the Daytona Beach Inn, over?"

Joa was now getting to the point of wanting to strangle Joe, wishing he would get to the facts, but this comment had left her a little disconcerted.

"Roger, damn Joe! How do you know this, spit it out, over?"

Joe began speaking quickly:

"Roger, Joa momentarily you will feel a warm sensation, let us call it your intuition, for now. Listen to it, it is very important and may even save your life as well as those of your team. Are you listening, over?" Joa was more than concerned, and now all her professional instincts were on red alert. Joa now began to wonder if she's in the process of talking to an absolute nutcase. However, Trojan is there with him and seems to know and believe Joe, even if he did seem more than just a little off the wall.

"Roger, Joe, I am listening, over."

So, Joe hurried even more to get this important information to her, he begins to get nervous and afraid of losing his voice:

"Roger, as I said Joa the sensation you will feel is like a warm feeling in the center of your body going up to your stomach, similar to your intuition, you must and I repeat, must listen, you must believe I am not a nut case and I am not off-the-wall. I could not possibly know what I know and I certainly could not get past Lieutenant Trojan."

Joa was surprised to hear that Joe seemed to know what she was thinking as she was thinking it and that made her uncomfortable, very uncomfortable.

“Roger, do you want me to go on Joa, over?” Readjusting herself in her seat, she began to listen more intently.

“Roger, Joe make it quick state your traffic, over.”

Poor me Joe, I was hoping I would not have this beautiful, smart and professional woman angry at me; I dearly wanted her as a friend:

“Roger, you know that we humans cannot understand everything that goes on in this world and that there are strange things that occur and are difficult to explain or understand. These things are sometimes much stronger than we are. I believe, however, when we meet face to face in the near future you will have come to understand what I am telling you now. Please let your intuition or that sensation guide you to do what is necessary to protect yourself, your team and put an end to, or if not, a dent into the wicked which currently occupies this little planet of ours. Should I tell you more or will you act on your intuition, over?”

Joa with some trepidation and a sigh:

“Roger, OK Joe! Give me the information you have, I will act accordingly, over.”

This time it was not Joe who spoke but the person who made her heart beat faster.

“Roger, Joa, this is Trojan. Listen to Joe very carefully. I do not want anything to happen to you. We should be there soon. Here is Joe, over.” Joe gives Trojan a knowing smile.

Joa found herself listening to her intuition as requested by Joe. In all reality, she had no choice. Not only was Joe armed with more intelligence and information than humanly possible, but in addition, SOMBRAJ was now able to access her volition and was doing so. This latter part she could neither see, nor understand, although she did know that something was happening very much out of the ordinary, and that she somehow felt that she must trust whatever this was. After all, this was the intuition that had enabled her to determine that "The Pouilleux" was the trigger in the Daytona Beach massacre; that she had felt and seen a photographer in the window of the neighboring building at the back of the Inn; that a shadow of a cat had stopped her from entering the Inn enabling her to avoid being shot.

Unbeknownst to her at this moment, she was coming to accept the help of SOMBRAJ and me, Joe. Before her operation began I needed to give her certain facts concerning what must happen during the operation, she was now embarking on with her team. All of the facts could not be provided by her intuition, so I began the process of providing the information to her, knowing that this information was well protected by the marvelous technology within her powerful 54-TI.

SOMBRAJ Was Also at Work

SOMBRAJ was also at work. He provided me with the necessary information that Joa would need. Amazingly, his method this time had been partly on my video cam, but now he brought it all together in a most unusual way. He allowed me, upon closing my eyes, to see what was going to happen in the next hour, as if looking at a colored television drama. It was more than my cam could provide. I had already shown the cam to Trojan. Speaking to Joa, I began relaying the information that was now being depicted in my mind's eye under the skillful guidance of SOMBRAJ.

While feeding Joa, SOMBRAJ was able to have a little excursion in the whole agglomeration that use to be a sisters' congregation. The whole quadrilateral was a convent, a gymnasium and a church with a big parking. The too old church had been blocked up and forbidden, the big Gym converted in two warehouses and the convent restructured in the deluxe DK Palace offices. The secret of it was the hidden tunnels interconnection with rooms, that use to be reclusion rooms.

Details were not available from Dennis's mind, so SOMBRAJ had to get more precisions to not risk Joa's life and her team's life too. Now more detailed information was available from the Dennis bunker. As Dennis trying to come closer, he is becoming more scared, but he can't imagine somebody could penetrate his, so dear to him, souvenirs of his craziness.

The Secret Brownstone Building

Joa's mind was more reachable and I was feeling like she was finally ready to embrace cooperation. In my head, it was something like watching a video in my brain, although that in all honesty is a really poor description. I could not hope to accurately describe a SOMBRAJ experience with words. What I could do was describing this video cam, documentaries, news reels, call it what you will but word by word I had to create a word picture for Joa and so I began:

"Roger Joa, make your way to the secret brownstone building on the site, I believe you know the one I am talking about. You do not have to answer. It is the one you last saw Dennis enter and disappears. Remember twice you waited for nearly two hours and the last time you waited for over four hours and he never came out, over."

Still Joa was having difficulty believing in Joe's words but like a true professional she continued listening and trusting her intuition:

"Roger, how do you ....?" Joa did not get time to finish because Joe became insistent and continued rapid-fire:

"Roger, Joa time is short. Your question will be answered in good time. Listen, do not mention, I repeat, do not mention the place in question, as you are the only one who knows it's real location! Be careful which of your superiors you advise, I also believe I do not have to tell you why. You will have a maximum of 'twenty minutes' from the time you pass the step of the basement door at the lowest stairs of the building, until you leave it, OK?" "Once you have entered and pass that door, that never was opened a destruction protocol to obliterate the bunker will be activated."

"Joa, to get the most of your time, prepare everything and give your orders before going through that door."

"The only and faster way to enter this particular building, without activating destruction, will be through the pyramid shaped stained-glass skylight. It is well hidden by a roof top garden and, as you know, most of the buildings in its vicinity also have rooftop gardens. Once your helicopter drops you and your team on the roof you need to use grappling hooks which you will attach to the weakened south corner of the triangle and pull it towards the north side of the building, over."

Joe needed to ensure that his instructions were clear:

"Joa, for now, you must contact the team that is waiting at the Tampa airport, and get them to prepare with explosives, chains and hooks, crowbar, and a dolly in case you need to bring the whole cabinet instead of drawers one by one. Be prepared with strong men to lift all as fast possible; I will wait until this is accomplished to allow you to provide them with the necessary coordinates in scrambled format. Use coordinates which are close by, but not exact. Ensure they are on board and understand the secrecy of the operation. Make sure that they are well equipped with explosives, hooks, chains and ropes. Concentrate on this operation and only this operation, once this is accomplished the other Dennis's office locations will be straight forward. Joa, you may need a few minutes to give your team orders and then, I will wait you get back to me and continue our conversation, out."

Joe became silent, letting Joa get her team ready to undertake this operation.

Joa must prepare her team for Tampa

While Captain Franklin was preparing for the operation requirement as specified by Joa, Captain Franklin with his Black Hawk ready, with men and equipment, was waiting Joa's OK.

Only 18 minutes after advising Captain Franklin to prepare, Jamari Joa's pilot, had cleared with Tampa MacDill air force base tower as incoming commercial, using their cover call sign, and set down beside Captain Franklin's Black Hawk who was waiting there and ready to go for top fly out action: BULLSEYE.

The original rendezvous

Since Joe's SOMBRAJ, had nourished Joa's mind with the new destination, the bunker, that was completely unknown from Joa and anyone, the whole rendezvous had to be modified, but for better. Before, Joa was going on a guesstimating, with something good too, but was not sufficient to get in the deep inner of the consortium and (WTB).

Once Joe had signed off, Joa began to prepare to contact 54-TI. Joa was still concerned about Joe's instructions, however felt that Trojan would not have approved if this would put her and her team in danger. With some trepidation but trusting her intuition she called Maurice: "54-TI this is two-one-six. What is your ETA, over?"

"Roger, Joa our ETA to your location is Two Five, repeat Two Five, over."

"Roger 54-TI, can you advise of disposition of teams and ETA of any personnel to our known location and wait for orders for the next coming secret location that I will tell you soon, proceed rapidly and be ready, as always, to help because war is on his way to all of us, over?"

"Roger, Maurice here is our coordinates in scrambled format, keep it for you only, this is a covert operation, and you know what is required of the team at this point: Operation BULLSEYE is now in effect, over."

BULLSEYE Operation, now in effect

"Roger, Joa just did that. Affirmative Operation BULLSEYE is now in effect, over."

Joa turns to her communication panel, giving Maurice the coordinates.

When the information had been transmitted, Maurice replied:

"Roger Maurice, 54-TI out."

Maurice has organized the whole team to be at the new secret destination that was the old church parking behind the DK Palace and wait for the whole team to get out with what Joa calls the package. Joa returned to her secure frequency with Joe Trakker:

"4137, Joe are you there, over?"

"Roger, Joa, is everything in place and are we a go, over?"

"Roger Joe, over."

"Roger Joa, when I have provided you with the following details, listen only to your intuition and especially do not doubt it, even if it seems unlikely, because doubt is interferences. The whole financial world depends on you and your team. Joa when you land, all of you will have is your confidence in your intuition. Let it guide you and do not forget a very strong force known as SOMBRAJ will help you and protect you, over."

Joa's intuition, with more than a little help from SOMBRAJ was now telling her to follow Joe's instruction:

"Roger Joe, SOMBRAJ, who the............. OK! OK! Joe let me get going. Time is a wasting and my team is ready, over." Joa is excited and concerned but she proceeds like a true professional even if she was trembling of optimism.

Joe with concern in his strong voice reiterates his warning:

"Roger, Joa follow your intuition and the following steps, make sure you are well aware of your surroundings as you proceed to the known SPOT, over." Joe's comment does register with Joa:

"Roger Joe, over." Joe reinforces his comment:

"Joa, do you understand all my instructions, over?"

"Roger, yes, out." Joa was 5 minutes to touch down at the appointed rendezvous point at the old church parking lot.

"Joa, after the stain glass stood out of your way to go in, get down the north stairs leading to the basement, arriving at the door marked DANGER in huge red letters, pry and open that tunnel door. Once inside, into the right branch of the tunnel, rush to a set of stairs ten feet in. And then stand up on the first step of the stairs, pressing down simultaneously on the corner of the upper and central molding located on the wall on your right and wait, two second pause, and the step will vibrate. And then go up quickly on the next step and the bunker door at the top of the stairs will silently open. You have two minutes lost."

- "After opening the lower stairs door with DANGER on it 'that never been opened,' that door is the trigger for destruction, so get to the west cement block wall and blow off a hole with explosives, to get all out the fastest you can."
- "Then, prepare stuff while the wall blowing off and then rush as fast as you can. Shaking the file cabinets may tell you if it's possible to dolly faster the whole cabinet out."
- "First, get the GREEN FILES at all price, next the ones with P followed by X in red, next the plastic cases with hart drives and the black dossiers with yellow and white lettering. If possible, get the Magic Egyptian Medallion. The rest will be a gift for victimized justice."
- "Try to throw away, the farther than you can the other side of the west wall, what you cannot carry out, maybe to get it later."

More strong guys with you in there will take out more documents in less than 18 minutes. Keep yourself a two-minute loss to evacuate by the church ways because the church is a safe solid construction.

Upon completing my instructions to Joa, I had fallen silent. I was hoping she had understood the importance of my instructions and had believed that SOMBRAJ would help her. I knew that Trojan and everyone in the helicopter were hanging on every word as I talked to Joa. They were in total awe of the details I was providing and probably were wondering what planet I came from. So, until that moment there was no time to lose...

The whole spider web was building in the same time; Joa's teams were on their way to help too.

Tampa secret rendezvous

The various units, including 54-TI, were all well versed in their orders and were to proceed to their designated coordinates once Operation BULLSEYE went into effect, under, of course, the worldwide: Operation CONSO-DOWN.

The ETA of the Coast Guard Thomas, 4137 with Trojan and Joe on board was not until well after Operation BULLSEYE was underway, their orders were to remain clear of the Kildem DK Palace, then proceed as cover for 54-TI when it left the church parking and headed to the new coordinates, The Guardia Fortress.

Trojan had been informed by Joa that 54-TI would advise Thomas when they were ready to leave the church parking accompanied by the General Bentall OSHKOSH JLTV and his huge air support. This meant that 54-TI had received—the package—which consisted of a highly sensitive Green Files and a "Magic Egyptian Medallion" from Joa, and would require air and important ground cover to their destination because passing through Tampa important populace.

Just prior to 54-TI leaving the church parking, Joa would leave in her Sikorsky, accompanied by Captain Wayne Franklin in the Black Hawk and Commander Graham's ground unit in a ploy to draw any mercenaries away from the vicinity of 54-TI. When secure, Joa and company deemed they would change direction, so that she would be on through courses for her leg of the mission? By this time, 54-TI would be on route for The Guardia Fortress. And if something unattended appends, 54-TI would run in a new running direction, provided by Joa, to get the Green Files and the whole (package) to destination. But this last Joa's part of the plan is changing due to Joe Tracker but all others still amplified by the need to succeed in the Operation BULLSEYE, the US part of the international CONSO-DOWN operation.

The Whole Area in a Sky and Ground War Alike

The whole area was in high level national security. Every street was blocked by local police, and state Sheriff, even FBI was cooperating. General Bentall, who is a member founder of S.I.I.T.F., had deployed, the ever-seen air and land, armed forces to protect the area, in case of mercenary invasion and eventual bombing or explosion warning. The vicinity was evacuated and 22 brand new Oshkosh JLTV's were patrolling the area. General said to the whole organized forces cooperating in the same unified goal Operation BULLSEYE:

"No one should be able to come close to the critic point,

Where the BULLSEYE Operation is in progress?"

Only the seven well-identified news channels helicopters that were there before being tolerated, any others were interdicted and push away by the military forces. It was looking like unproportioned to everybody and no one knew what to tell their auditory. Speculation had to be stopped because Tampa has one of the most petroleum bulk storage and distribution in the region, because of its natural deep-water navigation seaway through the Tampa Bay.

Victims Are Claiming Justice and Even Death If Need Be

And for this particular significant, ever, retracing of incriminated evidences, many SOMBRAJ spirits were floating all around the site. This was not about money or business, this was about crooks controlling the world against honest people by killing anyone in their way or in contradiction with their dictatorship...

SOMBRAJ was there for victims claiming justice. This is why, sometime, the real justice has to wake up beyond human ability and apply justice by death to the killers who deserved death.

SOMBRAJ said in an understanding way:

"When Justice has to be death, it is for protecting their eventual innocent victims, because the inside feeling of an assassin is as the pleasure he resents by killing others as he was killing himself... And later, after another killing, his deception is that he is still alive, and he will need to kill again."

Justice is predominant in this whole operation that has been orchestrated by the SOMBRAJ summit of the whole world. Not easy to believe for those who are sectaries pro-dependent, but all around the area, about 31 bodies were found holding arms whom were known to already have killed innocents, for criminal organizations. No one of them had fired a single bullet but they were there to kill. A butterfly has passed around their head and took away their miserable life, not because they were there to kill, but because they had killed before. Life is only gifted for a while and can be taken away from anyone criminals.

Those who think that they have the right to kill innocents with impunity is wrong and even if they are hiding behind believing, they will have their butterfly visit very soon because SOMBRAJ is here to stay for a while; they have to pay a visit into many jails where many killers are waiting for their butterfly. The good of it is, nobody feels anything, the life goes away first and slowly after two or three heartbeats... The body is dead, gone forever...

SOMBRAJ is righter of wrongs to the body of the killers. If it would be a vengeance, those who had unfledged so much suffering to innocents would be punished with the same suffering, but SOMBRAJs only take away the life they do not deserve to have. That is when justice has to be death and because the actual judiciary systems are not fast and effective enough to serve justice to innocents.

Dennis Weakness Serve the Mission

But the Dennis mental state was a good door for SOMBRAJ's feeding. When being scared, he was weakening his inner protection shield. (Carapaces.) Seen by a SOMBRAJ a carapace is built by education, mostly from childhood, it's like filaments crisscrossed over a lot of bad experimentations that protect your-self, to stay mentally healthy alike. In another word, it's to not become crazy. So, when Dennis loses control, it makes spaces between filaments and then anyone becomes easily penetrable to his real inside being.

In the meantime, SOMBRAJ had been able to penetrate again, into the mind and psyche of Dennis, in a very unusual fashion. As Dennis became more enraged and fearful because he was in the process of losing control of everything, the incoherence and near complete lack of control allowed SOMBRAJ to enter deeply into Dennis's interior castle, enabling him to obtain Dennis's extremely well hidden, deepest and darkest secrets. Individuals like Dennis, quite often build up such intensive hatred that they want to kill whoever or whatever gets in their way. In some instances, this madness allows them to forge another personality contrary to what it could be in reality. Even a most powerful SOMRAJ has difficulty in dealing with these individuals whose, sick mentally distortion is not just surpassed, but given birth by, then fed by the inner workings of the mentally ill. They are beyond immorality or they become irrational and illogical when it comes to humanity.

SOMBRAJ was now beginning to comprehend, allowing him to sort out and find pathways into the inner workings of Dennis's convoluted mind. SOMBRAJ made his way through this maze, avoiding directions which would lead him to nothingness or pure rage. SOMBRAJ believed that, until that only moment, he could plant a seed or cause Dennis to blunder; perhaps even causing he, to destroy himself mentally if not physically, even committing suicide was a possibility.

A SOMBRAJ had to flow into a human mind along a pathway made by thought patterns. Rage and insanity disturbed these patterns to such a degree, that there were no familiar thought structures for the SOMBRAJ to follow. It was like going on a journey with your eyes closed.

CHAPTER 14

Dennis Approaching DK Palace,

Meanwhile Dennis and his mercenaries were approaching the DK palace and he wondered if they had arrived in time to retrieve the sensitive information that was contained in his bunker and in his office. Dennis was concerned that an attempt would be made by unknown criminal factions and, or, the international law enforcement to get their hands on his office documents but would never have imagined one instant that somebody would find his bunker. Dennis who is not wearing a headset taps Robert on the shoulder. Robert puts the helicopter on auto pilot and turns to Dennis wondering:

"What does he want now?" Robert in a voice that could melt butter responds:

"yes Mr. Kildem." Dennis heard the note of sarcasm in the mercenary's voice:

"Robert! What is our ETA to DK palace?" He points to the complex ahead of them, replying with a hint of tired exasperation in his voice:

"Approximately one minute." Robert then returns to his controls and disengages the auto pilot, dismissing Dennis.

How Robert had answered him did not go unnoticed by Dennis; feeling dismissed and getting Trotter under the collar, Dennis turns to Dino his companion since ever, and overtly questions and instructs him:

“Dino, are you ready when we arrive to head for DK palace? Remember, you must disengage the security or we will be blown up within minutes. You are faster than me so I will let you proceed to the panel at the top of the stair, you know how to disengage the protocol, but you must hurry.” What Dennis failed to mention to Dino was that the protocol also had a second command if it had already been triggered, meaning that there was only five minutes left. But he deeply taught that it was impossible that somebody knew something about his bunker:

“It’s there since more than 30 years, it’s only in my head, and otherwise it does not exist.” Dino’s responds in a curt manner:

“Yes, sir! I will follow your instructions to the letter. I know what can happen if I don’t. Dino thought to himself:

“If I don’t get blown to smithereens by the security system, Dennis will blow my brains out. This is a no-win situation. My only chance would be to access the bunker and make my way out with some insurance and go underground.”

There was a brief respite of silence as everyone is deep in thought, then hurried activity among them checking their firearms as Robert came about 2 miles to get there.

“What’s that? Hey... Is there a war or something? Two war jets were on sides, signaling to go down and more! Just in front was coming 4 army combat helicopters and the radio got louder, warning us to land down?

“Last warning! You land down or we hunt you down!

Dennis became even more anxious as his thoughts turn to how he would handle an infiltration into his private domain:

"How could they…? After all, this is my place and how dare they invade the area? All that force, you think it's for DK Palace?" And he shouts:

"Robert! We have no choice go dawn! Have any news about the Humvees?"

Knowing Dennis was becoming more irrational, responds in a calm detached voice:

"Sir, we're only a few minutes from the DK palace but every street look like blocked down there so, we may try to get something else to go truly." And while landing:

"You know so many guys all around here; this place is your home."

As they came down in a big shopping center parking, his anger turned to white rage and he began one of his all too familiar rants:

"Robert gets me down there now by the fence"!

"But sir…………"

"I said get me down NOW! THERE! By the fence entrance close to the street"!

Robert, an excellent pilot, thought to himself:

"I think he has gone off his rocker or maybe he is trying to kill us all." He saw his opportunity and was able to set his helicopter down safely. No sooner has he touched the ground, but, Dennis jumped out of the copter in a dead run towards the street. Dino hit the ground a split second behind Dennis and was headed at full speed to follow him.

"Maniac!" Robert muttered. The remaining men simply sat looking indifferently at the floor in the idling helicopter, having not been given any other orders by Dennis, so he decides to wait there until he comes back.

Dennis stops a taxi passing by. The taxi stops, only to tell him that he was going on a call:

"I'm on a call I'm calling the dispatcher to send you one, OK?

Dennis pointed his gun, got in the taxi with Dino and ordered without asking:

'Go! I said go!' They went the closest they could, before the police barricades and they walk in the backyard of several houses, crawling and hiding behind parked cars to finally arrive close to the northeast of his warehouse. They were now hiding, waiting to have a chance to infiltrate the northeast fence that he was supposed to repair, but happy he didn't.

By this time Joa's team was in the bunker but he was sure that nobody could be in there. But he was doing the dirty stupid hiding and crawling, that he would never imagine to do in his whole life. He thought whispering:

'What? Me, with my $ 2 bricks silk mohair costume.....No.....No more ever, but I need my Green Files or I'm better be dead if I don't get them.

The team at the bunker site

And now, getting out of my cam viewer,

We are becoming, right now, in the crucial moment that you do not want to miss out.

So, stay close, for this little break will not last long.

Get closer again, and see!

SOMBRAJ was feeding Joe with up-to-date movements on the site; as Dennis was close to enter the Bunker by a secret back door, while he was still connected to Joa.

Close to 2 minutes after landing in the church parking she gives a little fast last briefing, and then, another minute, they were all on the spot on the top of the building. Joa had now set the plan in motion; everyone was ready to proceed with the mission. Jamari positioned the helicopter near the south side where there was more cover for the team to rappel to the roof. Joa gave the nod and the assault team was out the doors and dropping like black spiders on magic webs.

Lieutenant Logan Pike had the grappling hook, attaching it to the south point of the pyramid frame, while the remainder of the team prepared to follow Joa into the opening once the pyramid will be breached. The timing of the mission was extremely critical or Joa could lose not only evidences but also her team and her own life as well. The rappelling from Tiger had gone quite smoothly, the team was ready; Joa seeing everyone was in position said:

"Logan is the grappling hook in place?" Over the roar of the helicopter turbine whine, Logan quickly responds:

"Yes, Joa, ready to go?"

Joa nag and hands signs too Jamari up there:

"Jamari, grappling hooks attached. Lift and pull!" The turbine's whine turned to a low roar and with a crash and shattering into millions of little shards of beautiful colored glass and bent, twisted metal, the pyramid was lifted and flung to one side. Jamari had dropped the cables and was gone to the Church parking. Before the coupler hit the roof, Joa and her team had dropped through the opening to the floor below and disconnected their lines.

The Black hawks and her helicopter the Tiger had the order to get back at the entrance of the church and waiting for the signal to get in to help, after the explosion, proceeding securely to the church entrance. After the explosion, they had to run to the opening for helping getting out the most of the material. Joa said loudly:

"If we get everything out of there, we may be able to help a lot of victimized innocents."

Hurriedly, Joa ran to the north stairs leading to the basement, arriving in seconds at the door marked DANGER in huge red letters. Following Trakker's instructions to the letter, Joa motioned to Pike and Dewitt, and with one thrust on a door, pry the tunnel door, let go of its hinges with a loud, (s-p-la-n-g). Once inside, Joa led her team into the right branch of the tunnel to a set of stairs fifty feet in. Joa stood up on the first step of the stairs, pressing down simultaneously on the corner of the upper and central panels located on the wall on her right. A brief two second pause and the step vibrated. She stepped quickly on the next step and the bunker door at the top of the stairs swung silently open. She said aloud:

"THANKS Joe or SOMBRAJ, who or whatever?"

The team followed Joa up, taking the stairs two and three at a time into the vast bunker chamber. This was definitely not a safe. However, it was their immediate goal, where all the sensitive files, documents and important objects were neatly stored like a treasure, awaiting its imminent plunder.

Hank, Open a Doorway

Joa was now following her intuition, which she always took into consideration, but at this moment she seemed to be guided more so, as if being led. Was it true what Joe Trakker had said that something called SOMBRAJ would guide her? Joa had no time for this type of questioning as it could endanger the mission, so with speed and care she proceeded to do what she had been told by Joe. She and her team continued to advance quickly and carefully on the treasure trove of information contained in the bunker.

Prior to the start of the operation Joa had given orders to her team and specified their responsibilities during the operation. On entering the bunker, knowing there is little time; Joa had shown Lieutenant Hank Dewitt her explosive expert, further into the cavernous bunker, telling the Lieutenant as he is making his way towards the west wall:

"Hank, there we need it, big enough to allow us to escape quickly. Keep in mind it is a reinforced bunker."

Hank was already striding to the chosen site, and said over his shoulder as he swung his backpack full of plastic explosives and detonators off to the floor:

"Joa, got the plans in my head!"

Hank has made a test with his impact gun first and then yelled: "Blowout stays safe!" At that moment, there was a loud muffled crunch as Hank magically created their doorway.

The job was done after massing the loose debris around the open way to the west wall.

The team had come up with a very good exit plan, which would allow them to leave through a tunnel leading to a wooden door of the basement access of the old church, and an alternative escape route through a northeast tunnel leading to the warehouse. The door leading into the old church had been easily breached by more guys running to help from the other way. General Bentall had sent some more guys to help Joa's team.

Inside the old church basement in a very secluded area, Hank had discovered a low alcove where some of the file boxes could be put for safekeeping until the (SIRS) team had time to recover them. The immediate team would be able to move the Green Files, Magic Egyptian Medallion and Dennis's personal accounting files, both paper and electronic which was the most important part of the package through the church into waiting transportation located in the massive parking lot of the church and away from the perimeter of the DK palace.

Locate the Green Files First

Without hesitation she said:

"You all know what is required of you, make haste we have little time to accomplish this mission, take care there may be booby traps." While they were all getting stuff out, Joa made her way to where the most sensitive information might be stored and said to Lieutenant Wexford:

"Nicole, come with me." Joa points to the east side of the bunker where a group of black file cabinets were located. There were large white and yellow lettering on their fronts in seeming random order. She had been told that the Green Files would be found in the first group of cabinets:

"Nicole, we must locate the green folder as it is extremely important and is at the top of our list."

The filing cabinets in question were protected by a single padlock and bar assembly. The case-hardened padlock was no match for the laser cutter Nicole unsheltered, and in seconds it clattered to the floor.

Joa says to Nicole jokingly as they rapidly yanked open the drawers:

"Well I guess Dennis relied on the bunker's security protocol to protect it and did not think he needed heavier protection on the cabinets. However, he is very devious and probably has set up something else to challenge any intruder."

Finally, Found the Green Files

The two were tearing through the drawers, intent on extracting the files they needed, into one of the leather satchels readied on the floor. It was not until the third drawer that Joa came across the Green Files. Nicole had found the black folders imbedded with yellow and white lettering, and these too went into the leather satchel. Joa, after finding the Green Files makes her way to Nicole and hands it to her saying:

"Finally found it, yes, that's it! OK Nicole move it now with these they are too important to delay your departure from here."

Nicole shouldered the satchel and said to Joa, her voice suddenly rapid and a bit strange:

"Joa, what about the Magic Egyptian Medallion"? Nicole at that moment with files in hand, instead of heading towards the west wall was instead hurrying towards the north end of the bunker where they had entered. She seemed on a mission, as if she knew something or was being guided by some unknown force.

Joa shouted with concern:

"Nicole, there is no time"! Nicole intent on her quest says to Joa:

"I will only be a minute. I think I know where it might be. If it is not there, I will leave immediately." Nicole disappeared behind the rows of cabinets as she ran towards the north end of the bunker.

With a cold feeling in her stomach and no choice or time to argue, Joa replied:

"OK Nicole! Hurry! The rendezvous! We have no time to lose!" From many briefings prior to the raid, Nicole knew her first rendezvous point was to be the other side of the breached wall near the northeast tunnel exit leading to the old church. However, Nicole understood if she was not there at the appointed time Joa would proceed to the next rendezvous point which had been agreed to during the formulation of the escape route.

For the moment Joa put Nicole aside and made her way to the center of the bunker, where she had a good view of the operations and would be able to ensure the remainder of her team would be gathering only the boxes and files that Joa had stipulated beforehand that needed to be taken.

Lieutenant Michael Rampart was having difficulty with the heavy plastic file storage boxes which were quite awkward to carry, so, Lieutenant Logan Pike arrived to assist him.

Logan had removed many of the file boxes which included those specified by SOMBRAJ which included documents identified by black, white and yellow markings. Moving at almost a dead run under his burdens, Logan had stored them in the church basement in a safe area where they could be picked up by Commander Herckel and her team. Logan Pike picked up two of the white boxes as if they were paper bags and made his way to the west wall grabbing two other boxes which had the letter "P" followed with a red "X" embossed on the side. Michael, having been Pike's shadow on many operations picked up the remainder of the boxes and followed Pike without breaking stride. These boxes were important as they contained photos that may provide details on victims and where their remains could be found, according to Joe.

Joa had noticed why Michael was having difficulty with the boxes, he was holding the round silver box which was bigger and heavier than she had anticipated. She was hoping that it was the one she wanted, which had the word “Police” in black lettering on the lid.

Joa could see more guys adding to the team, coming from the church entrance, and were removing other documents contained in boxes, beginning from the top right-hand side and making their way to the bottom as requested by Joe Trakker. Joa spotted Hank leaving with three other white plastic boxes which SOMBRAJ said contained many hard drives which Dennis had kept, depicting many of his past operations.

Joa turned around from observing the team to see if Nicole was still in the bunker, but outside of the central work area, the other was nowhere to be seen. Joa hoped Nicole had found the Magic Egyptian Medallion, she was feeling like, it was very important to her.

Explosion in 2 minutes, everybody out! Get out NOW!

Joa looked at her watch to determine the remaining time, when suddenly seemingly out of nowhere a sleek Siamese cat appears and runs across her path hissing at her and disappearing towards the West wall where her team was heading. It was a strange and overpowering feeling of dread that swept over Joa, making her shout orders to her team: **“EVERYBODY OUT, GET OUT NOW!** Take what you have and head to the west wall! There is no time left!”

Just as Joa reached the breached west wall, he heard first two gunshots and right after a thundering explosion shook the building, behind her, a pall of smoke and dust engulfed the interior of the bunker, obscuring everything. The team was now far ahead of her, but she hesitated for a glance to the northeast branch of the tunnel to see if Nicole was there. Despite the smoke and dust, Joa could clearly see that the small exit door at the far end of the northeast tunnel was now open. She assumed, she hoped, that Nicole had left for the next rendezvous point when the explosion had happened.

There is rubble scattered all over and a huge pile of debris where the wall of that northeast tunnel had caved in. Joa knows she cannot go in that direction because of imminent danger of further collapse. Another explosion rocked the entire structure from deep inside the bunker, and now the entire building began to tremble with ominous crashing and cracking and tearing noises coming from the bunker as the building trembled and chucked in the throes of agony.

Joa's guts were telling her, while running in the dust:

"I must get out immediately," then she turned and ran towards the tunnel that the team has taken, hoping she would still be able to get out. Acrid smoke and dust are now rolling through the tunnel, and there is absolute obscurity, yet Joa believes, or does she really see, a light or glow at the far end? She does not hesitate, following her reliable intuition, running at full tilt towards that light.

The Team Got Out from Smoke and Dust

After what seemed like an eternity, coughing and eyes tearing from the smoke and dust, she finally arrives to where the doors of the old church have been removed; a sure sign that the team had left and were making their way to the rendezvous point, where they would be loading the many file boxes and recovered items into 54-TI that, according to plan, would now be waiting in the church parking lot.

Once her eyes had cleared, Joa noticed that the building that, a moment earlier, had stood above the bunker was now badly damaged with one corner a pile of rubble. She had a weird feeling that something was not quite right. Joa noticed that the Oshkosh carrying Captain Corrigan's crew had arrived and were assisting in the transference of the boxes to 54-TI. Joa said to Maurice to start scanning the most files that seem important only and transfer back the boxes, those of less concern, in the 4 Oshkosh, 2 of her team and 2 of General Bentall forces. They have to be prepared to leave before we get Dennis's mercenaries on our back.

Nicole and Green Files Still Missing

Lieutenant Logan Pike, just a few minutes before, when he saw Joa completely gray and dust covered, stumble out of the church, he had made his way to assist her, fearing she had been injured:

"Joa, are you injured?" Coughing from her encounter with the smoke and dust, Joa said:

"No Logan, just dirty. Has everyone made it out? Is the package loaded on 54-TI?" Logan's response is quick and concise:

"Joa some of the package is with 54-TI. Is Nicole with you?" Concern now on Joa's face:

"No Logan. Where is she?" Logan with a note of apprehension in his voice said:

"I did not see her, we thought she would be with you." Joa begins to turn and head back shouting over her shoulder:

"Hell Logan! I got a go back in. I must get the Green Files and the Magic Egyptian Medallion, Nicole had them! Oh no... Dennis! That damn Dennis was there, I have heard guns shot just before the explosion. Dennis may have shouted her,"

Shouting, Dennis may be at the bunker.

At that moment, Cristopher had overheard Joa's comment:

"Mam. My team and I will go back and will find her and get the items in question."

"OK Cristopher! Go ahead and get Nicole and the Green Files. We need you here and we leave no one behind. Joa gives a strange questioning look to Cristopher, as if the Captain could read her mind.

"Thank you, Cristopher, you are right, be careful, Dennis may still be there. Find her and get the items to me first or 54-TI!" Cristopher summoned his crew and they grabbed the needed gear, heading in the old church entrance that still was full of fluctuating dust.

Familiar thumping sound of helicopter rotors were all around so, General Bentall was still protecting, and the parking was safe to wait for Nicole and the Green Files. She was surprised to see that the Cristopher team was no longer there. Joa thought to herself:

"WOW that unit moves fast." She was unaware; however, that Cristopher had sensed something very important.

Waiting with hopes Joa was mad at herself to not have taken the Green Files in her one satchel. She was remembering Joe's warnings:

"Joa, the whole world is counting on you, remember, the Green Files are the most important files of your mission, as it provided precise information on the entire Kildem old and new operations, as well as their associates around the world. The information within these files also identified many senior governmental officials around the globe, and their link to worldwide money laundering and the creation of an underworld criminal bank, known as (WTB) WORLD TRADERS BANKS, that would enslave the world economy. It is also the key, linking the rest of the files and data that they were collecting to the criminal organizations. Without the Green Files, the entire mission is at risk."

Nicole had orders that these green files made it to the proper hands, if anything should happen to Joa. Also critical was the Magic Egyptian Medallion. Once these were located, Nicole was to exit through Hank's west wall doorway to a predetermined rendezvous. The all other files and more, they had them. The second most important files were, a series black folder embossed with yellow and white lettering, those Joa had them and they were already on the scanner.

We Live No One Behind

Joa was really cared about her friend Nicole, she was sure she got out with the Green Files package. Cristopher is getting in there but it's so dangerous that we maybe lose some precious time.

Cristopher and his team are into the entrance of the church and address his men:

"Shot off your laser Sargent, there is too much dust; if somebody is there they may see your laser through it. Take 2 men and move in to engage whatever incoming we may get, take sides position where it would be easier to handle them and perhaps set up a sniper position."

After giving his orders to his team, Cristopher quickly entered the building, and concerned about more explosions or about the building collapsing even more, but he was being driven to head inside the debris and the almost non-existing northeast passageway. Cristopher, through the clouds of dust and piles of debris seemed to have the ability to see clearly what was ahead of him. Just as he was approaching the far end of the passageway, he thought he saw the shadow of a cat, or was it an iridescent light near a pile of rubble. He followed what were not his normal instincts and headed towards the pile of rubble, only to see dust emanating from the pile, and not the shadow of a cat:

"Good," he thought, "I am not seeing things." Suddenly he heard a moan coming from the debris. He tore at the pile of rubble with his bare hands. Moving a large piece of drywall, a hand groped feebly up towards him, and he redoubled his efforts to remove the ruins of bricks and drywall, to found a young woman barely alive.

She opened her eyes and looked at Cristopher as if she knew who he was, and in a very weak voice said:

"Take the medallion and satchel to Joa or Maurice. Only them, no one else..." She coughed great clots of frothing blood:

"World depends ... they get this." It seems she was waiting to complete her mission, to die. Then with her last words, and to his astonishment, she coughed again, saying:

"Go Cristopher! No time!" She closed her beautiful clear blue eyes one last time in her death shudder.

Cristopher could not believe the strength of commitment she had. He knew death was there, her heart transpierced by bullets stop expelling blood.

With a heavy heart, Cristopher took the leather satchel and a beautiful "Medallion" and because of the importance of the package he was going to run out, but he said in a low voice:

"We leave no one behind." When he saw the most beautiful iridescent blue butterfly hovering over her, he felt she was gone, she looks like all her blood was out of her, and she got several bullets through the center and left side of her body. The one who did that, did it to kill. It was too difficult to liberate her body from all the debris securely and rapidly so they had to get out of there. He knew the young woman was Nicole. He whispered a solemn to the fallen warrior:

"Go in peace Nicole, we owe you, we will bring you home."

Before the bunker explosion

Dennis and Dino, close to enter the bunker

In front of a wall with no apparent door, Dino surprised he thought:

"What the hic is it there?" There was 4 little siding alike decoration from 2 feet of the ground, about 4' x 12' high, something done like for blocking windows. Dennis pushes one and then push a second one and returns to the same he had touched and finally the last one not touched on the right suddenly has opened as magically.

He touches an old pad with numbers as a phone dialer and the door behind there has opened. They hurriedly got in, close the doors one on the other one, and they were in a long tunnel after going down the stairs.

Dennis in the Bunker, Too Late Again

On entering the building through his secret door in the northeast wall, Dennis could hear a great deal of commotion taking place at the far end of the hall. This was unusual because no one could possibly enter the bunker from there, as the entrance is at the front or the southeast end of the building, and the only other entrance was from another secret door in his office on the top floor. That entrance is invisible and only, he knows where and how to open it, and there is a trap if anyone but me open it. Dennis called Paul, a friend and his office neighbor since ever. Paul said:

"Hey Dennis, it's as war here, I think the whole US forces are here, they are emptying your office, a lot of police is blocking every street. I'm having a look with the magnifier you give me from your yacht. They moved a lot of stuff, computers, file cabinets, even your big black old safe. They are there since almost 2 hours."

"Hey, Ben called me from the marina, saying they're gone with your yacht. I think Uncle Sam really want your ass."

Dennis, astonish, feeling disloyalty to see somebody in his Bunker, thought to himself:

"Dino? No! He was the only one who knows the existence of my Bunker, so he is the betrayer, that son-of-a-witch. I'll shoot... No; it can't be him... NO?

Dennis was not thinking clearly. He was angry, and he failed to consider a point of serious contention to his security: it was his beautiful skylight. Dennis decides to head towards the noise instead of making his way up the stairs to his office. He pulls out his gun and as quietly as he can, makes his way down the dimly lit passage way, when there before him was running her way out the opposite way, a woman in dark fatigues carrying a dark satchel and a glowing object.

Without a moment hesitation, he aimed and fired, to kill, 2 shots in her back, the woman stumbling backwards with a horrified look on her face as she crumpled to the floor. And he turns to face Dino:

'You were disloyal to me! What for, Money or vengeance? I trusted you; you were the only one to know about my personal secret Bunker! How could you?' Dino didn't even have time to respond, Dennis empty his gun on Dino. Only his face had time to say no! No...

At that precise moment came a rumbling from deep inside, the entire building shook and trembled, debris was falling all over the passage way and a few seconds later the wall collapses where was the woman. Shock registers on Dennis's face. Something has triggered the explosion. It is too soon! Then it dawns on him, thinking: the skylight. Dennis knew he was too late; he whirled and ran out and the same way he came at his place, retracing his steps, hoping his helicopter was still there, ready and waiting to lift off.

Robert and his men had heard and seen the explosion, the blades on the helicopter were turning, and it was ready to lift off. Robert shouts to his three men as they are scrambling into the helicopter:

'Hey guys we wait! Here comes the boss, get ready to leave. I do not see Dino.'

Dennis arrived at the helicopter, now ready to lift off, his curt command to Robert:

'Lift off, now!' Robert questioned Dennis:

'Sir, what about Dino?' Without skipping a beat Dennis says:

'Go! He's dead, under a ton of debris!'

Robert lifted off, simply wanting to put distance between them and the troubles below. What they did not see was the two mercenaries black Humvees abandoning the area they had just vacated.

Dennis Feels More Than Angry for the Green Files

As they flew, Dennis sat in silence, but his face spoke the words his mouth did not. Inside he was seething with anger, frustration, bitterness and hatred. Not long into the flight he erupted like a corrupt volcano, disgorging vile words like balls of fire and brimstone, spurting off about the Boa and what he would do to this snake, believing that she was the cause of all his problems. Dennis wanted to know who in all the unholy corners of hell this witch was. In his fevered mind, he hoped she was the one he killed in the northeast tunnel of the Bunker. The only thought that the Boa had managed to slither her way out and that he would have to endure her constant wound, simply fed his despicable mood and he fumed on, seemingly with no end in sight.

The more he pondered on whom the Boa is, the more agitated he got. How did she know about the meeting in Daytona? How did she find out about the old church and the Bunker in the back of DK palace? She seemed to be everywhere and keeping ahead of him and his next move. The first time he had heard the Boa's name mentioned was on a newscast out of Daytona. He had briefly seen a clip while escaping in a yacht, but unfortunately, it was very brief; and he had not seen or heard further details on this Boa who had become far more than a dagger in his side.

He vowed on his mother's grave, on his ancestry, as his last word, as his last breath, that as soon as he could, when he reached Miami, he would at any and all cost find this vile witch, and visits upon her a death that would give Satan himself a reason to catch his breath. The more he dwelt on the matter, the angrier he became. He had become irrational; his head was now going, back and forth, and he kept clenching his fists. The men were aware of this assassin's explosive temper, nervously but quietly wondering what Dennis would do next.

Suddenly Dennis exploded again, raving in a voice loud enough for the mercenaries to hear:

'I will get my revenge on this venomous Boa! I will cut the head off this snake with my teeth!' The mercenaries did not know who Boa was. However, whoever it was, this snake had incurred this assassin's wrath, and to a man thinking that whoever it is, he, or she was, glad that it was not one of them.

'Yes, oh yes I will be more than bad with you BOA! You don't know me but you'll soon do! But for now, I need the Green Files, yes, oh yes, I need the green Files. Watch me Boa!'

CHAPTER 15

Out of the bunker with the Green Files in hands

As Cristopher was about to exit the still dusty building with the Green Files, he could hear firing going on to the north side of the two warehouses. He thought:

“It might be Dennis running away; I wish they catch him for good, that assassin.” A close by, General’s Oshkosh, drove by Caporal Balderstone, forwarded closer to the church exits when he spotted Cristopher coming out of the building, to cover him to get out securely. Balderstone pointed his Oshkosh in Cristopher’s team direction and advance closer to the exit to keep them out of harms’ way.

Cristopher, carrying the satchel and the Medallion, saw the Oshkosh heading his way and stooped, at the ready to get in. As he jumbled up through the open door of the vehicle, a bullet whistle passes his head to ricochets off the Oshkosh door. Quickly shutting the door, he checked to see that his whole team was present, and ask the driver to get closer to 54-TI, about 30 feet away. His hope was to reach 54-TI to give Maurice the most important part of the incomplete package before they get away to The Guardia Fortress. But he hesitates thinking that he must see Joa before doing anything, so he asks the driver to go closer to Joa’s helicopter the tiger.

A few minutes later only and the shootings were over, a sniper did his job very precisely. Cristopher ran to Joa waiting for him with relief, in "The Tiger." And he said:

"Joa we have it all, finally, we have the remainder of the package, Joa, didn't have time to ask about Nicole:

"Joa it is with deep regret, I must tell you that we have retrieved the body of Lieutenant Nicole Wexford, there was no more help to do for her and we had to get out without her body because of the mission.

"Thank you, Cristopher." Joa is struck deeply by this information, but her professional side took over, and she continued to listen attentively to Cristopher's message:

"Yes, difficult to lose one of your teams." But she has to stay focus, because Joa's decisions affect the whole team and it is important that she remains at the top of her game.

"Cristopher, I have the feeling that we may rest on the Package until the surround calms. We keep it here, but stay close and wait for the next move."

"OK Joa, I feel so bad about Nicole but feel so happy that we succeed this so important part of the mission."

"Yes Cristopher, I feel great about this part of the mission too. Thanks Cristopher.

Cristopher went back to his Oshkosh where his team was now ready to go.

Bad feeling, one of us is not strait

In 54-TI, the driver, a Joa's friend, is suspicious, thinking he is really private and secure by himself, Simon has closed the cab door, made a quick mental calculation. He entered his own secured frequency and made his call.

The majority of Joa's apprehensions as to the safety of the Green Files were now somewhat relieved after being advised by Cristopher that he was in fact in possession of the Green Files and the mysterious Magic Egyptian Medallion. Her thoughts turned to the question troubling at her heart as to what had happened to Nicole, for deep inside she knew that Nicole was no longer of this world.

Harry, the 54-TI electronic top bowl was at his post doing his job, which was to know everything electronic going on in 54-TI. He immediately detected the antenna load meter moving up, from the cab transmission. What he also noticed too, it was not on any of their frequencies, it was scrambled, and the security was not theirs either. Concerned, Harry calls Maurice to his com station, putting his finger to his lips. Maurice and Harry both look at each other with questions and concern reflected in their faces. It may not be the right time to trouble more Joa, but it was important so, Maurice was the only one to know her confidential S.I.I.T.F. cellular number, so he did it...

Surprisingly her personal phone rang. She knew it was Maurice. But in the same time, Joa's intuition was telling her to take special care in informing for now 54-TI or her superiors about having or not the complete package. Anyways, nobody was supposed to know anything about the Green Files.

'Yes Maurice, it might be important for calling in this line?'

"Yes Joa, we have bad feeling about Simon behavior since a while, but now we have a certification that he communicates out with his own secure frequency."

“OK Maurice, I’m coming, we have no time to lose, from the now moment every second count.”

A sense of bad intuition was present or was SOMBRAJ trying to tell her something. She assessed comments made by Joe, and mostly backed by her well-honed foreboding, she agreed that the operation was, or maybe, compromised, not only at the senior level in S.I.I.T.F but also in 54-TI. This shocked and pained her to no end. It was like being betrayed by a family member. Her team and her organization were more than co-workers, and it was so deeply more than a job. She began to take the necessary steps to determine the extent of the damage in order to ensure that the Green Files which Cristopher was still had in his white Oshkosh.

“I have an idea Cristopher, give me the Green Files, I get back with a safer package.”

“Yaw Joa, you always have ideas, wait I’ll drive you closer, we never know when a bullet will fly around here.”

“OK, stay close!”

With a traitor on board

With a traitor on board at the wheel of 54-TI, it was absolutely critical Joa be on board.

When entered the communications area of 54-TI, Joa said:

“I’m proud of you guys! Harry motioned with his head towards the cab of 54-TI. The door to the cab begins to open slightly as if Simon was hoping to listen in on an important conversation, perhaps of plans being formulated, which he could impart to his accomplices.

Joa, with head signs and whispering, mention to Maurice giving him the whole Green Files:

“Fast scan priority.” Maurice responds the same way and give the files to upload ASAP, and in a fairly loud voice greets Joa and told her:

“Joa, we have been informed who the leak was in S.I.I.T.F.” At that precise moment Joa pulled the door of the cab, open it completely and told Simon:

“Step out of the cab.” Simon begins to protest when she told him:

“Out! Jacques Roux will take over the steering wheel!” Simon’s initial reaction was to become resistant, forcing Joa to pull out her handgun and aim it at his chest. Simon begins to babble, accidentally dislodging the unauthorized communication earpiece, which simply with its initial possession was in itself sufficiently incriminating evidence against him and his accomplices. Shortly thereafter, Harry’s analysis of the device would turn it into a tiny electronic hangman’s noose.

With an air of abject discuss, Joa says to him:

“Simon how could you, I trusted you and picked you myself.” Joa was angry and disappointed.

“You’re the only one who knew where 54-TI was going to go and no one in 54-TI knew the existence of the Green Files.” Simon begins to whimper and says to Joa:

“They have my wife and children; they will kill them if you don’t give them the Green Files. You can’t do anything to them, they are more powerful than you think, and they can buy everything.”

“Yes! Yes, as you said, everything as you are, a bad thing who didn’t care risking our life! Shame on you Simon!”

“No.... No!”

"Simon, you knew the danger before you became part of S.I.I.T.F., we need to secure everything now, and I do not have the time nor the patience. Talk! Now!"

"I have done nothing wrong Joa, I did not know that you had hidden the Green Files with Cristopher in the Humvee. It is he who told me."

"Who is 'He,' you speak of"? Joa is getting anxious.

"Yes, absolutely I will tell you." Simon responds with an air of sincerity.

"Simon, are you saying that there is another mole among us? Be careful on how you answer."

"OK, OK!" Simon responds totally encouraged by Joa's mentioning of another mole in S.I.I.T.F.

"Joa, you know among us is one or several people who put their lives at risk for the money of these villains! Perhaps these people or their families have been threatened. Most likely they quite often are offered millions of dollars and jump at the chance of having no more money worries or living the high life."

"Simon, enough! You are not telling me anything new. You have three seconds to tell me whom you have contacted regarding the location and who told about the existence of the Green Files." In a rarely seen or heard level of anger and impatience, Joa began to count: One—two ... before she could carry out whatever penalty Joa would have enacted, Simon, realizing he was beaten, responds again and tells Joa.

"Joa you know of Dennis Kildem, he is a murderer and a criminal."

"Stop!" Joa has now had her fill, he seemed to know too much of what for all intents and purposes he would have overheard here in 54-TI.

Simon, knowing he had no choice and perhaps hoping for leniency makes a desperate attempt to bargain, and he knows that this is all he has to offer:

"Joa, do you wish me to make contact?" Joa agrees and tells him to make the call on the unauthorized earpiece which Tobi had picked up. Tobi extended the device, and with trembling hand Simon took the earpiece and proceeded to do as he had been told.

Joa Called Dennis

Dennis was taken aback when he received a call on his confidential number. He wondered who would have this number and would dare call it. He decided he needed to know. In a voice laced with such emotion no one would dare to respond to him, unless they knew him well and were one of his accomplices.

"Who the hell dares call me on this number? You'd better have a good reason if you value your life!"

The short silence at the other end is deafening, then a strong female voice violated whatever dregs of peace he may have had.

"No, it's not Simon, this is the Boa." Dennis's face turns white, his eyes full of pure hatred. Without a moment of hesitation, he responds:

"Witch! I want the Green Files and the information you have dared to take from me, if you value your life at all. It was me who placed the bounty on your head, and I can buy anyone or anything."

"Well, well! Have a quick look at the news! I think that most of yours and family money and WTB that you have stolen are now frozen forever and will be returning in the right pocket, so now you are a hunted man. Watch your ass and you will realize what it is, to be scared to die!"

Joa's response inflames his anger even more that he was not able to place a word:

"Dennis, your house of cards is about to fall, and for your information, so is the Consortium, your friend's organizations, and, of course, yours." By now Dennis was screaming and becoming irrational, the electronic communication device he is holding is being strangled to the point of breaking:

"I... I will find you and show no mercy when I tear you apart. If you give me the Green Files, you can name your price."

"Now because of that poor little puppet Simon and his accomplices, the Consortium and their members personally, are after the Green Files too. And they're going, I bet, after your ass too. Bravo!"

"Tennis! We will find you before, hope the consortium let you live!"

There was absolutely no doubt in her mind, who, this distorts people was. He is the assassin Tennis, and she knew she would find the information confirming his identity in files which had been located in the bombed-out warehouse. Joa's intent now was to keep him talking a little longer so that Harry would be able to trace his exact location.

"What do you propose Tennis, and where should this exchange take place?" Now Dennis was livid; did she really know he was Tennis or was she fishing?

"I want the Green Files and also the Egyptian Medallion too! At any price, do you hear me? I will give you

$500 million, come by truck to the coordinates I will give you."

"Dennis, Tennis, whatever. You wanted fame and fortune. You got your fame, and your fortune is not money any more. Now you too have a price on your head so, get lost!"

He was angry, livid but not stupid. Coldly Dennis responded to Joa's taunt, realizing that he needed to stop the discussion if he wanted to fight another day.

"What are you saying? Do not play with me Boa! I know where the Green Files are! I have been informed it is not with you, but with one of your teams making its way to The Guardia Fortress. You will die, I promise." The line goes dead before Dennis gives up his location. Joa, sadly turns to Simon.

"OK! You had your chance"! Simon probably thought even to the last minute that his lies would work and that she would give him safe passage if he put her in contact with Dennis. Joa, had a gentle heart and she had known him a long time. Prior to today, she would never have imagined him capable of treason; for those reasons, he had felt safe. Unfortunately for him, he really did not know Joa. Yes, she had a gentle heart, but first, and foremost she was a warrior in the name of justice, and the fact that her team, her "family," had been put at risk, sold essentially, and infuriated her.

Simon was arrested and would be delivered to the proper authorities. Later it would be discovered that, after some calls by Harry, it was determined that his family was never in danger, it was only greed on his part. Joa felt violated by one whom she trusted.

The Green Files were being scanned and upload with other important documents. But Joa got out with a fake Green Files that she gives to Cristopher.

While so many things happening on the church side, where they all got out from the bunker, Joa was expecting the Bridget Herckel arrival from Daytona for taking care and securing the whole complex of buildings.

**Things are unrolling too quickly,
We need to take a break and place parts together,
Let's forget about my cam viewer for a while and see what is happening,
All in the same lapse of time.**

Activities have to be precise

- Dennis was there in the bunker, but now gone, will do anything to get his files back.
- The green Files now in Joa's hands.
- They have to be scanned and upload ASAP, to protect them.
- While this time unrolling, Bridget is now into cleaning and protecting the other evidences.
- Fixing problems with Simon mole.
- The bad Colonel Warfront treason.
- A leak coming from the aggressive Dennis, betrays himself, getting on the run everybody for the worldwide now known, Green Files.
- Joa, gets warning calls from FBI: "get rid of the Green Files, everybody will run to get them, hundreds of millions are offered."
- While waiting finishing the scanning the whole team is preparing to roll on the road again.

- Finally, the General Bentall forces are waiting for the Joa's Go on the road again...

We now can go back to my cam viewer

While being sure to catch up with the next frames.

Commander Bridget Herckel arrival at DK Palace

Bridget after releasing partly the Daytona crime scene to local police for security, and to FBI for their investigation, and assisted with CSI Miami drug department, she had to fly off to Tampa as fast as possible, to help Joa at the known Tampa site DK Palace. But surprises were waiting for her. Hearing Joa:

"Bridget, report when 2 minutes close to Tampa."

Oh! Bridget, we had a new urgent mission, over." She had to clean fast and get to Tampa ASAP and wait for new coordinates.

"OK Joa, already on my way at one zero, over." The whole team was in their private channels, communicating frequently. About 8 minutes later Bridget calls for new coordinates. It was about 10 minutes after the DK Palace explosion, but Bridget didn't know anything about the bunker and not even about the so hot Green Files. She even had problems to go through the area. She had to identify her helicopter registration numbers many times. Joa had to certify time to time her appurtenances to S.I.I.T.F. that is not known to everyone's. But General Bentall knew her personally, that helps.

Finally, Joa was happy to see Bridget cleaning teams around on the east side of the agglomeration where PK Palace site is. As she cleared out with Daytona, she had to do her job in this whole area too. S.I.I.T.F. is not there for extensive crime investigation. (SIRS) cleaning team is the last one on a crime site and their job is to secure evidences and deliver the crime scenes ASAP to local law enforcement or to the entitled authorities as FBI, state Marshall, county Sheriff, depending on the case by case implications.

The Neighbors Were Terrified

The neighbors were terrified in the whole around areas, and they had the right to know if it was war or what. The successive explosions and noise coming from the DK palace had attracted much more than the news media. Home owners and business owners in the surrounding area were frightened, and wondering if a terrorist attack was underway, or if war had broken out. 911 calls were flooding the local switchboards and the national anthem of slum areas was now being played on the approach roads in the form of police sirens, impressive army vehicles and up the air full of all kinds' helicopters and jets. This area, close to the Tampa port is an important oil storage transit and in and out manipulation, so people were scared to death.

Herckel arrived at the DK palace to find hell and mayhem running at full volume. Emergency responders were close inside the local law enforcement barricades. News helicopters were warned by General Forces to stay away. The Television vans, the other side was trying but not succeeding to get through the barricades and it seemed like every civilian within a thousand miles were all converging on this one site with everyone arriving as if choreographed to the split second. She had seen worse and this entourage from hell did not begin to challenge her training. She had already been in touch with each of the units involved in the assault to determine their status, and now it was time for Bridget and (SIRS) to get control and secure the DK palace and the other now new sites, the church parking, the underground bunker and the warehouses.

On seeing all the activity, Bridget first needed to ensure she had complete control of the site. So, she sets her Chinook down on the east side of the DK palace, where moments earlier, Trotter had informed her he was now in control of the area or the mercenaries were either down or obstructed the other side of locals, all around police barricades. She sends Captains Baker and Barilla to assist Plotter in rounding up the scattered mercenaries and help the county Sheriff to handcuff them. No one needs them around to escape and try to destroy the convoy when they are on their way to The Guardia Fortress. Captains Arleen, Heilder and Lieutenant King, exited the helicopter and make their way to the building's northwest and the northeast secret entrance, to secure what is left and ensure that it is safe for the team to enter and prepare for a thorough search of the premises.

Bridget, assessed the remaining situation, to take the necessary steps which would give her control of the office building and the perimeter of the DK palace, including the west church side.

Stay away! News units, air and ground

Using the S.I.I.T.F. priority channels giving her access to all radio bands, Bridget has sent a clear message. Even if the General Bentall forces were pushing them away.

Bridget began the process of contacting the News organizations to ensure their cooperation on reporting what is occurring at the DK palace, to avoid panic by the civilians and misrepresentation of the facts. She requested one trustworthy media contact point who would serve as news liaison for all media and press. She understood the News Media helicopters were hard pressed to show anything of interest, especially when it had to do with explosions and highly volatile activity.

She issued an immediate and terse warning to any and all occupying both ground and air space:

"Keep well clear! Do not interfere in official law enforcement works in any way, or face possible arrest, or seizure of your vehicles or aircraft by United States Air Marshall or ground law enforcement!" She advised local law enforcement to still keep all civilians clear of the area; the situation was under control and in the hands of federal level authorities and any interference could cost lives and would be dealt with severely. She sends Lieutenants Watson, Mason, Cox and Young to fan out and to ensure the perimeter remains totally secured. Manpower was limited, so she requested some assistance of the local law enforcement officers, for dealing with bikers and help for perimeter control, as well as a team of two bomb-sniffing dogs and their handlers.

Jose Morales & gang at DK Palace

looking over his shoulder: "damn boa!"

After the altercation in Daytona Beach, it took very little time for Tonito's gang to reorganize and seek revenge. The new leader was a young Puerto Rican, José Morales who told his members they would revenge Tonito's death and other dead brothers. However, for the time being they would track the loco Dennis, and their justice would be his death. José knew he was on solid ground, he was well aware he had the backing of a wealthy and well-organized gang in Miami, who had ties to Costa Rica.

Their tentative at intercepting Kildem at the DK palace had failed, every time, being blocked by police armed to the teeth barricades, but now by happenchance it seemed they had sprawled on a battle between two factions they were not familiar with. Even though they could see other bikers were also involved, the young José was very perceptive and decided it was in the gang's best interest to wait. Looking up in the sky, towards the main battle currently taking place all around, José could see what looked like two well-equipped helicopters circling around them, tripod-mounted weapons in their open bay doors. Further, another barricade of Oshkosh bumper to bumper were imposing their strongest scaring armored sheath compared to their bikes

José decides it is time for them to leave the area. Dennis was not there, and too many others were. It was time for them to call a special connection in Costa Rica to request their guidance regarding the gang's next move. José told his members, they need to head for Miami to plan their next move if they want to get justice for their dead's. There was no arguing. With a simple nod and a "let's go amigos" from his second in command, the members turned their rides southwards. They would reorganize there, bury their dead friends, and let the Dennis vengeance for another day.

Scan and secure the green files before moving to The Guardia Fortress

While Bridget at work, Joa on the west side of the buildings in the church parking, was dealing with the most important situation ever happened: scanning and securing a bunch of vital information for the world economic stabilization.

The security situation in 54-TI was now solved. The operation had been compromised for a little while, but so far, the damage was under control, thanks to the ever-watchful Harry.

And Bridget's team was finally on the spot to help.

They still had to make it to The Guardia Fortress but may be obliged to report moving after securing documents with all of their data, and so Joa returned to the urgent task at hand, that was not long to come.

FBI director calls: Joa, get rid of the Green Files ASAP

Joa received a call from Bernard Sandcastle, the FBI director, telling her that she needs to get rid of the Green Files ASAP, because of picked up conversation from everywhere:

"Anyone, who knows Dennis Kildem now known as Tennis Beaten, is scared about what could be in those files. Even here in FBI, we have tons of documents about this guy, but confidential, and this guy in the past was feeding us about almost everybody, I'm not sure but he might have been protected because of that..." Bernard was becoming fair with Joa.

"Yes Bernard, that's what we're doing with our Mobil Lab 54-TI and you can't imagine how fast she could do it. Thanks Bernard for cooperating, but we need your help here."

"Yes Joa, we are all around, pushing those guys away; any airport 50 miles around had interdiction to fly, they are nailed down for another hour. All radars are watching and warnings and are dispatched to Tampa air force base, where I am now!"

"That good to know Bernard, we are all together on that. Oh! In one warehouse here, there are a lot of arts stuff and relics kind, it's not urgent but you may find something about drugs too and other useful info's. But you know that we are cooperating with all and any Law enforcement agencies worldwide, but we need anything papers you find related to Dennis Kildem—Tennis Beaten that could help us putting down the Consortium. As soon we can, any evidences that are not related to our Operation will be back yours."

"Joa, you have full FBI cooperation."

"Bernard, thanks I must go."

“OK Joa!”

What a woman, he was thinking; SOMBRAJ was now connected to Bernard for future cooperation and also for reminding his words. At the beginning, Bernard was skeptical about Joa and the S.I.I.T.F. (Special International Intelligence & Tactical Forces). He was saying to anyone ears:

“Ah, it’s only another force we go have in our legs.” But after a while, was saying to his subalterns:

“Hey, guys! They’re really fast and efficient; so, let sit down, they’re doing the work for us!”

Only 54-TI Can Secure the Green Files ASAP

Dennis—Tennis became the best known, wanted dead in the whole world and that’s because of the wonderful media: TV news. All around the world his double face, now only one, was still showing on and on, without stop till the Daytona Beach killing; when Dennis coldly killed an unarmed family father, only because he was Spanish. After 30 minutes, it was about the Kildem RV’s treasure trove. And after only 2 hours later, it was about the most dangerous files, circulating, called the (Green Files) that could bring to light the most ever worldwide banking fraud of the century. And on and on, TVs were contaminating the whole world with the reality of our capitalist financial system wheeling.

When Joa has realized that everybody wanted the Green Files, it became imperative to secure the Green Files and the other very hot documents too. Nobody knew the existence of the Green Files before this leak, but till now the dangerously matter of having it in our possession was multiplied by thousands. Our advantage was to be able to act fast and stay on the spot and upload those files to different data banks; it was the only fast way to secure and succeed, and get rid of that dynamite ASAP.

We are teams organized, protected by General Bentall's forces and ready to act, and the opponents are a vast disorganized mercenary organisation, and their worst side is, they get into action only for the big money, they work separately, and they are hiring case by case only.

The great 54-TI has a real function that no one has yet. Even the pentagon and CIA are not electronically equipped as the last up-to-date technologies that have the 200 million $$$ 54-TI. Only 54-TI can secure files, documents, tons of data, or any scanned and scrambled evidences at the fastest speed and simultaneously at many different secret data banks. The internal computer, while taking a fast copy in memory, is able to upload instantly anything, everywhere, at the same time, in a 432K scripted ZIP format and not losing a second.

SECURITY Priority

SECURITY meant: the top-notch security is when everybody has all the same information, then, no one can scheme anything for their one good or falsify the information or denying it. Joa, after a quick look on the files, she called the international S.I.I.T.F. Headquarters, telling them about the incredibly dangerous content of the Green Files and told them:

"None of your names are in these files, so I am not scared about sending to you some of the files concerning the rest of the world. We are securing the whole package, right now in 54-TI, but we cannot do anything more, before a centralized general meeting with all of you, take place urgently."

They were all ears, and Joa had to give them her professional advises that they were expecting:

"I can certify that the Operation BULLSEYE is a great success! And I still encourage you all to get a solid hold on anything pertaining to the Consortium and (WTB), Maxim is receiving the same files as yours and there is so much in there that no one could imagine." 54-TI was still connected to the whole S.I.I.T.F. Headquarters, including Maxim at the Guardia Fortress.

Sorting Document Priorities

"Guys, we cannot stay still too long. We had a considerable advance on Dennis Kildem but he is now in the area and according to the 54-TI wave scanning system, there is an army of mercenaries coming in our direction. All forces will not succeed blocking all of them. We are protected but we still need to be vigilant." Joa, while expecting more documents from the bunker was dispersing boxes equally in four Oshkosh JLTV and the most important ones were loaded in the Trojan HH 65 and one HH 65 of the General Bentall forces. And important convoy, land and huge General's air protection will help Joa's team, small but strongly armed.

Colonel Warfront calls Joa

Just after the 54-TI driver Simon treason and calling Dennis Kildem, Joa received a call from Colonel Warfront from the Tampa Air Force Base, identifying himself as a member of the S.I.I.T.F her intuition was telling her that there was something suspicious, so she calls Trojan with her personal phone:

"Hey Gordon!"

"Joa? What a surprise, how did you know this number?'

"No time Gordon, I just fixed a mole problem with 54-TI and I have the feeling that a certain Colonel Warfront is something I do not feel happy with. Would you call your friend Jeff about it?"

"OK Joa, Joe told me about you were going to call me with your personal private phone."

"OK Gordon, do not abuse of it, ah.....Ah."

Yes, she was feeling happy when talking with him, but she was too busy to even think about that kind of feeling. Just 5 minutes later Trojan called:

"Hey Gordon, you're fast, and what?"

"Yaw Joa, Jeff was able to find out that the group led by Colonel Regis Warfront were without doubt the moles in S.I.I.T.F., and were on their way to retrieve the documents from you, at any cost." Trojan told Joa with concern in his voice:

"Joa, Jeff and a team, had them under surveillance and would pick them up once Joa had transferred the documents to them." Trojan's voice had a note of concern as he said to her:

"Joa, this man is dangerous, I fear for you. I'm getting close to your now site, do you wish us to come and provide more close air cover for you, over?" This is a man using his heart and not his well-honed tactical expertise.

"OK Trojan because any plan is now changing, everyone is now protecting the area to cover 54-TI while scanning and securing evidences. Even with the strong General Bentall forces, we will need our one closer assistance. Once I have accomplished this part of my plan. I am not sure right now if we will be able to get through the city streets with 54-TI. We need a safer plan to not endanger the population. Thank you for your concern but I believe you know that the mission is first, and foremost on my mind, out." Joa smiles a little but it fades quickly as her warrior mind takes over, and none too soon.

Just after fixing the mole problem with Simon, she asks Cristopher to get the same number of papers from some of the office non-useful files and exchange them with the green cover of the original Green Files. Joa had a feeling about taking an extra precaution for securing the Green Files.

Falls Documents for Colonel Warfront Visit

After fixing problems, Joa got out 54-TI with documents in her hand, the same thickness of the Green Files. This was done before in prevention or from SOMBRAJ suggestions. Joa was joining Cristopher in his Oshkosh JLTV with his team, telling them:

"Guys, we won't change anything, you all have to act as your orders, but it will be with these fake documents. So, act realistic. Keep a strong hand on your weapons and if something turns bad, to my signal, you open fire. Keep your motor idling as if you were almost ready to go."

"Cristopher, we will exchange the current contents of the Green Files which you have, with germane information good enough to fool anyone at a cursory glance. You have to act as you are to continue to make your way to The Guardia Fortress and deliver to Maxim Kgnu the contents of the Green Files, which is the fake ones that I am inserting into this brown waterproof pouch. Shortly I will be meeting with one of the S.I.I.T.F upper echelon, whose intentions are questionable. I will provide him with this Green Files containing information which I obtained at the DK palace office, in hope that this will be enough to satisfy him. It is a long shot but my intuition tells me it will work." Cristopher smiles knowingly at Joa. She made her way at the north end of the parking lot to meet with an S.I.I.T.F representative.

Colonel Warfront slaved to Kildem's Family Trust (KFT)

Joa thinking loudly: "May not be alone, who is corrupted in politics and armed forces.

Colonel Warfront was hailing her on her com headset. One end of the parking lot was entirely without vehicles, and she moved to its perimeter, telling Warfront to meet her there. Moments later a helicopter touched down in the parking lot a short distance away from the Cristopher Oshkosh, its engine held far above idle, prepared for a rapid exit. A band of five well-armed individuals exited and fanned out in an aggressive attitude, their weapons aimed in the direction of the Oshkosh, their intent poorly disguised by their semi-casual manner. Joa exited the Oshkosh, and smiling, approached a tall man with insignias on his uniform denoting he is a Colonel. Joa with respect, yet wary of the small army, she addressed Warfront.

"Sir, I am Joa, what can I do for you."

"Joa, you are in the possession of files and information which your superiors in S.I.I.T.F wish you to give me, so I can secure them and bring them to S.I.I.T.F. US HQ for dispersal to the proper authorities."

Still smiling, Joa replied in her best professional manner:

"Sir, I may give them to General Bentall, he said he was landing down now soon."

"No, you need security here, let him do his job."

"Yes sir, I understand completely. I had The Green Files safely secured ready to go in that Oshkosh, and all those Oshkosh around there, are close to protect us and you too. One moment please. I will get them for you." Without waiting or allowing time for his reply or response, she turned and went quickly to the passenger door.

Caught slightly off guard, the Colonel stared at Joa with somewhat of a quizzical look. At the Oshkosh, with her back to the Colonel, Joa extended her hand for the files, at the same time whispering to Cristopher team to fire on the Colonel if need be. She glanced at two of her team who seemed to have blended into the back of the Oshkosh. Cristopher quickly gave Joa the files, she turned and retraced her steps towards the Colonel, who now seemed impatient.

"Sir, here are the files with the documents you have been sent to recover. Some of the information and other files were dispatched to 54-TI which was uploaded to Maxim Kgnu at the Guardia Fortress. As for the rest of the many boxes of files and information, we were unable to save any of that material due to the destruction as you may see, of the buildings at the DK palace."

"OK Joa, you did a great job!" The Colonel, well aware of Joa's integrity, believed her, and told his small well-armed force, to fall back as they were going to deliver the package which was now in their possession.

Once in his helicopter, Colonel Warfront may have looked quickly at the contents of the files, and satisfied with the information it contained, and may have contacted his accomplices to advise them that the Green Files were in his possession. Unbeknownst to him, everything was being recorded and transmitted to S.I.I.T.F. US HQ where surveillance of this group and their accomplices was underway, and an arrest was imminent. Evidences of acts of treason, was necessary to catch him and his group. The capture of this group of traitors and their accomplices was left for the capable hands of S.I.I.T.F. international Headquarters forces, because they had accomplices in Europe too. Billions can buy so many people.

Intuitive Bad Feelings

But Joa was feeling bad about something strange and she only had the time to go back to 54-TI, looking Colonel Warfront getting away south and not far, over to the Tampa Bay on his way to the air force base, the helicopter may have been knocked down by a few rockets, because the explosion was complete destruction. The explosion was fatal, but out of habit, a helicopter loses the tail, spin and fall, but this time it was like a destruction to eliminate the presumed evidences. They badly paid their treason. But was it from the Consortium or Dennis criminal mind?

Joa's intuition told her in-self that, the Consortium may think the Green Files are destroyed now, so they, SOMBRAJ and General Bentall, may have a slow down with tacit understanding, pushing away mercenaries. She thought: I have to call General Bentall, and did it:

"General Bentall!"

"Yes, Joa I saw it too! They did it right in front the whole News helicopters running around, it looks to me that this action is over Dennis Kildem wishes, it could only be the Consortium, they wanted a complete destruction."

"Yes, General Bentall I agree with you."

"I think Maxim can do something more effective now."

"OK, thanks general"

Joa has called Maxim and he had called Mrs. Hall already for giving her more precision according of some received documents. Maxim give her details and names and mentioned to her that the Green Files have been destroyed in the Colonel Warfront helicopter explosion.

Life Is Only Lent and Can Be Withdrawn at Anytime

Seemingly, from nowhere, the distinctive sound of Harley Davidson motorcycles began to permeate the air. Like sound effects from a B grade movie, the distant roar of the motorcycles grew, now obviously coming from the road east of the warehouses. They were stopped at barricades but any were able to cross over and try to shout a few bullets, but it was a crazy effort with so many Oshkosh around and police and helicopters up there. And the worst of it was the SOMBRAJ's doing their job, taking off and away their miserable life, as SOMBRAJ said:

"Live is only a lent gift, anybody can go along with it for a while, but no one knows when it's going to be taken from anyone..."

"And killers have made their choices by killing coldly, innocents, they condemned themselves and any cold killers that still alive, are only on respite and even in repentance they are in the waiting room for SOMBRAJ to withdraw their last breathing and get away with their miserable life. And it is, the only way that justice can be served, by death of their useless body possessed by a sick disturbed inner mind."

These bikers were no slouches in gangs, they knew how to fight. However, if push came to shove, they had air and land cover from General Bentall forces, and Bridget team had them outgunned, at least with size of armaments, and training of personnel. It was pretty difficult to carry heavy weapons on a Harley and he grinned grimly at the thought of what his 50 calibers could do to one of their fancy machines.

They were gone away fast, for them it had to be easy because gang bravery is only in the back of their gun, without it they are only the real cowardly mirror of themselves. But five of them were killers, and time was there to payback with their one life. About two miles on their way back, one of them manage strangely, zigzagging, entraining others to lose control of their bike and the five of them died suddenly with almost nothing apparent.

There was a rumor since that certain morning at Daytona Beach killings: many gang guys died naturally with no clinical explication, their heart had ended beating, strangely.

The leak: Dennis losing his head again

When somebody is scared and feeling that everybody is against him, he shouldn't be asking his one supposed closest friend for help. Dennis losing his head again, making his worst move, has released the Green Files existence to one of his old partners, asking him to get, at any price, what he called the green archives and all documents pertaining to him and specially the GREEN Archives.

Since everybody now knows about Dennis—Tennis, the worst of the most horrible, now hunted man, he was foolish again to divulge what would be killing him for real. Sylvester Pity, a known bandit and bandit killer, who did execute for Dennis many contracts on many poor guys, was also known by any of the Consortium members; so, the information about the Green Archives "dynamite" start to go around the world and came to Colonel Warfront, who had no other choice of getting back the files Known as Green Archives, at least for erasing his own name on it. After half an hour, circulating around the world, the file name became what everybody's most wanted thing: the real name became the (Green Files).

Sylvester, now in the sight of SOMBRAJ, because anybody who becomes in relation with Dennis who has his permanent SOMBRAJ connected to his deep inside, become a member of his network, so, susceptible to eventually receives a butterfly visit and payback for killings done to innocents. As already seen since the morning at Daytona, life is fragile and lent only for a while... Until then, Sylvester is giving a lot of needed information about other killers of his own network. But he is not stupid enough to do more business with an ambulant future dead. His thinking was about the 100 million offered by Dennis:

"Why not 500 million, a dead body has no money. And he called his contact from the Consortium. So, that was the leak of the century, but will it succeed to pave the way to Joa?

A leak has unclenched a crook's world war against each other's.

Crooks are solidary when thing goes well, but when things get really bad, it goes the opposite way; BUT, when crooks are driven in chaos, then, it becomes—everything's for me! And they run in a free-for-all.

Any thief is scared to be stolen and any killer is scared to be killed and the ball goes loose, and machine-guns talk. **And everyone blames the others.**

Since the world knows about important documents that could kill the Consortium and about Denis Kildem and Tennis the killer, anybody, whom anyone, that has been in contact with the both of him, are scared to see their names in those documents. The leaks about some information contained in those documents were on any news channels around the world.

TV news channel wanted attention:

"Stay tune, more to come, important divulgations of worldwide criminals known names, stay tune, more to come!!!

Till this moment, any organized criminal groups wanted those documents; especially when they heard about the GREEN FILES. The ethnic mafias, the Cartels, the crooks banks dealing with the consortium bank (WTB), everyone was in an overall turmoil.

A deeper look shows that the whole world was close to tremble

The known Tennis Beaten face, now known to be the big business Dennis Kildem, is scaring the whole illicit and political world, worldwide because Dennis Kildem was always dealing on cover with intermediaries. So, when he was dealing, buying, selling, spying or exchanging information, he was Tennis and had a passport on Tennis Beaten, a very good tennis player (was). He uses to deal with the known Mr. Edgar in the past and compared himself to his Idol. He knew everything on anybody in the illicit world and a lot about the political ones too. So, since his double faces apparition on TV, anybody who did business with him was scared to death, of the kind of information about them-selves is going to get out of the bag…

In his entire career (if it's one) he paid millions for investigation. His saying was:

"No deal with unknown dealers."

Incredible, one-in-a-life treasure discovery

While scanning the Green Files, Joa was having an eye through the enclosed documents, and this one time of the best, adding all this information to what was seized from the Dennis RV, she yelled with enthusiasm:

"What a....!"

"It is a fantastic prize of a big fish catch, a perfect gift to the whole world economic revitalization!!!" But Joa had to call Maxim Kgnu for telling him the bad of it:

"Maxim we are in real danger now!"

"What, Joa, what? What is it happening Joa? I never heard you with so much passion!"

"Yes! Yes Maxim, there was a leak, I already send to you and to the S.I.I.T.F. Headquarters, some of the files, the Green Files, those they are talking on TV and radio everywhere. Now, everybody that has been in contact with Dennis Kildem or for any reason, they will run for the files and other stock. And I think, some of them maybe even paid to destroy, to eliminate us and the whole compromising stuff."

"But what are those files?"

"For now, believe me, it's a question of life or death for them and us."

"OK! What you want me to do Joa?"

"We cannot move from here, because we are more protected here with General Bentall forces and we can't go anywhere in Tampa's streets without endangering the population."

OK....Yes.....Yes!

"Maxim, we have to slow down the mercenary's angry voracity, running for money. Would you ask Ms. Hall for me, giving her the exclusivity that all the Kildem money was being ceased according to worldwide fraud and industrial espionage transactions and money laundering?"

"OK Joa, let me have a quick look on those files."

"No time Maxim! What is in there is an atomic bomb for them and only imagine what more we are going to find, I'm shaking dramatically about what that guy has done, he is a monster! I tell you he is a real sick predator monster! Money and business is nothing compared to the killing and what he has done to innocent people."

"OK Maxim, I got a go."

Joa was connected with the S.I.I.T.F. Headquarters in the same time, while Maurice's team was uploading very hot stuff to them. They were all busy looking and taking concrete actions. There was munch we knew about the whole implication into the world economy but S.I.I.T.F. needed proves, evidences, irrefutable evidences. And that was unfolding right in front everybody all around the world in the same time. Information was equally available for the whole S.I.I.T.F. Headquarters worldwide, because the whole world was dangerously implicated and deeply concerned too. Since that moment, the earth economy was quaking, but even if Dennis Kildem was expended in a big part of the world, most of his operations were operating in North and Sought Americas.

Proves are now known that Dennis personally holds financial statements on organized crime and he is one of the instigators, of the worst financial fraud and economic extremism in the history of our world. He and his accomplices have begun to throw the world economy into a tail spin. Dennis Kildem is only a part of the Kildem Family Trust, but he has long fingers on it. With the Consortium that was already known, they were preparing to control the world economy with the already in action (WTB) World Traders Bank. What 54-TI has uploaded is only the 1% evidences getting out, and it shows that the Consortium bank, of major proportions with many other banks, is holding thousands of billions if not trillions of dollars in all major currencies. They already have infiltrated banks, multinationals, hundreds of businesses, thousands of buildings and organizations around the world.

Joa was communicating with the whole S.I.I.T.F. Headquarters and they connected her to the whole Law Enforcement agencies, united worldwide for the Operation CONSO-DOWN.

Everywhere in the world, they were waiting for those irrefutable evidences to finalize all the requisition in course. Heads that were on hold will all fall in the same time everywhere on the planet.

Dennis Kildem Loses Everything

Believing him-self invulnerable; was this a colossal error in judgment, or a point of sheer madness, on the part of what the world usually saw as a stoic and businesslike powerhouse? Has Kildem lost everything? The story unfolds...

Whatever friends he had were now in flight and no longer wanted his name associated to theirs, for fear of reprisal or financial impact on them personally.

His family especially, they wished that he had never been born and proceeded to disown them. Benjamin Den Kildem, who loved his grandson, could not believe that a Kildem could make such a mess of things, but he knew something other than Dennis's business acumen, had driven him to commit this highly visible murder. The story had long been buried in his psyche, and unfortunately had reared itself at a most inopportune time. Only he knew the secret and it would die with him, as a Grandfather's promise is sacred. Benjamin had a decision to make, one he did not wish on his worst enemy.

His gang and close friends had been obliterated. Others were in the process of disappearing and going into hiding, feeling Dennis had betrayed them by, his stupidity of being caught on camera, committing a brutal and senseless murder that did not serve the organization in any way. And those documents now spread with names all over the world...

Those who trusted him now want his hide, fearing Dennis would cop a deal to save his sorry skin.

A Bargain to be struck:

A deal is sometimes offered by law enforcement agencies, or the powers that be in order to obtain information which would enable them to capture some of the most difficult criminals, or allow them to infiltrate and dismantle well-established organizations. Some of Dennis's friends were aware of these deals, and feared that perhaps one would be offered to Dennis. They were now deathly afraid that if he were captured by authorities and offered some sort of plea deal that could guarantee one giant noose around their collective necks.

Dennis had an honorable and distinguished face. What the public saw and remembered now, however, was the twisted face of a man in the grip of uncontrolled murderous rage? He was now on the run and fleeing anyone who would denounce him. Now his enemies could be found in every corner of the world, he seemed to have nowhere to hide.

Those in high places who have known him for over many years, and for whom he had made millions if not billions of dollars, will now need to take drastic steps to safeguard themselves. These individuals are unscrupulous as their master is the almighty dollar and they will do anything to ensure that no harm comes to it. These individuals, know they cannot take it with them when they die, so they are going to make sure they can spend their ill-gotten gains come hell or high water. In most cases, it will be hell.

The fortune that Dennis had amassed, and now was in the process of losing, was in reality not his. These gains had been obtained through crime that is why many countries now have a law, on their books, which addresses the dispersion of ill-gotten gains. One must also look a little further and deeper inside, to ensure that the victims are provided for the use of this money that would be a start to right a wrong.

More Than a Billion Invested in Politic

According to a fast-visual information extraction from the Green Files, The Consortium has invested more than a billion in dirty money for finance members of governments all over the world, especially in the United States and Europe. But none to Russia, because they are already investing in and part of the Consortium. They preferred to invest in anything chaos, it's in chaos that they make big money. But it shows in a prime view that the Consortium is the bad guy who owns the bank (WTB) that has a completely different view and operation.

Is money could buy anyone?

It is why Joa will have to change her whole evasion plan, because of the now precariously situation of having in hands that vital information against the whole Consortium. Money could buy anyone they use to say, we will see...

There is no way that the convoy with that dynamite could pass through Tampa streets without endangering the population. No one can take that risk and Joa will not go out of there for taking that risk, if she is not completely sure to have a tactically organized protection from her team, the whole General Bentall forces and the cooperation from the whole law enforcement agencies, if working together to block streets and push the mercenaries away.

General Bentall's Super Power Forces to Be Deployed

Joa called the general expressively:

"General Bentall here's Joa; we are in real danger, more than ever. I think I would need some of your guys to push the barricades further; the local police won't resist the mercenaries. And due to the importance of the documents we now have, the consortium and everyone would kill to have what you cannot imagine, we have. We are scanning and uploading files, on the spot, it would be too hazardous for the civilians, for us and for the documents to drive through the city. I even think it is perilous to fly out of here because they would think we use ambulances or medic helicopters to switch out the Green Files. What you think general?"

"Yes, I think so too, I'll send down six helicopters with 24 men well-armed right now and send 6 Moskito-Spy and drones to patrol around when you all be ready to go! Joa we have 20 more Oshkosh JLTV blocking streets everywhere along your way, in combination with FBI's Humvees and county Sheriff's Bearcats, even the state Marshalls are there now. It's really a statewide assistance Joa, we never saw a so big partnership."

"Thanks general, here is the now plan, we are loading the most important documents into two HH 65 helicopters, because they are so fast, and they can simulate going away east where is no mercenaries and go around coming by the northwest side of the bay and land directly at Guardia Fortress. Then for our convoy, we would need your escort to get out of here with our little but strong army."

"It sounds good Joa, then I will send two of the Moskito-Spy to open securely their way there by providing scanning to snipers, of eventual land shooters."

"General Bentall, here is my last scrambling plan: I would like to be sure that you will still be using your communications channels, because as soon as we are ready we will scramble the whole communication waving, with our new hi-tech-com center, we will initiate the scrambling of all communications pertaining to the current operation, but 54-TI team will try to allow your military waves to communicate together, but in the case we can't, it will last for 15 to 20 minutes only, for the time being able to get to The Guardia Fortress."

"OK Joa, we will switch to a special unique channel, I'm waiting for your GO call!"

Thanks general, I owe you one!" Preparation was rushing on.

Snipers and Moskito-Spy to protect the whole area of 54-TI

The surround is already well protected, with the General Bentall forces patrolling the whole area air and ground. The brand new Moskito-Spy is on its first show, but they are so fast that when they fly around, you're not sure if it is a real mosquito, because of the sound, or the Moskito-Spy that nobody had ever seen yet.

Indications were that this armed mercenary's confrontation, even if disorganized because of the impromptu unimaginable situation that came up beginning with Daytona. They were facing an army of determined mercenaries with a lust for blood, and an even more intense lust for the millions of dollars of bounty offered for this Green Files. Hoping they are blocked everywhere by all united police forces.

Even with the General Bentall huge armed land and air protection, they are expecting the worst. That is why 6 Moskito-Spy will be patrolling with infrared scanning. Their up-to-date gadgets are very effective in identifying hidden armed bodies, even hidden over cement walls; giving instantly coordinates to snipers deployed everywhere. Helicopter fears of being hit by rockets from hidden launchers. Moskito-Spy is so fast, invisible to radars and almost impossible to catch, so they don't fear rockets. The HH 65 helicopters are top armed and any of the fastest ones.

But, 54-TI on its way to The Guardia Fortress, a known mercenary direction would maximize the risk. A simple hidden man, sitting and waiting since an hour or more, along 54-TI's way to The Guardia Fortress could be fatal. A few rockets could hit badly 54-TI and put at risk the files and data uploading to security. So even if 54-TI was protected from 2 sides, east and sought, secured by the buildings and the church, Joa decides to move 54-TI in the warehouse, were Dennis use to store his luxurious RV, beside his other toys. But it had to be done tactically, simulating getting our way true the city streets. As soon they see that we are preparing they will move to a sure position to get a win target.

She said to Maurice: “Tell Jacques, to be prepared to move in the warehouse.” She asks everybody, helicopters and Oshkosh:

“Be ready to move, simulate as if we’ll be living to our way out!”

“Jacques, you simulate as quitting out the parking, placing 54-TI to back up and at my signal you back up fast as the warehouse door will open, OK.” Jacques Roux, the driver was ready, but nervous. And the move was fast, Jacques has backup 54-TI as it was only a car.

This was only for the time to upload vital documents, for the worldwide operation. With all those evidences, they will be able to proceed higher with ceasing money and take them off from power. News goes fast, so Joa’s thinking is:

“If they have no more money, the mercenaries will go back home, giving us a break to move to Guardia Fortress.

Preparation still on, boxes are moved by priorities in different Oshkosh and the two HH-65 helicopter which one is Trojan’s and Joe aboard. SOMBRAJ went for a quick ride around and will suggest an evasion plan, according to where the mercenaries are expecting the convoy to make its way out through the city.

CHAPTER 16

Everything is about timing and simulation

Joa has a plan for escaping with the whole team, but because everything is happening in the same time, Bridget has now to continue terminating her work. Let's go back to my cam viewer.

Bridget, Securing DK Palace

By now Bridget knew who was where and what they were doing. The security of the perimeter had now progressed to the point where she could do an assessment, an inventory really, of what they had found that would better their mission. She made two calls to her teams and stopped briefly to question local law enforcement.

A few minutes later, with the perimeter well secured, Bridget met with the first responders. The DK palace sites were in a war zone shamble but everything was firmly under the control of Bridget and (SIRS). Now that the proverbial dust had settled, Bridget began her assessment and determines her next steps prior to contacting Joa.

The other west side church parking was secured by Joa's team while, she told Bridget, still securing the whole package on the spot instead of running to the Guardia Fortress. Bridget asks Joa:

"Joa you need any of my guys there?"

"Not for the moment Bridget, but tell me when you're ready to move."

"OK Joa, we still have to secure down there, the sniff dogs look like ready too."

"Be careful, over."

Ms. Sylvia Hall: Channel 18 DBN news

The whole US operation was monitored by Maxim Kgnu, installed comfortably in the Guardia Fortress. Many financial specialists were assisting him and were suspended to the next Joa's revelations about more evidences. The whole worldwide S.I.I.T.F. Headquarters were also connected directly to the Joa's BULLSEYE operation in concordance with the worldwide CONSO-DOWN Operation. So, Bridget was advised to tell Ms. Sylvia Hall the minimum. The team and operation security were depending of not expanding what we had in hand for not having the whole mercenaries at our tail. Or, for the all other criminal ethnic mafias that would like to have, for their one use, the enormous Dennis information's he had. For any crooks, Dennis was the most influential dangerous man, for the information he had on everybody known, criminals, crooks or politically.

For the present, all the information being released should be to appease the local populace that they are not under attack and that everything is under control. Bridget explained to Ms. Hall that the situation here was of national and international security issues and that principally, there was a fire and explosion at a local warehouse that was of suspicious nature and currently being investigated as a probable case of arson, not related to terrorism and that when any other “facts” became known, Ms. Hall would be given the exclusive. After ending briefing Ms. Hall, Bridget ask her to certify Maxim about what is favorable to tell the public for not to endanger the actual operation.

Bikers in the Process of Leaving

Ryan informed Bridget, the bikers all around the other side of the barricades were now in the process of leaving, and that the east gate was now closed and secured. He was presently on his way to verify that the north perimeter was secured to his satisfaction, and was also currently under the watchful eye of their air cover.

After taking casualties to receive medical attention, Trotter located Bridget advising her both northwest and south gates were closed and secured. Trotter is to remain on the east side of the office building and ensure protection for the remaining medics and other first responders in that area. Due to the important state of the situation, Bridget asks the medics to dispense cares locally because of the risk of road danger by mercenaries. They may think that we use ambulances to take out what they badly want, the Green Files as now showing in the news channels.

The Bomb-Sniffing Dog at Work

Meanwhile Captains Arleen, Heilder, and Sub-lieutenant “Kojak” the bomb-sniffing dog and his handler, were in the process of checking the bunker and the various tunnels, to ensure their structural stability and whether there were any further explosive traps. Things were progressing well, however, as they made their way through the tunnel near the church basement in the far corner of a semi-lit alcove, they came across a number of file boxes, which Joa's assault team had left for them to retrieve. This area had much rubble, but the file boxes were visible due to an unusual iridescent light which seemed to be highlighting the area. Arleen could not figure out where this iridescent light was emanating from, because the church alcove did not have any windows. Arleen shook his head and proceeded carefully to ensure the area was safe. He contacted Lieutenant King requesting assistance in the removal of the boxes to a safe and secure place, so their contents could be verified and secured as necessary.

While the S.I.I.T.F teams were about their business, within what was left of the DK palace, Arleen, Heilder, Kojak and his handler, were making a safety sweep through the bunker below a secret entrance of the office building. In the dark ruins, near a collapsed wall, Kojak alerted to the rubble there. Approaching cautiously, they heard a faint moan coming from under the debris. Arleen contacts medics and assistance, but told them to wait outside, until he advises them that it is safe to enter the building's front door. Kojak did his job and returned to his handler; meanwhile Heilder moved in and began to carefully remove the rubble of bricks, avoiding more debris tumbling on the site. As she removed a brick which is pinning a piece of drywall, she could see the back of a man's head partially buried beneath the collapsed wall.

Taking care, she continued to remove the debris until she had exposed the entire body. While ensuring that the badly injured man could breathe, she told Arleen to request two of medics with a stretcher, but to warn them of the danger and to be extremely careful. In short order the two medics had the man on the stretcher, quickly making their way to the awaiting ambulance. After ensuring everything in the area was secured, Heilder and Arleen followed by Kojak and his handler, returned to the bunker, to ensure that everything of importance had been removed from the area. They continued making their way through the tunnel, back through the secret entrance, on the northeast side of the office building. Heilder stopped and began to stare at the light coming from the entrance, to the northeast tunnel, but she shakes her head as if to clear cobwebs. Kojak senses something as well, he makes a low growl from deep within.

"Arleen, did you see that?"

"See what?"

"Damn! I swear I saw a cat near that fallen wall."

"Oh, come on Heilder! What have you been drinking; it is not like you to see things, and besides, a stupid stray cat is somehow important?"

"I swear .... Oh well, it may be the light playing tricks."

To humor her, Arleen looked in the northeast direction where she had indicated. To his surprise, he could see a beautiful blue iridescent butterfly, surrounded by a bright white light located over the top of a pile of rubble. He turned to Heilder, his quiet voice reflecting his surprise:

"You now have me seeing things. OK. You're right. There must be a reason for this and my intuition says to go and investigate." Both made their way very carefully towards the pile of rubble. As they approached they saw the body of a young woman in army fatigues. They know without doubt they have found one of theirs. They gently removed the remaining debris and Arleen noticing that she is small and light, tells Heilder that he will carry her out. Heilder gets on her com to advise the team to meet them at the exit area, at the east side of the wall, as they are bringing one of their own out. Bridget was noticed by Joa that Nicole had been shot dead by Dennis:

"Tell me please when you find her." At the exit, those near the entrance solemnly removed their hats and bowed heads, as the body was carried past to the coroner's car. There would be time later to honor their fallen comrades. For now, there was a job to do, and one must continue to do what they have been trained to do. Bridget called Joa:

“ Yes Joa, we have found Nicole and she is out right now, and we found a man also but he has been gunned shouted and he is in a really bad shape.”

“Oh! Nobody is supposed to be in there, he might be a Dennis’s man, did you checkout his identity?”

“No, I think a part of his pant might still be under debris, we get it later.”

“Have him look by the medic, we can’t let him go truly the barricades if it’s a Dennis man they will probably kill him, this man might be a witness, I presume, that Dennis thinking nobody knew about the bunker; he might think he betrayed him and shouted him, I don’t see another reason.” Joa was right because she knew how a sick twisted man as Dennis is thinking.

“You might be right Joa; we’d better send an agent to protect that witness, as soon the medic could go out securely.”

“OK Bridget let me know, over.”

Bridget found bundles of money at DK Palace

Bridget and Ryan were now approaching the rubble of the bombed-out warehouse. Lieutenant Cox met them near the crater which had been secured by Kojak and company. Janice reported to Bridget that there were no other bodies to be found. Bridget thanked Janice and began making her way to the bombed warehouse when she was hailed on her com set by Captain Bill Trapp.

After an enlightening discussion with Bill, she made her way to the rubble which at one time was a fairly imposing brick warehouse. Ryan noted Bridget's resolute manner as she walked towards a specific area of the damaged warehouse. Walking through and over debris, she entered a hole which seemed to be the remnants of a doorway. Ryan followed, as she proceeded carefully towards what seems to be an impassible staircase leading down to a subterranean level.

Bridget hesitated, and as if guided by an unknown force, she began to remove some debris exposing a door leading to three passage ways branching out just the other side of it. Ryan noticed, as he helped her pull away the rubble, that in some way Bridget seemed strangely different somehow. She proceeded towards the entrances to the passageways, almost as if she were drawn or possessed.

Suddenly, a brilliant white mist appeared in a passage leading off to the right. She motioned him to follow, pointing with her torch to a steel door which stood partially opened. Ryan examined the door and checked inside as best he could. Believing that it was safe, he used gentle cautious pressure to open the door further, allowing them to enter a room which was not large, but held much.

Upon cursory glance, they saw pallets of money bundled, which on closer examination they estimated to be in the amount of several hundreds of millions. The bills were of high denominations, new, and looking alike never been circulated. Murmurings of counterfeit were made; however, it was impossible to determine here and now if this money was counterfeit. If they were looking at counterfeit money, Bridget said:

" I hope it would not be too late finding the plates. If this amount of currency was still being printed or in circulation, it would weaken the local economy." And not having to look around this place or around the whole warehouses, Bridget said:

" OK guys, for now on, we forget about plates, let's say that's enough dishes to wash with the Consortium and the villains Kildem family.

Wanting to know more, Bridget opened one of the many file boxes, noting that some dated back more than twenty years. She picked up one of the files and began to read, concern showing on her face as the name Tennis kept appearing over and over. Bridget thoughts: "hey, Joa told me about this guy." Ryan prowled the corners of the room, finding crates of priceless art objects and relics, but for the time being they were only of secondary importance:

"Let's live that for the FBI." Time was limited. She needed to get these files to Joa as quickly as possible, and make sure that the money and other physical properties were immediately taken into secure custody and being compiled and calculated.

Bridget has loaded the 19 big boxes in the Trotter's Oshkosh JLTV, and just got in the other side of the main building where Joa still was uploading files and documents for securing them. The last changes were:

" We stay here to be sure we secure everything, because going through Tampa would be too risky with mercenaries to increase dramatically civilian casualties."

So, Bridget with more documents, plus the others waiting close to the church passageway, Joa needed help to determine what's the most important to secure, now, before driving on a risky road way to The Guardia Fortress.

She took a deep breath and dispatched several men to the subterranean room to retrieve their latest finds, with admonitions of care. The way was hazardous and there could be further collapse at any second. It's enough losses for one day.

Bridget's assessment of the situation at DK palace was now completed; she made her way to the Chinook and contacted Joa, and said nervously in French:

"Sécurité ! Sécurité ! Sécurité!" NA216, Joa, this is Bridget NA404, over."

100 Million Bounty on Joa's Head

Bridget continued her report:

"Joa we are in the possession of several file boxes which were retrieved from the church basement alcove, and others just now recovered from the bombed-out warehouse as well as a king's ransom in money paper. I have received some information from Bill Trapp from Daytona. Apparently, there is a bounty, 100 million dollars on you, and something known as the Green Files currently in your possession. Making this bounty highly volatile is the fact, if a group of individuals are responsible for retrieving this file, they will each receive the same amount of 100 million dollars. This has aired on an underground network and the name Boa was mentioned. Bill told me he was unaware of who was at the origin of this bounty, however, his intuition was that it emanated from Costa Rica. Joa, I tend to trust in Bill's deductive reasoning. I believe he may be right. Please take the necessary precautions, as the forces they will throw at you will be well armed and merciless. As far as the files recovered from the Church alcove and the ones retrieved from the bombed-out warehouse, do you wish these files to make their way to 54-TI, or to The Guardia Fortress, over?"

"Thank you, Bridget, for the warning about the bounty, and yes, my intuition also tells me to take extra precautions. I believe that in the immediate future, the entire team will have their hands more than full. In that respect, it is imperative that you release the DK palace as soon as possible to local law enforcement. Let them secure the money on the spot, for the moment. Files are very important and we can deal with the money later. We need your help as immediate cover and backup crossing the City and getting our cargo to the Guardia Fortress. It's Priority One! Please thank Bill for his astute deduction regarding the transmission. I too tend to believe his insight is excellent in a Colombo way. If Ryan is still with you, and you are no longer in need of his services, have him and his team load the files in his vehicle and make their way here to join the convoy, and I repeat immediately, we are, one zero, to GO, over."

"Joa, I am at this very moment in the process of turning the DK palace over to local law enforcement and the capable hands of Trotter, King, Dewitt and Rampart will assist them and ensure our evidences are not compromised in any way. I should be on my way momentarily with the cavalry, over."

"Bridget, as usual take all precautions on your way there, warning your guys 'trigger ready' these bad guys are a scurvy bunch, over."

"Affirmative NA216, NA404 out."

US General Bentall's Oshkosh JLTV to clear our way

Concern for the security of the area had been heavy on Joa's mind. She had absolutely no doubt that the enemy knew they had to cross via the City and that, this place would be their gauntlet, and the attack she feared was now a reality. But, Joa had friends in high places, in fact, in most high places in existence. She had placed, 30 minutes before, one such strategic call, and within minutes some more of the local law enforcement including county Sheriffs and State Marshalls and even FBI forces were there to help establishing road blocks, keeping the civilian population out of the area. It was most certain to have some effect on the mercenaries, who without doubt were already in place lying in and wait for their prey. But they probably will be detected by the Moskito-Spy and have the sniper's gunshot them down, if SOMBRAJ does not pass before them and get away with their miserable life...

But nothing was sure because up to this moment, Joa was always in advance on them, she was prepared and ready to go. But the advantages Joa's team had on the mercenaries were their disorganization, first they had to be called and join together and prepare, and this is time consuming. They may be a lot of them, but they are not working organized and united and their communications are obsoleting and tunes on close FM's waves. They are grouped by small mob with old Humvees or Bearcats, those vehicles are cheaply armored, easy to destroy.

So, with the General's forces armed, up there, with new fast helicopters and on the ground with his new armored Oshkosh JLTV armed to the teeth, they will face a war defense, if they can come close enough over the barricades.

The GO signal is (Switch-4)

But Joa, always try to get all chances on her side and for jeopardizing their efforts, nothing is better than putting them in chaos, mixing them up with false coordinate's direction for about 2 minutes. 54-TI will completely squelch their FM radio bands or marine channels, sorry for local police that are too easy to scan by today's equipment.

Joa's last-minute tricks: **Switch-4**.

Too bad for mercenaries, without knowing where it's coming, just before ready to go, 54-TI will scramble their communication signals, in the way that they will be impossible to communicate together. 54-TI is preparing a squelch sound mixed with "war-march-music," called: **(Switch-4)**

At the simulated GO signal: the convoy will be engaging their way, all in coordination for two minutes, aiming west as if the convoy was going through the City streets. All General's helicopters must go blowing up their ways west too, in simulation; six Oshkosh JLTV's, two each 54-TI's sides and two in the back. All the other Oshkosh already moving through the city to help reinforcing barricades will come to help. And after that 2 minutes simulation, the mercenaries will be moving too, and there is the Joa's trick:

At the **Switch-4** signal, all mercenaries radio in scramble mode with a nice squelching-march-music will be moving fast and warning their acolytes that the GO is on, but:

Switch-4 tells everybody what they were previously projected to do according to Joa's plan.

- First, the convoy goes west in simulations for 2 minutes, and at the signal switch-4, the complete radio signal become scrambled for everybody mercenaries.
- The 54-TI convoy turn around to east direction, takes the tools highway, enable them to cross the city on an over streets level, fouling the enemy.
- While the General's helicopters are circling around to protect, also with the six Moskito-Spy patrolling in the lower city buildings for shooters.
- As previously organized, the two Joa's team fast HH-65 well-armed helicopters quit the General's air crowd for going around east and then north and west on the court building, The Guardia Fortress, with the most important

physical originals of the most ever-important physical evidences against the Consortium.

While the mercenaries, hiding and waiting in their spots, unable to communicate with their team, the 54-TI convoy has escaped truly the top of the City, avoiding firing for nothing risking civilian's casualties. But the war was not ended; the convoy had to quit the highway, turnaround the ramp and still had to cross a little part at the west Esplanade along the canal up north to the Guardia Fortress. The mercenaries were not expecting the convoy by that way, so the roadway was clear up to the Esplanade entrance. The west side of the bay, where it could have been dangerous was protected by the Coast Guards Vessels and the Moskito-Spider for infrared scanning for eventual snipers' coordinates.

The Esplanade

Without such precautions in such a highly populated high traffic area, such a battle would otherwise most assuredly involve innocents being injured or killed. The Esplanade to get to The Guardia Fortress runs south to north, over a shallower part of the inter-coastal water way due to natural incoming sediment from the local inlet. On the water side on the southeastern side is a narrow public dock, which boaters use to make their way to the business area. The well-maintained asphalt roadway known as the Esplanade enables homeowners and businesses of the islands to access their properties from the old highway on side.

The Esplanade east side entrance is wide, flanked by a few vacant lots east and small parcels of, what had at one time been, a small orange grove; but has remained sporadically populated. The west side of the bay, however, is a completely different picture; completely comprised of prime waterfront. It is populated from the inter-coastal water side to the golf and filled with development. It is a typical mixture of middle class and high-class people, many lavish homes, a commercial area, and an affluent industrial park, and it is densely populated.

Alike a citadel or a fortified fort, The Guardia Fortress is a large imposing two stories well-appointed building with its portico supported by impressive Roman pillars and separated by deliberate zoning. It is located on the intercostal side of the bay land, nestled in a buffer zone between the populace and the commercial business park. The two-story building is sitting on a huge bunker base, hiding under an immense grass-covered land, was constructed at the middle of the last world war in 1942. It is all high cement fenced and highly protected, once inside and even at the surround, anybody armed could be killed after a little siren warning, security is seriously applied there, it's almost as the White House.

The expected enemy, with reinforcements closing in on The Esplanade from both east and west sides, would be intent on one thing only, and respect for the populace or regard for any human life would not be on their agenda. It is why... So many armed forces were involved as one united force to protect civilians... Joa was able and only her, with her team, capable to bring together the whole armed forces and law enforcement agencies to work unified, for the first time ever.

Jacques Roux was at the control of 54-TI, and the wheeled warrior was prepared to fight near northwest side of the entrance to the bay side, if need be, but again, two Oshkosh JLTV open fire just to scare them. The General Bentall forces action had become more intensive, Joa, on board 54-TI, had advised Maurice to make use of the heavier weapons from the on-board arsenal at their disposal, if need be, before they entered the populated area, but again General Bentall was prepared for a war alike and Joa's team and other imposing Oshkosh JLTV made their way in The Guardia Fortress without firing a bullet. Confronted with a so huge armed force, the mercenaries were not stupid enough to risk their life for nothing, so they finally quit.

Five major reasons for the success

There were five major reasons for the success of the BULLSEYE operation coupled to the international CONSO-DOWN operation.

1. The team work synchronization and help from communication intervenient.
2. Joe and SOMBRAJ assistance with crooks' brain scanning for crucial information.
3. Rapidness, effectiveness and believing in intelligent and tactical organization.
4. General Bentall forces protection and the cooperation of the whole law enforcement agencies: local police, county sheriffs, state Marshalls and FBI great cooperation with the Tampa Air Force Base radars assistance.
5. And 54-TI technologies and great intelligence and tactical agents.

There were more interveners, but the success of the whole operation owns to the whole world economic systems, that is why any forces are there for: to protect and defend, against the faulty instead of applying competition against each other.

CHAPTER 17

Cristopher meets the man

After a rough ride, then escorted by S.I.I.T.F elite force, Cristopher and his battered team made it to the confines of The Guardia Fortress. The emotionally and physically exhausted warriors, dirty, tired, hungry and followed by their rearguard escort literally stumbled through the elaborate entrance of a beautiful well-built building. The Guardia Fortress is two stories in height, its stone and granite facade giving it the allure of Roman architecture. The front portico is flanked by two majestic Roman pillars leading to two impressive doors, elaborately carved from solid oak with bronze inlay whose patina showed age. They were in fact treasured antiques imported from Greece.

Inside, The Guardia Fortress itself, takes up the first floor, the interior lobby and office area done in white Carrera marble and aged oak. Other heads offices are in hallways leading off to either side of an ornate staircase. The staircase itself is a wonder to behold and leads to a second floor which holds a Clearance Room at the center, with offices leading down each side. The entire building simply reeked of money, old, new, and of world industry and trade; a given that this building is much more than a Fortress.

The security around was normally high, but as a result of Joa's call, the local law enforcement had added several members of the General Bentall forces around the front entrance. Inside, things were more or less as normal, but normal here meant several well-armed and well-trained security officers on both levels, as well as the S.I.I.T.F agents stationed there. Anyone considering any form of illegal activity within would be well advised to consider a simpler form of suicide.

An Asian woman beyond mere beautiful, with porcelain skin, jet blue-black waist length hair and dressed impeccably, met them at the entrance. Cristopher sensed gratitude from her, as she extended a beautifully manicured hand and in a powerful yet very cultured and feminine voice, introduced herself as Lee Ling Konu. She assured him that they were now safe, in the confines of a secured building under the auspices of an international force known as S.I.I.T.F. She advised him that his team would be taken to a comfortable area and cared for, while she escorted him to the individual to whom he will be delivering the files and the artifact. Cristopher's face showed concern. He refused to be separated from his team. His job was not finished yet.

The choice was made for them. Unexpectedly, a sound of footsteps emanated from the staircase. They all looked towards the top of the ornate staircase. Standing there was an imposing tall dark man, perhaps six feet six in stature. He was wearing a well-tailored suit that did very little to conceal a well-muscled body. The striking man descended the staircase stopping a few feet away from the team.

In a slow and precise movement, he extended his well-manicured but enormous hand to Cristopher. With the most brilliant and warm white smile, he spoke with a slight accent:

"I believe you are known as Cristopher? I am Maxim Kgnu, Head of the International Finance Task Force dealing with money laundering and financial extremism. I have been expecting your arrival." His handshake was firm and friendly.

"Yes sir. I was ordered to deliver this original package containing the Green Files to you and only you, as the uploaded copy you may have received from 54-TI."

"Thank you, Cristopher. I have been well informed of what preceded our meeting. The entire world owes you and the team, an enormous debt of gratitude. You have offered and were willing to sacrifice your very lives, for the service and protection of others. Joa was correct, you would not fail her. All of you have exhibited great courage and bravery."

"Thank you, sir, but you know, we did it as Joa's team!"

"Joa is a true professional and guardian of justice. I agree to your request. We will proceed to the fortified area where our financial assessors, money laundering investigators and financial extremism experts are located. Once the upload of the data is accomplished we will return you to your team to await Joa's arrival."

After making it over the city on the tool highway without too much problem, under the General Bentall protection, it was a sight to see the wounded mammoth arriving at the magnificent front portico of The Guardia Fortress, which was under the protection of the S.I.I.T.F elite international force and the General forces. Joa was now confident that her plan would come to a satisfactory conclusion. But as she said:

"However, there was still considerable work to be done."

Maxim heard the commotion taking place in the lobby, and stepped out from the secured room to see what was happening. He rapidly made his way to the head of the ornate staircase. Surprised, nevertheless delight still registered on his intelligent face, when he realized that the origin of the disturbance was none other than his beloved beautiful Joa, with Lee Ling at her side making her way towards him. He walked to the top of the staircase, and like a father with his child said with a slight French inflection:

"I was worried, and I had a right to be, as there is a very large bounty on your head. Your disheveled look tells me you have slithered from between the hands of your archenemy, on your way here." With a smile that lights up a tired dirty face, she said to Maxim:

"Remember, it is teaming Boa and they will need a far bigger force to take us out. I am Boa!" Has she approached Maxim, there was no handshake there but, a warm embrace from her mentor. Always has a warrior she inquiries, regarding the state of Cristopher's team. As they made their way towards Maxim's office, he told her that the team is well and are located in a salon to allow them to relax until she had arrived:

"I must say Joa; you know how to surround yourself with the best there is."

"You have taught me well, Maxim! Thanks to you and your incredible teaching skills, my growth will be exponential. Thank you, Maxim." Joa smiles because the terminology (growth being exponential) falls in Maxim's domain of finance, and she knows her words would please him to no end. After all, was she not his pupil?

More Than a Fortress

Maxim requested that Lee Ling ensured that Joa's team in 54-TI is attended too. He further instructed her to acquire the assistance of special financial agents, to obtain the boxes of files including the electronic hardware from Maurice and have them moved from 54-TI to the secure room in the Fortress. Joa agreed with Maxim but wished to see the secure area, so they make their way down a well-lit hallway seemingly without end. Joa noticed a small shadow move quickly from one side of the hallway to the other, and then suddenly, vanish. Maxim took a superb gold pen from his pocket and pointed at a beautiful abstract frieze on the wall to his left. And silently a hidden door opened to reveal a beehive of activity.

Joa was impressed, nonetheless not surprised. She knows Maxim and recognized, he will spare no cost to ensure everything will be done to bring justice, in dealing with the atrocious crimes perpetrated on so many innocents. He will do everything in his power, to restore financial stability to the world order and economy, by taking power of the complete activities of the whole Consortium operation and the Bank (WTB) and sub activities of dependencies.

The well-lit and appointed cavernous room holds not only people with credentials which would make any organization envious, but also electronics which would make technical experts salivate. Joa turns from the activity that is taking place in the room, questioning her friend:

"Maxim, have you gone public with the information yet?"

'Only what you ask me about tranquilizing the whole mercenary's aggressive angrier as you said for money."

"Oh yes and it did work!" But the question was about the whole financial situation, and he answered:

"No, however, shortly we will make some information public. This release will only be the tip of the iceberg. We have begun, however, the process of freezing some organizations' financial accounts. Personal accounts are more involved, but we were able to have one of the legitimate financial institutions in Germany freeze one particular patron's account. It is only the beginning of many across the globe." And after a little sigh:

" Needless to say, the net is cast and very soon it will be full of very large fish, and the smaller ones will quickly follow, and I might add, I am rather fond of—ahem— "gold fish." It will take some time to explore all the information, but they will find, we are rather good fishermen." Joa chuckled at his pun and spoke of an important detail for her:

"If that is the case Maxim, I would like Sylvia Hall to have the exclusive on public dissemination of the information. She has been of great help to Bridget. I know her news station is small compared to the mega networks and other larger global news media, but I trust Sylvia's good judgment, and I am confident she will ensure the truth is exposed, without making a sensational spectacle or fear-mongering from the horrendous wicked doings. She will treat the information in certain cases, with dignity and will without doubt infuse certain of her personal warnings, for, that malicious will always arise from the ashes." Maxim smiled at Joa, telling her:

"Joa, be happy! Sylvia had already been contacted, because I know well about her integrity. I knew her mother well, and she is her mother's daughter, continuing to carry out her mother's news mandate, having all of her morals and qualities, and then some..." Maxim chuckles a little, saying to Joa who is now all ears:

"Her father was no slouch either, he was a highly sought-after reporters, and my dearest friend." Maxim and Joa were two good friends, they were able to elaborate long and interesting discussions, but they both had a lot to do, so...

CHAPTER 18

The Consortium attending annual meeting in Costa Rica

In the last two days before the vast operation CONSO-DOWN, originated from the Dennis Kildem meeting at Daytona Beach Inn, there was an important meeting somewhere, near the remote area of Puerto Jimenez on the Osha Peninsula, Costa Rica. An incredible looking mega yacht on its standing slips was attending the Consortium's bank elite annual meeting. That special meeting has been arranged to deal with the huge founds investment coming in from other found rising meeting all over the world. The party kind meeting was more like a fiesta, because the growing stage of the bank WTB was on its last stage to become the first important World Bank internationally.

The House of Cards Is About to Fall

After three days partying, something had to wake them up just before hitting the top of the wall, money was getting in from all unattended sources. Fiscal Paradises were emptying, cartels were coming in with billions on pullets, and even Switzerland Paradises numbered accounts were transferring huge money. Bundles of any currencies were getting transferred in WTB bunkers all around the world. It was a euphoric moment: taxes avoiders, bandits, killers, crooks, and criminals of all kinds without scrupulous senses, were almost winning over the world. Multinationals were adhering and applauding WTB success too. Those who put money before any humanity sensitivity were winning controlling the capitalist systems of the whole world. Those money believers were fascinating; some of them were on their knees praying to get more money from hell and more dictating power to govern.

But SOMBRAJ was not there for money, the SOMBRAJ's intervention was there for the suffering caused by their unscrupulous killing ways to get their money. Money believers put money before anything and they even believe to bring it in their coffins, yes, they could be granted for a little, but not it all...

So, after a late breakfast following the effects of a drinking night, the next meeting was reported to dinner time so everybody had a little while to get back on their feet. Relaxing, all of them were very far from any news channels, especially not for Costa Rica's news. But the Italian chef was a music lover flooding the kitchen with his preferred tunes, when all his preferred channels were talking about the same thing: the cold killing of a Porto Rican, only because he had a Spaniard looking. He always had the TV on, for watching images once in a while, but switching channels, seeing a known face Dennis Kildem killing an unarmed man front kneeing him, what! Louis turn on the sound, hearing the same story again and again certifying in words the scandalizing images, it was too much. The man had the only default to be a Latin Spanish speaking alike.

The chef, Louis Lazaretto, scandalized, asks the Captain to pay him a little fast visit at the kitchen, for something might be very important. Alfredo, the Captain, came in the kitchen faster than ever, usually he was not very fast to come in the kitchen for hearing Louis lamentations. After listening and seeing, the Captain first words were:

“Cancel everything on the set menu for the next coming days.” George was completely astonished, so much that he didn’t know what to do and how to tell Dennis Grandfather. So, they decided to call Mister Benjamin, to come to the kitchen to see is very good friend Louis. George didn’t want to be there, he was too affected, knowing closely so much Dennis. No TVs were on, nobody knew anything yet.

While coming in at the door kitchen, Mister Benjamin was in conversation on his cell, he first asks for a chair and put his phone in his pocket. He addressed Louis:

“How are you my friend?”

“I am affected right now, Mister Benjamin, see by yourself.”

“OH! That is bad, but according to my French friend Bertrand Dubois, the worst might be coming.”

Without a word or a sign, Mister Benjamin quit slowly the kitchen and asks the Captain George to call for an immediate directors' meeting in the little front Captain saloon.

When they had, all filed in, with an unseen hand Benjamin touched a hidden place, and the door to the boardroom closed as if in a whispered omen behind them. His figure was imposing but, what left everyone uncomfortable were his iced blue eyes which seemed to be looking right into your soul.

“Come in gentlemen, we have much to cover.” The Don spoke with a cultured voice of command yet of genuine concern. He was standing up to the group sitting around the table and spokes slowly weighing every word, as he addresses the gathering:

"My friends, finances and business are our bounties, riches our life blood, mistrust becomes our failure, united we may stand, but an hour ago we were to our supreme utmost, but according to our friend Bertrand Dubois's call, the worst has arrived to Daytona's meeting."

"What has...?"

"Please, see for yourself!" The big screen suddenly opened and images worth it all. Benjamin let them see what was very bad for Mister Benjamin, but he was waiting for telling them the worst. After 10 minutes, everybody was ready to congratulate him, but he said:

"Please, stay sited. The worst is coming." He briefed them with the minimum, letting the worst to eventually show them slowly the right picture. And Gunter asks to talk:

"Benjamin, you speak our credo, however, it is your great-grandson who has brought judgment on the Consortium because of his stupidity. We need to remedy the situation if it is not too late.

The Benjamin's face did not reflect his concern and he responded accordingly:

"Yes, Gunther you are correct, and I have taken the necessary measures to deal with Dennis and his indiscretions. This meeting was called on to last longer, but things are amplifying too fast. Now I must request that you ensure that your financial institution deals with..."

A knock is heard, interrupting Benjamin in mid-sentence. He pressed a button to release the door lock and allow it to slide open. The Captain entered and made his way to Benjamin's right side, whispering in his ear. Once the Captain has delivered his message, the Don addressed the man from Brussels:

"Gunther there is an urgent message for you, please follow my captain, he will take you to our communication center."

Gunther had a look at the Don with concern on his face, and he leaves following closely behind the Captain George addressing the remaining members:

"Gentlemen, the problem is now here, our house has become a house of cards and it is about to fall. But do not forget, they will have to deal with us. I will prepare a report for you with the latest updates that I have managed to obtain. I would suggest that you study it and consider its suggestions carefully, and contact each of your holdings to ensure their stability."

"Life is talking to us, when we are close to the utmost, we always have to prepare for a beginning of something, but this one hit, as a hurricane, will get us to rebuild everything different from the base, but stronger."

The current President of the (WTB) Consortium's bank, Benjamin Den Kildem, also one of the Consortium's member, well-respected financial gurus and business aficionados, was preparing to pass the presidency to his Great-grandson Dennis Kildem, who has reversed the vapor to the worst. He has committed the most shameful blunder possible by keeping in his possession detailed and damning records of the Consortium, most of its organizations, their mandates, financial records, businesses, members' names. And worst, their involvement and connections, money laundering networks and banking information including detailed accounts information in one thick concise file called the Green Files. It was literally a hangman's noose for thousands of high-powered high profiled individuals, and a lawman's license for the seizure of billions of dollars.

It had come to light that Dennis's greatest sin was being so egocentric, that he believed this information could never fall in the hands of the law, or anyone who would use it to bring down what they now had, the house of cards. Dennis believed that he was infallible, and that one decision to set up a meeting, in an area which would be susceptible to have vital information being taken, when openly available in a questionable luxurious RV, at an event called Bike Week, was beyond foolish on Dennis's part. He believed himself invincible and untouchable by law enforcement. From his bounced extravagant ego, and from exotic precautions regarding personal security, it did not allow for his fate that it would draw him into the deadly coils of the determined special agent Boa.

Serious damage done to the Consortium, possibly sufficiently serious to cause irreparable damage or even destruction of the Consortium, its many organizations, their way of life, and perhaps their elimination entirely by worldwide united law enforcement agencies, both known and unknown.

They Will Have to Deal with Us

Benjamin Den Kildem is a master in finance, so he had to tell them a little word of encouragement:

"My friends, I had prepared a communique for the whole worldwide financial corporates, our members and law enforcement agencies. Our com system has already sent thousands of copies and will complete its faxing soon. The tile is: they will have to deal with us."

"I will call an end to this meeting, allowing you to return to your organization and business, to deal with the fallout which I believe is about to explode. I am sorry for this disaster but some may be able to save certain parts of their organizations. I too must now deal with this matter. But, do not be in a hurry to live, if you feel like staying, you are welcome." And there was to be an end...

"Have a good day, till we can meet again."

The exit from the room was quick, and arrangements were made to assist the members to leave and return to their own organization.

After a few deep respirations, the Don, as they call him since a very long time, gets out of his chair and told the Captain:

"Please George, make plans to get underway at an appropriate time, but, take care to avoid raising anyone's curiosity." The Don stands tall and confident as he makes his way to his stateroom.

Communique faxed to members and law enforcement agencies, worldwide

RE: They will have to deal with us

Benjamin Den Kildem

President of the:

(WTB), World Traders Bank. And member of the Consortium

Dear world finance members and law enforcement agencies,

To whom it may interest.

Money laundering is politic but not a fault

This is a warning that the true could not be hidden anymore. We have thousands more information than you all have. We succeed where any financial institutions have failed, where any Government administration has failed. We are the only one who has the right picture of the worldwide real economy, because we have the best administrators of the world.

Money laundering is politic but not a fault, the fault is to the governments who let it happen intentionally for hiding the politician's money and their sponsors. Any banking world has found a way to cash what is called dirty money, and fiscal paradises are there only to amortize banking transactions. The big-money world players are regularizing the switching by absorbing by vacuum in their own money lever, playing with warranties and credit margins or floating losses and gains.

WTB has its own system that works successfully, we secure bundles of any money in our bunkers, no matter where it comes from, for only 20% and WTB give an 80% credit margin of clean money and this is not worse than, hiding sleeping money in a numbered account in a Switzerland fiscal paradise. WTB is already financing thousands of buildings and business all around the world, with money coming from fiscal paradises and, supposedly called, dirty money that we have cleaned, for the good of the whole world economy. Money has been printed for exchanging services, and the wrong of it, is freezing it in bunkers or fiscal paradise for not paying taxes. Devises could not be dirty, they have no smell but the signature on it is the warranty of its real value, even if governments are playing with its real value or are printing new money when needed.

My friends, this is the most important ever meeting in the world, because we are holding close to 38% of the world economy, and we are the most dangerous weapon that the whole capitalist system has ever encountered, no government is stronger economically, we can create the worst crises the world has ever lived on. But we will not, because we are profit makers, not looser. Our head office is out of your jurisdiction sovereignty and untouchable and all dependencies dealing with us are independent and self-owned, we only lend intangible assets or warranty their bounded operations electronically.

So, my friend, do not be worried, the whole united economic world central banking cannot live healthily without us. So, they are going to be obliged to deal with us. They may hold some of you in a luxurious jail for a while, but be peaceful; they will deal with us, because I have prevented that state of the worst. I only have to push a mental button and the whole world is going to hate themselves.

Most patrons of the whole financial system ignore the reality of the amalgamated wheeling of the world capitalist catalyzer. The Universities ignore reality; they propagate dreams only for future business doers. Past knowledge has built Spain's Castles alike, but experience has shown practical understanding of the world economy wheeling. The world economic system is like in a war, somebody has to lose for others to win.

In our system, all dependencies are there to win, because they have nothing more than papers and a commission on what they do... WTB is everywhere, but nowhere, they control everything but could not be controlled.

The world's economic system is only a toy for genius calculation, it is built and based on the abuses of 98% puppets of the world population, and the puppets are themselves their one activator of that slave system. The system has reversed the whisk, no need to be beaten to work harder. Buy now and pay later, and then, they have to work all their life to pay for their dream and their get-up-and-go to work. The known system is: get into debt and then work all your life to pay it or you lose it!

The worse side of our system is for those who get a drug momentary feeling knowing deeply that they'd prepared themselves for being future zombies.

We, bank up dreams! The whole system is money laundering: any business is money laundering, you buy Asiatic for a 10 Cents and you sell for $ 10 Dollars that is what we call business. The puppets buy drugs with their money, fruit of their work, but they are financing cartels, gangs, mafias, wars, believing, sects, and so much more, but stopping and arresting them is the law enforcement job. Money holds the system going on and on, money is our business. Money is always clean but you can buy dirty things with it. All the banking system is money laundering for taxes evasion and bigger profit and the essence of it is the 98% puppets. Money has no identification smells, what our members have done with it, left no trace on it, but there is always some work to get it, even if it is only genius calculation...

No Evidence of Dirty Money

Anyone who has bundles of money is welcomed to WTB because we never see printing signs on bundles that the money is dirty, so we always presumed the money is clean because there is no dirty evidences on it. Contrariwise, we always presumably give to our member the benefice of doubt until any law enforcement has proven the opposite. To WTB's policy, any money is clean in our members' hands, unless the holder has been arrested and brought to justice to be judged and declared guilty.

What we have done for the economic system is more than calculation, it is realization and rebuilding of the whole international banking system:

We have brought new hidden capital and we were almost ready to release them in the whole world economy, new funding sources are coming from:

- Fiscal paradises, all over the planet.
- Bundles of billions of devises, hiding in private bunker safes.
- Bundles of devises sitting in business money carrier bunkers.
- Private hidden values, as gold diamond and money, siting in bank private cases, doing nothing or for avoiding paying taxes.
- Even Switzerland fiscal paradise's hidden numbers accounts, has been revived and recovered, reanimating billions of moneys of sleeping taxes evasion accounts.
- Most of riches got most of their money out of fiscal paradises and transferred their fortune to our (WTB), World Traders Bank.

We have realized what, no one of the biggest government powers has ever been able to materialize, and for the only reason that they are all in competition against each and others. And the other reason is that they are not interested to show up, publicly, how they balance the value of their devices with printing more new money when needed.

Global financial crisis averted by:

A vigilant international financial watchdog

News banners were now flashing across TV Stations around the world, under the by-line of Ms. Sylvia Hall well respected anchor of DBN Channel 18 News.

Ms. Hall stated that she was informed of the following actualities by the proper authorities. The following facts have now been verified and confirmed. I do not wish to cause panic, please rest assured that the global economy is safe and the WTD "World Traders Bank" has not suffered any undue harm. The following arrests have transpired.

Sergio Berardi, a highly resourceful business mogul was arrested upon returning to Italy from a business meeting. Witnesses observed that Sergio was not surprised to see the Italian "Policia" waiting with an arrest and seizure warrant on his return. He had been informed by one of his senior officers in his organization that Francine Chevalier a long-time friend and business associate had also been arrested at the Paris airport on her return from a Costa Rica said vacation.

An arrest warrant was also issued for Baxter Heinz from Germany, well known global investors and businessmen who was also out of country. His assets were now in the hands of international authorities for exhaustive investigation.

There are to be more arrests pending the review of documents now in the hands of Maxim Kgnu, Head of the (IFTF) International Finance Task Force dealing with money laundering and financial extremism. This financial fraud, worldwide operation is the most ever-important happening in this century that was controlling close to 40% of the world economy.

We all know the many threats the global community must endure but, we must remain vigilant at all times and be thankful for the many tentacles of global law enforcement who continue their unending search for law and order, so that the public may remain safe and live a peaceful well-ordered life.

Money was the rat trap

In this vast operation, money was only the part that has settled the crooks together in the same rat trap, but the real reason for SOMBRAJ only justification to come alive, was the innocent-suffering cause by the coldly assassins, who are capable to kill anyone for money. And in this case the money became alike excrement: if dispersed all around it smells a little but when piled up on big heap, it stinks far around...

Under the incomprehensible meaning of the invisible, SOMBRAJ will accomplish its journey butterflying from malicious spirit to criminal spirit and take away forever what was lent only: their miserable life. SOMBRAJ has let me know that many cold killers were going rotten in jails everywhere in the world and as soon SOMBRAJ has some spare time, he will be paying them a visit. There is no reasonable situation to let the sufferers pay forever because of the cold killers' fault:

- First the killers have judged and executed innocents who had done nothing to deserve to be cold killed.
- Innocent families suffering, was intentionally afflicted by the killers.
- Law enforcement has to prove and bring them to justice.
- Justice gets them in a long trial that cost a lot of money and may get out with an agreement sentenced.
- And, at the end the killer will get rotten for years in jail, while innocent families will pay again all along his incarceration.

The innocent families are paying for all those stages that are a huge amount, and they still have to pay to nourish them, to keep them alive and healthy while behind bars.

Why innocent families, do have to pay all their life for something that has been coldly committed by the killers, while the killers have nothing to pay to stay alive? This is like paying unjustifiably thousand times for something they have not done.

“This is why Justice has to be death, for the cold killers!”

Well, SOMBRAJ told me that they will soon be visited by a beautiful butterfly, until then, SOMBRAJ is telling them:

“Wait, stay awake, I know where you are, I’ll see you soon!!!”

Since then, many jails have been visited and many miserable life’s has been taken back. Even those killers thinking they are free, because justice fails to check them on their slow system. SOMBRAJ is busy:

“But you turn is seconds away and no one will be forgotten”

CHAPTER 19

The loss of one comrade-in arms

After the passing, Bridget turned away for a brief moment, her head down. Their work so dangerous, the need so intense, the loss of even one comrade-in-arms hit everyone deeply, regardless of how they showed it.

"Let's take a little rest and give a break to my cams! The goal is attained, the worst Consortium crooks are arrested, for the moment, and all the money is in hold. All of us do not care about Dennis, he was only another trigger kind, for that vast operation and he may have many mad guys after his ass. But for us, we want to know what the HIC has triggered that Daytona Beach KILLING. Do you? Joa did a lot of work on this report that she starts preparing while flying to Tampa. Here it is, come closer and see by yourself, ACTION."

Conclusion of the Daytona Crime Scene

Every law enforcement agency wanted to know what happened to Daytona Beach, so Joa was there to present her conclusion of the crime scene. Those who were in charge of an important part of the operation were there to assist and applause Joa and her team determination as General Bentall, Bernard Sandcastle and Maxim Kgnu.

So, Bridget had advised all the law enforcement agencies interested, but the information has spread as fast as a virus. News media of all categories, down land vehicles with direct air transmission antennas, helicopters circling all around finally came down, and a crowd as ever seen, with their little digital registering gadgets, microphones with extension as giraffes with long neck over in Joa's direction. The rendezvous was as a fiesta.

While Joa was shaking hands, she was scrutinizing the whole crowd as if she was a mental scanner. She didn't know yet that she has been invested of super power, about 3 hours before, by the SOMBRAJ's summit. Joa had to wait until the crowd stop arriving, even if some were there since 2 hours.

General Bentall with about 60 of his team members and the FBI director Bernard Sandcastle were there with about 30 of his agents. Medic staff was there by their own vehicle, and the cherry on the cake was Jose Morales and his Southern gang, but no one was armed, after being checked, they only wanted to know what had happened to their dead friends.

Joa, ask Bridget to go and arrest three well dress men, on left at the back:

"Bridget, there is three men just arrived, be careful, go there about 60 feet at left, just beside the blond women with a red cap, be discreet, you see her?"

"Yes Joa, what's there?"

"Bad intention armed guys, they might be here to shout us all, but I think they were not expecting a so huge crowd of armed soldiers and police officers."

"Take five armed guys, pass right first and go around and point the 3 men in black suits at her right. Then look at me, I'll nod you, if they are the right ones. Be tactical Bridget!"

"OK Joa, 2 guys are in the back already." Bridget radioed her guys, to come slowly from the back as if they were patrolling, but directly at left. They had to avoid shootings in the crowd. They join together and aimed the 3 men and all those around; Bridget did wait for Joa's nodding and those guys add new small Chinese machine-gun hid on their back.

They were arrested and took away by FBI. Joa ask Bridget to go around in case they had backups for escaping after their shouting plan. They were alone maybe, waiting to have their best shots. She said it all only to Maxim:

"It might be better not to show in public for a while, until things are fixed up and all over. We keep it silent for now; FBI will get it out after the meeting. Do not be preoccupied with that, they were not kamikazeing and too many armed people around, they were more scared than us."

"Yes Joa, I think you are right, but better I get to know you, more you surprise me!"

That was a local offense; S.I.I T.F. is there for international operations in cooperation with any country law enforcement agencies, where an international operation is needed. But the offense has to be perpetrated in two countries, simultaneous for being international.

Nobody knew what was happening; Joa put her finger on her mouth, telling Bridget to keep silent. But Bridget was still questioning herself:

"How did she know that? Do not ask, she wouldn't know how, either."

Joa's Meeting for Exercise Recapitulation

"Hi everyone! Thanks to all of you, that has participated to that ever so huge, criminal and fraud, international operation. The whole world and each person were concerned personally about that world economic issue, and every law enforcement and armed forces worldwide did participate together, to finally freeze and dismantle an important part of their operation. After what you came here for, my report prepared by my teams, I'll let Maxim Kgnu, the US Director of the Special International Intelligence and Tactical Forces (S.I.I.T.F.), to explain what we all together have done for our world economic stabilization and against assassins and criminal organizations."

"A report had to be done. All united law enforcement agencies, have their one Daytona crime scene speculated definition, but my team and I were the only ones, installed, investigating, collecting information, and sighting the Kildem organization at the Daytona Beach Carnage. Oh, I'm forgetting, the 2 gang shooters were there too, but unfortunately for their family and friends, many of them are no more witness."

"This report as you will receive a copy is based on observations and videos that were preliminary but was impartially complete and accurate with accordance expertise in police forensics and crime scene evidences. Precise information obtained from the 54-TI laboratories analyses and observations were given credence once certified and compared from different video sources."

"54-TI team is quite capable of contributing information and analysis, as to what had occurred at the crime scene, using the information, witnesses' accounts and videos provided by the extremely thorough and well qualified 54-TI team. And I was also able to provide an eyewitness account in the area visible to me, because I walked in as the incident in question was taking place."

"Conclusions were based on videos, eye witness testimonies, and forensic indices which will include the location of the bodies, type and position of wounds which were inflicted, the direction of blood spatters after impact as well as powder marks or residue, the analysis of blood samples for identification and matching to the various profiles and bodies; determining the type of the weapons used, number of shot fired according to witnesses' accounts, the position and number of spent cartridges as well as their trajectory."

"Lieutenant Gordon Trojan has arrested 9 witnesses that were unable to fly away as others and they were a good source to identify dead friend bodies; and he gives his report to Commander Bridget Herckel to complete the on-site investigation and dispatching responsibilities to relating law enforcement agencies."

"In the meantime, this is an account of how the crime scene played out. The details substantiated by eyewitness testimony and it including an equally comprehensive record of information, which was captured on video and sound equipment located in most of the strategic points of the Inn. Some of the surveillance equipment is the property of the Inn security. Earlier on, other equipment had been installed by S.I.I.T.F to ensure complete coverage of the Kildem meeting, which was to take place."

Bridget was beside Joa and she continued explications:

"Hi I'm Commander Bridget Herckel!"

"What Joa and her teams had prepared would be 'courtroom evidences' grade information and testimony, and its quality at Joa's level, irrefutable by the slimiest of defense lawyers, if need be."

"Profiles and information on guests and bikers were gathered and provided by local, regional and international law enforcement agencies. Other than the Dennis Kildem group conference, which was taking place on the premises, everything seemed to be fairly routines, when Bike Week is underway. Many of these individuals were here under the guise of Bike Week."

"Once Joa will have satisfaction with the contents of the report, she would ensure that the required authorities received a copy. Thanks!"

"And between you and me, this crime scene was easily determined that two gangs defend themselves from each other and the trigger was an innocent rage man called the Pouilleux with no identification yet.

After a little break, Joa add some more tanks:

"It is with a sincere thankfully gratitude that we own our life to the General Bentall forces for close protection, to local police for holding bad guys the other side of the barricades, to the county sheriff for blocking roads and streets and State Marshals for maneuvering their Humvees and Bearcats in the fields around for blocking and chasing mercenaries.

"And a special appreciation to Bernard Sandcastle with his FBI troops who were blocking air traffic and nailing down mercenaries from all airports 50 miles around." "Bernard was dispatching by himself all over his agents to be sure no mercenaries will get to our proximity."

"This was a united coordinated effort from all forces that took place naturally to protect our country while protecting the whole world economic stabilization, against the ever so important attack from the most organized criminals grouped linked in a crook Consortium."

"Thank to you all! Let me present to you Maxim Kgnu, my S.I.I.T.F. director and (IFTF) member."

Maxim Kgnu, the S.I.I.T.F. Director, US Headquarters

"Good morning everybody, Joa ask me to give you a little detail about the financial side of that so vast criminal operation that took place all over the world. It is a so complicated happening, but I will resume with the simplest important lines, that brought to light the possibility to take back in our hands the volatile world economy."

"From that operation that mainly began at Daytona Beach, there was a so huge impact derived from the success of the final Tampa operation, but at this stage it is only the tip of the iceberg that was revealed."

"From Joa's investigation about Dennis Kildem, we have so much crime and assassination evidences that it will take months to decorticate some of the encloses and elaborate the atrocities of it."

The Most Ever Worldwide Financial Fraud

"A mirror image of the (WTB) World Traders' Bank known to be the Consortium owned was in the process of being established to undermine the global economy. This organization would be allowing their vast organizations to launder monies received from illicit gains and to hold the global financial world hostage, allowing the executives to add to their personal wealth. The World Traders Bank (WTB) is now safe and under the ever so vigilant eye of (IFTF) an international Finance Task Force watchdog, that I am honored to be a head member."

“Further, we have been advised by the world main S.I.I.T.F. Headquarters that in excess of thousands personal and business bank accounts have been frozen; billions of dollars were retrieved from illicit gambling houses; more than hundred fifty investment organizations are being investigated for fraudulent representation to investors; more than hundred thirty-nine questionable businesses as well as a total of hundred fifty major corporations perhaps involved in the process of laundering money. The number of funds currently frozen internationally is up-to-date, in excess of thousands of billions in many currencies. Detailed information will be made available to the public once they are determined and vetted.”

“Money will be redistributed accordingly to which countries and banks that have been crooked braided. This, to assure that the power of that capital is still on the market to not destabilize the world economy.”

“But my last word would be something brought to your imagination:

- Let say that for not paying taxes you hide your money in a fiscal paradise.
- Crooks do the same after laundering their dirty money.
- Fiscal Paradises hiding thousands of billions in numbered accounts.
- And so much more ways to hide money and richness.

‘For now, allowing your imagination to come to reality; This CROOK’s Consortium has succeeded in what no other financial forces have ever been able to attain; because the Consortium has given a push, to any kind of currencies, to emerge from the dirt and come alive again. The richness got out of almost every Fiscal Paradise (for them to fall down), bringing now the money up front, with their owners identified. Cartels did the same emptying their bunkers, big criminal organizations did the same:

- Some of them are killers and they will have to pay a visit to jail waiting for their trial with their money seized.
- Others will have to pay taxes on the big amount even if they deposited by little amount, and will have to prove the source of that money.
- Drug cartels will have their money seized and brought to justice with an international arrest warrant.'

'But the conclusion is: we cannot have everybody arrested in the same time, jails are not ready for that, but important changes will be made, even our world financial way to transit and control the tracing of any kind of currencies transactions will have to change.'

'From the very bad Consortium, laundering money for their international bank WTB (World Traders Bank), there is a lesson to be taken: the bank has the most sophisticated controlling system from the complete money manipulation in the world. Even from North Korea, China, Russia and any places around the world, the WTB has the most effective out of market gadgets to spy electronics systems. They also have the best pirates of the world to operate them.

The bad will eventually bring good things to our weakened banking systems.

Thank you, ladies and gentlemen, let me now pass back the very hot microphone, because of money, to Joa, my dearest friend.' There was a strong applauding and getting stronger when Maxim has passed the microphone to Joa.

Joa's report: Daytona crime scene, the Story to be told

After a few shots of fresh water, Joa did present the scene actions as in a video, so, open your own sensitive imaginative cam or get an eye at my cam viewer!"

Joe Trakker is saying that to you:

"Action!" And Joa's telling is to be ear-drunk by a silent crowd with not even a fly around. The trigger began with Tonito words. You remember? They were all at the beach bar:

"Hey, Ramon! It is your turn, CUIDASE (you, be careful in Spanish). Go check around to ensure all our toys are OK. Have a look on our beauties! OK?"

Then laughingly, Tonito shouted in broken English to his men on the other side of the bar:

"We do not leave our beautiful toys without supervision, too long, especially in Daytona Beach during Bike Week! Not? Ah, ah, ah."

Joe Trakker knows what has triggered the carnage.

"Now every moves are as a film and will need your own imagination, or come closer to me and be a voyeur again, because you want to know what has happened to Daytona, and what did trigger that massacre!"

"Come closer and see through my cam viewer!"

According to an informant and confirmed on videos, Ramon Blanquez and his close friend the muscular Carlos Blondo, who was like a brother and protector to the slightly built twenty-two-year-old Ramon Blanquez, had headed to the north parking lot of the Inn close to the beach. Shortly before, Tonito had been heard shouting to Ramon:

"Go check on the toys and make sure that no harm came to them."

After leaving Tonito and the Southern fire gang on the beach, enjoying their beer and games, as they approached the bikes, Ramon noticed an itinerant-looking-man walking among them and every so often he would kick one. He made his way to the bad looking guy, while Carlos walked towards Tonito's bike with his back turned on the ugly guy and Ramon. Ramon, approached the man and in a sudden move a knife appeared and slashed his arm, and in a flash, the attacker had leaped with rage on Carlos, who still had his back towards them. No one of them was armed and The Pouilleux was trying to hit again without stops as a sick crazy man. Ramon surprised, clash, hurt, and in shock, backup and ran to get arms.

The Carlos Blondo body lying in an awkward position over Tonito's motorcycle with his two arms hidden under an overturned bike. In a vicious attack, his back had been punctured multiple times and he was immobile as dead. As proceeding with the investigation, it became clear that Carlos Blondo, collapsed on Tonito's motorcycle after the surprise attack by the extremely strong deranged assailant.

Their Special Alarm Sounds Had Warned Tonito's Gang

Carlos falling over resulted in three others of the gang's bikes falling over like dominoes, causing some of the alarms to be set off. Recognizing their special bike alarm sounds, everyone ran off the bar. Five of them have run first and followed by Tonito and his seven other guys.

In the same time, the tinny unarmed Ramon, his arm bleeding and seeing Carlos looking as dead, ran to the first of their bike trailers to get something to turn around his arm, as an improvised bandage, and got a machine-gun to bring down that crazy mad man; while another unknown man, just passing by, was trying to warm the mad man. According to videos that Good Samaritan was Jim Ballenger the Dennis driver and long-time friend who were sent by Dennis to notice his invites, taking a foot bath on the beach, about his soon beginning meeting.

Jim arrive directly on the macabre scene, warned by bike alarms, seeing a dirty man (the Pouilleux) still assaulting, a fallen immobile man, with a knife. So, Jim came to the rescue, shouting with a booming voice:

"Look out," but he was too late to divert the impending attack. Jim ran and launched himself to the aid of the victim, not knowing that the biker was a member of a rival gang. Jim must have grabbed the assailant to remove the weapon from him but 'The Pouilleux,' still in a maniacal trance and rage, turned and before Jim was able to react to defend himself, "The Pouilleux" inflicted three stab wounds in the stomach. Eyes wide in disbelief, Jim doubled over, but with a last-ditch effort of strength, he was successful in deflecting and removing the attacker's knife by kneeing him in the groin and grabbing the blade, however "The Pouilleux" continued to unleash his hatred of society on Jim by cutting his throat.

Always within seconds, Ramon hurrying out of the bike trailer with a machine-gun, seeing an unknown man (Jim) trying to stop the Pouilleux, still hitting the Carlos immobile body, he fired six shots just before the Pouilleux cut Jim's throat and finally brought down the Pouilleux, while Paul arrives at the mistaken scene first impression.

Everything is happening in the same time, while Dennis dispatched Paul Belfast, his body-guard and right-arm man, to find out what was taking Jim so long to return. Paul was in the RV having a coffee, with friends, he grabbed a small Chinese machine-gun. Dennis had turned presumably heading back to his suite. Paul seemed in a hurry, as he was seen leaving the RV site and heading for the beach area. Paul apparently had arrived on the scene, to see Ramon firing at The Pouilleux while Jim was falling over Carlos, Paul thinking Ramon was firing on Jim.

Gun Shouting Has Awakened the Two Gangs

A video confirmed the witness account, that he had seen Paul quickly made his way to the beach way and without hesitation pull out his gun first and fired on Ramon back and The Pouilleux, then fired with his machine-gun with rage and so many shots. The battle between Jim and his attacker had left spatters of their blood, covering many of the motorcycles in the vicinity, as well as on Carlos's body.

One witness in proximity to the ensuing carnage stated that suddenly hell broke loose and bullets were flying from every direction, of both front and side north parking lots, close to the fallen ones over the bikes. The witness stated that he saw and this was later confirmed by video, those five guys from the Southern fire gang, had upon hearing the motorcycle alarms, had come running from the beach bar direction. The fastest of the them, Benito Montana, with gun in hand was firing in the direction of Tonito's motorcycle, where Paul was standing over the body of Ramon, Jim and Carlos while the four others were getting arms in their bike trailer. Benito was instantly shouted down by Dennis's men arriving at the scene too, while Paul and Ramon were down motionless.

Always in the same time of fraction of second, five of Dennis's men hearing gunshots got out the RV with machine-guns too, and running where was gone Paul. In the same time, all the Tonito's man hearing gunshots were already running out from the beach bar, but only a few had a gun, but in the same time Pedro and his three friends got out of their bike trailer with three machine-guns and handguns to give to their friends. Two of them ran to Pedro getting a machine-gun, while the five Dennis's men arrived at the same carnage and were shouted down instantly.

And the Rage and Vengeance Took Place

According to witnesses, the both gangs were firing towards the north parking lot as well. Unfortunately, other people trying to get out of harm's way, had been hit by stray bullets, or was this intentional?

Alfredo Morandez, not known for his intelligence and called Machete, had arrived in shooting distance ahead of the others and upon seeing the bodies lying down over Tonito's bike, and his unarmed fallen friends, came to a most unfortunate conclusion and got his hands on the Ramon machine-gun. With revenge on his mind, he aimed his machine-gun and without warning fired on anyone passing by even the five warm ones coming from the beach in bathing suits. Four Dennis guests died instantly: Joa had the order to arrest four convicted killers that had an international warrant against them: Julien Patois from France, Heinz Dertker from Germany, Roberto Benito from Mexico, and Petro Capitez from Columbia. And, justice was served, when justice has to be death, they were known Killers.

Seconds later after hearing gunshots seven of Dennis's men were seen exiting the north parking lot door shortly after Paul. Shots rang out and they saw Paul crumbling to the asphalt. And Luc Bendix, Ed Filling and Frank Galotti were the first to be gun fired down.

The rest of the gang proceeded Tonito on their way out, firing their hand gun, while trying to find cover of which was very little. They continued to engage in the ensuing gun battle against those armed with semi-automatic guns. Unfortunately, this group of fighters would end up dead, any of them, due to the severity of their wounds.

Tonito and seven of his gang members were captured on video arriving on the scene taking guns on dead bodies, and with his men engaging in a gun battle. Unfortunately for them, one of Dennis's men armed with a sub-machine-gun came running from Dennis's RV located on the other side of the tree line in the north parking lot and opened fire on the Tonito's guys.

The whole scene was almost quiet, with a shot weaseled once in a while, it was the unfitted (Machete) Alfredo Morandez, walking free as he was untouchable, he fired on the last three men who were assigned to protect the Dennis's RV with their life. He receives five shots and was still walking as a zombie. Alfredo, while Joa arriving on the scene, fired a bullet that had almost hit her, rolling over she shouts Alfredo to finally stop his Zombie walking and he felt down dead. It was determined that Joa received the last Alfredo bullets, because his machine-gun charger was empty.

Tonito's men were grossly under armed, as they had been partying on the beach and doing what bikers enjoy doing, which is drinking and having fun. Five of them had really no chance to defend them-selves, they were too intent on what was occurring in the parking lot when Dennis's men assaulted them from behind. There exists also the question of inebriation from their partying. At any rate, the five bodies of the Tonito's men were laid close together in a mixture of blood and guts, so garbled that they were initially unidentifiable. Positive identification has still yet to be confirmed.

Only 9 persons, who were hiding at the dumpster back behind the cement block wall, were in security but scared. Lieutenant Gordon Trojan has arrested 9 armed witnesses that were unable to fly away as others and they were a good source to identify dead friend bodies.

Dennis Didn't Like Latinos

Perhaps Dennis, after returning from the lobby had heard gunshots, and looking out his balcony patio door, had seen people running every direction as they came in from the beach. The only man guarding Dennis was Dino Delatti, a gentle giant of a man whose eyes told another story, but whom Dennis trusted implicitly with his life and had been in his employ for a long time. Dennis's pent-up anger must have surfaced, possibly on seeing the Latino bikers, he was heard shouting to Dino: "come with me NOW! ... Those bastards! Those sons of witches"! In a fit of rage took off ready to inflect hell as he made his way to the lobby behind his only protection, Dino.

As they entered the lobby, Dino saw the onslaught of people coming their way, and pulled out his gun ready to defend his boss. Dennis, seeing what he perceived, one of them, to be a Latino directly in front of him, no longer could hold back his seething rage. Registered from the gadgets installed everywhere, the Dennis's voice was heard laud and crystal clear, he was yelling at Dino: "kill that damn Puerto Raccoon dog! Kill that son-of-a-witch! F-f-u-n-k! What the hell are you waiting for! Kill the good-for-nothing bastards!"

In the next instance, Dennis grabbed the gun from a stunned Dino, who could not believe what he had heard coming from Dennis's lips. Dennis, while making his way towards the hysterical oncoming crowd and his victim, fired a few shots, adding further panic to the crowd and sending patrons scattering in all directions with both bullets nearly hitting them.

Unfortunately, through happenstance, that victim Paolo Caballero was also in the lobby making his way to what he hoped was safety. Then he heard and saw Dennis, red-faced, and in a rage with his gun pointed at his chest. Paolo Caballero's only reaction as he stumbled to his knees was that he was heard saying to Dennis:

"Oh God... Please, my family!"

At this point, Dennis was deaf to all logic and out of control, and with the cold stare of an assassin, aimed his gun at the victim's forehead and pulled the trigger. Paolo had no chance at all with this sociopath, his last thoughts were of his family. And that phrase was still heard on TV all around the world.

Dennis, after shooting his victim, was seen high tailing it through a door at the far right of the salon with Dino following close behind. This seemed to have been a planned exit as it led directly to where Dennis's RV was located, and the video cameras were not functioning. Their whereabouts are currently unknown. How was this possible?

Investigation: many unanswered questions

The shootout at the Inn unfolds as the two gangs converge on the scene trying to defend themselves, or was it finally to unload their hatred of each other which has gone on far too long.

In the lobby of the Inn, one victim known as Paolo Caballero was shot in the forehead by Dennis. This tragic story unfolded on DBN news was captured by an unknown individual who was on the scene. The information contained on the aired video was established by 54-TI's own surveillance equipment and was also confirmed by Joa's observations, as she had arrived on the scene at the instant the incident took place.

But the investigating authorities still have many unanswered questions; where is Dennis? Where and how did Dennis vanish? Who killed two of the RV guards? Who were some of the individuals in Dennis's RV and where are they now? How could they all of them vanished so fast?

Another major question, is the identity of the five bodies who were shot by automatic weapons near the entrance to the north beach parking lot? Is Tonito Vasquez one of the bodies? Bodies still in the RV vicinity still remain to be identified. Dennis is still on the run, it is believed to Tampa. The investigation will proceed until all questions are answered. Also, information will become clearer as the various forensic teams finish their analysis.

The Joa's report was to be faxed, to any law enforcement agencies concerned who took the releases, to continue their own final investigation. Joa finally terminated the meeting in answering a few insignificant questions but finalized by saying:

"It's no to your request! There will not be any tour visiting 54-TI, my Mobil Lab, because of the secrecy about special equipment and unique armaments. It's not a toy, even if I love her for her so helpful technical efficiencies."

"Thank you any one, but the crime scene is now yours, because we were there for the Dennis Kildem criminal economic part. The drug concern about the Miami gang is completely yours too, all those other concerns about Dennis-Tennis's investigations are yours too. The only concern was, what we did successfully yesterday, about the most important ever fraud economic operation here in the United States and simultaneously all over the world. And our investigation will follow with all the information we now have."

Au Revoir Not Goodbye

It was now time to release the team from Operation BULLSEYE, but the worldwide CONSO-DOWN operation was still braking down crooks' castles. This was just the tip of the iceberg. The whole operation had obtained good results in this battle, but the war had not yet been won. She may shortly need to call on them again, as part of another covert operation. There was no finer, braver and selfless group of men and women, she was very proud of them. It was one thing to show up for work, to give your time and talents for a paycheck, but these individuals, as a routine on a daily basis laid their lives on the line for their fellow mankind. There was no greater thing that any person could do. It was a thing, almost above understanding.

Her thoughts turned to Gordon Trojan. He was not only a friend or fellow law enforcement officer but something more. She was tired. The late afternoon sun warmed her, her head slumped to one side and she began to dream.

Joa's hopes and dreams...

Will they ever come to fruition?

Life is not straight forward and not always what you wish. Is Gordon Trojan the one? She was flying, soaring high above... Someplace there was light, everything shone almost sparkled, and the sparkling air flowed over her body like flowing warm water and it was delightful. She arched her head back and arms outstretched and soared up and back, doing a complete circle, then was aware of another soaring beside her. She could not see his face was drawn to, but pulled away in fear, as if afraid he would give her an embrace, and in doing so, take away her ability to soar ...... Her phone jarred her abruptly awake and she looked at the screen to see who it was before answering: "yes Joa here..." She waits too long to answer...

Joe Trakker on Joa's Mind

On her way to the hospital parking lot, going to pay a visit to Dino who was shot to kill by Dennis, thinking he might become a serious witness. Thinking is free, so anyone can let it go while it's a kind of feeding up your brain. There was an unspoken awareness within Joa hoping Joe Trakker would become an integral part of her team. His demonstration more than once, of his knowledge and intuition of upcoming events, had convinced her that he would be a valuable asset to the team.

She did not know how, she did not know why, nor did she know to what extent Joe's strange abilities could go to. So far, these visions or predictions or whatever they were, had been legitimate.

She had begun to piece together, many of his comments and things he had introduced to, over the short while of knowing him. In her thoughts, she was beginning to slowly piece things together, but as yet, they still did not make sense. However, she thought, neither did a nuclear-powered reactor, but they worked.

She pondered the various things that Joe had said:

"The butterflies are not solitary in their work, one must keep in mind that the SOMBRAJ spirits do not confine themselves to the criminal element; remember, SOMBRAJ and I share my body and we will do what is necessary to eliminate the malevolent, which is now playing havoc with our world." She felt almost odd, like she was believing in some sort of split personality sideshow psychic, yet both she and Trojan were witnesses to his very legitimate work, and those and other things he had said:

"There are many stories which are independent of the Dennis case and must be told, each will require telling on its own merit, with your help, I will cover the unimaginable atrocities of their crimes as they perpetrate their assassinations, their cruel and sadistic games under the eyes of police forces no matter how vigilant they may be. SOMBRAJ with his tremendous abilities can infiltrate the criminal mind no matter how devious that individual is. Joa I believe you understand my meaning."

As of yet, there was no logical explanation, but Joa was all too aware that Trojan knew of Joe's amazing intuitions and mystic cam viewers. That is why she would have a chat with Trojan regarding bringing Joe in, as part of the team, in search of the real sick distorted doers which still threatened the global community. This was not the only reason, it was also personal. Joe could perhaps shed some light on her beloved adopted sister's whereabouts and the mystical impact of the "Magic Egyptian Medallion" which was now under the protection of 54-TI. For the moment; all she could do was take things on face value, and remain critically vigilant.

Life Is Not Only Work

Joa was completely immersed in uploading her analysis and suggested plan of action on one of the hard drives seized from Daytona, when she heard a familiar warm voice behind her:

"All work and no play make Joa a dull girl." She turned to see Trojan, arms crossed nonchalantly, leaning against the door frame with a too warm and inviting grin on his face. He was dressed more casually than normal, and there was something about him this moment that left her feeling like she had never felt before, and those feelings were both exhilarating and frightening at the same time. Without thinking, she smiled at him warmly, and suddenly stuck for words she said what first came to mind, wishing that she didn't feel so out of control of the situation, and feeling that what she said was a bit lame:

"What brings you to the neighborhood? I uh-h..." He sat in the chair beside her, still grinning this wicked grin, tented his fingers and the delight in his blue-green eyes could not be hidden, even if he had wanted to:

"Here on police business; stolen motorcycle." Joa knew him, up to something, and that he was playing with her. It troubled her how much she liked it. She stood, hands on hips and with mock anger in her face that could not hide the sparkle in her eyes she bent and was in his face with:

"OK, mister police man. Just what are you up to? Out with it or I'll have my agents hog-tie you and feed you to some criminal element."

He chuckled at her rise to the bait, "promise?" She prodded him with her foot, and still with that grin, he held both hands up in surrender:

"OK, you win. Have something I want to show you. Close up shop here."

"It's late."

"Common." He stood and held out her sweater. She backed into it, turned briefly, clicked safe and shut down, and allowed his arm to caress her out the door to his waiting beamer.

Looking up into his blue-green eyes:

"OK, so what's this about a stolen motorcycle?" With the right emphasis on his words, he looked at her, his smile was not wicked but warm:

"Not 'A' stolen motorcycle, 'YOUR' stolen motorcycles." She looked at him slightly confused, fairly sure that he was not talking about her bike, really being stolen, but she knew he was up to something and that he was playing with her, and it felt good. More than anything, with him she felt peaceful. She grinned at him her most wicked grin, and replied:

"You can, and will be made to pay. So there! ....." The ride was a short one. Their joking banter went back and forth until Trojan wheeled his classic antique into an exclusive, and expensive motorcycle shop, strode to her side and opened the door for her. Then, her interest piqued to the max, she followed him into the office where he simply nodded to the girl at the desk and they continued through and into the shop behind. Trojan stood aside and with a simple gesture of his arm, presented her Harley.

Joa's hands went to her mouth, for a moment speechless, what she saw almost took her breath away, questioning herself:

"Somehow, Trojan had taken my bike from the repair shop where I had left it, and brought it here." The crash bars had been replaced and the work that had been done on the Harley was incredible. The entire machine had been hi-lit and outlined with subtle LED lighting, and a beautiful airbrushed "boa" coiled around the fuel tank. The colors were iridescent blues and greens and gold's, and the artist had outdone himself. Joa stepped up to the machine, stroking the new hand worked leather and the beyond beautiful paint work, and she said:

"Wonderful! Even the wheels had been changed for sporting colored rims that match the color theme." She was moved almost to tears, turning to Trojan, looking up to her huge friend not knowing what to say:

"Well......You're 'go-n-n-a' take me for a ride or not"?

As expressive she is, she hugged him warmly, and motioned to the rear seat. After some additional o-o-oh-s and ah-h-h-s from Joa over them as well, they put on the two new color-themed helmets, and the bike roared to life. And within minutes they were cruising for a while. Joa delightfully chatting on the new helmet intercoms that Trojan had done for her. Eventually hunger caught up with them and they stopped at a roadside diner for burgers and milkshakes. As they ate, Joa looked at Trojan and asked, the question:

"OK Gordon. Got to ask why?" Trojan was in a playful mood, knew that she damn well knew the answer to her own question, knew what he wanted, and where he was going, and so with the baldest of Trojan grins on his face he responded in kind:

"Why what Joa?" Smilingly...

Love at Work

Joa looked at him, trying to control the almost adoration in her eyes, and with all the seriousness she could muster, turned to him and put her cards on the table, so to speak:

"Gordon, you are the only man to get through my defenses, my walls. You did that because I allowed you to. You need to know that I am Joa, and I mean I AM Joa, and nothing more. This job, who I am, is what I breathe and live. Without it, I would die! I will not and cannot let anyone, including you, take this from me. It means too much to me. I can't...!" He put a finger to her lips, cutting her off:

"You know, for a super-intuitive and ultra-intelligent detective, sometimes when it comes to you, you are not the sharpest tool in the shed." Before she could respond, he continued:

"We just came through the most intense work, bang-bang shoot-them up mega-war, hell-on-wheel affairs that any agency could imagine. They don't make films with shit like we just did. Nobody would believe it!" Joa wanting to return with a one-liner of her own:

"So, what's your point?" Trojan was not going to let her win this one, he was going to put up a strong logical defense:

"My point is this. Was I an asset, or a liability? Did we work better together and support one another because of ... of... us? And before you answer that, I have felt this way about you for a while now, and I know damn it well what you feel for me too. I am just as much Trojan as you are Joa. If I felt you had to change, or I had to change, or either of us had to lose who we are, I wouldn't be here at this moment. In law enforcement, and outside of our jobs, me, plus you equal three, not two. There is Trojan being Trojan, Joa being Joa, and then there is us, working together, when it is appropriate. I like who and what you are now. I like what you do and how you do it."

With that, he leaned forward slightly, placed his two massive hands gently on either side of her head and slid his fingers into her now loose hair, and drew her into their first kiss, soft, long, and passionate.

She did not resist. She could not resist. He was right; her fears were just those fears. Her arms went around his neck and she responded with a part of her that she had held dormant since a while. It was so powerful because it was passion fed by both of them. They kissed again, then sat for a short while, her head on his chest, his arm around her, sharing new lover's thoughts and concerns.

She stood, smiling down at him, pulled him to his feet, indicating the bike with a nod of her head:

"Wan-n-a show you a special place."

"Ho! Gordon, do not be upset if sometime I call on you Trojan, I like to say Gordon, but because we work together, at work it might be Trojan, OK?"

"Yaw Boa do not worry about that, hey!"

He followed her to the machine and they were off on the highway again. She skillfully wheeled her Harley into a small, little used park she had found, and frequented when she needed someplace beautiful to just be, or decompress. They dismounted and walked for a short while in silence, Joa delighting in Gordon's wordless pleasure as he discovered her special place. They sat by a fountain disguised as a waterfall, chit-chatting, and just feeling the pleasure and warmth of the newness of their mutual surrender.

Day had transformed into a warm moonlit evening. Joa and Gordon strolled on through the beautiful little park near the river's edge. Gordon turned to Joa and said he would be back in a minute, as he stepped behind some bushes. Joa smiled and shook her head gently. She felt relaxed and at peace with everything. She continued to walk slowly down the pathway between gardens, caressing the many beautiful plants and flowers barely visible in the moonlight but oh their scent so intoxicating.

As she looked to see if Gordon was anywhere to be seen,

Joa looking at Gordon, and a small whimper escaped her lovely lips. He took her into his arms and gently led her down the path towards home. He knew her strength and when the time is appropriate for her, she would tell him what he needed to know. He felt her whimper had come from deep inside her trembling body and may have something to do with the Magic Egyptian Medallion that she told him about feeling a strange energy out of it.

Joa, Invested of Super Powers

After many risks to receive a shot, or being hit by a lost bullet, something not easy to control for a SOMBRAJ, there was something to be applied to Joa without hurting her.

Even SOMBRAJ, or a BRAJ, where not able to prevent everything and they had a conclude example as when Joa was hit by a bullet once, from the interaction with the mercenaries. She was not aimed precisely, it was a lost bullet. Joa being killed, it would have been a disaster for the MISSION that was not completed; because Joa is UNIQUE. The SOMBRAJ in me, did not know how special and unique she was until he had to deal with her. And she is too dedicated to her profession to be matched with a SOMBRAJ spirit in her body as I am. SOMBRAJ did recognize in her a strong intelligent intuition and a deep controlled sensibility.

Because of the risk she may encounter in the fight of dreadful mercenaries and unscrupulous crooks, or warrants on her, Joa needed to be protected with Super Powers.

There was a brief meeting at the SOMBRAJ's summit and they decided to invest Joa with Super Powers. But SOMBRAJ needed unanimity from the whole high spirit power of our planet, the Earth.

Any power we have must be activated, so Joa will notice her new power while processing any action that will trigger her new powers.

When Joa has touched the Magic Egyptian Medallion, she activated something that was in her deep inside since her childhood, something that she did not noticed yet, but soon, that will match with the Super Power she will deploy...

Brain disturbances

Anyone who will think about her, with bad intention, will encounter brain disturbances as:

• She will have the power to vanish from the eyes of anyone who has a bad eye on her.

• She will have the power of disturbance and manipulation on memories and brain wash of anyone bad guys.

• She will read thoughts, intentions on her, instantly, and will be able to build by herself a crook and killer's network from the past actions and follows files mentally.

• She will be more receptive to SOMBRAJ communications and will be able to manage BRAJs for help.

"But she will still need both of us, SOMBRAJ, and my help for holding the cameras and seeing crooks planning actions in the possible future."

How it works:

Brains articulations are dispersed all over our intentions and memories and manipulations are often made by our own illusions, and applied by our own individual cerebral cortex. The cortex is the gray exterior substance of the brain. It's a sheet of neural tissue in the outer part of the cerebrum that plays an important role in human attention, perception, thought, language, and consciousness. So, Joa will have the power to apply illusion, as in a dream in the back of the eyeball while applying the surrounding tissue and muscles tension, and that may apply a temporary trauma like when necessary and can provoke and effect similar to a temporary schizophrenia.

Everybody knows that thought is energy, so when anyone is thinking to you, you have immediately an intuitive energy call in your brain, but it's so fast that most of us do not detect anything, we are used to telephone and cellular now. The waves, exchanged between each other, called intuition or sixth sense, will now be real expression from Joa's communication. In one word, she will not be there, vanished to anyone she wants or project herself from your mind somewhere else... Well... Watch what you're thinking about.

Trakker: Death Never Sleeps

Now speaking to all of you:

"Here I am, yes me Joe Trakker, sitting in my comfortable van, yes, my bubble, shutting off my cams for a while; if you wish to know my true feelings for it, well I am just a few feet from the tumultuous yet magnificent ocean. It has been a few hours since my meeting with Joa and Trojan, and I am making notes on what I have been involved in during the last little while. I was satisfied to know how; SOMBRAJ and I had assisted Joa and Trojan in the capture of some of the wicked crooks impacting the world global economy and without all of us would have cost a few million jobs all over the world."

"But, crimes occur all over the world, and nobody knows where we may possibly, SOMBRAJ and I fly to help. It may not be with Joa's team, but at least you can sleep quietly, because the S.I.I.T.F. is serving all over the world and Joa's team too." Now as I relax, thinking to head up North to Canada for retreat, that's what I only want for now!"

Here's my one specification:

"Me, Joe Trakker, as SOMBRAJ knows me, I am too independent to be dedicated to one cause as running for crooks' injustices and killers, for all my life. I like traveling and writing and playing with my cameras but for now, I need to rest for a while and I think SOMBRAJ may like that too..."

"Joa's teams are going to be busy for many months with all those files, videos, and computer files to decorticate and get criminals arrested and put behind strong bars..."

"Dennis was one of the worst killers, for his one business, for others by contract, and for the crooks' consortium too. He was known as 'Tennis' with a mention: 'the fighting tennis player.' So, they are going to be busy finding dead bodies all over the world: according to Dennis's videos and documents specifications. So, very soon, I will head up North for my summer life where the temperature is so clement for that season."

"But I will be back as a snow bird and you may watch my next new books soon; I have three more breath taking and very, very, bad crook story for you; particularly those stories about new technologies, as new computer operating systems, drones new tech killings. Why bad guys? Why are they becoming worse than ever? But we have to stop them and get them off the living world."

EPILOGUE

The story never ends. Morally distorted spirits are always present and renew themselves. You eliminate one faction and another replaces it. We all know that goodness conquer badness, but for now this story will have no end.

And much more to come for Joa, there are a lot of not open documents from the Dennis's bunker, to reveal something very bad... SOMBRAJ told me... So, let's jump to the next titles!

A CAST OF PLAYERS

MAIN CHARACTERS

Joe Trakker

Joe is an integral part of the story as a narrator, novelist, owner of the cam which shows incidents of morally distorted spirits proportions, which are occurring or about to. Joe becomes the vessel of the entity 'SOMBRAJ, who wants to eradicate the malicious on this planet; at least to rebalance the innocents' suffering. The only thing you must do is that you have to stay close to his camera viewer and snick a "voyeur eye" into it and let the story unfolding before your eyes.

SOMBRAJ

The Mystical spirit who can take many forms, which allows him the flexibility to fight criminals mind on this planet called, Earth. SOMBRAJ is standing as a dual spirit, dual essence twined with Joe.

Joa Kara "Boa"

The beautiful dedicated and vivacious Law Enforcement Agent responsible for a Finance Task Force under S.I.I.T.F her responsibilities are far-reaching as they pertain to the investigation of money laundering, international organized crime, gambling, and economic extremism.

At the loss of her parents at an early age, she was raised by her well-known archeologist adopted sister who heightened her curiosity of Egyptian archeology. Her concentrated interest in the mystical cat, the Egyptian Mau, could not deter her from following her love for law enforcement. Was Joa's interest in the pursuit of justice due to her love for law enforcement or was something else at work?

Gordon Trojan

The handsome, intelligent and resourceful Lieutenant Detective assigned to Bike Week festivities in Daytona Beach. Trojan had a penchant for classic cars and would on occasion go to the auction at the impound yards. This is where he had obtained his blue gem, the classic 1960 Beemer convertible, the envy of his close friends. Gordon has more than respect for his capable friend Joa and in many instances, work related partners. His feelings for the beautiful lady S.I.I.T.F agent must remain his own special quest in order to allow himself to be her protector, if she gets herself in harm's way during her fight with crooks.

Dennis Kildem

The savvy dapper and dark curly hair businessman with family ties to the Kildem, all crook's family. The Kildem family is an important founder of the consortium and one of the Heads of a multi-billion organizations preparing to assault the world's financial stability with their multi-billionaire partners, who are spread all over the world. Dennis is an unscrupulous crime boss with a very volatile temper and believed to have a dual personality. When you look into his very dark eyes it leaves you with a feeling of foreboding and makes your hair stand up.

He believes himself untouchable by law enforcement and known to use many alias names, one of which is Tennis, Francis, Bezel, and has double nationality, American and Australian.

Blake Grimes

Police sergeant: with expertise as a sniper and Gordon Trojan's long-time friend and confidant. Blake tends to speak his mind using his ability to make comical comments at the most opportune time.

Bill Trapp

The Daytona Beach Police Captain, a Colombo type cop, smart, hard-nosed, and very protective of his territory and his police force. He earned the name "Bible Bill" because he goes by the book it has been rumored that he put his brother behind bars for a minor infraction when he was a small-town sheriff. He tends to be tenacious and ask many questions leaving individuals a little perplex as to his capabilities as a law enforcement officer. Passed over for promotion many times have left him jaded and quite often ornery, but never let it be said that he is not good at what he does when it comes to enforcing law, and getting to the bottom of things leading to the capture of many criminals.

Bridget Herckel

The Commander of (SIRS) special operations assigned from Germany's elite combat and tactical force. She is responsible for a CH-47 Chinook, C.S.... NA404...... And elite team of specialists in tactics, recovery, security, covert operations and cleanup team.

Over the many assignments with Joa, she knows their goals are the same and they have now become very good friends.

Maxim Kgnu

Head of the International Finance Task Force: (IFTF) responsible for money laundering and financial extremism; renowned business guru, in his own right and Joa's friend and financial mentor, also responsible for the US S.I.I.T.F. sited at Guardia Fortress.

About the Author

The author is a publisher since 1979 and has registered more than a thousand periodical newspapers, magazines and diversified books. He is still writing for the pleasure of creating stories instead of watching TV. Three more Joe Trakker police stories are coming, one is almost done.

Thanks for visiting Jasselin.com

www.ingramcontent.com/pod-product-compliance
Lightning Source LLC
Chambersburg PA
CBHW070802180626
46818CB00001B/65

* 9 7 8 1 9 2 7 6 5 2 0 9 1 *